Operation: Excitement!

Camp Club Girls

Operation: Excitement!

Camp Club Girls

3 STORIES IN ONE

BARBOUR
PUBLISHING

Contents

Camp Club Girls

Kate's
Vermont
VENTURE

Janice Hanna

Three Blind Mice

"Ahhh!" Kate Oliver screamed as she ran from the Mad River Creamery. Her heart raced a hundred miles an hour. "Wait, Sydney!"

Her friend half-turned with a frantic look on her face. She kept running, nearly slipping on the icy pavement. "We can't stop! N–not yet!"

"B–but. . .you're too fast! I can't keep up!" Kate paused to catch a few breaths. Then she ran again. The sooner she could get away from what she'd just seen. . .the better!

From behind, she heard others crying out as they ran from the building. She'd never seen so many people move so fast! Kate had a feeling none of them would ever visit the Mad River Creamery again!

Whoosh! Kate's feet hit the slippery patch of ice. She began to slip and slide all over the place.

"Nooooooo!" she hollered as her tennis shoes sailed out from underneath her. She slid a few more feet, finally plopping onto her bottom on the icy pavement. Her tiny video camera flew up in the air. Thankfully Kate caught it before it hit the ground. When she screamed, Sydney finally stopped running and turned around.

"What are you doing?" her friend asked, sprinting her

way. "We've got to get out of here! I can't stand. . ." Sydney's voice began to shake. "I can't stand. . .*rats*!"

Kate shuddered and the memories flooded back. Not just one but *three* jumbo-sized rats had raced across the floor of the creamery during their tour. One had scampered across her toes! Kate shivered—partly from the cold Vermont air, and partly from remembering the sight of those horrible, ugly creatures! *Oh, how sick!* And—just in case no one believed them—she'd caught the whole thing on video!

Sydney's hand trembled as she helped Kate up. "Let's go, Kate. I'm never coming back here. Never!" Sydney's dark braids bobbed back and forth as she shook her head. Kate saw the fear in her friend's eyes.

"But I *have* to come back," Kate argued as she brushed ice off her backside. "My school report! We'll only be in Mad River Valley a week. I have to get it written! I'll never get an A in science if I don't finish it."

"Just choose a different topic. Your teacher won't care— especially if you tell her what happened!" Sydney said as they started walking. "Vermont has lots of great things you could write about. Why don't you write your essay on your aunt's inn? Or about the ski lifts? They're the coolest I've ever seen!"

Kate shrugged, still feeling sore from falling. "I don't know anything about skiing, remember? You know I'm not into sports. And nothing is scientific about my aunt's inn. This is supposed to be a *science* paper not a *What I did on my Christmas vacation* essay!"

"Well then, what about the Winter Festival?" Sydney suggested. "I read about it in the paper at the inn, and I even saw a poster advertising it. They're having all sorts of races and prizes. Maybe you can write about competition from a scientific angle."

Kate groaned. "I guess, but none of that is as exciting as the creamery. I had so many ideas for my paper, and now. . ." She sighed. "Now I probably won't even get to go back in there."

"The Mad River Creamery is exciting, all right!" Sydney agreed. "Just wait till your teacher finds out about rats in their cheese! She'll tell her students and they'll tell their parents! Before long, supermarkets won't even carry Mad River Valley products anymore."

"I guess you're right," Kate said with a shrug.

Sydney laughed. "If you *do* go back, you should get extra credit for this paper, that's all I've got to say!" Her eyes lit up. "I know! Show your teacher that video! That will get you some bonus points!"

Kate sighed. "It does creep me out to think about going back in the creamery, but I wanted to write about all the electronic gizmos they use to turn milk into cheese. It's so. . . fascinating!"

"Yes," Sydney agreed, "but *rats* are not fascinating." She squeezed her eyes shut. Opening them again, she said, "They're awful, disgusting creatures! I hope I never see another one as long as I live."

Kate laughed as she trudged along on the snow-packed sidewalk. "I've never seen you scared of anything, Sydney. You're the bravest person I know."

"Just because I'm athletic doesn't mean I like rats and snakes and stuff." Sydney shook her head. "No thank you! I'll scale the highest heights. Ski down the biggest mountain. . . but don't ask me to look at a rat! Ugh!" Her hands began to tremble.

Kate looked at her friend curiously. "Why do rats scare

you so much, anyway?"

Sydney's eyes widened. "I can't believe I never told you! A couple of years ago at summer sports camp, one of the boys put a mouse in my lunch sack."

"No way!"

"Yes. I opened the bag, and the rodent stared at me with his beady eyes." Sydney's voice shook. "I threw the bag halfway across the room."

"Aw." Kate giggled. "Was the mouse okay?"

"Was the *mouse* okay?" Sydney looked at her with a stunned expression. "What about me? Why aren't you asking if *I* was okay? It scared me to death! Seriously!"

"Still, it's kinda funny," Kate said, trying not to smile.

"Well, not to me. I've never liked mice. . .or *rats*. . .since. And especially not in a creamery." Sydney shook her head. "Not that the creamery will be open for long. I'll bet the health inspector's going to come and shut the place down permanently. That's what I'd do, anyway."

"That's just so sad!" Kate sighed. "For the owners, I mean. I'd hate to be in their shoes right now!"

"Me, too!" Sydney said. "'Cause their shoes. . .and their feet. . .are still inside that awful creamery!"

Kate finally started to relax as they walked together the three blocks to her aunt and uncle's inn—the Valley View Bed and Breakfast. When they drew close to the building, Kate saw her brother, Dexter, outside building a snowman. "Just wait till Dex hears about the rats!"

"Hey, Dex!" Sydney hollered. "Do we have a story for you!"

The nine-year-old rose and brushed snow off his wet knees. Then he jogged toward them, his cheeks bright red from playing in the cold. "What's up?"

"We saw *rats* at the creamery!" Sydney began to tell the story with great animation. Before long, Dexter's eyes grew so wide they looked like they might pop out.

"No joke? Rats! Ooo, that's so cool!" He rubbed his hands together. "Let's go back. I want to see them. Do you think they'll let me keep one? It's been ages since I've had a pet rat!" He rattled on about how much fun it would be to share his room with a rat.

Kate shuddered. "This isn't the day to ask. They've closed the creamery for the afternoon. I bet they won't even be open tomorrow."

"And besides. . .those weren't pet rats." Sydney squeezed her eyes shut and shivered. "They're probably disease-carrying rats."

Dex scrunched up his nose and said, "Sick! Never mind, then!"

A voice rang out from the front of the inn, and Kate saw Aunt Molly at the front door, waving. Then Uncle Ollie joined her.

"Come inside, kids. Lunchtime!" Uncle Ollie hollered.

"I've made homemade vegetable soup!" Aunt Molly added. "Perfect for a cold day like this. And we have apple pie for dessert!"

"Everyone in Mad River Valley knows your Aunt Molly bakes the best apple pies around!" Uncle Ollie said with a wink.

Kate smiled at her uncle. He looked so much like her father they could almost pass for twins. Uncle Ollie was older. And mostly bald. But she still saw the family resemblance. How funny that Uncle Ollie had just married a woman named Molly! Kate still giggled, when she thought about it. Ollie and

Molly Oliver. Their names just tripped across her tongue.

"Apple pie!" Dexter began to run toward the house. "My favorite!"

"Mmm!" Kate smacked her lips. Aunt Molly's great cooking would surely take her mind off what had just happened. . .unless she served cheese on top of the pie!

Inside, Kate and Sydney pulled off their mittens and scarves, snow falling on the front rug. Kate's dog, Biscuit, jumped up and down, excited to see them. Then he licked up the little puddles of water from the melting snow.

"Sorry about the mess, Aunt Molly." Kate sighed.

"Never apologize for falling snow, honey," Aunt Molly said. "I always say snowflakes are kisses from heaven. So I don't mind a little mess. You girls have just left kisses on my floor!"

"You're so sweet." Kate hugged her aunt, noticing the familiar smell of her aunt's tea rose perfume.

"So. . ." Aunt Molly flashed a warm smile as she helped Sydney with her jacket. "What do you think of Mad River Valley? Did you kids find anything exciting in our little town?"

"Oh, more than you know!" Kate shrugged off her heavy winter coat. She explained what had happened, then added, "I don't know if I can ever look at Mad River Cheddar Cheese the same way again."

"I bet supermarkets all over the country stop selling it!" Sydney added.

Her aunt's brow wrinkled. "Oh dear! I know the Hamptons, who own the creamery. They're such nice people. This is terrible. . .terrible!"

"Very strange," Uncle Ollie added, shaking his head.

14

"Highly unusual goings-on over there lately."

Aunt Molly led the girls into the kitchen, and Kate's parents soon joined them. After they sat down at a fully laden table and asked God to bless the food, Kate told her parents about their adventurous trip, but Sydney interrupted and told the part about the rats. "It was d–d–dis–*gus*–ting!" she added.

"Not a rat fan?" Uncle Ollie asked.

Sydney shook her head. "No, sir!"

"When Dexter was younger, he had a pet rat named Cheez-It," Kate's father explained. "I'll never forget that little guy. He was pretty cute, actually."

"Only, he bit me and I started calling him Cheez-*Nips*," her mother added, then grinned. "I never could stand rats. Still can't."

Sydney shivered, but Kate laughed. "They're okay in a cage," she said, "but not running around in a creamery."

Suddenly the food didn't look very appetizing, even to Kate, who usually loved to eat. And she couldn't help but notice the cubes of cheese in the center of the table. She closed her eyes and pretended they weren't there.

Aunt Molly clucked her tongue as she scooped up big bowls of steaming vegetable soup. "That poor, poor Hampton family. Haven't they had enough trouble already? Now their creamery will be shut down. It's a shame, I tell you."

She set a bowl of soup in front of Kate, and suddenly her appetite returned. She took a yummy bite and listened to the adults talk.

"Has this happened before?" Kate's mother asked.

"Sadly, yes," Uncle Ollie said.

"This isn't the first time the health inspectors have come,"

Aunt Molly explained. "They've been out twice before. Can't imagine what's causing this."

"Sounds like they'll have to shut the place down permanently, then," Kate's dad said.

Aunt Molly shook her head. "Just seems so sad. I've known the Hamptons since I was young. They're good people. And the creamery has had such a great record of cleanliness. Until a week ago. First I heard about an ant infestation. Then spiders. And now. . .rats! This is all so. . .shocking. Folks around here just find this all so unbelievable!"

"Hmm." Kate pondered her aunt's words. "Why *would* they have a rat problem now, after all these years? Out of the blue? Seems. . ."

"Suspicious?" Sydney whispered.

"Yes."

"Highly unusual goings-on," her uncle added, shaking his head. "Quite odd."

Kate looked at Sydney, her excitement growing. "Are you saying what I *think* you're saying?"

"Maybe they don't *really* have a rat problem at the creamery," Sydney whispered. "Maybe someone is just trying to make it *look* like they do, to sabotage them!"

"But, why?" Kate asked. "And what can we do about it?"

"I'm not sure, but I'm gonna pray about it." Sydney nodded.

"Me, too. And maybe, just maybe. . ." Kate smiled, thinking about the possibilities. This wouldn't be the first case she and Sydney had solved together. No, with the help of their friends—the Camp Club Girls—they'd almost become supersleuths! They even had a page on the Internet and a chat room!

"I'm glad you're going to help figure this out," Dex said with a frantic look in his eyes. "If the Mad River Creamery shuts down, I won't be able to eat my favorite cookies 'n' cream ice cream anymore!"

"Oh, that's right." Kate clamped her hand over her mouth. "It's not just the cheese customers will be losing. . . it's ice cream, too."

"And milk," her mother added. "Their milk is the best in the country."

"But I'll miss their ice cream most," Dexter said with a pout.

Kate forced a serious expression as she said, "Especially their newest flavor."

"Newest flavor?" Sydney and Dexter looked at her with curious looks on their faces.

"Rat-a-tat-tat!" She almost fell off of the chair, laughing. "Get it? *Rat*-a-tat-tat!" She doubled over with laughter.

"That's horrible, Kate Oliver!" Sydney said, standing. "I'm never going to be able to enjoy ice cream again."

"You don't eat sugar anyway," Kate said with a shrug. "You're the healthiest person I know. But me. . ." She sighed. It really would be tough for her to give up Mad River's famous ice cream.

But how could she eat it now, knowing they had a. . .what would you call it? A vermin problem. That's what they had: vermin. Vermin in Vermont.

"Ugh!" A shiver ran down her spine. Vermin in Vermont. Would she ever think of the state again without thinking of. . .rats?

Only if they solved the case!

I Smell a Rat

After lunch, the girls took Biscuit for a walk and talked about the case.

"I wonder if this is a case of sabotage," Kate said, kicking up a pile of snow with her boot. "I think so. Don't you think?"

"Probably if they've had so many problems they've never had before. But, why?" Sydney asked, looking worried.

Kate sighed as she pulled her coat tighter to fight off the bitter cold. "We need to call the other Camp Club girls. Surely one of them would know what to do."

Sydney giggled. "Knowing Bailey, she would also want to fly out here and join us."

Kate laughed. "Yes, and Alexis would be telling us just how much this case is like some book she read, or some movie she watched."

"Elizabeth would remind us to pray, of course," Sydney added. "And to guard what we say so that we don't falsely accuse anyone."

"Yes, and she'd probably quote that scripture she loves so much. . . .'Vengeance is mine; . . .saith the Lord.'" Kate smiled, just thinking about her friend. Elizabeth loved the Lord so much, and it showed in everything she said and did.

"What about McKenzie?" Sydney asked.

"She would keep searching for clues till she found the culprit!" Kate explained. "You know McKenzie! She would examine the motives of every suspect until she solved the case."

"Can we call a meeting of the Camp Club Girls in our chat room tonight?" Sydney asked. "Does the inn have Internet access?"

"Uncle Ollie has a wireless router," Kate said. "I know, because I've already checked my e-mail on my wristwatch."

"Your wristwatch?" Sydney looked at her curiously.

"Yes, remember?" Kate stopped walking long enough to hold up her watch. "I have an Internet wristwatch. One of my dad's students at Penn State invented it. He's a robotics professor, you know."

"I know, I know." Sydney laughed. "And you're going to be one when you grow up, too!"

"Yep," Kate agreed. She looked at her watch once more. "I have to be close to a wireless signal to get online on my wristwatch," she explained. "We're too far from the house now or I'd show you how it works."

Sydney grinned. "Okay, Inspector Gadget! I always forget you've got such cool stuff."

Kate laughed when Sydney called her by the familiar funny nickname. "Well, that's what happens when your dad is into electronics like mine is! He gives me all of his old stuff—cell phones, digital recorders, Minicams, and all that kind of stuff—when one of his students invents something better. And this watch. . ." She glanced down at it with a smile. "It's the coolest gadget of all. I can check my webmail and even send instant messages with it."

"And check the time, too!" Sydney chuckled. "Which is

about all I can do on my watch. . .period!"

"Speaking of the time, I think it's nearly time to meet Uncle Ollie and Dad in the big red barn out back." Kate squinted to catch a glimpse of the building through the haze of the drifting snow. "They're in the workshop."

"Why are we meeting them, again?" Sydney asked.

"I think Uncle Ollie wants to introduce us to someone. There's a neighborhood boy who's been helping him with some of his projects. I think his name is Michael. We're supposed to be nice to him." She shrugged, unsure of what to say next.

"Is he cute?" Sydney asked with a twinkle in her eye.

Kate shrugged. "I don't know. Could be. I just know that Uncle Ollie said he's kind of a loner." She shivered against a suddenly cold wind that tossed some loose snow in her face.

"A loner?" Sydney wrinkled her nose. "Meaning, he doesn't have any friends? That's kind of weird."

"Maybe." Kate sighed. "Molly told me he's just sad because his grandfather died last month. So Uncle Ollie's been playing a grandfatherly role in his life. I think that's pretty nice, actually."

"Oh, I see." Sydney looped her arm through Kate's. "Well, why didn't you just say so? I'll be extra-nice to him. Poor guy."

With Biscuit on their heels, the girls trudged through the now-thick snow to get to the barn. Kate pulled back the door, amazed at what she found inside.

"Doesn't look like any barn I've ever seen!" Sydney said with a look of wonder on her face.

"I know." They stood for a moment, just taking in the sights. "Look at all of Uncle Ollie's electronics! This place is even better than my dad's workshop in our basement."

"I can sure tell your dad and his brother are related!" Sydney said.

"No kidding. Except, of course, Uncle Ollie is a lot older. And he is so smart!" Why, next to Dad, he was the smartest man Kate had ever met.

Off in the distance they heard voices. Kate followed them until they reached a small, crowded work space filled with all sorts of electronics and robotic goodies. "There you are!" she said as she caught a glimpse of her father and uncle.

A boy, about fourteen, stood in the distance. *That must be Michael.* He was tall and thin with messy hair that needed to be combed.

Michael turned to look at them with a nervous look on his face. At once, Biscuit began to growl.

How odd, Kate thought. *Biscuit gets along with everyone!*

"Stop it, Biscuit!" She tugged his leash and he stopped, but she could tell Biscuit was still uneasy. Very, very unusual. Something about this boy made Kate suspicious right away. She immediately scolded herself. *Stop it, Kate. He's never done anything to you. Be careful not to pass judgment on someone you don't even know!*

Sydney didn't seem to notice the tension in the air. She went right up to Michael and introduced herself with a welcoming smile. After taking a seat on a nearby chair, she asked, "Have you lived in the area long?"

He shrugged, but never looked her way. "I grew up in Mad River Valley. Why?"

"Oh, I just wondered." She looked around the workshop then glanced back his way. "Do you ski?"

"Of course. Who doesn't?" He looked at her as if she were crazy.

"I don't," Kate said. "Never have."

He shrugged and went back to working on some electronic contraption. "That's weird."

"So, if you ski, are you going to enter the Winter Competition?" Sydney asked.

"Maybe." He kept his eyes on his work. "I usually do, but I don't know if I feel like it this year."

"Oh, you should! It would do you good." Uncle Ollie patted Michael on the back then turned to the girls. "You should see him ski! He's the best in his age group. Wins every year."

"Humph." Sydney crossed her arms at her chest and looked him in the eye. "We'll just see about that."

"Oh yeah?" Michael turned her way. "What do you mean by that?"

"I mean, this year *I'm* entering, too." Sydney nodded, as if that settled the whole thing.

"You are?" Kate turned to her friend, stunned. "Really?"

"Did you see the grand prize?" Sydney said, her voice growing more animated by the moment. "Three hundred dollars! That's exactly the amount I need to go on my mission trip to Mexico this summer."

"Oh, I see." Kate pondered that for a moment. Sydney would have a wonderful time on a mission trip. And Mexico. . .of all places! Sounded exciting.

Sydney sighed. "My mom doesn't make a lot of money." She shook her head. "And things are really tight right now. But she told me I could go if I could raise the money on my own. So, that's why I have to win that competition! I've read the article in the paper a dozen times at least. And I've stared at the poster in the front room of the inn a hundred times!"

"You have?" Kate looked at her, stunned. "Why didn't you say something sooner?"

"I don't know." Sydney looked down at the ground. "I still have to come up with the entrance fee. Twenty-five dollars. But I think my mom will send it if I ask."

"Wow." Kate stared at her friend. "So you really want to do this."

"I do."

Michael crossed his arms at his chest and stared at her. "Well, maybe I *will* enter after all. We'll just see who's the best."

"Fine." Sydney shrugged. She stuck out her hand and added, "And may the best skier win!"

Michael shook her hand then went back to his work. Kate could see now that he was putting together an electronic resistor board. *What are they building out here, anyway?* she wondered. She drew near to Sydney and whispered, "What can I do to help you win the competition?"

"Hmm." Sydney pursed her lips and squinted her eyes. "I guess you could help me find the perfect skis. I'll have to rent them, probably." A sad look came over her. "I guess that will cost even more money, so maybe not. I don't know."

"Maybe Aunt Molly can help with that," Kate suggested.

"Maybe. And then I have to find out where the competition will be held. I want to hit the slopes in advance. Get in plenty of practice." Sydney's eyes lit up. "Oh, you need to come with me!"

"Me? Put on skis? I don't know. . ." Kate hesitated. "I never. . ."

"I know you've never skied before, but there's a first time for everything. Besides, I need someone to clock my time. So you won't really be doing a lot of skiing. I think it will be good for you, Kate! You'll learn something new, and I know you love learning things."

"Maybe." Kate shrugged. "Just usually not sports! But first let's go talk to Aunt Molly and see if she knows where we can get some skis."

"Hope she has two pairs!" Sydney said, looping her arm through Kate's. "Then it'll be you and me. . .off to ski!"

Another shiver ran down Kate's spine. This one had nothing to do with the cold. How could she possibly make Sydney understand. . .she didn't like sports! Not one little bit! And the very idea of soaring down a hill with boards strapped to her feet scared her half to death!

Sighing, she headed back toward the house to ask Aunt Molly about the skis. Hopefully she would only have one pair!

CHAPTER 3

The Mousetrap

Kate and Sydney tromped through the snow, finally reaching the back door of the inn, which led straight into Aunt Molly's spacious kitchen with its big, roaring fireplace. As they stomped their snow-covered boots on the mat, Biscuit jumped up and down excitedly. Must be the smell of gingerbread that had him so excited!

"Oh, yum!" Kate looked down at a large tray where several cookies were cooling. "I love these!" She pulled off her coat and hung it on the coatrack, then turned to her aunt with a "Can I have one?" grin.

"I'm glad to hear that you like gingerbread." Aunt Molly handed each of the girls a warm cookie. "Taste and see if they're any good."

"Oh, they're the best I've ever had!" Kate spoke between bites. She snapped off a little piece and handed it to Biscuit, who gobbled it up and begged for more.

"I saw that, Kate!" Aunt Molly said. "You shouldn't be giving sweets to a dog!"

"I know, I know." She sighed and pulled off her mittens. "I know I spoil him. . .way too much! But he's such a good dog, and he's been great at crime-solving, so every now and again I like to treat him."

"Treat him too much and he'll be as big around as a turkey at Thanksgiving!" Aunt Molly laughed.

"I know, I know." Kate hung her head in shame, then looked up with a grin.

"I've got some good news!" Aunt Molly said as they nibbled. "The creamery is open again. The health inspector came this morning and couldn't find any rats. In fact, they couldn't even find a hint that there had ever *been* rats. Strange, isn't it?"

"Wow! That's amazing," Kate said. "I need to go back for the tour and get some more information for my essay. Do you think Mr. Hampton would give me an interview? Maybe on video? I'd love to share it with my class. My teacher might even give me extra credit!"

"I'll call him and ask," Molly said. "Surely he will do it for me. I'm an old friend." She winked as she said the word "old" and Kate grinned.

"Do we have to go back there?" Sydney asked, looking worried. "I don't care what the health inspector said. We just saw rats in that place yesterday. Besides, I need to go skiing. I need the practice, remember?"

"Yeah." Kate leaned her elbows on the counter and sighed.

"What's wrong, Kate?" Her aunt gave her a curious look.

"Sydney wants to enter the ski competition at the Winter Festival to raise money for a mission trip to Mexico," she explained.

"Well, that's a lovely idea!" Aunt Molly stopped working long enough to grin at Sydney. "I think that's wonderful." She set two steaming mugs of hot apple cider down in front of the girls.

"Only one problem. Well, two, actually." Sydney shrugged.

"I don't have any skis, and I don't have money to enter the competition. At least, not yet. I'm going to ask my mom."

"I can help with the skis. I have a wonderful pair," Aunt Molly said with a wink. "They're in the barn. Want to go see them?"

"Well, um. . ." Sydney looked a little embarrassed.

"What, honey?"

"Well, Michael is out there, and he's going to be competing against me," she explained. "So I don't really want him to see what I'm up to."

"Oh, I see!" Aunt Molly giggled. "So this is a covert operation, then?"

"Covert operation?" Kate looked at her, confused.

"Top secret mission," Aunt Molly explained. "Is that what this is?"

"Oh yes!" Kate and Sydney spoke together.

"We don't want anyone to know anything!" Sydney explained.

"Excellent idea." Aunt Molly nodded. "And I've got just the pair of skis for you. I used to ski a little, myself. These were mine from years ago. And I've even got an extra pair for you, Kate. They're not the new, expensive kind, but they will do for a beginner."

"Oh no!" Kate argued. "I don't ski, Aunt Mol. Seriously. Not ever. And I don't want to start!"

"Hmm. Well, we'll see about that." Aunt Molly snapped the leg off a gingerbread man and popped it into her mouth. "We will just see about *that*." Biscuit stood at her side whimpering until she finally gave him a tiny piece of the cookie. "Go away, goofy dog! You're going to eat me out of house and home!"

Kate looked at Sydney, hoping to convince her. "I don't mind if you go, of course. You need the practice. I don't. And maybe I can go with you tomorrow. Today I need to stay here and research cheese-making for my essay paper."

Sydney rolled her eyes. "C'mon. Are you serious? You want me to believe you'd rather work on a school paper than hang out on the slopes?"

"You don't understand." A lump rose up in Kate's throat. "I *have* to get the best grade in the class because. . ." She didn't finish the sentence. No telling what Sydney and Aunt Molly would say if they knew the truth.

"Tell me, Kate." Sydney took another bite of a gingerbread man. "Why do you have to have the best one in your class? Why is it so important?"

"Because. . ." She shook her head. "Never mind. It's no big deal."

"Must be," Aunt Molly said, her eyes narrowing a bit. "Or you wouldn't have brought it up. Go ahead and tell us, Kate. Confession is good for the soul."

"Oh, okay." She bit her lip, trying to decide where to start. Surely Aunt Molly would understand. "There's this boy in my science class," Kate said, finally. "His name is Phillip. He's the smartest person I know."

"Smarter than you?" Sydney's eyes widened. "Impossible!"

Kate shrugged. "I don't know. Maybe. But we're always competing to see who gets the best grades. Kind of like you and Michael are going to do on the ski slopes. Lately, Phillip has been, well. . ." Her voice trailed off and she sighed.

"He's been getting better grades than you?" Aunt Molly asked.

"Yes, but that's not all." A lump rose in Kate's throat as

she remembered the things Phillip had said. "He made fun of my last science project. I did a great job on it, and the teacher really liked it, but. . ."

"Oh, honey. I'm sorry he hurt your feelings." Aunt Molly shook her head.

"I don't like to be made fun of."

"No one does," Aunt Molly explained with a sympathetic look on her face.

"He doesn't sound like a very nice guy," Sydney said.

"He's not. He even told me. . ." Kate felt the anger return as she thought about him laughing at her. "He even told me that I would never be a professor like my dad. . .because I'm a girl."

"Ah." Aunt Molly nodded and handed her another cookie. "So, you're going to try to prove him wrong by being better than him at something."

"M—maybe." She shrugged and bit off the gingerbread man's head. The yummy, warm cookie slowly dissolved in her mouth.

"Kate." Aunt Molly reached over and placed her hand gently on Kate's. "It's not wrong to want to be the best you can be. But in this case, I question your motives. You've got to examine your heart, honey."

"Examine my heart?" Kate swallowed a nibble of the cookie and took a drink of the hot apple cider. "What do you mean?"

"I mean, you need to start by forgiving Phillip for what he said."

"Oh." Kate sighed and took another sip of the cider. "I never thought about that."

"Holding a grudge isn't a good thing. Besides, the Bible

says the Lord will only forgive us to the extent that we forgive others."

"W—wait. What do you mean?" Kate stared at her aunt, stunned. "You mean God won't forgive me if I don't forgive Phillip?"

"Well, Ephesians 4:32 says we should be compassionate and understanding toward others, forgiving one another quickly as God forgives us."

"Whoa." Sydney and Kate both spoke at the same time.

"Forgive quickly? But that's hard to do." Kate drew in a deep breath as she thought about it. "Sometimes it takes a while to forgive, doesn't it?"

"Sometimes. But here's the problem with holding a grudge," Aunt Molly said. "It might start out small—like competing over whose essay is best. Then before you know it, a grudge can turn into revenge. Anger. And that's never good. So, it's better to put out that spark before it becomes a raging fire."

"Wow." Kate thought about her aunt's words as she continued to nibble on the cookie. It was all starting to make sense.

"Think of it like this." Aunt Molly appeared to be deep in thought for a moment. "Let's use what's going on at the creamery to illustrate. Imagine you're a little mouse and you see what looks like a beautiful piece of cheese. You run over to it and grab it, then. . .*snap!* You're caught in a mousetrap."

Kate nodded, "I see what you mean."

"Unforgiveness is a trap," Aunt Molly explained. "And as soon as you're caught in it, you're in trouble. So, let go. Forgive. It's always the best choice."

Kate stared at the fireplace, listening to the crackling and popping sounds the fire made. "I never thought about that before, Aunt Molly. I guess I have been holding a grudge but didn't realize it. Will God forgive me for that?"

"Of course He will! But you have to pray about it. And then—while you're at it—pray for Phillip, too," her aunt said. "And you never know. . .you two might end up being friends when all is said and done."

"I can't imagine that." How could she ever be a friend to such a mean person?

"I know it seems impossible now, but trust me when I say it is possible." After a wink, Aunt Molly added, "Ask me how I know."

"How do you know?" Kate asked, nibbling on her cookie.

"Because your Uncle Ollie and I met when we were competing against each other in a square-dancing competition. We were both mighty good, though maybe I shouldn't say that."

"Oh, wow!" Kate giggled. "So, who won? You or Uncle Ollie?"

"In the long run, we *both* won," Aunt Molly explained with a sly grin. "Though it certainly didn't seem like it at the time. In the second round of the competition, my partner hurt his leg. And Ollie's partner got sick. So, we ended up competing together. . .as a team." She giggled. "And the rest is history!"

Sydney's eyes sparkled. "You fell in love on the dance floor? He danced his way into your heart?"

"Well, not that first day, but it didn't take long." Aunt Molly winked. "Ollie Oliver is a godly man and a great dancer. What a charmer!" Her cheeks turned pink, and she giggled.

Sydney sighed. "That's so sweet!" She grinned at Kate. "So maybe you and Phillip will fall in love and get married someday!"

Kate shook her head. "No way! But maybe we will end up as friends like Aunt Molly said. I just never thought about it before."

Sydney nodded. "And who knows? Maybe I'll even learn to like Michael." She shrugged. "It's possible."

"I hope so," Aunt Molly said. "That would be nice. He's such a great boy."

"Hmm." Kate wrinkled her nose. "I guess we need to give him the benefit of the doubt, even though he didn't make a very good first impression."

"I still plan to beat him in the skiing competition," Sydney said. "And I do need to practice. But I'll make you a deal, Kate. Today I'll go back to the creamery with you *one* last time. But tomorrow, you have to come skiing with me. Promise?"

Kate paused. She didn't know if she should promise such a thing or not. After all, she'd never skied before. "I—I guess so," she said, finally. "But for now, let's get back to cheese-making!"

Sydney made another face then shuddered. "I sure hope there aren't any rats this time."

"Surely not," Aunt Molly said. "But if you *do* happen to see one, just remember that story I told you about the mousetrap. It's better to forgive than hold a grudge."

"It's better to forgive than hold a grudge," Kate agreed. Then, with a happy heart, she looped her arm through Sydney's and they headed back to the creamery.

CHAPTER 4

The Big Cheese

Kate and Sydney walked the three blocks to the creamery with snow falling all around them.

"Don't you just love Vermont?" Sydney asked. "It's so pretty here." She began to describe the beautiful trees and the crystal-like snowflakes. On and on she went, sounding like a commercial.

"Mm-hmm. I like it here, but it's so cold!" Kate shivered.

"It's cold in Philly, where you live," Sydney said. "And in D.C., where I live, it gets really cold in the wintertime. So, this doesn't feel any different to me. No, I love the cold weather. And I can't wait to put on skis and glide down the mountainside. Oh, it's going to be wonderful! You're going to *love* it, Kate. I promise!"

"If you say so."

As the creamery came into view, Sydney groaned. "I can't believe I offered to come back here. This place is so scary. Do we really have to go back in there?"

"We do. But maybe we'll have a better time if we think happy thoughts," Kate suggested. "We'll focus on the good things. For example, I've been saving my allowance so I can buy different cheeses to take back to my class. You can help me decide what flavors to buy. Should I get swiss or cheddar?

And if I get cheddar, which kind? There are so many, you know." She went off on a tangent, describing her favorite kinds of cheese.

"I can't believe you're actually going to *eat* something made there." Sydney scrunched her nose. "I'd be scared to! Aren't you worried?"

"Nah," Kate said, shaking her head. "And besides, I have the *strangest* feeling about all of that, Sydney. I'm convinced someone is sabotaging the Hamptons. But, why?"

"Hmm." Sydney walked in silence a moment. "Maybe we should put McKenzie or one of the other Camp Club Girls to work, figuring out who their main competitor is. Maybe someone from another creamery is jealous and wants to put the Hamptons out of business."

Just before they entered the building, Kate caught a glimpse of someone familiar off in the distance. "Hey, look, Sydney! It's that boy. . .Michael! Are you going to tell him that you're entering the competition?"

"No way!" Sydney grabbed her arm and whispered. "It's top secret, remember? I don't want him to know."

They walked inside the store at the front of the creamery, and Kate took a deep breath. "Oh, it smells so deliciously cheesy in here!" She closed her eyes and breathed in and out a few times. "I totally believe this is what heaven it going to smell like."

Sydney grunted. "Heaven. . .smells like *cheese*? I sure hope not! Doesn't smell so good to me." After looking around the empty store, she added, "Look, Kate. Have you noticed? We're the only ones here. That should tell you something! People are scared to come back."

"Or maybe we're just early." Kate looked at her Internet

wristwatch. "Ooo! I have an e-mail." She quickly signed online and smiled as she read a note from Bailey that said, "Have fun in Vermont!" Kate quickly typed back, "Having a blast!" then pressed the tiny SEND button.

"I don't blame people for being scared to come here," Sydney said.

Kate looked up from her watch and shrugged. "Well, let's not think about all that. Since we're here, let's sample the cheeses."

"I guess so." Sydney shrugged. "But you can do the sampling. I'll just watch."

They walked around the large glass case, looking inside. "Oh, I *love* Colby Jack!" Kate reached for her camera and took a picture of the tray filled with chunks of orange and white swirled cheese. Then she lifted the clear dome top from the cheese tray and took a piece. With her mouth full, she pointed at the tray next to it. "They have every kind of cheddar imaginable! Yum!" She lifted the top on that tray and took several pieces. "Wow, this is great!" She'd never seen so many different kinds of cheeses. . .and all the samples were free! But which one should she buy for her classmates?

"My favorite is the swiss," Sydney said, taking a tiny piece. "Mom puts it on my turkey sandwiches."

"Ooo, you're making me hungry." Kate took a couple of chunks of the swiss cheese and ate it right away. "Let's order something to eat." She pointed at the Cheese-o-Rama Snack Shack in the corner of the room. "Look! It says they make the world's best grilled-cheese sandwiches, and you can pick the kind of cheese you want. I'm going to ask for the Colby Jack on mine. What about you?"

"Kate, we just ate breakfast a couple of hours ago,"

Sydney said. "And then we ate your aunt's gingerbread cookies. I don't need the extra calories. And I still think we should be careful not to eat too much cheese from this place."

"Calories, schmalories." Kate shrugged. "Who cares?"

"I do." Sydney gave her a stern look. "I have to stay in shape to win that competition next weekend."

"You're already the fastest, strongest, most athletic girl I know!" Kate said. "What else do you want?"

"I want to win."

"Well, I'm not competing, and I'm hungry. Besides, it's almost lunchtime and we'll never make it back to the inn in time for Aunt Molly's food. So, let's eat!"

Kate went to the counter and ordered a cheese sandwich with a side of cheese-flavored chips. Mr. Hampton—her aunt's friend—prepared her sandwich. He looked a little worried.

As he placed her plate in front of her, Kate whispered, "Mr. Hampton, did my Aunt Molly Oliver call you?"

"She did." He gave a hint of a smile.

"Could I speak with you. . .alone?" She looked around, hoping not to be overheard, then remembered no one else was in the shop. "I'm working on a paper for school and would love to get some information—straight from the source!"

"Sure, I'd be happy to help." His shoulders sagged as he looked around the shop. "Doesn't look like we've got many customers today, anyway." He sighed. "What a mess this is! We can't afford to lose customers right now."

"I understand." Kate gave him a sympathetic look. "And I want to help you with that. In my essay I'll tell everyone how wonderful your cheeses are. That should help your business! But I'll need your help. Thanks for answering a few questions for me!"

Just then, a cheerful female voice came over the loudspeaker. "Ladies and gentlemen, the Mad River Creamery will conduct a tour of its facility in exactly ten minutes. The tour is free of charge, and complimentary cheese samples will be given along the way. Join us for the tour of a lifetime."

"It's the tour of a lifetime, all right," Sydney whispered in Kate's ear as she drew near. "Complete with rats."

"Shh!" Kate ignored her and turned her attention back to Mr. Hampton. "Maybe after the tour you could answer some questions for me? I'll be sure to give you credit in my paper. And I'll need to purchase lots of different kinds of cheeses to take back for the kids in my class, so I'll need help picking those out, too."

"Of course!" he said with a smile. "I'm always happy to help a customer."

Just then, a couple more customers came through the door—a woman in a beautiful white fur coat and a man with a sour look. He shook the snow off of his leather coat and looked around the shop with a frown.

"Wow, he doesn't look happy," Sydney whispered in Kate's ear. "Do you think his wife made him come?"

"I don't know." Kate stared at the man then turned back to her sandwich. "Maybe he heard about the rats and is afraid."

"He doesn't look like the kind of man to be scared of anything. He just looks. . .mean." A look of fear came into Sydney's eyes. "I hope they're not coming on the tour with us."

The woman walked toward them and the man followed

closely behind, muttering all the way.

"Uh-oh." Kate let out a nervous giggle. "Looks like they're joining us. Just smile and be friendly. Maybe they'll turn out to be nice."

"Whatever you say," Sydney whispered.

Within seconds, Kate and Sydney were tagging along behind Mr. Hampton and the two strangers into the creamery. She couldn't get rid of the nagging feeling that the man and woman were up to no good. And Sydney made her a little nervous. She wouldn't stop talking about rats.

"I can't believe I'm doing this again!" Sydney whispered. "I still have vermin-phobia after our last tour!"

"Shh." Kate turned and gave her a *please-be-quiet* look.

The girls walked from room to room, listening as Mr. Hampton explained the process of cheese making. Kate pulled out her video camera and began to film his presentation. In one room, he pointed out something he called curds and whey.

"Just like Little Miss Muffett," Kate whispered.

"What?" Sydney gave her a funny look.

"'Little Miss Muffett sat on her tuffet, eating her curds and whey.'" Kate giggled. "Now I know what curds and whey are. I never knew before. Kind of looks like cottage cheese. Kind of chunky and. . ." *Gross* was the only word that came to mind, but she didn't say it.

"Doesn't look very appetizing!" Sydney made a terrible face. "It's enough to scare me away, too!"

"Well, in the nursery rhyme, a *spider* frightened Miss Muffett away," Sydney reminded her. "Not the curds and whey. And certainly not a. . .well, a you-know-what."

Mr. Hampton turned and gave her a warning look. He

put a finger over his lips, then whispered, "Don't even use the *r-a-t* word. And please don't talk about spiders, either. I'm having enough trouble keeping my customers without worrying them even more!" He nodded in the direction of the man and woman, who stood on the other side of the room, looking at the big machine that held the curds and whey.

Kate apologized, then added, "I'm sure your customers won't be gone for long. You have the best cheese in the state, Mr. Hampton. My mom has bought Mad River Valley Cheddar for as long as I can remember." Kate raised her voice to make sure the man and woman heard her. Sure enough, the woman looked her way. "I love, love, love cheese!" She licked her lips. "Without Mad River cheese, grilled cheese sandwiches wouldn't be the same!"

"Cheeseburgers wouldn't be as cheesy!" Mr. Hampton threw in.

"String cheese wouldn't be as. . .stringy," Sydney added, then giggled.

The woman in the white coat moved their way and nodded as she said, "Cream cheese wouldn't be as creamy."

Kate turned to the man, who crossed his arms at his chest and remained quiet. Hmm. So, he didn't want to play along.

Kate decided to change the subject. "This cheese-making stuff looks like fun. I wish I could make cheese at home," she said with a sigh.

"Why, you can!" Mr. Hampton said. "If you have a gallon of milk, you can make a pound of cheese. You would need the help of a parent—and it takes a couple of days—but it's worth it. I can show you how to make your own cheese press, if you like."

"Would you, really?" Kate grew more excited by the moment. "Oh, I would love that. I think I'll write my paper on that, then!"

"Let's finish the tour, and then I'll show you a homemade cheese press," Mr. Hampton said. He led the way into a large room with a huge rectangular contraption filled with what looked like thick milk.

Kate looked at it, amazed. "Wow, this is huge." She'd never seen such a thing!

Mr. Hampton explained. "Yes, this is just like we talked about earlier. Once the whey is removed, the curds are pressed together, forming the cheese into shapes."

"Wow!" Kate began to videotape the process. She didn't want to miss a thing. Something caused her to turn toward the woman in the white coat. She was whispering something to the man and pointing to the curds and whey. *Hmm, I wonder what they're talking about?*

Just then Kate saw something out of the corner of her eye. She turned her camera toward the floor, just to make sure she wasn't imagining it. At that very moment, Sydney screamed. Kate jolted and almost dropped the camera.

"It's a. . .a rat!" Sydney jumped on a chair and began to squeal.

Sure enough, the brown furry critter headed right for them! He was moving so fast Kate could hardly keep up with him. For a few seconds he disappeared from view in her video camera lens, and then she caught a glimpse of him again. *Oh, gross!*

The woman began to scream at the top of her lungs and fainted. Her husband caught her just before she landed on the floor. He fanned her with the creamery brochure and called, "Abigail! Abby, wake up!"

The rat scampered close to the woman and Kate gasped. *What's going to happen next?* She whispered a quick prayer.

Holding a tight grip on the camera, Kate continued videotaping the vermin. Thankfully, he scurried to the other side of the room, leaving the woman alone. But something about the little critter seemed. . .odd. It ran in circles. Round and round it went, in a never-ending cycle. Maybe it had had too much cheese! Something was definitely wrong with it.

Mr. Hampton came around to their side of the room and his eyes grew large. "No! Not again! We took care of this. I promise! Mad River Valley Creamery doesn't have. . ." He didn't say the word. He didn't have to.

The rat finally stopped running in circles and took off under the vat of cheese. The woman regained consciousness, and Kate turned her camera in that direction. The woman began to cry out and her husband hollered, "Turn that off! I don't want you videotaping my wife!"

"Oh, I'm sorry, sir. I didn't mean any harm." Tears sprang to Kate's eyes. The man headed her way. When he got close, he grabbed her camera and shut it off, then pressed it back into her hand.

"Get on out of here, kids. . .before I lose my temper. Or maybe I'll just call the police and tell them we were being illegally videotaped!"

Sydney turned on her heels and sprinted like an Olympic track star toward the door. Kate followed, shaking like a leaf.

What a mean man! She never meant to do anything wrong! And how awful. . .to see another rat! Kate couldn't figure out why, but something about that fuzzy little creature still puzzled her.

"I'm never. . .eating. . .cheese. . .again. . .as long. . .as I . . .live!" Sydney hollered as she ran.

Kate groaned, trying to keep up. So much for helping Mr. Hampton and the Mad River Creamery. Another rat had interrupted her plans. But who was behind all of this? And why?

With the help of the other Camp Club Girls. . .she and Sydney would figure it out!

Hickory Dickory Dock

Kate and Sydney ran all the way back to the inn. When they arrived at the front door, Biscuit greeted them with wet, slobbery kisses.

"D—down, boy!" Kate panted. "N—not right now."

Between the cold air and the excitement of what had just happened, she could hardly breathe!

"Is everything okay?" Aunt Molly met them as they raced into the big room. Kate headed toward the fireplace to warm herself. "N—no," she said through chattering teeth. "We saw another r—rat!"

"Oh dear, oh dear!" Aunt Molly's cheeks flushed pink. "That's just awful! Was it inside the creamery again?"

"Y—yes!"

"Oh, how terrible!" Aunt Molly began to fan herself, looking as if she might be sick.

Kate's mother entered the room with a worried look.

"Did I hear you say something about a rat?" When Kate nodded, she said, "Honey, I don't want you and Sydney going back to that creamery. You'll just have to write your essay paper on something else, Kate."

"But that's just it." Kate sighed and plopped down on the large leather chair in front of the fireplace. "It's not dangerous at all. Something is definitely up. I can feel it in my bones!"

Aunt Molly laughed. "Oh, you can, can you? Well, what do you feel?"

"I'll know more after I look at the videotape. Do you mind if I hook my camera into your big-screen TV, Aunt Molly? I want to see everything close up."

"Ugh!" Sydney grunted. "We have to see the rat on the big screen?"

Kate laughed. "You don't have to watch."

They gathered around the television as Kate hooked up her camera. When she hit PLAY, they all watched the action.

"Here's the curds and whey part," Kate explained, pointing at the screen. "And here's the part where—"

Her mother and Aunt Molly screamed when they saw the rat run across the floor toward the woman in the white coat.

"Oh, how awful!" Aunt Molly clasped her hand over her mouth. "That poor woman."

"That man who's with her looks really angry," Kate's mother added.

"Oh, he was." Kate shivered. "But look at this."

She paused the video for a moment, focusing on the rat.

"What?" Sydney drew near, looking at the television.

Kate pointed at the pesky vermin. "Take a good look at this rat."

"Do I have to?" Sydney squeezed her eyes shut. "What about him?"

"Something about him is. . .odd. First, he's a little too big. Not your average-sized rat. Not even close!"

"Well, on your Uncle Ollie's big-screen TV, everything looks bigger than it is," Aunt Molly explained.

"Yes! Look at my ears!" Sydney laughed. "They're huge. Someone please tell me they're not that big in real life!"

"They're not, silly!" Kate groaned. "I know things appear larger than they are, but even so, this is one giant rat. And look at his fur. Have you ever seen rat fur so. . .furry?"

Sydney came a step closer and looked for a second. "No. But I'm no expert on rats."

"I've seen a few in my day," Aunt Molly said, drawing close. "And he does look a bit odd. Must be an interesting species."

"I know what it is!" Sydney said. "The rats at the creamery are well fed! That's why they're so huge!"

"Could be," Kate's mother said. "I just know we don't grow them that big in Pennsylvania!"

"Or in DC!" Sydney added.

"Most rats have really short hair," Kate observed. "And most aren't this color. This is more like the fur you'd see on a hamster or something."

"So, you think it's not a rat after all?" Sydney asked. "Maybe it's a giant hamster?"

"That's just it." She drew in a deep breath as she thought about it. "Hamsters are smaller than rats. I'm not sure what it is, but it's not a typical rat, that's for sure. I'll have to get on the Internet and research all different types of rodents."

"Doesn't sound like much fun to me!" Sydney said. "We're on Christmas vacation, Kate. Remember?"

"I know, but this is really going to bother me if I don't figure it out!" Kate backed up the video and watched it again. With a sigh, she said, "Something about this frame really bothers me. After all, rats are very agile. This one isn't."

"Agile?" Sydney groaned. "I'm gonna have to look that one up in the dictionary, Kate. Why do you always use such big words?"

Aunt Molly laughed. "I hardly use that word myself!"

"Oh, sorry." Kate giggled. "I just meant most rats move fast and can make quick turns. This one. . ." She stared at the stilled photo again. "This one makes choppy movements. Jerky. You know what I mean?"

"Maybe he's had too much cheese." Sydney laughed. "That would do it. Once I ate too much string cheese, and I could barely move at all!"

"You should see me after I've had a big slice of cheesecake," Kate's mother said with a nod. "I just want to curl up in a chair with a good book!"

"Yeah, but this is different. He didn't look like he'd eaten too much. He was. . ." Kate couldn't think of what to say next. "He's shaped weird."

"Yeah, a little." Sydney shook her head. "But can we stop looking now? I've had enough of rat talk!"

"Right, right." After a moment's pause, Kate added, "Oh, I just had an idea!"

"What?" Sydney's brow wrinkled. "What are you thinking, Kate Oliver? What are you up to?"

"Well, I was just thinking this would be a great project for McKenzie," Kate explained. "She loves to search for clues. I'll send her a picture of this. . .creature. She can research it for us."

"Okay. That's a good idea." Sydney began to pace the room as she talked. "Let's send out an e-mail to the girls and ask them to meet us in the chat room tonight at eight o'clock our time. That will give us plenty of time to hang out with your family first. What do you think?"

"Perfect."

"In the meantime," Kate's mother said, "we're still

planning to go to rent a family movie and order Chinese food. Does that sound good?"

"Great! What movie?" Kate asked.

"We thought you girls could decide," her mother said. "So be thinking about it."

"Oh, I know!" Sydney clasped her hands together. "Let's rent the Nancy Drew movie. That's one of my favorites!"

"Ooo, perfect!" Kate agreed. "That should put us in the mood for solving a mystery!"

●—●—●

A short time later, everyone gathered around the television to watch the movie and eat Chinese food. Kate started with a big plate of moo goo gai pan, then refilled her plate with General Tso's chicken and pepper steak. Between bites, she commented on what they were watching on Uncle Ollie's big-screen TV.

"See, Sydney! See how good Nancy is at solving crimes? See that part where she kept searching for clues, even when it seemed impossible? We've got to think like that!"

"You want to be like Nancy Drew, eh?" Her father flashed an encouraging smile. "Well, you're certainly adventurous."

"And you know a lot more about technology," Sydney added. "Back when the Nancy Drew books were written, cell phones hadn't even been invented."

"No computers, either," Kate's dad threw in. "And the Internet was unheard of!"

"Wow!" Kate could hardly imagine a time without computers and Internet. She glanced at her wristwatch, thankful for modern-day technology.

As soon as the movie ended, she glanced at the clock. "Oh, it's ten minutes till eight! Time to meet with the Camp

Club Girls in our chat room!"

Sydney tagged along on her heels until they reached their room. Using her dad's laptop, Kate signed online in a flash and went to their website chat room.

As usual, Bailey was already there. The words, *"Hey, what's up?"* appeared on the screen.

Kate: *We need your help.*

A couple of minutes later, all the girls arrived in the chat room. After explaining what had happened at the creamery, Bailey typed, *"LOL. . .I just watched* Ratatouille! *I have rats on the brain!"*

Kate: *Oh, that is ironic! Didn't the rat in that movie work in a restaurant?*
Bailey: *Yes, he was a great chef.*
Kate: *Well, maybe the rats we saw at Mad River Creamery really want to become cheese-makers!*
Bailey: *LOL.*
McKenzie: *Somehow I don't think the rats are wanting to do anything but scare people! But it sounds more like someone is putting them up to it! What can we do to help?*
Kate: *McKenzie, I'm uploading a photo of the rat. I want you to take a good look at it and compare it to other rodent photos you find online. This is a weird-looking creature. We need to know for sure what it is.*
Bailey: *Icky!*
Kate: *Alexis, would you mind doing a little research online? See if you can find out any information*

> about Mad River Creamery. See if anyone might
> be holding a grudge against them.
> Alex: *I'll find out who their competitors are! And I'll
> check to see if anyone is blogging about the
> creamery.*
> Bailey: *I'll help with that. And I'll see if any
> complaints have been filed against the company,
> or if the cheese has ever made anyone sick.*
> Elizabeth: *What about me? What can I do?*
> Kate: *Can you put a prayer request on our blogsite?
> Please let people know how much we need their
> prayers. Also, ask them to pray for Sydney. She's
> competing in a skiing competition at the Winter
> Festival this Saturday. If she wins, the prize
> money will cover the cost of her trip to Mexico
> this summer.*

All the girls started chatting about Sydney's trip. When they ended, Elizabeth suggested they all pray together. She typed her prayer for all of them to see.

> *Lord, please show us what to do. We don't want to
> falsely accuse anyone. Please give us wisdom and show
> us who is doing this awful thing to the Hamptons. Help
> Kate and Sydney and keep them safe. In Jesus' Name.
> Amen.*

As she signed off the Internet, Kate thought, once again, about Nancy Drew and the movie they'd just watched. If Nancy could solve a crime. . .surely the Camp Club Girls could figure out who was sabotaging the Mad River Creamery!

CHAPTER 6

The Rat Pack

The following morning—bright and early—Sydney came in the kitchen door, her cheeks flushed pink. She shook the snow from her jacket and pulled off her scarf. "Oh, it's beautiful out there!"

"How far did you run today?" Kate asked. Seemed like every day Sydney exercised a little more and ran a little farther!

"Only two miles." Sydney shrugged as she pulled off her scarf and gloves. "I'm out of shape. Been eating too much of your Aunt Molly's good cooking. I'm really going to have to be careful once I get back home or I'm never going to stay in tip-top shape!"

"Oh, posh!" Aunt Molly laughed. "As much as you exercise, you could stand to eat even more. Never seen anyone eat as healthy as you. Well, no one your age, anyway."

"It's important! I want to do well in the competition on Saturday." Her eyes sparkled as she added, "And you know, I want to compete in the Olympics someday, too."

"She's already been in the Junior Olympics, Aunt Molly," Kate explained. "Sydney is a serious athlete." She stressed the word *serious*.

"Well, that's wonderful." Aunt Molly patted her own round

tummy and laughed. "I could stand to be more athletic. These days I just work out in the kitchen, not the gym."

"Cooking?" Sydney asked.

"No, *eating*!" Aunt Molly let out a laugh that brought Uncle Ollie in from the next room.

"What's so funny in here?" he asked.

"Aunt Molly is just telling us how she exercises," Kate said with a giggle.

"Aunt Molly. . .exercises?" Uncle Ollie looked at them with a funny expression, as if he didn't quite believe them.

Aunt Molly giggled and lifted a fork. "Like this." Opening her mouth, she pretended to eat. "I exercise my jaw." She closed her mouth and everyone laughed.

"I hope I'm as funny as you when I'm. . ." Kate stopped before finishing.

"When you're *old*, honey?" Aunt Molly laughed. "It's okay to say it. I'm no spring chicken."

"Did someone say something about old people in here?" Kate's father entered the room, yawning. "I'm feeling old and stiff. These cold mornings are really getting to me!"

"I could use a cup of coffee, myself," Kate's mother said, entering the room behind him. "Good morning, everyone!"

"Good morning, Mom." Kate reached over and gave her mom a huge hug. "We were just talking. . ."

"About me being old," Aunt Molly threw in. "But that's okay. I don't mind admitting it. Maybe I don't work out as often as I should, and maybe I can't ski like I used to when I was young, but I can certainly pay the entrance fee for Sydney to do so."

"W—what?" Sydney gave her a surprised look.

"That's right. I paid the twenty-five dollar entrance fee

for you this morning," Aunt Molly said. "I prayed about it last night and felt a little nudge from the Lord to do it. Hope you don't mind."

"Mind? Mind? Oh, Aunt Molly!" Sydney threw her arms around Kate's aunt and gave her a warm hug. "Of course I don't mind! How can I ever thank you? My mom will be so grateful!"

"Just go out there and ski the best you've ever skied." Aunt Molly patted Sydney on the back. "But take care of yourself. It's cold out and you'll be in unfamiliar territory."

"Where do we go?" Sydney asked. "Where's the best skiing around here?"

"You need to ski the Rat," Uncle Ollie explained. "That's where the competition will take place, and it's great for skiers at every level."

"The. . .what?" Sydney looked stunned.

"The Rat," he repeated. "That's the name of the most famous ski run around these parts."

"Ooo!" Sydney let out a grunt. "Why did they have to name it *The Rat*? Of all things!"

Uncle Ollie laughed. "I see your point. But don't let the name stop you. It's a great ski run. And if you make it from the top to bottom without falling, they give you a T-shirt." He went into another room and returned a few minutes later with a brown T-shirt in his hand. "I got this one back in the eighties when my ski legs were still strong."

"Wow." Kate laughed as she looked at the shirt that said THE RAT PACK on the front. "That's really cool, Uncle Ollie."

He turned it around and showed them the picture of the rat on the back.

Sydney shuddered. "I never dreamed when I said I'd

compete that I'd have to ski on. . .a rat!"

"It's just a name, honey," Aunt Molly said. "And besides, you'll never overcome your fear of rats without facing it head-on. So, if you're going to teach Kate to ski, the Rat is the perfect place."

Kate shook her head. "No thank you. No skiing for me, thanks. I'll just hang out here and work on my supersleuth blogsite."

"Oh, come on, Kate," Sydney implored. "If I can overcome my fear of rats, you can overcome your fear of skiing! And you can work on the blogsite anytime! We're on vacation now!"

"I've been a member of the Rat Pack for years," Uncle Ollie added. "We've got to keep the tradition going in our family."

"I—if I have to." Kate trembled, just thinking about it!

"Aw, don't worry," Uncle Ollie said. "I wish I could go with you girls, but I've got a project going in my workshop. Should I send along your Aunt Molly as a chaperone?"

Aunt Molly laughed. "A great one I'd be! I'd probably tumble right down the hill."

"Well, maybe I could. . ." Kate's mother started the sentence, but didn't finish it.

"Could what, Mom?"

"Well, it's been years since I skied," her mom said, "but I'm willing to give it a try. To help Sydney out, of course."

"Woo-hoo! We're going skiing!" Sydney began to squeal, but Kate's insides suddenly felt squishy!

Less than an hour later, she and Sydney arrived at the ski lift, along with Kate's mom.

"Let's put our skis on before we go up," Sydney instructed.

Kate didn't have a clue how to do that, but with help from her mom, she got the long, skinny boards strapped onto her feet.

"Now what?" she asked. She wrapped her scarf around her neck as the cold wind sent an icy shiver down her spine.

"Now we go up!" Sydney pointed up the hill.

"And we have to go up. . .in *those*?" Kate felt sick to her stomach as she looked at the little chairs.

"Oh, it's a lot of fun," her mother said. "Something you'll never forget as long as you live."

"I'm sure you're right about that!" Kate said. Somehow she knew this whole experience was something she would never forget!

"This is the coolest ski lift ever!" Sydney said. "Like something out of the past. It's so cute."

"Cute?" Kate shook her head. "Doesn't look cute to me. Looks scary."

She stared up at the contraption, trying to figure out how it worked. After a minute or two, she relaxed. "It's really just a pulley system, isn't it? I know how pulleys work, so we should be safe."

"See! You just have to look at this like you do one of your science experiments, Kate," her mom said. "I'll help you into a chair, then I'll be in the one right behind you."

"Let's do it the other way around," Kate implored. "You two go first and I'll follow behind you."

"No way!" Sydney laughed. "If we do that, we'll turn around and you'll still be standing on the ground. We need to make sure you actually make it to the top of the hill."

After a groan, Kate agreed. "Just help me, okay?"

"Of course."

A few seconds later, Kate was in one of the chairs, rising up, up, up into the air.

"Wow!" she hollered, her voice echoing against the backdrop of snow. "It's beautiful up here!" She looked around, mesmerized. Everything was so white. . .so perfect. "I can't believe I never did this before. It's so fun!"

She reached inside her pocket and pulled out her tiny digital camera. Unfortunately, she quickly learned that taking photos from the air—especially when the ground was covered in glistening white snow—was almost blinding! She put the camera away and held on for dear life.

When they reached the top of the hill, Kate carefully scooted off the chair, doing her best not to fall as the skis slipped and slid underneath her. It was so hard to balance!

"Now what?" she asked, as Sydney's feet hit the ground.

Her friend offered a playful grin. "*Now* your mom and I teach you how to ski."

"I can't promise I'll be a very good teacher," Kate's mom said, looking down the hill. "It's been awhile since I've done this. Skiing is a little scary for me, too! I'm pretty wobbly!"

"I'm sure we can teach Kate what she needs to learn to make it from the top of the hill to the bottom," Sydney said. "And before long, she'll be as fast as lightning!"

"Hmm." Kate shook her head as she looked at Sydney. "I doubt that. Have I mentioned that I'm no good at sports?"

"Only a thousand times. But don't think of this as a sport." Sydney's eyes lit with excitement. "I know! Think of yourself as one of those robots you and your dad like to build down in the basement at your house in Philly."

"Huh?" Kate gave her a curious look. "Me? A robot?"

"Sure." Sydney grew more animated by the minute. "If

you had to build a robot that could ski—one that could get from the top of a hill to the bottom without falling down—how would you build him?"

"Well. . ." Kate demonstrated by putting her feet together and bending her knees. "He'd have to be really flexible. And he'd have to be able to shift to the right and the left to get the right momentum going, so his knees would have to bend. And he'd have to have a way to come to a quick stop, so I'd have to build him ankles that turned so he could stop in a hurry!"

"Exactly!" Sydney giggled. "You've got it! Just pretend *you're* that robot."

Kate laughed. "Okay. So what would you name me?"

"Hmm." Sydney paused, deep in thought. After a moment her eyes lit up. "I know! We'll call you Snow-Bot!"

"Snow-Bot it is!" Kate nodded. "So, show me what to do, O Sports Star, you!"

Sydney looked at her with a grin. "I can't believe I'm saying this, but let's hit the Rat!"

Kate looked down at the track winding alongside some trees. "Where does it lead?"

"Who cares?" Sydney called out. "That's half the fun. . . finding out! So, c'mon! Let's go!"

Just as they started to push off, a boy whizzed by them. He wore a red jacket and cap, but looked familiar. Kate watched as he soared down the hill, faster than anyone else.

"Oh, look Kate!" Sydney pointed with a worried look. "It's that boy. . .Michael."

"I wonder what he's doing here." Kate frowned. Hopefully he wasn't really going to enter the competition. Sydney needed to win, after all!

"He's a great skier." Sydney watched him closely as he

zipped down the hill, moving gracefully around every curve. "Doesn't look like he needs the practice." They watched him ski all the way from the top of the hill to the first curve, where they lost sight of him. At that point, Kate groaned.

"Wow." She didn't know what else to say. Michael *was* good.

"I'll bet he already has his Rat Pack T-shirt," Sydney said with a sigh. "He probably has a whole drawer full! Let's face it. . .I'll never win that competition on Saturday if he skis."

"Don't say that," Kate's mother said. "I'll bet you're just as fast!"

"Probably even faster," Kate added. "I don't know anyone who can run as fast as you. So surely you're just as fast on skis!"

"Only one way to know for sure." Sydney's expression brightened. "Let's go!"

She pushed off and led the way. Kate looked down, took a deep breath, said a little prayer, and then inched her way forward with her mother at her side.

To her surprise, she went slip-sliding down the tiny hill without falling. In fact, she went even faster than her mother, who tumbled into the snow at the first big curve.

Down, down, down Kate went. . .feeling almost like a bird taking flight. The cold wind blew against her cheeks, but she didn't mind. And though skiing was a little scary, Kate had to admit it was a lot more fun than she expected. *Maybe I really am a Snow-bot!*

On the other hand. . .she looked ahead. Sydney had almost made it to the bottom of the hill. Kate had almost caught up with her when something caught her attention. "Look out!"

Kate swerved to the right to avoid hitting a baby fawn.

She tumbled head over heels, hollering the whole way. *Thump!* She ran straight into Sydney, who also took a tumble. Thankfully, Kate wasn't hurt. But when she looked up, Sydney was sitting in the snow, holding her ankle.

"Oh man!" Sydney's eyes glistened with tears.

"What is it?" Kate asked, drawing close.

Sydney groaned. "My ankle hurts. I guess I twisted it."

"How bad is it?" Kate knelt down in the snow, shivering from the cold. "Is it my fault? Did I hit you with my skis?"

"No, you didn't hit me. It's my own fault. I wasn't paying attention."

"Is it really bad?"

"I think I can walk on it." Sydney took a few steps, groaning the whole way. Each step looked more painful than the one before it.

"Do you think it's broken?" Kate asked. *Poor Sydney!*

"No. It's just twisted. I'm sure it'll be fine. When I get back to the inn, I'll put some ice on it and elevate it." After a few more steps, Sydney added, "Sure hope this doesn't keep me from being in the competition."

"We'll pray about that," Kate said. "The Lord knows you need that money for the mission trip. He's going to provide it one way or another."

Mrs. Oliver arrived. She took one look at Sydney and apologized. "I'm sorry we got separated! I made it down around the next curve before I realized you weren't with me. I took a little tumble, then came back up to look for you." She looked at the tears in Sydney's eyes and gasped. "Have you hurt yourself, honey?"

"A little," Sydney said. "My ankle hurts. I don't think it's very bad, but we should probably go back to the inn, just in case."

She hobbled beside Kate as they walked back to the car. Just as the girls reached the parking lot, Michael passed by. He gave them a funny look, but kept walking without speaking a word.

"Hey, there's Michael again." Kate watched as he disappeared into a crowd of people. *Something about that boy seems. . .weird.* Just as quickly, she was reminded not to judge him before knowing all the facts.

"He's really going to beat me now, especially if I'm injured." Sydney groaned.

"Don't talk like that!" Kate said. "You'll be fine. And you were almost to the bottom of the hill when I knocked you down. It's wasn't your fault."

"No, you don't understand. It was already hurting before that. When I rounded the first turn, I think I twisted it!"

"When we get back to the inn, we'll elevate your ankle," Kate's mom said. "I'm sure it'll be fine in no time."

They drove back to the inn, where Aunt Molly greeted them with hot chocolate and peanut butter cookies, straight from the oven. She scolded Sydney, her gray curls bobbing up and down. "Sydney, you need to be careful! You could have hurt yourself out there."

"Oh, I'm fine." She forced a smile, but Kate could tell her friend was really in pain.

"Still, I've been skiing for years and I've never gotten hurt before." Sydney groaned. "It would have to happen the day I'm trying to teach Kate."

"I'm not a very good student." Kate shrugged. "I'm the reason she fell in the first place." She buried her face in her hands, trying to stop the tears. "I told you I was no good at sports!"

"Of course you are! You were doing a great job," Sydney said. "And I think you would have passed me, too!"

"You do?" Kate looked at her, stunned.

"I do." Sydney nodded. "So, don't be so hard on yourself!"

"You're a natural, Kate!" her mother added. "You need to stop saying you're no good at sports."

"Saying we're no good at sports is an Oliver family trait." Aunt Molly laughed. "Most of us in the Oliver family are more into technology." She turned to Kate. "Did you know your Uncle Ollie is working on a new mixer for the creamery? Michael's been helping him."

"Michael sure isn't helping him today," Sydney explained. "We just saw him skiing. He's really, really good."

"Ah." Aunt Molly nodded. "He's decided to enter the competition, then."

"I guess."

"Well, don't fret, Sydney. Let's just pray and see what God does. In the meantime, you girls scoot on out to the barn and take a plate of these cookies to your Uncle Ollie. They're his favorite."

"Maybe I can help him with his project," Kate said, growing excited. "I'd love to see all of the gadgets he's working on out there. Maybe I'll learn something new!"

Sydney laughed. "That sounds just like something you'd say, Kate. You're always more excited about learning than anything else."

"That's a special gift God has given her," Aunt Molly explained. "He's gifted her with. . ."

"Lots of brains?" Sydney asked.

Everyone laughed.

"Well, I *do* get a pretty big head sometimes," Kate said

with a giggle, "especially when it comes to my science projects. But that doesn't mean I have more brains than anyone else."

"Still, you're the smartest girl in our club," Sydney said. "And I just know you'll figure out what's going on at the creamery. Before long this mystery will be solved."

"Yes, but who knows if the creamery will reopen." Aunt Molly sighed. "I talked to Geneva Hampton today, and she said the county health inspector is coming back for another inspection. Everyone is nervous they won't pass this time around."

"I still say there was something strange about that rat on the video," Kate said. "It looked different from other rats I've seen. I can't wait to hear back from McKenzie."

She thought about it as she trudged through the snow to get to the barn, where Uncle Ollie greeted her with a smile. Enough worrying about rats! For the rest of the day, she just wanted to do what she did best. . .work on gadgets and gizmos!

CHAPTER 7

Hi-Ho, the Dairy-O

After the long day of skiing and helping Uncle Ollie in the barn, Kate finally fell asleep. Every muscle in her body ached from skiing, so she tossed and turned all night trying to get comfortable.

When she finally did fall into a deep sleep, Kate had a crazy dream. She was skiing through the Mad River Creamery, chasing rats! At the end of the dream, she fell into a humongous vat of curds and whey. For some reason, the woman in the white fur coat was swimming in there, too, with the mean man! And Michael was standing nearby with skis in his hand, talking about what a great competitor he was.

When she finally awoke, Kate found herself quoting the lines from "Little Miss Muffett." Totally strange!

She rubbed her eyes and looked at the clock. Seven thirty in the morning? Too early to be up, especially on a vacation.

She rolled over in the bed, wondering where Sydney was. Had she been swallowed by a giant rat, perhaps?

Kate rose from the bed, brushed her teeth, and dressed in her warmest clothes. She had a feeling she knew just where Sydney would be. Sydney's foot had felt back to normal when they went to bed the night before. Minutes later—after shivering her way through several snowdrifts—Kate arrived in the barn and made her way back beyond Uncle Ollie's workshop to the small gym in the back. Uncle Ollie had added the gym, primarily for guests, a few years earlier. Sure enough, Sydney was on the treadmill. She looked at Kate and smiled, but never stopped walking.

"Hey, you're up early." Sydney dabbed at her forehead with a cloth.

"So are you." Kate yawned. "But you actually look like you're happy about it. I still want to be in bed!"

"I get up early every day now. Got to stay in shape, you know." Sydney stopped the elliptical machine and turned to face her. "Morning is the best time to exercise. It wakes up your body and gives you the energy to face the rest of the day. But the roads were icy this morning, so I decided this would be safer since my ankle is still a little weak. Uncle Ollie said it would be okay."

"He's probably just happy someone is actually using his workout room." Kate looked out of the window back toward the inn. In the early morning light, it looked even more beautiful, especially with snow stacked up in lovely white piles all around. "But can we talk about working out later? Aunt Molly is making oatmeal, and I never like to think about exercising and eating at the same time! Makes me nervous. Besides, I'd rather eat any day!"

"I suppose." Sydney shrugged, slowing her pace on the machine. "I can eat oatmeal. It's loaded with fiber and lots of vitamins. That's what I need to stay in shape for the competition. I just have to cut back on the brown sugar and butter, that's all."

Kate slapped herself in the forehead. "Good grief."

They trekked through the snow to the back door. As Kate

swung it open, the wonderful aroma of cinnamon greeted them. "Yum!" Her tummy rumbled.

Minutes later they sat at the table. Kate warmed her hands against the steaming bowl of oatmeal. She breathed deeply, loving the smell of the cinnamon.

"I want to go back to the Rat today," Sydney said, taking a bite of her oatmeal.

Kate started to grumble, but then remembered how much she had enjoyed skiing. *Maybe I need to stop saying I'm no good at sports! I actually found one I like!* She took a bite of the oatmeal, smiling as she tasted the sugar, cinnamon, and butter. *Mmm. Aunt Molly knows just how I like it!*

Sydney fixed her own bowl, careful to add only the tiniest bit of brown sugar. Kate sighed as she watched her friend. Maybe if she tried—really, really tried—she could be athletic like Sydney.

Or not.

Thankfully, her little brother interrupted her thoughts. "I'm gonna build another snowman," Dexter said. "My other one fell over last night. Besides, he didn't look very good. He was kind of lumpy, and his nose fell off. I heard one of the kids in the neighborhood laughing at him. I think I'd better start over."

"You go right ahead and build a new one, honey," Aunt Molly said. "But remember to forgive those kids who made fun of you first!"

"I will." He nodded and skipped off to play outside.

Aunt Molly looked at Kate and winked. "You know what I always say. . . 'A snowman is the perfect man. He's very well rounded and comes with his own broom.'"

Kate laughed. "You're so funny, Aunt Molly."

"Why, thank you very much." Her aunt handed her a mug of hot cocoa.

"I want to go back to the creamery today," Kate said, then sipped the yummy cocoa.

"Go back?" Sydney gave her a funny look. "But it's closed down, right?"

"I don't mean go inside. I just want to look around outside. To. . ."

"Snoop?" Sydney asked. "Is that what you mean?" She paused for a moment then added, "I know what you're up to, Kate Oliver. You're determined, aren't you?"

"Well, maybe a little." Kate shrugged. "We'll only be in town till the end of the week, and I want to solve this case. If we spend all of our time practicing for the competition, we won't figure out who's sabotaging the creamery."

"Or *if* someone's sabotaging them," her aunt reminded her. "We still don't know."

"And we never will if Sydney and I don't get busy."

"True, true," Aunt Molly said.

Just then, Kate remembered something. "Before we leave, I need to check my e-mail to see if any of the other Camp Club Girls have written." She signed online and checked her e-mail.

The first was from McKenzie:

> *Been checking every species of rodent on the Web. Gross! The creature in the photo you sent has the body of a rat, but is a lot larger. It also has unusual fur. I can't find any other critters with fur like that! I will keep researching, I promise! In the meantime, keep me updated!*

Operation: Excitement!

The next e-mail was from Alexis:

> *Kate and Sydney, I have been researching the*
> *Mad River Valley Creamery. It's been in the area*
> *for over seventy years—owned by the Hampton*
> *family. The current owners—Luke and Geneva*
> *Hampton—inherited it from Luke's parents in*
> *1986. Sales last year were higher than ever before.*
> *There is another creamery called Cheese De-*
> *Lite in a town about fifty miles away. Their sales*
> *aren't as high as Mad River's, but they claim to*
> *have the best cheese in the country. Cheese De-*
> *Lite is owned by Mark and Abigail Collingsworth.*
> *Their photos are on their company's website.*

Kate clicked the link and tried to go to the website Alexis was talking about, but just then the Internet stopped working. With a sigh, she rose from her seat. "I guess we should really get over to the creamery anyway. We can go skiing tomorrow, I promise."

The girls bundled up in their heavy coats and grabbed scarves and mittens.

"It's extra-cold out today," Kate's mother said, "so don't stay out long. Promise?"

"I promise, Mom." Kate kissed her mother on the cheek. "Please pray for us, okay? I want to solve this case!"

"I will, honey. I'll pray that the Lord reveals every hidden thing! Oh, and take Biscuit with you. I'll feel safer knowing he's there. He's a great watchdog!"

"And a great crime solver!" Sydney added.

"Okay." Kate reached for Biscuit's leash. He jumped up

and down, excited to be going with them.

Minutes later, the girls headed on their way to the creamery. Kate noticed how much colder it felt today. "M–man!" she said with chattering teeth. "Maybe we picked the wrong day for this!" She clung tight to Biscuit's leash and kept an eye on him.

"It's perfect ski weather." Sydney took a couple of steps, then slid a little. "Whoa." She paused to rub her ankle. "I've got to be more careful on this weak ankle! I almost fell."

"Better watch out! We've got to get that ankle healed by Saturday, so no more falling!" Kate said.

When they arrived at the creamery, they found it closed, just as Kate suspected. There were no cars out front—not even the Hamptons' SUV.

"So sad," she said, shaking her head.

"Now what do we do?" Sydney pulled her scarf tighter and looked at Kate. "How can we snoop if the place is closed down?"

"Let's go around back. We've never seen the back of the building before."

"You're not thinking of sneaking inside, are you?" Sydney asked. "'Cause if you are. . ."

"No, no. I wouldn't do that. I'm just looking to see. . ." Kate shrugged. "I don't know. Something. Anything."

Biscuit tugged on the leash, leading them to the back of the creamery. Once there, they looked at anything and everything— the doors, windows, even the alleyway behind the back parking lot. All the while, Biscuit kept his nose to the ground sniffing, sniffing, sniffing. Kate wondered what he might be smelling. *Probably all of that cheese!*

"This place is huge!" Sydney said. "I had no idea it went back this far."

"It *is* big. And it's different from any building I've ever seen before." Kate pointed. "Oh, look. There's the Dumpster."

"So?" Sydney gave her a funny look. "You're not going to make me climb in and look for evidence, are you?"

"No." Kate laughed. "But it would make a funny picture to send the other girls. I'm just looking to see evidence of rodents."

"Rodents. . .gross!" Sydney shuddered. "You think they've been hiding out in the Dumpster?"

"If they're looking for leftovers!" Kate giggled.

"Dis–*gus*–ting!" Sydney said, then laughed.

They looked all around the Dumpster, but saw nothing suspicious. Kate even checked the edges of the building, finally noticing some footprints in the snow. "Oh, Sydney, check this out. These look like tennis shoe prints."

"So?" Sydney shrugged. "Mr. Hampton probably wears tennis shoes."

"No, he wears hiking boots. I remember looking the other day. These prints start at the edge of the parking lot and go all the way to the back door." Kate pulled on the door handle, but it didn't open. "Hmm. Locked." Biscuit began to whimper and pawed at the door. "Looks like he wants in there, too."

"He's a cheese-a-holic!" Sydney said. "He wants inside so he can eat all of the cheese!"

Kate laughed and said, "Probably," then pulled Biscuit away from the building.

"Lots of people probably use that door," Sydney said, rubbing her hands together.

"I don't think so." Kate shook her head, deep in thought. This looked like the kind of door that rarely got used. "Maybe someone snuck in through this door to put rats inside."

"If so, wouldn't we see evidence of the rats? Maybe. . . droppings." Sydney looked like she might be sick as she said the word.

"Ooo, so true!" Kate dropped to her knees and looked around. After a few minutes she rose back up again and shrugged. "Don't see anything."

Pulling out her camera, she began to take pictures of the footprints. "At least we have this evidence."

"Little good it does us," Sydney said. "Just footprints in the snow. Big deal."

"But it might be a big deal," Kate reminded her. "You never know."

She snapped several photographs as she followed the trail of footprints back to the edge of the parking lot. "They disappear right here." She sighed. "Oh well."

An idea came to her. "If we measure the footprints, we should be able to determine the shoe size."

"How will that help?" Sydney asked, wrinkling her nose in confusion.

"It will help us eliminate suspects," Kate explained.

"Are you saying you have a measuring tape with you?" Sydney looked at her as if she didn't believe such a thing was possible.

"I do! It's a digital measuring tape and it records the measurements. I can't believe I haven't shown it to you before." She pulled it out of her pocket and measured the prints. "Hmm. It's 10.31 inches. I wonder what size that is."

"Well, it's not as big as your dad's shoes," Sydney observed. "But it's lots bigger than Dexter's." She stuck her foot in the footprint and shrugged. "Bigger than mine, too, and I've got pretty big feet!"

"I'm guessing it's a size eight or nine in a men's shoe," Kate said, putting the digital measuring tape away. "But we can ask my dad later."

Her cell phone rang, startling her. Kate looked at the number and smiled when she saw it was her dad. "Hi, Dad! Wow, that's a crazy coincidence! I was just talking about you."

"You were?" He laughed. "Good things, I hope."

"I need your help. We've measured some footprints. They're 10.31 inches long. What size man's shoe would that be?"

"Hmm. I might have to look that one up on the Internet," he said. "Or, measure my own feet! But before I do that, let me tell you why I'm calling. We've decided to go to the restaurant in town for lunch. Want me to swing by and pick you girls up?"

"Oh, we can walk," Kate said, her teeth chattering.

"No, honey. The temperature has really dropped. Your mother is worried you and Sydney will get frostbite. We're coming by that way, so meet us out front. Besides, we'll need to drop Biscuit back off at the inn before going to the restaurant. Oh, and Kate. . ."

"Yes, Dad?"

"How's the investigation going?"

She sighed. "Other than a few footprints, we haven't found anything suspicious. This case might just turn out to be a dead end. Maybe the creamery isn't being sabotaged, after all."

"Well, don't sound so depressed about that!" He laughed. "We want a happily-ever-after ending to this Christmas vacation, don't we?"

"Sure. But if there's really no case to solve, then I've wasted a lot of hours on our family vacation when I should have been hanging out with my family. And I've spent way too much time outdoors when I could have been sitting next to the fireplace drinking Aunt Molly's hot cocoa."

"Aw, honey, your mother and I know how much you girls love to investigate. So you go right ahead and do what comes naturally."

"Are you calling me a natural-born snoop?" Kate asked.

"If the shoe fits. . ." He laughed again. "But I am a little concerned about how much time you kids have been spending outdoors in this weather. I don't want you catching cold. . .especially right before Christmas!"

"Yes, and poor Biscuit is shivering," Kate said. "I feel bad for him. We should buy him a sweater!"

"We'll do that," her dad said. "In the meantime, we'll be by to pick you girls up in about ten minutes."

"Okay, Dad. Oh, and Dad?"

"Yes, honey?"

"I love you. Thanks so much for understanding."

"Love you, too, kiddo."

As they ended the call, something caught Kate's attention. A car pulled around the back of the creamery through the alley. She and Sydney slipped behind a Dumpster and watched. Kate did her best to keep Biscuit quiet, but he kept whimpering. "Hush, boy!" she whispered.

"Wow, that's a great car. A Jaguar!" Sydney whispered, her eyes wide with excitement. "Do you suppose the Hamptons own a car that fancy?"

Kate shook her head. "They don't seem the type. Besides, I saw Mr. Hampton drive away in an SUV the other day, not a Jaguar."

"Seems kind of weird that a fancy car like that would be in an alley behind a creamery," Sydney said. She peeked out once again, then pulled her head back with a worried look on her face. "We'd better be careful. I think they're slowing down."

The tires crunched against the icy pavement, finally stopping. A woman stepped out and looked around in every direction, then signaled and a man got out. Biscuit began to growl. Kate pulled on his leash to get him to stop, but he refused.

Kate gasped. "Do you see who that is?" she whispered. "It's the woman who fainted the other day. . .and her husband."

"Oh yeah." Sydney squinted. "The woman in the expensive coat and the man with the sour look on his face." Sydney paused a moment to look at them. "Ooo! He looked this way. I hope he didn't see us."

They watched as the man and woman walked across the back of the building. He seemed to be looking for something. At one point, he stood on his toes and tried to look into a window. Biscuit yipped, but Kate tapped him on the nose and whispered, "Shush!"

"Why do you suppose that man is looking inside?" Kate whispered to Sydney. "He just went on the tour the other day, so he knows what the building looks like on the inside."

"I don't know," Sydney said. "But it's really suspicious. Oh!" She paused, then looked at Kate with a gleam in her eye. "Kate, look! He's wearing tennis shoes!"

Kate squinted to see the man's white tennis shoes.

"Wow!" she whispered. "You're right."

That didn't necessarily make him a suspect, but it did

make her wonder!

They continued to watch the man. He put his hand on the doorknob of the back door and tried it, but it wouldn't turn. Once again, Biscuit started to growl. Kate tried to quiet him. "He's trying to break in!" she whispered.

"We don't know that for sure," Sydney said. "After all, we tried that knob, too, and we weren't trying to break in."

"True." Kate shook her head as she watched the man. He walked to another window and looked inside, then continued across the icy parking lot to the side of the building.

"It's like he's looking over every detail of the building," Sydney whispered. "Like he's scoping it out. But, why?"

"I wish I knew! Something is odd about him, for sure," Kate said.

"Do you think they have something to do with the rats?" Sydney asked. "Maybe we should find out who these people are and see if there's any connection."

Just then Kate's cell phone rang. . .loudly! Then Biscuit started barking even more loudly!

"Oh no!" she whispered. She reached to silence the phone, but the man turned and looked in their direction. "Hush, Biscuit! Hush!" Kate pressed the IGNORE button on her phone and took a couple of deep breaths. "Look the other way. Look the other way," she whispered as she watched the man.

However, instead of looking the other way. . .he began to walk right toward them! Kate's heart felt like it might explode.

"Lord, help us!" she whispered. "Please!"

The Plot Thickens

Kate's heart raced as the stranger's shoes crunched through the snow in their direction. *Oh no! Please turn around!*

"What is it, Mark?" the woman called out. "What are you doing over there?"

"I heard something behind the Dumpster," he hollered back. "I'm checking it out."

Kate squatted and tried to hide on the farthest side of the Dumpster, praying he wouldn't see them. Unfortunately, the closer he came, the more Biscuit growled.

Just when Kate was sure they would be discovered, a car horn beeped from the front of the creamery.

"It's Dad!" Kate mouthed to Sydney.

The woman hollered out, "Mark! C'mon, let's get out of here before we get caught!"

"I'm out of here!" The man ran back toward his car, and the woman joined him. Seconds later, they went speeding off.

The car disappeared back into the alleyway and Biscuit ran after it, barking at the top of his lungs. Kate sat shivering behind the Dumpster. "I c–can't b–believe they didn't c–catch us."

"I know! That scared me *so* bad!" Sydney said, her eyes wide with fear. "I've never been that scared!"

"Me either! What do you think they were doing here?" Kate asked. "Do you think they put the rats in the store the other day? Seems pretty obvious, if they did!"

"I don't know, but it sure is suspicious!" Sydney said. She glanced Kate's way, still looking nervous. "Oh, by the way, who called?"

Kate glanced at the caller ID on the phone. "Bailey. I'll call her back later. No time to talk right now!"

"Just wait till she hears what she interrupted!" Sydney said.

The girls heard a horn honk again.

"That's my dad," Kate said. "He's probably getting worried. Let's make a run for it!"

Sydney took off running and Kate followed. As always, she could barely keep up with her friend. "I've. . .been. . . eating. . .too. . .much. . .cheese!" she said as she slid back and forth across the slippery pavement. "It's. . .slowing. . . me. . .down!"

"Just. . .keep. . .going!" Sydney called out. "You'll make it!"

As they rounded the front of the building, the girls saw the Olivers' car. Kate was never so happy to see her parents. She opened the car door and climbed in, happy to find it warm inside. Biscuit jumped in on top of her, his wet paws making her colder than ever. "Sit, boy!"

He curled up next to her on the seat, panting.

"I th—thought I w—was going to f—freeze out there!" she said with chattering teeth. Her hands were shaking so hard, she could barely close the door.

"So, any more suspicious stuff to report?" Dexter asked, looking up from his handheld video game.

"Is there ever!" Kate told the whole story about the man and the woman.

Her mother gave her a stern look.

"Kate Oliver, this is getting dangerous. You're in over your head. I think it's time to call the police."

"I understand your concerns." Kate's father reached over to pat her hand. "But let's not get too worked up. It was just a car in a parking lot. No one set off any alarms or anything. And the girls are fine." He looked at them both. "You are fine, aren't you?"

Kate nodded and Sydney muttered a quick, "Uh-huh." However, inside, Kate still felt like a bowl full of jelly! She quivered all over! Was it from the cold. . .or fear?

"We'd better get Biscuit back to the inn," Kate's mother said. "He looks tired."

Minutes later, they dropped him off at the inn. The adults chatted all the way to the restaurant, but Kate couldn't seem to say a word. Instead, she just kept thinking about the man. Why was he scoping out the building? Were the footprints his? He was wearing tennis shoes, after all.

They arrived at the restaurant in just a few minutes. As they started to get out of the car, Kate's father turned her way.

"Before we go inside, give me your digital measuring tape and I'll measure my feet," he said.

"Why in the world would you do that?" Kate's mother asked. "And in a restaurant parking lot, of all places!"

"I'm trying to help Kate solve a big case!" He pulled off his shoes and Kate handed him the measuring tape. After a moment, he said, "My feet are 10.7 inches long and I wear a size ten. So I'm going to guess your suspect is probably a size nine in a men's shoe."

"What makes you think it's a man?" Aunt Molly asked. "Maybe that woman with the white coat has extra-large feet!"

"Good point." Kate shrugged. "We really don't know." As they walked into the restaurant, she leaned over and whispered to Sydney, "Hey, what size feet do you think that man had? The one behind the creamery, I mean."

"I wasn't looking at his feet, Kate," Sydney said, shaking her head. "Honestly! I was too busy trying not to get caught!"

"Yeah, me, too." Kate sighed, then whispered a prayer of thanks. *Thank You, Lord, that we didn't get hurt back there. Thanks for sending my dad at just the right moment!*

As they entered the restaurant, Kate's wrist began to buzz. "Oh! I have an e-mail on my Internet wristwatch." As they waited to be seated, she checked it.

"Who was it?" Sydney asked.

"Elizabeth. She just wanted to let us know she was praying for us this morning."

"Wow!" Sydney smiled. "I'm glad she was! What a cool coincidence! We really needed it, didn't we? Her timing was perfect!"

"It sure was!" Kate agreed.

"That's how God works," Aunt Molly said with a nod. "He works out every detail in His perfect timing."

The hostess led the Oliver family to a booth, and everyone sat down. As soon as she got the menu, Kate began to look over it. Her stomach was rumbling, and she could hardly wait to eat!

Just then she heard a familiar voice. Looking up, she saw Michael in the next booth, talking to the waitress.

"Hi, Michael," Kate called out. She waved, trying to be friendly.

He looked her way and nodded, then turned back to his handheld video game, not even pretending to be nice.

"Humph." Kate crossed her arms at her chest.

"Be quick to forgive, honey," Aunt Molly reminded her. "Even when others don't respond the way they should. That's the perfect time to forgive. . .before you get upset."

"Yes, but he *never* responds the way he should," Sydney said quietly. "And have you noticed he never looks happy?"

"And why is he sitting all alone in a restaurant?" Kate asked. "That's weird."

"Oh, I can explain that part. His mother is a waitress here." Aunt Molly pointed at a woman with dark hair pulled back in a ponytail. "That's who he was talking to. Her name is Maggie. She's worked here for as long as I can remember, so Michael spends a lot of his free time here. Keeps him from being lonely, I guess."

"I see." Kate raised her menu, trying to hide the fact that she was snooping.

"The poor kid's been through a lot," Uncle Ollie said with a sad look on his face. "His dad left when he was only three, and now, of course, Michael has lost his grandpa. So anything we can do to keep him from being too lonely is a good thing."

"Oh, I know, but there's something about him that worries me." Sydney shook her head. "I don't know what it is, exactly. Just. . .something."

"Are you worried he'll beat you in the contest?" Uncle Ollie asked with a mischievous twinkle in his eye. "'Cause I have it on good authority you're pretty fast. I wouldn't worry if I were you."

"Oh, I'm not worried. I promise."

Kate looked at her friend, wishing she could read her thoughts.

Uncle Ollie rose from his seat and invited Michael to join them at their table. He came, but he didn't look happy. When he sat next to Kate, she tried to smile. . .tried to be friendly. But he didn't make it easy! He sat there like a bump on a log, just staring at his Nintendo DS Lite while everyone else talked.

Kate's cell phone rang, and she looked at the number. "Oh, it's Bailey! I forgot to call her back." She looked at her mother and asked, "Can I answer it? Do you mind?"

"Go ahead, honey," her mom said. "Just don't be long. We need to order our food soon."

Kate nodded then answered the phone with a smile. "Hey, Bailey! What's up?"

"I found some information online," Bailey said, sounding breathless and overly excited, as always. "Did you know the Mad River Creamery fired their security guard several months ago?"

"No. How did you find that out?"

"I googled the name *Mad River Creamery* and went to every site that came up. Every one. Way down on the list I found a blogsite that belongs to some nameless person, complaining about someone being fired from the creamery this past summer."

"Really? But you don't know who owns that blog? That's weird."

"Really weird!" Bailey said. "It was all very suspicious. Just sort of a warning for readers to stay away from the creamery. I guess this person was the one who got fired. Or maybe a relative or a friend. . .something like that."

"Ooo, the plot thickens!" Kate looked at Sydney in anticipation and whispered, "There's more to this than meets the eye!"

Sydney looked surprised, but didn't say anything. Instead, she stared at Michael out of the corner of her eye, as if she didn't trust him.

"Did the website mention anything about rats?" Kate asked Bailey.

As she said the word *rats*, everyone at the table looked her way. Kate's mother shook her head, as if to say, "This is not appropriate dinner table conversation, Kate!" Kate mouthed the words "I'm sorry," then put her hand over her mouth, waiting for Bailey's response.

After a moment, Bailey said, "No, but there was plenty of stuff on there about getting even!"

"Very suspicious. Makes me wonder. . ." Kate started to say more, but noticed the look on her mom's face. "Bailey, can I call you back later? We're in a restaurant right now, and I need to order my meal."

"Sure. I'll text you if I find out anything else."

"Please do."

Kate ended the call and turned back to everyone at the table with a cheery voice. "So, what's everyone going to order? I'm starved!" She opened the menu and pointed to a large baked potato with all the trimmings. "Mmm! This looks good. I'm going to get this." After a moment, her gaze shifted to a picture of roast beef with mashed potatoes and gravy. "Or this! Yummy! I haven't had roast and potatoes in ages. And can we order dessert after, Mom? I'm starved!"

She pointed to a picture of coconut cream pie. "They have my favorite!"

"I like the cherry pie," Dexter said, pointing at another picture.

"Their apple pie is great," Uncle Ollie added, "but not as

great as your Aunt Molly's!"

"Pie has a lot of empty calories, Kate," Sydney whispered. "It's not really good for you."

"Empty?" Kate looked at her friend, curious.

"That just means it's not really good for you, but it's fattening," Sydney explained. "Most sweets are nothing but empty calories."

"Oh." Kate closed the menu and thought about that for a minute. Finally, she cheered up. "But I feel full after I eat pie, not empty. So it can't be all bad, right?" She flashed a smile at Sydney, who laughed.

"I love you, Kate," Sydney said. "You always see the good in everything."

"Especially in food!" Kate giggled. "And I'm starving right now!"

"Solving mysteries makes you hungry, eh?" her father asked. "That's my girl. But you'll never *really* starve, that's for sure!"

"Nope! I have the best appetite in town."

"And the best nose for snooping," her mother added. "And I'm assuming Bailey was calling with news about the creamery?"

"Well, yes, but. . ." She shrugged. "I don't want to bother you guys with this while we're eating."

"Tell us," Aunt Molly said. "We want to know."

"Well, Bailey thinks maybe she's stumbled across a clue. Something that will help us figure out who's sabotaging the creamery."

"*If* someone's sabotaging the creamery," Aunt Molly reminded her. "We still don't know for sure."

"Yes." Kate nodded. "That's true." Even as she spoke the words, however, she knew that it *was* true. Someone was trying to sabotage the creamery. And she would figure out who. . .and why!

"What's the deal with you girls?" Michael rolled his eyes. "Why is it so important to figure this out? What are you trying to prove, anyway?"

"Trying to prove?" Kate asked, confused. "Nothing, really."

"We just like to help people." Sydney shrugged. "It's what we do."

"And they're good at it!" Dexter added.

Michael rolled his eyes. "Why do you want to help those Hamptons?" He muttered something under his breath.

"Don't you like the Hamptons?" she asked.

Instead of answering, he got up and left the restaurant without even saying good-bye.

"Well, that was strange," Aunt Molly said with a stunned expression.

"Very!" Kate's mother added.

"Not like him at all," Ollie added. "In fact, I've never seen this side of him. Very odd."

"I'm telling you, something about that boy bothers me," Sydney added. "I can't put my finger on it, but he's just. . . weird." After a second, she looked ashamed. "I'm sorry. I shouldn't have said that. I'm trying not to judge people, and look what I just did." She sighed.

"We all make mistakes," Kate added, "but you're right about the fact that something about him seems suspicious."

Thankfully, the waitress showed up at the table.

"Hi, Maggie!" Aunt Molly said with a smile. "Good to see you."

"Well, it's great to see you, too," she said. "You're my favorite customers, you know."

"She says that to all of her customers," Uncle Ollie whispered in Kate's ear.

"I heard that, Ollie Oliver, and you know it's not true!" Maggie grinned. "You folks are my very favorite." She looked around and asked, "Hey, what happened to that son of mine? I thought I saw him sitting here with you."

"He was." Uncle Ollie shook his head. "Not sure what happened, but he left in a hurry."

"Hmm." She shook her head. "He's been acting mighty strange since my pop. . ." Maggie's eyes filled with tears, and Kate suddenly felt very sorry for her.

"I'm sorry," Kate said, feeling a lump grow in her throat. How terrible it must be to lose your father! She looked over at her dad and tried—just for a moment—to imagine it. The idea was so painful she pushed it away immediately.

"Sorry to get all emotional on you." Maggie wiped the tears out of her eyes with the back of her hand and smiled. "What would you like to order, folks?"

Kate ordered the soup and sandwich combo then listened as everyone else ordered. Everything sounded so good! At the end, she changed her order to a burger and fries to match her dad's.

While they waited for the food, Sydney changed the topic to the upcoming competition.

"Do you think you're ready, honey?" Aunt Molly asked.

"I don't know. I've only had one practice," Sydney said. "But Kate and I are going back to the Rat tomorrow so I can try again."

"I'm glad you're learning to ski, Kate," Aunt Molly said. "And you never know. . .we may turn you into a sports fan after all!"

"That would be the day!" Kate's father said. "My girl is far too busy helping me with all of my gadgets and gizmos to think about sports when we're home. That's one reason I'm glad we're in Mad River Valley. She can stop thinking about electronics and start thinking about just being a kid!"

Kate shrugged. "Skiing is okay, but you know me, Dad. I'd rather be working on one of the robots with you."

After a moment's pause, she added, "Oh, and by the way. . .speaking of robots. . ." She went on to tell him Sydney's idea about the snow-bot.

"Snow-bot?" He looked at her with a sparkle in his eyes. "What a marvelous idea. Maybe when we get home, we could actually build a little snow-bot and use it for ski demonstrations! Can't you see it now?" He went off on a tangent, talking about how they could sell the robot to people who wanted to learn how to ski.

"Wonderful idea!" Uncle Ollie threw in.

"Hey, it was my idea," Sydney said with a pretend pout. "If you make millions off of this robot, do I get some of the profits?"

"Of course, of course!" Kate's dad laughed. "You'll get a percentage and so will Kate. Who knows. . ." He grinned from ear to ear. "Snow-bot might just be a big hit!"

"Oh, I hope so!"

Everyone went on to talk about skiing, but Kate's thoughts were on something else. She kept thinking about what happened at the creamery. The man and woman in the car. . .what were they doing there? Something about them just didn't seem right. And what was up with those footprints? Did they belong to the man. . .or someone else? How would she ever find out?

Glancing out of the window, she happened to notice Michael passing by. The minute she saw him, a chill came over her. Something about him made her very nervous. Very nervous, indeed.

With a sigh, she turned back to her family and friends, determined to stay focused on the important things. *Lord, don't ever let me forget the people who are right in front of me! They're more important than any case!*

Right now, the investigation could wait!

Lost in the Maze

On Friday, just one day before the big competition, Kate went with Sydney to ski one more time. This time she wasn't as nervous as before. In fact, she almost looked forward to it.

"I'm getting faster every time!" Sydney said, looking more confident than she had in days. "But there are still a couple of areas that slow me down. I need to figure out how to pick up speed in those places!"

"Yes, there are some crazy twists and turns on the course," Kate agreed. After all, she'd already fallen several times and had the bruises to prove it!

"I think I can make it to the bottom without falling this time," Sydney said. "But I want to increase my speed in the tricky places. So let's do our best to get to the bottom in record time today, okay?"

"Sure. And I'll time us." Kate pointed to her super-duper wristwatch. "I'll bet you're the fastest one out there!"

"Hardly!" Sydney laughed. "But maybe I'll do better today than last time."

The girls dressed in their warmest clothes and prepared to head off to the slopes.

"Do you think you'll be okay without me?" Kate's mom asked. "Molly and I have plans to visit Michael's mother today. She seems a little lonely, so we want to cheer her up by taking her to the tearoom for some girl time."

"That's sweet, Mom," Kate said. "But don't worry about us. Mad River Valley is a safe place. Nothing'll happen."

"They'll be fine," Aunt Molly assured her. "It's a safe course, and lots of people are around. Don't fret!"

"Well, just stay as warm as you can." Kate's mom handed her some money. "And if you get cold, go inside and buy some hot chocolate. Promise? And don't forget to call if you need anything. We're just a few minutes away."

"I promise, Mom." Kate grinned. "But don't worry! I'm twelve now, remember? And it's not like I haven't been to the slopes before. We just went the other day. This time I'm sure it will be even easier than before."

"I know, but it's hard to watch your children grow up and do things on their own!" Kate's mom shrugged and her eyes misted.

Kate gave her a hug and whispered, "I promise not to grow up *too* fast." She wondered what it would feel like to be a mom, watching your child do something alone for the first time.

A few minutes later, Uncle Ollie drove Kate and Sydney to the ski area. As he stopped the car, he gave them a warning. "We're expecting more snow this afternoon, girls, so finish skiing early. I'll be here to pick you up at two o'clock. I think that will give you plenty of time. Try to be here waiting so I don't have to come looking for you."

"We'll be here!" Kate said. She waved good-bye as she and Sydney headed across the parking lot with their skis.

When they arrived at the ski lift, this time Kate wasn't as scared to get on it. In fact, she looked forward to it. As they rode up, up, up the hill, she breathed in the fresh morning air and hollered, "I love it here!" to Sydney, who was in the seat below hers. Her voice echoed against the snow-packed mountain. *This place doesn't just look awesome; it sounds awesome!* she thought.

Finally, they reached the top of the slope. Even though Kate wanted to ski, she still felt a little nervous. She and Sydney made their way to the Rat, and Sydney looked at her with a grin. "I'm overcoming my fear of rats by skiing here!"

"Me, too!" Kate giggled. "Funny, huh? Think of all the stories we'll have to tell the other girls!"

Kate rubbed her gloved hands together for warmth before reaching for her poles. Then she and Sydney took off soaring down the hill. The crisp, cold wind whipped at her face, making it tingle. In fact, it was so cold that her arms and legs began to ache.

The first big turn caught Kate off guard, and she almost fell. Thankfully, she got control of herself and made it without tumbling. A short time later, she came to a small drop-off.

"Woo!" she hollered as she soared into the air, then landed gracefully below. *I can't believe I did that!*

Now for the hard part. The next part of the course was filled with twists and turns, and there were some trees ahead. *Better steer clear of those, for sure!*

She bent her knees and leaned into the course, picking up speed as she rounded the first sharp turn. Then the second. As she came to the section of trees, she leaned to the left to avoid them.

Just as Kate sailed into a clearing, she heard a terrible cry. To her left, Sydney tumbled head over heels into the snow.

"Oh no!" Kate got so distracted watching her friend that

she lost her footing and tipped over sideways. She landed on her bottom in the snow. It didn't hurt too badly, but then she rolled a couple of times and banged her elbow into a rock. "Ouch!"

Finally coming to a stop, she pulled off her skis and ran to Sydney's side. "Are you okay? What's happened?"

Sydney sat in the snow, gripping her ankle with tears streaming down her face. "Oh, Kate. It's my ankle! It's worse! *Much* worse. I think I've really hurt it this time!"

"What did you do?"

"I don't know. It was already hurting this morning when I walked on the treadmill. I guess I should have told someone, but I didn't. I thought I could make it stronger by walking on it, but I guess I was wrong."

"Oh, Sydney!"

"I feel like I've twisted it again. But it hurts so bad! Much worse than before."

"What should we do?" Kate asked, looking around. Oh, if only someone else would come by and offer to help! What made her think they could come to the slopes alone?

"I—I think we need to go back," Sydney stammered. "Do you mind?"

"Of course not!" Kate looked around again, hoping for some help. The mountainside remained empty. The only thing she heard was the sound of her voice echoing against the snow. "Will we have to walk down to the bottom?"

"I guess." Sydney looked around. "But I don't think I'll make it, to be honest. Maybe there's a trail closer to the trees. It's too dangerous to be out in the open like this. Any moment a skier could come flying down the hill and run us over!"

"Oh, I never thought of that!" Kate held tight to her

limping friend's arm and led her to some trees.

When they got there, Sydney gripped her ankle and began to cry harder. "I can't believe I did this! I'm never going to get to go on my mission trip now."

"Don't worry about that right now," Kate said. "One thing at a time."

She looked around, a little confused about where they were. Just then a bit of falling snow caught her attention. "Oh no! It's snowing again. Uncle Ollie said it wasn't supposed to snow till this afternoon."

"That's not good, Kate. We can't get stuck out here in the snow, especially if my ankle is too weak to go to the bottom of the hill!"

"I know, but what can we do?" Kate started to tremble.

"We've got to get back to the parking lot somehow." Sydney dabbed at her eyes with gloved hands. "Do you think you can help me?"

"I'll try." Kate looked around. "But which way is the parking lot? I'm confused."

"I think it's east?" Sydney looked up with pain in her eyes. "Do you have a compass?"

"Yes." Kate pulled out her digital measuring tape with the built-in compass. "Okay, east is this way." She pointed to their left. "You're sure it's east, right?"

"I think so." Sydney shrugged. "But right now I'm in so much pain, I'm not sure about anything."

A cold wind blew over them, making an eerie sound against the backdrop of the mountain. Kate shivered.

"Wow. That was creepy. Sounded like the mountain was crying."

"No, I'm the only one crying," Sydney said, forcing a smile.

"Would it be better if I went after someone to help carry you back?" Kate offered. She hated to leave Sydney here, but she didn't know what else to do.

"No, I think I can hop on my good foot, as long as we go slow. Just help me, Kate. Please." Sydney rose to her feet, almost falling over. She leaned against Kate.

"Take slow, steady steps," Kate said. "And let me do most of the work."

She had never seen Sydney like this before. Usually Sydney was the one running races or playing sports. But now—with an injured ankle—would she even be able to ski in the competition? It was tomorrow. What would happen if she didn't win the three hundred dollars? Would she get to go on the mission trip?

After the girls had been walking a few minutes, the snow began to fall even harder.

"It—it's blinding me," Kate said, shivering. "I can't see more than a few feet."

"And I'm getting colder by the minute," Sydney added. "It's making my ankle hurt worse."

They followed what looked like a trail. It wound in and out, in and out, and seemed to lead absolutely nowhere. They faced dead ends at every turn!

"Now I know what a mouse feels like, hunting for cheese in a maze," Kate said, then groaned. "No wonder they call this slope the Rat. It just like being trapped inside a gigantic trap!"

Minutes later, Sydney shook her head. "I have to stop for a minute, Kate. It hurts too much to keep going. Stop. Please."

"Of course." Kate stopped, grateful to find a spot under

some trees where the snow was packed tight. After watching Sydney rub her ankle, Kate had an idea. "Oh, I can't believe I didn't think of this sooner!"

"What?"

"I have a GPS tracker on my cell phone. I can type in the name of the lodge next to the parking lot, and the tracker will lead us back. . .no problem."

The wind began to howl louder and louder, and the girls huddled together. Off in the distance, the skies began to look heavy and gray.

Kate opened her phone and waited for a signal. "Come on." She shook the phone, frustrated. "Work! Please work!" A few seconds later, she had a faint signal. Kate quickly typed in the name of the lodge.

"Pray, Sydney," she said. "This has to work."

"Okay. I'm praying." Sydney's eyes were filled with tears, and Kate knew her ankle must really be hurting. Sydney never complained!

A couple of minutes later, just as Kate started to get her hopes up, she lost the signal on her phone. She closed it with a sigh. "What's the point of having GPS tracking if I can't get a signal?"

A burst of cold air caught her by surprise, and she began to shake. "Is it getting colder, or am I just imagining it?"

"I—it's g—getting c—colder. And the snow is really coming down now. See?" Sydney pointed to the skies then huddled next to Kate, shaking. She closed her eyes. "I don't know why, but I'm suddenly getting tired."

"It's the altitude. And the dark skies."

Kate looked up. The sky hung heavy over them, a sure sign that a heavy snowfall was on its way.

"W—what are we going to do?" Sydney broke down in tears.

Kate had never seen this side of Sydney before. Usually her friend was the strong one. . .the brave one.

Now I have to be strong and brave!

"They're going to find us," Kate said, doing her best to sound confident. "We've got the transmitters on our snow boots, remember? That's the very best tracking device."

"Yes, but your Uncle Ollie's not coming back till two o'clock," Sydney reminded her. "It will be hours before they even realize we're missing. No one will know to look for a signal till then, and I'll be frozen stiff by two o'clock!"

"Don't say that!" Just the thought of it sent a shiver down Kate's spine.

"I'm sorry." Sydney pulled at the scarf around her neck. "I don't know why I'm so scared."

"It's normal when things go wrong. Just keep praying, Sydney."

"I need to," her friend said. "My throat is starting to feel funny. And my eyes sting from the ice."

"Would you be okay for a minute if I went to look for someone to help?" Kate asked. "I'll come right back, I promise."

Sydney leaned against the tree and nodded. "Just promise you won't stay gone long. And leave a trail so you know how to get back to me. I don't want to get stuck out here alone."

"Me either. I'll follow my footprints back." As soon as Kate spoke the word *footprints*, she remembered the footprints they'd found behind the creamery. Would they ever figure out who was sabotaging the Hamptons?

This isn't the time to worry about that!

Kate hated to leave her friend, but she wanted to check something. If she was remembering correctly, there was an old red barn just south of here. She'd seen it yesterday when the skies were clear. If they could just make it to that barn, they could warm up. And maybe she could get better reception there, too. If so, she could call her father or Uncle Ollie on her cell phone. They would come in a hurry!

A few minutes later, Kate found a trail. It wound through tangles of brush and snowcapped trees. She turned to the right and then the left, trying to get her bearings. *Lord, help me. Please.* A tree branch slapped her in the face, and snow flew everywhere.

"Oh!" The pain shot through her cheek, and she ducked to wedge her way underneath the low snow-covered branches.

A few seconds later, she heard the strangest sound. . . like something falling and hitting the earth below. Taking a step, she heard a *c-ra-ack!* The ground underneath her shifted, and she started to tumble forward!

Down, down, down she went. . .praying all the way!

CHAPTER 10

Along Came a Spider

Kate tumbled down through several layers of snow and ice until she landed with a *thud* on an icy patch of ground. She rubbed at her backside and cried out in pain. "Oh, help!" Right away, she began to pray. "Lord, get me out of here. Please!"

Pushing her weight backward, she landed on sturdy ground. However, the place where she stood just seconds before collapsed. Down, down, down it went, making a crashing sound below.

She peeked over the edge, realizing she'd almost stepped off the edge of a drop-off. Somehow she had stopped. . .just in time! Kate's heart thumped hard against her chest. How close she'd come to falling! Another look convinced her it was a long way to the bottom. *I could have died!* Something—or *Someone*—had saved her, just in the nick of time!

And where was the crackling sound coming from? She still heard it off in the distance. Squinting against the blinding snow, she saw something that looked like a frozen waterfall to her right. Pieces of the ice had broken off and fallen into the spot way down below. The frozen water led down to the place where she might have landed, if she'd taken one more step.

Whoa! Talk about a long drop! Thank You, Lord! You saved my life.

Kate scooted backward on her bottom, finally confident enough to try to stand. Only one problem. Her clothes were now damp and so cold. Straightening her legs was tough. And her feet suddenly ached. "Lord, just a few more minutes," she whispered. "I have to find a safe place."

Struggling against the strong wind, she kept her balance. Kate tried her cell phone once more. No signal. Determined to succeed, she turned toward the right. *I can do all things through Christ who strengthens me. I can do all things through Christ who strengthens me.*

For whatever reason, she thought about Phillip and her science project. Suddenly—with her life in jeopardy—it seemed so silly to hold a grudge against someone else. Really, the only thing that mattered right now was getting help for Sydney!

After a few treks through the deepening snow, Kate finally caught a glimpse of something red in the distance. "Oh, good!"

An old, dilapidated barn stood alone against the backdrop of white snow.

It's a long way away, but I think we can make it.

She used her own footprints to run back to Sydney. Kate found her in tears, seated on the ground next to a tree.

"I've found a safer place to wait," Kate explained. "Do you think you can take a few steps with my help, as long as they're not downhill?"

"I can do all things through Christ who strengthens me," Sydney spoke above the rising winds. "That was our Bible verse a couple of weeks ago in Sunday school."

"Wow! That's amazing! I was just quoting that verse!"

With Kate's help, Sydney rose and leaned against her. Together they took their first step through the mounds of snow.

"I can do all things through Christ who strengthens me," Sydney said.

"I can do all things through Christ who strengthens me," Kate echoed.

They continued saying the words until they drew closer, closer, closer to the old red barn. Finally they reached the door.

"It looks really old, Kate," Sydney said. "I don't even think that door will open. The hinges are broken."

"It *has* to open. It just has to." Kate reached for the door, praying all the time. After a struggle, she managed to get it open. "There! See!"

"Oh, it's dark in here." Sydney took a few hobbling steps inside, and Kate followed her.

"I wish we had a flashlight. It's kind of creepy."

"You don't think there are any. . ." Sydney's voice trailed off.

"What?" Kate asked.

"Rats?" Sydney whispered.

Kate shuddered. "Oh, I didn't think of that. How strange would that be? To find rats here."

She squinted, her eyes finally getting adjusted to the dark. "Ooo! This place is filled with spiderwebs!"

She found herself caught in one and began to bat at it, pulling it apart. "Gross!"

"This is so creepy!" Sydney said. "I don't like spiders any more than I do rats. But this place is filled with them. Look!" She pointed as a large spider crawled up the wall.

"Remember your Aunt Molly said the creamery had spiders, too? I wonder if they were this big?"

"I don't know. But, look, Sydney. There are some mounds of hay over there." Kate pointed, getting more excited by the minute. "If we can get down inside the hay, I think we'll warm up. Then I'll try to use my phone again."

The girls had just settled down into the soft, cushy straw, when Kate thought she saw the door crack open. "W–who is it?" she called out. She began to shake all over!

The door slammed shut, making a clacking noise as the wind caught it and pushed it back and forth.

"Do you think that was a person?" Sydney asked. "Or maybe just the wind?"

"I'm too scared to look!" Kate pinched her eyes shut and sat in fear for a moment. Then, just as quickly, she felt courageous. "I'm tired of being a scaredy-cat! I'm going to look." She ran over to the door and inched it open. Staring out onto the open expanse of snow, she thought she caught a glimpse of someone.

"Come and help us!" she called out.

The person—who looked like a boy or maybe even a man—disappeared in the distance. He wore a dark jacket and carried a big backpack. But why would he be hanging out at an empty, abandoned barn? And what was in the backpack?

Or was he even real? Kate turned back to Sydney and sighed.

"Who was it?" her friend asked.

"I don't know." Kate rubbed at her eyes. "Maybe it was no one! Have you ever heard of a mirage?"

"A mirage?" Sydney yawned. "Like, something you see only in your imagination, but it seems so real you actually think it *is* real?"

"Right." Kate shrugged. "First it looked like someone. . . then it didn't. Maybe my overactive imagination is working overtime! My mom accuses me of that sometimes."

With the door still cracked, Kate opened the phone and saw a tiny signal. The GPS tracking system opened, but the signal faded almost immediately. Kate prayed a silent prayer: *Lord, I'm scared. And I don't know what to do. But I know You do. Help us, Lord. Please! I'm starting to imagine things— and they're not good!*

"My ankle hurts even more." Sydney's voice sounded weak. "And I'm getting so tired. Feels like it's nighttime, but it's barely even noon. Right?"

"Right. But I'm getting sleepy, too," Kate agreed with a yawn. "Maybe it's because it's so dark in here." She walked back over to the straw and curled up next to Sydney. She wanted to rest, but visions of spiders and spiderwebs kept her awake. What if she dozed off and one of those creepy crawlers crawled into her hair? Or down her arm! Ooo! What a terrible thought!

Minutes later, Kate's eyes grew heavier, heavier, heavier. Though she tried to fight the sleepiness, before she realized it, her eyes were closing—and she was sound asleep. She dreamed of rats and spiders, all chasing her down a big hill!

Kate couldn't be sure how much time passed, or if she was dreaming. But at some point, she heard the sound of a man's voice outside the barn and the sound of a dog barking. It sounded like a distant echo, like something from a dream.

"W—what is that?" She sat up, trying to figure out where she was. She could only make out shadows in the dark barn, but she definitely heard sounds coming from outside. The barking continued, sounding more and more familiar!

"Biscuit!" Was she dreaming? It sounded like her canine companion!

"Is anyone in there?" a man's booming voice rang out.

Kate jumped up, her eyes still heavy with sleep. "Sydney! They've found us."

Sydney awakened and rubbed her eyes. "W–what? Who's found us?"

"Sounds like Pop and Uncle Ollie!" Kate tried to stand but could hardly move, she was so cold. Every joint and muscle ached.

"We're in here!" she called out. "Help us, please!"

"We're here! We're here!" Sydney called out, sounding hoarse and tired.

The door to the barn swung wide, and Kate's father stood there. Uncle Ollie appeared next to him with Biscuit at his side. The dog ran straight for Kate, jumping into the pile of hay and spreading it everywhere.

"Kate!" her father called out, his voice cracking with emotion. "I was so scared!"

"Pop! I'm so glad you're here! How did you know where to find us? I couldn't use my phone."

"Michael came and got us," Uncle Ollie explained. "He told us you were here."

"Michael?" Kate and Sydney spoke at the same time.

"How did he know we were here?" Kate asked, more confused than ever.

Uncle Ollie shrugged. "I'm not sure. He just said he saw you girls go into the old red barn on the south side of the pass. He was worried you might be in trouble."

"We *were* in trouble, so why didn't he come inside and

talk to us?" Sydney asked. "That doesn't make any sense! He left us all by ourselves."

Uncle Ollie shrugged. "I don't know. I just know that he saved your lives by telling us you were here! We owe him our thanks."

"Humph." Sydney crossed her arms and made a face.

Biscuit jumped up and down, licking Kate in the face.

"He's happy to see you!" Uncle Ollie said with a nod.

"I'm happy to see him, too. I—I wasn't sure I ever would again." Kate burst into tears at once, realizing just how scared she'd been.

"How will we get back to the inn?" Sydney asked, looking nervous. "My ankle is injured. And I think it's really bad this time." Her tears started up again.

"Oh, we're on the snowmobiles," Kate's father explained. "But if you're injured, we'd better take you to the emergency room as soon as we get back to town."

Sydney's tears started flowing when she heard the words *emergency room*. "I'm never going to get to ski in the competition now. I can't believe this!"

"Remember, 'all things work together for good to them that love God, to them who are called according to his purpose,'" Uncle Ollie reminded her. "God will use this situation in a good way. Just watch and see."

"I don't see how He can, but I'm going to choose to believe that," Sydney said with a sigh.

Minutes later the girls climbed aboard the snowmobiles. Kate rode behind her father, and Sydney rode behind Uncle Ollie. As they made their way up one hill and down another, Kate thought about everything that had happened that day. Sydney's ankle. Almost falling down into a frozen creek.

Finding refuge in a barn. Michael.

Hmm. Thinking of Michael raised so many questions. He hadn't been a mirage after all. But why didn't he stop to talk to them? Why did he run off, even if it was to get help?

Something about that boy just seems wrong.

As soon as they arrived at the inn, Kate's mother and Aunt Molly ran out to greet them. The girls were showered with kisses, then Kate's mom called Sydney's mother on the phone to tell her what had happened.

She gave them permission to take Sydney to the emergency room, and the girls and Mrs. Oliver piled into the car. As soon as they got inside the car, Kate finally felt free to cry. Oh, what a day it had been! Her tears flowed—partly in relief for being safe and partly because of the things she had faced earlier in the day.

Just then, her cell phone beeped. *Now I get a signal!* She glanced down, noticing a text message had come in from Elizabeth. Strangely, it was a scripture verse, the same one she and Sydney had been quoting all day.

Kate almost cried as she read the words: "I CAN DO ALL THINGS THROUGH CHRIST WHO STRENGTHENS ME."

Somehow she knew this was more than a coincidence.

CHAPTER 11

Curds and Whey

Later that evening, after returning from the emergency room, Kate and Sydney enjoyed a quiet evening with the family. Thankfully, Sydney's ankle wasn't broken, though the doctor said it was a bad sprain. After putting a splint on it, he warned Sydney to stay off it for at least two weeks and to keep it elevated. She didn't care for that idea very much.

"That's my whole Christmas break!" she had argued. Still, she had no choice. Under Aunt Molly's watchful eye, Sydney kept it elevated for the rest of the day and kept ice packs on it. Every time she started to put it down, Aunt Molly would tell her she was going to call her mama. Then Sydney would put it back up again and groan.

As they ate their dinner, Kate kept thinking about the skiing competition. What a shame! Three hundred dollars lost! Sydney wouldn't get to go on her mission trip now, after all. But what could be done about it? And with Sydney's ankle in such bad shape, would they ever figure out what was going on at the creamery? Surely Kate's parents wouldn't let her go alone to snoop, not after what happened today!

After a wonderful meal, everyone relaxed around the fireplace and told stories. Kate told everything that had happened to them on the ski course, right down to the point where she almost fell into the frozen creek. Her mother's eyes filled with tears.

"Oh, I should have gone with you! I can't believe I let you go without an adult. Can you ever forgive me for letting you go alone?"

Kate rushed to her mom's side and leaned against her. "There's nothing to forgive, Mom! We wanted to go by ourselves, remember? But I forgive you, anyway. . .if it makes you feel better! I've learned to forgive quickly and not to hold a grudge!" She gave her mom a squeeze. "Not that I could ever hold a grudge against you—even if you did do something wrong, which you didn't!"

"Thank you, sweetie," her mother said, giving her a kiss on the forehead. "That makes me feel better."

"Forgiving quickly is always a good plan," her father said. "Remember that time I had to forgive the man who claimed he invented one of my robots?"

"Oh, that's right," Kate said. "I'd forgotten about that."

"And remember the time that woman backed out of her parking space and hit my car?" Kate's mom said. "She wasn't very nice about it, and neither was the insurance company— but I had to forgive."

"I remember it was tough—especially because she wasn't nice about it." Kate shook her head, wondering how some people could be so mean. *Why can't everyone just be nice. . .like my mom and dad?*

"Once, someone found my checking account number and stole some money from my bank account," Uncle Ollie said. "He took hundreds of dollars and I was really mad. At first. But I got over it. I read that verse about forgiving as Jesus forgives and decided it wasn't worth holding a grudge."

"It never is," Aunt Molly said. She turned to Kate with a wink. "And I'm sure you've already forgiven the boy in your class who made fun of you, haven't you, honey?"

"Yes." Kate nodded. "I've forgiven him."

Sydney groaned and everyone looked her way.

"What's wrong?" Kate's mom asked with a worried look on her face. "Are you in pain?"

"No." Sydney looked sad. "I guess I just have to learn to forgive myself. I got so excited, thinking I could win that contest, that I put all my hopes in myself instead of in God. And I let myself down by getting hurt."

"You can hardly be mad at yourself for getting hurt!" Aunt Molly said. "That just doesn't make sense!"

"Oh, I know. But I'm disappointed in myself because I was *so* sure I was going to win the prize." Sydney shrugged. "Just goes to show you I was putting my trust in the wrong person. Me." She looked at the floor, her eyes filling with tears. "I guess I do that a lot, actually. I'm pretty good at sports, so sometimes I think I can do things on my own without God's help. I forget that He's the one in charge."

"I think we all do that sometimes," Uncle Ollie admitted. "But God always forgives us, if we ask."

"I will. I promise." Sydney smiled. "And if He wants me to go on that mission trip, I'll go—one way or the other."

"That's right! He always makes a way where there seems to be no way," Kate's dad said. "That's a promise from the Bible. And you know God's promises are true. He is faithful to do what He says He's going to do."

Sydney nodded and smiled for the first time all evening. "I feel so much better. Thank you for reminding me. I needed to hear that!"

Kate didn't say anything, but she was glad for the reminder, too.

After dinner, they all gathered in the big central room, where they ate large slices of warm apple pie and drank apple cider flavored with cinnamon sticks. As Kate leaned back against the super-sized pillows on the sofa, she looked around the room and thanked God for the special people in her life. She also thanked Him for protecting her and getting her back to her family safely.

For a moment—a brief moment—she felt a little sad. After all, they only had three more days in Mad River Valley. She and Sydney hadn't solved the mystery, and now Sydney wasn't going to get to ski. Looked like things weren't working out the way they'd hoped. Still, she had to believe God would work everything together for His good, just like Uncle Ollie said.

"A penny for your thoughts, Kate," Aunt Molly said with a hint of a smile.

Kate turned to her with a grin. "Oh, I'm just thinking of how God always has bigger and better plans than we do!"

"He sure does!" Aunt Molly agreed. "And I have a sneaking suspicion He's got more plans ahead than you know!"

Kate thought about that. Maybe Aunt Molly was right. Maybe there were plenty of adventures ahead!

A couple of hours later everyone headed off to bed.

"It's been a long day," Aunt Molly said with a yawn. "I'm going to sleep like a bug in a rug tonight."

"Ooo! Did you have to say that?" Kate said. "Thinking of bugs reminds me of all those spiders we saw today in that old barn!"

"Sorry, kiddo," said Aunt Molly. "I'm going to sleep well tonight."

"I'm not sleepy at all," Kate admitted. "My mind is still going, going, going! I can't seem to stop thinking about everything."

"Well, try to get some rest anyway, honey," her mother said. "You need to enjoy our last few days in Vermont, and that won't happen if you don't get enough sleep."

Kate and Sydney dressed for bed and then climbed under the covers. Kate tossed and turned for at least an hour. She finally gave up and kicked off the blanket.

"What's up?" Sydney asked, opening one eye.

"It doesn't matter how hard I try, I just can't go to sleep," Kate said with a loud sigh.

"How come?" Sydney asked with a yawn.

"I have too much on my mind. Things are all jumbled up."

"Really? What do you mean?"

"My thoughts must look kind of like the curds and whey in that big container at the creamery. Everything is all mixed up. Lumpy."

Sydney chuckled. "Sounds funny, but I'm not really sure what you're talking about."

"Well, I have a lot on my mind. The competition. The creamery. The picture of that rat. The woman in the white coat. . .and her husband. Michael and the barn filled with spiders." She shook her head. "It's just a lot to think about. I'm having trouble falling asleep with my mind whirling like this."

"Well, try counting sheep," Sydney suggested.

Kate pulled the blanket back up and closed her eyes, but for some reason, all she saw were rats and spiders. "Ugh!" She tried to fall asleep with her eyes open, but that didn't work, either. Suddenly, Kate sat up in the bed and gasped. "Sydney! I just remembered something!"

Sydney rolled over in the bed and groaned. "We're never going to get any sleep!"

"I know, but this is important!"

"What is it?"

"The man behind the creamery. . .the one with the woman in the white coat. . ."

"What about him?" Sydney asked with a yawn.

"His name was *Mark*." Kate pushed the covers back once more, suddenly very nervous. "Remember? The woman called him by that name!"

"So?"

"So, Alexis said *Mark* was the name of the man who owns Cheese De-Lite, Mad River's main competitor. Right?"

"Ah." Sydney sat up in the bed. "That's right. And didn't she say his picture was on the website?"

"Yes, I think so. There's only one way to know for sure!"

The girls sprang from the bed and tiptoed out into the great room of the inn, where Uncle Ollie kept two computers for guests to use. Kate quickly signed online and typed in "Cheese De-Lite." When the web page came up, she gasped.

"Oh, Sydney, look!" She pointed at the screen. Right there—in living color—was a professional photo of the man and the woman they'd seen on the tour that day, and again behind the creamery. "Mark and Abigail Collingsworth, owners of Cheese De-Lite in central Vermont." Kate shook her head as she read the words aloud. "Do you think they. . ."

"I don't know." Sydney began to pace back and forth. "I suppose it's possible. Maybe they want to make Mad River Creamery look bad so they can steal their customers."

"Seems weird." Kate thought about it. "Why would they go to such trouble? Why not just hire an advertising firm to come up with better commercials or something?" She began to list several different possibilities, but none of them made sense.

"I don't know." Sydney shrugged.

Kate shook her head and continued to stare at the photo. "I just have the strangest feeling about these two. I can't put my finger on it."

"What are you thinking?" Sydney asked. "Tell me. . .please!"

Just then a light snapped on in the room. "What in the world are you girls doing up after midnight?"

Kate turned when she heard her dad's voice. "Oh, Dad, I'm sorry! We didn't mean to wake you up, but we just found another piece to the puzzle!"

All the noise woke up Biscuit, who began to yap and run in circles. Before long, Uncle Ollie came into the room. Then Kate's mom. Then Aunt Molly. Then Dexter, who rubbed his eyes and looked at them all like he thought it was morning.

"What's happening, girls?" Aunt Molly said, rubbing the sleep from her eyes.

Kate turned her attention to the website, showing it to the others.

"Do these people look familiar to you?" she asked.

"Not at all." Aunt Molly squinted. "Wish I had my glasses on. . .I'd be able to see better. But they don't look familiar to me. What about you, Ollie? Do you know these folks?"

"I don't recognize them." He snapped his fingers. "But, come to think of it, I did hear Michael say some couple was snooping around town, asking a lot of questions about the creamery."

"Michael said that?" Kate released a breath, then leaned back in her chair.

"Yes."

Even stranger. "This is Mark Collingsworth," Kate explained, pointing at the picture of the man. "And his wife, Abby."

"What about them?" Aunt Molly asked.

"They own a creamery about fifty miles away. A competitor. This is the man Sydney and I saw the other day behind the building. And this woman was with him."

"Wow. Very suspicious." Uncle Ollie nodded. "We'll have to call the Hamptons in the morning and tell them." He scratched his bald head and pursed his lips. "Do you think he and his wife are the ones sabotaging the creamery?"

Kate sighed. "Maybe. I'm not sure. We don't really have any proof, and I hate to accuse someone unless I know for sure."

"We just know they were doing something behind the building that day," Sydney added.

"Well, let's talk about this in the morning," Kate's dad said with a yawn. "There's no point trying to solve a mystery in the middle of the night. We all need our rest, especially if we're going to go to the Winter Festival."

Kate's heart twisted at his words. If Sydney couldn't compete, what was the point in going?

Just as the girls crawled back into bed once more, Sydney sat up with a silly grin on her face. "I have a brilliant-beyond-brilliant idea!"

"What is it?" Kate asked, yawning.

"Just because *I* can't enter the competition doesn't mean *you* can't."

"W—what?" Kate sat straight up and stared at her friend in disbelief. "Did you just say what I thought you said? You want me to take your place in the competition?"

"Sure! Why not? You did a great job skiing down the Rat. And I'd be willing to bet the people in charge of the festival will transfer my entry fee to you once they hear that I'm injured."

"But, why?"

"Because. . ." Sydney took her hand and gently squeezed it. "I think it would be good for you. For ages now I've heard you say you're no good at sports. I really think you would do a great job and it would prove—once and for all—that you can overcome your fear of sports."

"But. . .a competition?" Kate shivered just thinking about it. "That's not the best place to prove something to myself."

"Don't you see, Kate?" Sydney said. "The only person you'd be competing against is yourself. This wouldn't have to be about anyone else. Just you. Face your fears head-on like I did. Ski down that mountain and you'll be a winner, no matter how fast you go. See what I'm saying?"

"I guess so." Kate pulled the covers up and leaned back against her pillows. "But I'll have to pray about it. I just don't know yet. I'll let you know in the morning, okay?"

"Okay." Sydney chuckled. "But get ready, Kate! I have a feeling you're going to be skiing tomorrow afternoon."

As Kate closed her eyes, she tried to picture herself sailing down a mountain. For some reason, every time she thought about it, she pictured Michael. . .whizzing by her, going a hundred miles an hour.

Thinking of Michael made her wonder—once again—why he'd been at the old spider-filled barn. Just a coincidence, or were there darker forces at work? And why had he left them there without saying a word? Very strange, even for him!

Kate's eyes grew heavy and she finally drifted off to sleep, dreaming dreams of red barns, snow-covered mountains. . . and rats. Big, hairy rats.

CHAPTER 12

Racing the Rat

Kate stood at the top of the hill, staring down. Somewhere between her middle of the night conversation with Sydney and now, she had decided to do it. She'd entered the skiing competition. And now, looking at the steep hill below, she was finally ready to face her biggest fear. "I can do this! I can do all things through Christ who strengthens me!"

Off in the distance, she heard Sydney's voice calling out. "Go, Inspector Gadget! Ski the Rat!"

"You can do it, honey." Her mother's voice echoed across the packed snow.

"Join the Rat Pack!" Uncle Ollie threw in his two cents' worth.

Hearing the words *The Rat Pack* reminded Kate that they hadn't yet solved the mystery about the creamery. Thinking about the creamery made her think of the woman in the white coat and the man with the sour expression on his face. Thinking of the man and woman reminded her of the day she and Sydney had hidden behind the Dumpster. And for some reason, thinking of the Dumpster reminded her of Bailey and how her phone rang at just the right—er, *wrong*—time.

"Why am I thinking about that right now?" Kate scolded herself. "I'm supposed to be getting ready to ski, not solve a crime!"

She took her place and tried to prepare herself the best she could.

"I can't believe I'm doing this. I can't believe I'm doing this!" Kate bent her knees and looked down at the long, slender skis. "Lord," she prayed, her eyes now closed, "help me get to the bottom without falling. Oh, and Lord, if You could help me win, I promise to use the money to bless someone else!"

She opened her eyes and looked at the hill below. "It's just a hill. And I'm just like a little robot, about to glide from the top of the hill to the bottom. No big deal! What am I so worried about?"

Of course, there was that part where hundreds of people were watching her, but once she got started, she wouldn't have time to even think about them. No, all she had to think about was getting to the bottom without falling!

At the *pop* of the starter's pistol, Kate dug her poles into the snow and pushed off. As she began to sail down the hill, the cold wind whipped at her face. In fact, the wind was so strong it nearly knocked her down a time or two. Thankfully she managed to stay on her feet!

She came to the first curve and bent her knees, leaning into it. "C'mon, Snow-Bot!" she whispered. "You can do this!"

Kate managed to straighten out her position after making the curve. . .without falling! "Woo-hoo!" she called out to no one but the wind. "I did it!" Up ahead she saw a sharp curve to the left. "Uh-oh." She whispered another prayer then bent her knees to make it around the turn.

Picking up speed, she almost lost control. After a bit of wobbling, she sailed on down, down, down. The trees off in the distance seemed to fly by, their snow-covered branches nothing but a blur.

For a moment, she remembered what had happened yesterday. . .how Sydney had injured her ankle in that very spot. How Kate had searched for a trail through those trees to find help. How they'd ended up in an old red barn with spiders. How Michael was there with his backpack on.

Michael. Hmm.

"Don't think about that right now!" Kate whispered to herself. "Just stay focused! Stay focused!"

After a couple more twists and turns, the bottom of the hill was in sight. Kate crouched a bit, trying to get more speed.

"C'mon, c'mon!" With faster speed than ever, she soared over the finish line, then—like a good robot would do— turned her feet to come to an abrupt stop. Kate's heart raced a hundred miles an hour.

"I did it! I did it!" She pulled off her goggles and began to cheer at the top of her lungs. She could hear the roar of the crowd and felt a little embarrassed. Kate put her hands over her mouth and giggled. Making it to the bottom without falling felt so good! And Sydney was right! She *had* proven something to herself.

I'm not bad at sports! I need to stop saying that!

One by one, she watched the other skiers in her age group. A couple of them fell. One of them made it all the way to the bottom, but didn't seem to be moving as fast. One girl was really, really good. Kate watched her as she came sailing down the hill. Her bright blue snowsuit stood out against the bright white snow.

"Wow, she looks like a pro." At the very last minute, the girl lost control of her skis and went sprawling in the snow.

"Oh man! I hope she's okay," Kate whispered.

Thankfully, the girl rose to her feet and raised her hand to show everyone she wasn't injured. Everyone cheered and she skied down to the bottom of the hill and took a bow.

Finally it was Michael's turn. Kate had almost forgotten he was competing until she saw him. She could hear Uncle Ollie's cheers off in the distance.

Michael is really blessed to have Uncle Ollie in his life. He needs someone like that to support him.

Michael started off well and even made the first curve with no problem. But then, at the second big turn, he almost lost his footing. Thankfully, he didn't fall, but it did slow him down a little. He still skied very well, and Kate knew he'd made up for the lost time. At least, it seemed like it! She was surprised when she saw his time come up on the board. *Oh wow. It took him almost a full second longer to reach the bottom than me. Weird.*

Only one skier was left. Kate watched as the boy sailed down the hill like a professional skier.

"Wow, he's so good!" She watched in awe as he gracefully moved back and forth on his skis. Then, just before he reached the final turn, his skis somehow bumped up against each other and he toppled over! A loud gasp went up from the crowd.

"Oh, that's terrible!" Kate covered her eyes, not wanting to look. Hopefully he wasn't badly hurt.

It took a couple of minutes for him to stand, but he finally managed. The crowd applauded his efforts, and he responded with a dramatic bow. Kate laughed. *He's a great sport!*

After that, everything seemed to move in slow motion. Kate heard her name announced over the loudspeaker. "The winner of this year's Winter Festival junior level competition is eleven-year-old Kate Oliver from Philadelphia, Pennsylvania!"

It almost felt like they were calling someone else's name.

"Me?" she whispered. "I won?" Kate could hardly believe it! The whole thing seemed impossible. . .like a dream. Only this *wasn't* a dream! It was true. Every bit of it!

An older man gestured for her to come to the stage, which she did with shaking knees. She climbed a few stairs and stood before the people.

"Kate Oliver, congratulations on skiing the Rat! You're now an official member of the Rat Pack!" He handed her a T-shirt and opened it to show the icky-looking rat on the back.

Kate giggled and took the shirt. "Thank you so much!" She searched for Uncle Ollie in the crowd. When she found him, she held up the shirt and grinned.

"The Winter Festival of Mad River Valley is proud to give you this trophy for your performance today." The man standing next to Kate gave her a big silver trophy with two skis on top. "And of course. . ." the man continued, handing her a check, "the grand prize of three hundred dollars!"

Kate gripped the check in her hand and whispered a prayer. "Oh, thank You, Lord! I know just what to do with this!"

The crowd started applauding, and Kate felt her cheeks warm up. They always did that when she was embarrassed. No doubt they were as red as tomatoes!

She looked through all the people till she found her family and Sydney standing off to the left of the stage. Getting down the stairs was the easy part. Making her way through the crowd—with so many people patting her on the back and saying congratulations—was a lot harder than she imagined!

Finally she saw her mother. "Oh, Kate! You were wonderful! Congratulations! We're so proud of you!"

"I knew you could do it!" her dad hollered.

The others in her family gathered around, looking at the trophy. Kate held it up for all to see.

"She's a beauty!" Uncle Ollie said.

"That's the coolest trophy I've ever seen!" Dexter added.

"Wonderful, wonderful!" Aunt Molly added. "I'm tickled pink, honey. And even more tickled that you were wearing my old skis! What an honor!"

Biscuit jumped up and down in excitement. Kate reached down to scratch him behind the ears. "I know, boy! You're so excited!"

Sydney came hobbling toward her on her sore ankle. "Oh, Kate! I'm so proud of you! You're the fastest skier here."

Kate shook her head. "I still don't know how it's possible. And I know for a fact that your time would have been better than mine, if only. . ." She looked down at her friend's ankle and sighed.

"No *if onlys* today," Sydney said with a happy nod. "Today we're *all* winners."

Off in the distance, Michael walked by, his shoulders slumped forward in defeat. Kate noticed the sour look on his face. He looked her way and glared at her.

Wow. Not everyone is acting like a winner, Kate thought.

He reached underneath the stage and pulled out his backpack, but as he started to put it on, something fell out of it. Something small. And furry.

"Is that what I think it is, or is my imagination acting up again?" Kate whispered.

At once, Biscuit went crazy! He ran toward the small

fuzzy critter, barking like a maniac. Only when Kate took a second look, did she realize for sure just what she was looking at! Right away, she began to scream!

"It's. . .it's. . .a. . .*rat*!"

CHAPTER
13

The Mouse Takes the Cheese

As soon as Kate shouted, Michael dropped his backpack into the snow and began to run away from the crowd. Kate had never seen anyone move that fast! He shot through the throng of people, heading toward the lodge.

"Oh, I wish I could run!" Sydney said, wringing her hands together. "This bum ankle of mine won't let me!"

Kate raced after Biscuit, who now stood at the edge of the snow barking like a maniac. She couldn't blame him! *Did I really see what I thought I saw? Did a rat. . .a real, live rat. . . just fall out of Michael's backpack?*

As she got closer to the stage, she glanced down to see what Biscuit held in his mouth. He yanked it around to the right, then the left, then the right, then the left.

"Oh, gross! If it was a rat, it's a goner now!" Kate didn't want to touch it. *Oh, how disgusting!*

A crowd gathered around. "Look, everyone!" Dexter shouted. "Biscuit caught a rat. Good boy!"

"A rat?" one man said with a smirk on his face. "How ironic!"

It took Kate a minute to realize what he meant. They were standing at the bottom of the Rat ski course, after all.

People began to laugh, but Kate didn't feel like joining

them. Not yet, anyway. She had a sinking feeling.

"Look!" another man called out. "This dog is going crazy!"

Biscuit continued his chewing and chomping frenzy, and Kate actually felt sorry for the poor little rat. What a terrible way to die!

She grabbed the dog by his collar and scolded him. "Biscuit, let go! Stop! Enough already!"

After a couple of seconds, he finally dropped the furry little thing. Kate gasped when she looked down and saw. . . metal pieces? *Metal pieces inside a rat? What?*

"What is that?" Sydney hobbled up beside her.

"Oh, wow, Kate!" Sydney looked shocked. "It's not a real rat at all. It's a little. . ."

"Robot," Kate whispered. "It's a robotic rat! No wonder it ran in crazy circles that day at the creamery. And no wonder McKenzie couldn't find a photo of another rat that looked like this one. It's not real. It never was." Relief swept over her. "That means they never really had a rat infestation at the creamery. Not real rats, anyway. Just robotic ones. But why? Why would Michael do this?"

Uncle Ollie reached down into the snow to pick up the robotic rat, which Biscuit had almost destroyed. He rolled it from one hand to another, looking it over. "I don't believe this. I really don't believe this. I'm the one who taught him how to build robots, but I never dreamed he would take the things I'd taught him and use them to hurt someone!"

"There were three rats that first day at the creamery," Sydney said, reaching for Michael's backpack. "So there must be at least two more inside!" She looked up at Uncle Ollie. "Is it okay to open it and look inside to see?"

"I give you permission." Michael's mother, Maggie, drew

near. "We need to know for sure before. . ." Her eyes filled with tears, and Kate suddenly felt very sorry for her.

Poor woman! She's still sad about her dad dying, and now this!

Mr. and Mrs. Hampton walked up. They both looked completely shocked.

Sydney reached inside the backpack and came out with not just one but two furry critters! As soon as she saw them, she began to scream. "Ooo! More rats!"

One of them flew up into the air, then hit the ground. Kate reached down and grabbed it. "But they're not real. See?" She rolled it around in her hand. "I can feel the metal parts inside. And look, here's where the batteries go." She showed everyone the belly of the rat.

By now, several people had gathered.

"Step back, everyone!" Mr. Hampton said, drawing near. "Step back!"

He approached Kate and took the rats from her, examining them carefully. "Whose bag is this?" he asked, pointing to the backpack.

"It belongs to my son, Michael," Maggie said with tears in her eyes.

"Where did he go?" Mr. Hampton looked around. "Is he still here?"

"I saw him running toward the lodge," an older woman said. "He was going mighty fast!"

Mr. Hampton and Uncle Ollie led the way to the lodge. Kate and her family trudged along behind him in the snow. Kate prayed all the way. *Lord, please let Michael still be there. And help us understand why he would do something like this to the Hamptons!*

As they entered the main room of the lodge, Kate saw Michael sitting in front of the fireplace. As soon as he heard everyone come in the door, he turned and looked their way. Kate couldn't help but notice he had tears in his eyes.

What's up with that? What secrets are you hiding, Michael?

Mr. Hampton walked straight over to him and dropped the backpack down on the floor. "Is this yours, son?"

"Yes, sir." Michael looked down at the ground.

"And these, um, rats. They're yours?" Mr. Hampton continued.

Michael hung his head in shame. "Yes, sir. I made them. In my basement."

Maggie walked to his side and slipped an arm over his shoulder. "Michael, we just need the truth. Are you the one who. . ." Her voice cracked. "Are you the one who put the rats in the creamery?"

Kate's heart twisted as he gave a slow nod and then began to cry.

Why would he do such a thing? That's horrible!

Michael turned to Uncle Ollie, talking a mile a minute. "You don't understand what they did to my grandpa!"

With an angry look on his face, he pointed to Mr. and Mrs. Hampton, who stood in silence listening to him. "My Grandpa Joe worked for them for years as a security guard. He was a good man. . ." Michael's voice cracked. "But they fired him! Fired him. For no good reason. He needed that job. We had bills to pay!"

Mr. Hampton looked stunned. "We had good reasons for firing him, Michael, whether you know it or not."

Michael shook his head, growing angrier by the moment.

"After he lost his job, Grandpa started getting sick. I know it was because he was so depressed. He was never the same after that. And my mom had to work harder than ever to pay for his medical bills."

Michael began to shake uncontrollably. Kate watched as he clenched his fists.

"So you wanted to get even with them?" Uncle Ollie asked. "You sabotaged the creamery to get even?"

Michael nodded. "I. . .wanted to bring them down! They hurt my grandpa, and I wanted to hurt them!"

Ooo! Kate thought about the scripture she had learned from Aunt Molly. *So that's what happens when you hold a grudge! People really do end up getting hurt!*

"What did you do, son?" Uncle Ollie asked. "Tell me everything."

"I. . .I went to the old barn on the south slope and got lots of spiders. I set them loose in the creamery. But I could tell that wasn't going to be enough to convince people, so I. . ." He shook his head, then stared at Uncle Ollie. "I used what you taught me about robots. Made three of them. Figured if I could. . ." He paused and shook his head. "I just wanted sales to go down at the creamery. I wanted to hurt the Hamptons like they hurt us!"

Michael's mother drew near and wrapped Michael in her arms. "Oh, honey," she spoke with tears in her eyes. "First of all, it's wrong to get even with people, even if they really do hurt you. But in this case, you're completely mistaken! The Hamptons are good people."

"No, they're not!" He looked at his mother like she was crazy.

"Oh, Michael, there's so much you don't know about

your grandpa. He was a good man, but in those last few months before he lost his job, he was already very sick. The Hamptons didn't know it, of course. He didn't want them to know."

"What do you mean, Mom?"

"He told me he'd been falling asleep on the job. A lot. It was probably the medication he was on. I always suspected that, of course. And he never told the Hamptons he was on medicine for his weak heart, so they never knew. He didn't want anyone to know."

Geneva Hampton began to cry. "I always thought there was something more going on with Joe. He kept falling asleep on the job. But I didn't realize he was on medication!"

"He was," Maggie said. "And mighty strong medicine, at that." She turned back to Michael to finish the story. "One night your grandpa fell asleep on the job. It had happened before, but this time a fire broke out in the area where the cows were kept."

"I remember that night," Uncle Ollie said, scratching his head. "It was a close call! The Hamptons could have lost all of their cows that night."

"And it was your grandpa's fault," Maggie said softly to Michael.

Michael shook his head. "Why didn't you ever tell me this? Why did you let me think. . ." He looked up at Mr. and Mrs. Hampton and shook his head. "I just thought they were being mean to him. Now I don't know what to think."

"I think we're all confused and hurt," Uncle Ollie said. "And when we're hurt, we often do things we don't mean to do. I once heard a pastor say, 'Hurt people hurt people.' And it's so true."

Mr. Hampton shook his head, looking more than a little upset. "Oh, I feel terrible! I wish I had known about Joe's heart condition! We could have worked something out. Maybe cut back on his hours or something."

"No, he was really too frail to be working, anyway," Maggie said. "That's why I tried to pick up so many extra hours at the diner. I figured the more money I made, the less he would have to worry about finances. We were doing okay, until. . ."

"Until he had the heart attack?" Uncle Ollie asked.

Maggie nodded. "Yes. Then I knew. . ." She began to cry and Kate reached over to wrap her arms around her. "That's when I knew he would never work again. At that point, I just wanted to see him get better, to come back home."

"We just wanted everything to be. . .normal," Michael said, his eyes glistening with tears. "But then. . ."

"Well, we all know what happened next." Maggie sniffled then wiped her nose with a tissue. "He went to be with Jesus. And, of course, he's in heaven celebrating right now, but we still miss him so much."

"Enough to do some really dumb things." Michael kicked at a pile of snow with the toe of his tennis shoe. "I. . .I'm so sorry. I really thought you guys fired Gramps because. . .well, because you didn't like him."

"Oh no, honey!" Geneva Hampton wrapped her arms around his shoulders. "We loved your grandpa. And we were concerned about him. That's really why we let him go. Though he never told us about his illness, we knew something was wrong and we decided the job was putting too much stress on him."

"You did the right thing," Maggie said. "It wounded his

126

pride a little, but he needed the rest."

Michael looked at Mr. Hampton with tears in his eyes. "Can you ever forgive me? I'm so sorry."

"Of course we forgive you, Michael," Mr. Hampton said. "It would be wrong to hold a grudge."

"I'll do everything I can to make this better," Michael said with a hopeful look in his eye. "I know! I'll come to work for you. You won't have to pay me or anything. I'll work in the factory every afternoon to make up for what I've done. And I'll tell everyone I know to buy Mad River Valley cheese!"

Mr. Hampton laughed. "Well, we can always use the help, but you're a little young to be working, aren't you?"

Michael shook his head. "I'm turning fifteen in a week! I can have a job if my mom says so, right? I just want to make up for what I've done. I—I can't believe I let my anger get control of me like that. Next time I'm going to wait till I have all of the facts before acting!"

"Great plan!" Mr. Hampton gave him a pat on the back. "Now, I have an idea! Geneva made a huge pot of cheddar cheese soup for the festival. It's out in the car. Are you folks hungry?"

"Cheddar cheese soup?" Kate's stomach rumbled, just thinking about it. Man, did that ever sound good!

She turned to Sydney with a smile on her face and whispered, "I can't believe it! We were right! The creamery was being sabotaged!"

Just as quickly, she thought about the woman in the white coat and her husband. If Michael was the one who'd sabotaged the creamery, who were they. . .and what were they doing in Mad River Valley?

Christmas in Vermont

On the day after the big Winter Festival, Kate went to church with her family. She knew their time in Vermont was drawing to a close, and she wanted to enjoy every moment. She couldn't have been more surprised to hear the preacher's topic of the day: forgiveness. What a fun coincidence. Of course, Aunt Molly called it a *God*-incidence. Kate couldn't help but agree!

A couple of times during the service, Kate looked at Maggie and Michael who sat in the row beside them. He really seemed to pay attention to the sermon. And she felt pretty sure he'd learned his lesson about forgiveness.

But, had *she*?

As soon as they arrived back at the inn, they all ate lunch together, and then Aunt Molly and Kate's mother washed the dishes. Sydney settled into a chair across from Uncle Ollie to talk about sports, and Kate. . .well, Kate had something specific on her mind. There was something she needed to do. Something she should have done days before.

Heading over to Uncle Ollie's computer, she signed into her e-mail account. Then, thinking carefully about each word, she began to type.

Dear Phillip,

I'm in Mad River Valley, Vermont, on Christmas vacation with my family. I've been working on my science project. It's all about cheese! (Boy, have I learned a LOT!) I'm sure you're hard at work on your project back in Philly or wherever you're spending your vacation. Hope you're having fun!

I just want you to know that I'm sorry if I ever did anything to make you feel like you're not as smart as me. I think you're so smart and should have told you so instead of always trying to make it look like I'm the best!

When you made fun of my project a few weeks ago, it hurt my feelings, but I have forgiven you. Will you forgive me for the mean things I was thinking about you since then? Please? When I get back to school, I'm going to ask Mrs. Mueller if we can work together on our next project. The Bible says that one can put a thousand to flight but two can put ten thousand to flight. That's kind of a fancy way of saying we can do more if we work together!

I learned a lot about that this week in Vermont. I worked with my friend Sydney and together we accomplished great things. I can't wait to tell you all about it! The rest of the school year is going to be better if we're friends!

See you soon! Kate Oliver

She read over the e-mail once or twice then pressed the SEND button.

Just then, Kate heard her mother's voice behind her. "What are you doing, honey? The others are waiting to open Christmas presents!"

"Oh, just taking care of something I should have done days ago." Kate turned around and smiled at her mom, feeling contentment in her heart. "Forgiving someone. Or rather, *letting* that someone know I've forgiven him!"

"Wow. Well, I can think of no greater Christmas gift than that. You know, honey, God is in the forgiving business. That's why He sent His Son, Jesus, as a baby in a manger. He knew that we—His children—all needed a Savior."

Kate nodded. "I know. But I'm glad you reminded me. I'll never look at the baby in the manger the same again, Mom!"

In the next room, Kate heard voices raised in song. Aunt Molly warbled, "Deck the halls with boughs of holly" at the top of her lungs, and the others soon joined in.

"Come and join us, honey," her mother said, extending her hand. "We've got some celebrating to do. And lots of presents to open!"

"Yes, we do!" Kate thought about all the victories of the past week as she made her way into the great room, where flames lit the fireplace and her family members sang in several keys at once! In one week's time she had solved a mystery, won a competition, and forgiven Phillip. *That's a lot, Lord!*

Only one thing left to do. . .and oh, what fun it was going to be! Talk about a merry Christmas!

One by one the family members opened presents. Kate was tickled to get so many fun gifts—a hand-knitted scarf from Aunt Molly, a great journal from Sydney, and lots of cool things from her mom and dad. Even Dexter gave her a great present—a cool new digital recorder.

Finally the moment arrived. . .the one Kate had been waiting for. She watched as Sydney opened the gift she had so carefully wrapped. Everyone's eyes nearly popped when they saw the three hundred dollars in cash inside.

"W—what?" Sydney looked at her, stunned. "What have you done, Kate?"

"It's my Christmas gift to you!" she exclaimed. "The *only* reason I agreed to take your place in the competition was to help you go on your mission trip. Of course, I never dreamed I would actually win. . .but I did! It was a huge blessing for both of us! Don't you see? Now you can go to Mexico."

"B—but. . .I didn't earn this money." Sydney tried to hand it back to her. "*You* did."

"No, the way I look at it, it's really a miracle I made it from the top of the Rat to the bottom without falling on my face and embarrassing myself in front of hundreds of people! So, we'll call that our miracle money. And I can think of no better way to spend my miracle money than on a mission trip!"

"A—are you sure?" Sydney stammered.

"Sure I'm sure! Take it. Go to Mexico. Have the time of your life." Kate leaned over and whispered, "Just don't have any big adventures without me, okay?"

"Okay! I'll try!" Sydney giggled and hugged the gift tightly. "Oh, I don't believe it! Can I call my mom? Would that be okay?"

"Of course, honey." Aunt Molly pointed to the phone. "You go right ahead. But the rest of us still have presents to open."

Sydney headed over to the phone to make the call. Kate could hear her squeals as she shared the story with her mother. Oh, how wonderful it felt. . .to be able to do something so fun for a friend!

Several minutes later, after everyone had opened all the Christmas gifts, Kate heard singing at the door. At least, she *thought* it was singing. Sounded a little off-key to her!

"Sounds like carolers!" Uncle Ollie said.

He opened the door and Kate smiled as she saw Mr. and Mrs. Hampton outside, along with Michael and his mother. Together, the four of them sang "The First Noel" really, really loud. Oh, what a wonderful sound, to hear their voices raised in harmony! A little off-key, but harmony, just the same!

Thank You, God! Kate giggled. *This is what happens when people forgive one another! You fix their broken relationships!*

After they finished singing, Aunt Molly invited them inside. "You're just in time!" she said. "We baked Snicker-doodles and I've made wassail! Let's celebrate together!"

"We have a lot to celebrate, don't we?" Mr. Hampton said, smiling at Michael. "God has done such wondrous things this Christmas season. He's brought us all closer together and given us plenty of reasons to look ahead to a bright new year!"

"Yes, He has," Mrs. Hampton agreed with a twinkle in her eye.

They had all settled into chairs around the dining room table to eat cookies and drink wassail when Mr. Hampton cleared his throat to get the attention of everyone in the room. "I have some news," he said, clasping his hands together.

Everyone looked his way. Kate could hardly wait to hear what he had to say. She hoped it was good news!

"Geneva and I are selling the creamery!" Mr. Hampton grinned from ear to ear.

"W—what?" Everyone spoke in unison.

"Are you kidding?" Uncle Ollie asked.

"Please say this is a joke!" Aunt Molly added. "We don't want you to move away!"

"We're not moving away," he said. "I promise!"

"Oh, Mr. Hampton. . .please don't give up just because your sales are down right now," Michael begged. "I'll do anything. . .everything to help you get them up again."

Mr. Hampton laughed. "No, you don't understand. Geneva and I are ready to retire. And we have no children to pass the business to. God never blessed us with a son or a daughter. A wonderful couple from central Vermont has been talking with us about buying the place. In fact, I think you met them, girls. They were on the tour that day. . ."

"Abigail and Mark Collingsworth?" Kate stammered.

"Why, yes." Geneva Hampton looked stunned. "How did you know their names? That's amazing."

"Oh, trust me," Sydney said. "We know a lot more than that about them. They already own a creamery called Cheese De-Lite about fifty miles from here. They're Mad River's main competitors."

"Not anymore!" Geneva Hampton laughed. "They're moving their operation to Mad River Valley. From now on, there will be no Cheese De-Lite. But they will bring their signature cheese flavor with them. . .the low-fat version of cheddar."

"Low-fat cheese?" Kate wrinkled her nose. "No wonder that man has such a sour look on his face. That doesn't sound very yummy."

"No, he had a sour look on his face because he *really* thought we had rats at the creamery," Mrs. Hampton said with a laugh. "We had a hard time convincing him it wasn't true! But now that he knows the real story, he's made us an offer. And it's a good one. So the next time you see him, he will be smiling, I'm sure!"

"Still, low-fat cheese?" Kate said. "Icky!"

"Hey, we have to cut back on our calories every way we can!" Sydney said. After a sheepish look, she added, "Well, at least *I* do, if I'm going to be a sports star!"

Kate sighed. "I guess I'd better cut back on calories, too. Skiing was a lot of fun. You never know, I may end up liking sports, too! Wouldn't that be something!"

"I can hardly wait to tell the other Camp Club Girls!" Sydney laughed. "Can you imagine the look on Bailey's face when she hears you won a skiing competition!"

"And what about McKenzie! She's going to flip!" Kate chuckled, just thinking about it. "I'm excited to tell Elizabeth. I know she's been praying. I always feel better, knowing she's praying."

"Me, too," Sydney observed. "And I always feel better when I'm spending time with you. That's why. . ." Her eyes filled with tears. "That's why I'm so sad this week is almost over! We have to go home soon!"

"Let's spend every minute together. . .having fun!" Kate said.

●—●—●

A few minutes later, Michael asked if he could speak to Kate in private. She sat next to him on the couch wondering why he had such an embarrassed look on his face.

"You know, I bragged a lot about how fast I am on the slopes," he said.

"Yes, you did," Kate agreed. "But you *are* fast. I saw you with my own eyes."

"Yes, but I saw *you*, too! And you're amazing, Kate! Really amazing."

"You think so?" She felt her cheeks turn warm as an embarrassed feeling came over her.

"I know so." He grinned. "Are you coming back to Mad River Valley next winter? If so, I'd better start practicing now if I'm ever going to beat you."

Kate laughed long and loud at that one. "How funny! A boy actually thinks I'm good at sports! That's hysterical!" She giggled. "I don't know if I'll compete next year. I liked it more when I was skiing for fun. But I'm sure we'll come back for a visit if Aunt Molly and Uncle Ollie invite us!"

"Oh, you're *always* welcome!" Aunt Molly said, sweeping Kate into her arms. "Please come and see me as often as you like."

"Yes, I feel sure there are lots of mysteries to solve in Mad River Valley," Uncle Ollie said.

"Like who ate all the Snickerdoodles when I wasn't looking," Maggie said, looking at Uncle Ollie.

"Or who put too much cheese in the fondue," Michael threw in.

"Or who used my treadmill when I wasn't looking!" Uncle Ollie added, looking at Sydney.

"Wasn't me!" Aunt Molly proclaimed.

They all laughed at that one.

"It doesn't matter where Kate goes, adventure always seems to follow," her dad said. "She's my little supersleuth!"

"I just *love* adventure!" Kate said. "Love, love, love it!"

She and Sydney spent the next few minutes telling everyone about some of the cases they had solved with the Camp Club Girls. On and on their stories went, filling the ears of everyone in the room.

When she finished, her dad looked at her, beaming with pride. "I'm so proud of you, Kate."

"Here's to Inspector Gadget!" Sydney raised her glass of wassail.

Seconds later, everyone joined her, offering up a toast to Kate. She felt all warm and tingly inside. Solving mysteries made her feel good from the top of her head to the bottom of her toes.

But what made her feel even better—much, much better, in fact—was forgiving Phillip. Perhaps that had been the greatest lesson of all this week. Never again would she hold a grudge. No, from now on she would forgive. . .quickly!

"Be kind to one another, tenderhearted, forgiving one another, even as God in Christ forgave you." Kate smiled as she whispered the words. Yes, from now on, she would always be quick to forgive!

Aunt Molly stood and began to sing "Joy to the World." Uncle Ollie joined her, then Mr. and Mrs. Hampton. Before long, most everyone was singing, even Michael.

Sydney leaned over and whispered in Kate's ear. "We solved another case, Kate! Can you believe it?"

"Yep!" Turning to her friend, Kate whispered the words they loved so much: "Supersleuths forever!"

Sydney winked and added, "Forever and ever!"

Kate nodded, then happened to look over at the little manger scene on the fireplace mantel. She focused on the babe inside, remembering what her mother had said. *He came to forgive*, she reminded herself.

With a *very* merry heart, Kate lifted her voice and began to sing!

Camp Club Girls

McKenzie's
OREGON
OPERATION

Shari Barr

Lost!

"They're going to hit us!" McKenzie screamed, clutching the sides of the tiny sailboat, *Sea Skimmer*.

Alexis Howell reached back and grabbed the tiller, the steering device of the boat. She tried to move the sailboat out of the path of the motorboat speeding straight for them. But the steady breeze from earlier had died down.

Instead of moving out of the motorboat's way, the *Sea Skimmer* bobbed lazily, its sails hanging limp. Alex paddled frantically with her hands, but her attempts were useless.

"Watch out!" McKenzie cried. She waved one arm furiously, trying to get the driver's attention.

A man wearing a black baseball cap and mirrored sunglasses sat in the driver's seat. He stared straight ahead as if unaware of the girls. The woman in the front seat beside him looked the other way as they barreled down on the skimmer.

McKenzie and Alex yelled, but the roar of the motorboat drowned their screams.

Zoom! Splash! Suddenly the driver whipped the boat into a sharp turn.

But that caused choppy waves rolling right at the girls. Again and again. Higher and higher. They relentlessly beat the sailboat.

"Hold on!" Alex cried out.

The skimmer bobbed wildly.

Blam! Whoosh!

The sailboat toppled, dumping the girls into the blue-green ocean water.

Ahh! With flailing arms, McKenzie began to sink. Seconds later she felt an upward pull. Her orange life vest popped her out of the water. She bounced up and down as the waves slowed. She coughed and sputtered from the salty water that had gone up her nose. Craning her neck, she searched for Alexis.

"Alex!" McKenzie yelled, her eyes skimming the surface of the water. "Where are you?"

The capsized sailboat lifted slightly. Alex's sunburned face appeared. "I'm under here. You okay?"

"Great," McKenzie said between sputters. "Except for a major wedgie."

"Wow, what was that all about?" Alex asked. She slipped from beneath the overturned skimmer, clinging to its side.

McKenzie flung her wet hair out of her eyes. She swam to the sailboat. Then she draped her arms across the bottom until she caught her breath. "Man, was that guy trying to kill us or what? I thought for sure we were goners!"

"I don't think he even saw us until he almost hit us," Alexis said. She took a deep breath.

"How could he not see us?" McKenzie asked. "It's hard to miss this skimmer with its bright sails. And he didn't even stop to see if we were okay."

McKenzie squinted into the distance. The motorboat was idling about a half mile away. The driver appeared to be standing and watching them through binoculars. Was he checking to make sure they were okay? If so, why didn't he just come back and ask? She scanned the cove, but only saw a cloud of haze on the horizon.

"Let's swim this thing to shore," Alex suggested. "We'll never be able to turn it right side up out here."

The girls had entered a narrow inlet near Sea Lion Harbor on the Oregon coast. The nearest shoreline was an isolated beach about one hundred yards away. Kicking their legs, the girls slowly towed the sailboat to shore.

A few minutes later, McKenzie felt sand beneath her feet and stood in chest-high water. The girls flipped the sailboat right side up. Then they tugged it onto the sandy beach, far from the incoming tide.

McKenzie flopped onto the sand. Glancing around, she noticed nothing but a small sandy beach along the rocky coastline. "I wonder where we are," she said, slipping out of her life vest. She flung it to the ground.

"I think we're near your Aunt Becca's beach house," Alex said, brushing sand from between her toes. "I try to pay attention to landmarks. Dad taught me to always watch my surroundings. I haven't got lost yet. If we get out of this inlet, we'll be able to see the house just south a little ways, I'm sure."

"I'm glad you know how to sail." McKenzie wrung water out of her dripping curly auburn hair.

"My grandparents' home in San Francisco is on the beach, so my parents take my brothers and me sailing about once a month," Alex said, tucking her dark, shoulder-length curls behind her ears. "I didn't realize the ocean is so much rougher up here, though. No wonder we don't see any more sailboats out here. The water's colder, too."

"I have no clue where we are. I was just looking for the sea lions."

"Aren't sea lions cool? I've seen tons of them near my grandparents' home," Alex said.

McKenzie picked up a seashell and examined it. "Are they Steller sea lions?" she asked, glancing at her younger friend.

"Yes. Most of the sea lions along the Pacific coast are from the Steller family."

"Why are these kind called Steller?" McKenzie asked.

"They're named after the guy who first studied the animals back in the 1700s," Alex explained. "They're usually larger and lighter in color than other sea lions, the California sea lions. Sea lions are my favorite animal, and sea lion pups are so cute. I can't wait to find those two you were talking about—Mario and Bianca."

"Yeah, it's really weird," McKenzie said. "They're always with their mom, Susie. I saw them last night after my plane got in, before you arrived. But no one's seen them since. I want to put them in my video report."

"I can't believe this report is really going to be on TV. Can you?" Alex asked, shielding her eyes against the sun.

"Not really," McKenzie said. "I about freaked out when the public TV guy called and told me that I had won the essay contest about endangered animals. I couldn't believe it when he said I'd also won a trip to Sea Lion Harbor to film my report."

Alex smiled at her friend. "I am so glad you asked me to come up here and run the video camera. We'll have a blast."

"Mom and Dad would never have agreed to let me come if Aunt Becca wasn't already working out here at the resort.

They're too busy on the farm to take a vacation right now, so this is perfect. And it would have been no fun to spend every day alone while Becca's at work," McKenzie said, digging a broken seashell from the sand and tossing it aside. "Though it's cool to have an aunt who's a private airplane pilot with a company connected to a resort!"

She stood, hopping across the sand until the waves washed over her toes. This was her first visit to the ocean, and she absolutely loved it. The Oregon coast was a long way from her parents' farm in Montana. The salty air mixed with the scent of pine trees was so different from the woodsy smells back home.

Last night, after Aunt Becca had picked McKenzie up at the airport, she had taken her to a spot farther down the coast so McKenzie could see the Pacific Ocean. The roar of the waves had practically hypnotized her. She had never heard or seen anything like it. The water here at Sea Lion Harbor, though, was calm compared to the way the ocean had been the night before.

"Let's go exploring," Alex said, interrupting McKenzie's thoughts.

Alex had already started down the short stretch of sandy beach that lay between two craggy rock formations. McKenzie followed her, wet sand squishing between her toes. Alex hurried to the nearest rock and scurried to the top.

"Come on up." Alex motioned for McKenzie to follow. "You've got to see this."

The rocks were rough and hot beneath McKenzie's feet, but she scaled the rock to stand beside Alex. Below the girls lay a narrow sandy inlet that stretched into a gaping hole in the side of the cliff.

"Wow!" McKenzie exclaimed. "Look at this cave."

McKenzie climbed partway down the rock before leaping the last few feet. She fell to her knees, reaching her arms out to keep from falling on her face. She stood and brushed the sand off her legs. The sandbar was cool here, shaded by the craggy rocks towering above the opening to the cave.

McKenzie turned as Alex leaped off the rock beside her. The girls moved closer together. They stared into the opening of the cave that yawned like a huge mouth.

Alex's blue eyes gleamed with wonder. "Look how tall it is. You could drive a truck through there. That is, if you could get a truck out here."

McKenzie took a few steps forward. She approached the opening and felt the cool, damp air inside. She wrinkled her nose. "Pew! It smells like something died in there."

"Are you going in?" Alex sniffed the air with a look of disgust.

"I'm a wimp. You go first." McKenzie gave Alex a gentle shove forward.

"Why me?" Alex said, taking a step backward. "You're a whole year older than I am."

McKenzie sighed as she shook her head. "Okay, okay. But you're coming with me," she said, tugging her friend's arm.

McKenzie stepped inside the cave, letting her eyes adjust to the darkness. Nothing but a black hole loomed before her. She had no idea how far the tunnel reached into the cliff. She glanced downward and noticed a paper fast-food cup lying on the sand at her feet.

"Hey, look. Somebody's been here." McKenzie pointed at the cup.

"Maybe it's been here awhile," Alex said as she bent over

and picked it up.

"I don't think so," McKenzie answered. "The cup hasn't even started to get soggy. I think someone was here not too long ago. Or maybe somebody is still here."

McKenzie shuddered as she spoke the words. Standing in the cave without a light was starting to give her the willies. She turned to make sure Alex had followed her. *I'm thinking this isn't exactly the place I want to explore without a guide. On the other hand, maybe I don't want to explore it at all.*

"Maybe this isn't such a good idea," Alex said. "We can't see where we're going without a flashlight."

"I agree. I'm not about to get lost in this place. It's way too creepy for me. Besides, my feet are cold," McKenzie said, rubbing the goose bumps forming on her arms. Her wet swimsuit felt icy against her skin. Eager for the warmth of the sun outside, she hurried toward the entrance. After stepping from the darkness of the cave, she stopped in her tracks.

A thick blanket of fog was creeping across the smooth surface of the cove toward them. The sun that had warmed them earlier had disappeared behind the haze.

"We'd better go before the fog closes in on us." Alex sprinted toward the rock piling and quickly climbed to the top. "I want to be able to see our way back."

Dashing back to the beach, they hurried into their life jackets. Then they carried the *Sea Skimmer* to the cold water's edge.

"Hop on," Alex said as she steadied the boat. "I'll tow us out into deeper water."

McKenzie pulled herself up, the boat teetering as she climbed aboard. Alex waded out a little farther, pulling the boat behind her. A few seconds later she pulled herself onto the deck of the boat, tipping the skimmer slightly. McKenzie gripped the sides praying Alex wouldn't tip the boat over.

"I'll teach you to sail sometime," Alex said, grabbing a stick that was fastened to the floor of the sailboat. "But not today."

McKenzie watched in amazement as Alex's hands flew back and forth. "What is that thingy?" she asked, pointing to a sticklike device attached to the floor.

"It's called a tiller. It's connected to the rudder, so I can steer the boat. It will even let us sail against the wind," Alex answered. "But barely any breeze is blowing now. We're not going anywhere very fast."

Alex turned the tiller, trying to catch what little breeze they could in the orange, yellow, and blue sail. *Turtles can swim faster than this,* McKenzie thought as Alex steered the skimmer into deeper water.

Minutes later they sailed out of the inlet into the open waters of the cove. McKenzie focused on the fog pressing closer and closer. The water shimmered like an aquamarine stone, an occasional breeze causing slight ripples on the surface. Alex caught every puff of wind, no matter how small, and slowly sailed the boat toward home.

McKenzie had never sailed before. She had only ridden in speedboats and rowboats on lakes near her home in Montana. She gazed toward the shore, noting the unfamiliar landmarks. Nothing but pine trees and steep bluffs lined the shoreline.

"Are you sure you know where we are? None of this looks familiar to me. Shouldn't there be houses along the beach?" McKenzie's grip on the side of the boat tightened.

Alex kept her hand on the tiller and gazed at the overcast

sky. She looked up and down the mainland. Then she brought her free hand up and chewed on a fingernail.

Alex's eyes looked worried. "I thought I paid a lot of attention earlier, but I don't recognize anything. Those trees aren't familiar, and I don't see the resort. I'm not sure where we are. I guess maybe I was watching for sea lions more than I thought."

McKenzie felt her stomach lurch. "What do you mean? We aren't lost, are we?"

Alex fixed her gaze on the mainland, struggling to keep the sailboat from going too far into the open cove. "I'll figure it out in a minute," she finally said.

Uh-oh, McKenzie thought as she stared at the isolated shoreline. *I sure hope she figures it out, because I have no clue where we are.*

"Alex, I just had an awful thought," McKenzie stammered. "Aunt Becca was already at work when we left. I forgot to tell anyone we were leaving."

Alex blinked her eyes nervously. "We were supposed to tell Mr. Carney if we went sailing, weren't we?"

Mr. Carney, or Mr. C. as the girls called him, rented the cabin next door to Aunt Becca. He was an elderly man who, he said, had rented the same cabin every summer for the last twenty years. Since Aunt Becca had rented the same cabin for the previous three years, the two knew each other well. Mr. Carney had volunteered to keep an eye on the girls if they needed anything while Becca was at work.

"Nobody knows where we are," McKenzie said, her voice trembling. "Aunt Becca won't know we're missing until she gets home from work. That won't be for hours yet."

"Mr. C. will notice that our sailboat is missing," Alex said, trying to sound reassuring.

"What if he's not home?" McKenzie asked, growing more worried by the minute.

Alex didn't answer. The girls sat in silence, watching the fog roll toward them. It settled over them like a cold vapor. McKenzie could barely see past Alex on the other end of the boat.

The sails of the little sailboat hung limply as the breeze died. The *Sea Skimmer* bobbed idly. McKenzie shut her eyes briefly, feeling the gentle rise and fall of the boat. *Dear God,* she prayed. *Keep us safe and help us find our way home.*

"Have you figured it out yet?" McKenzie asked as she cautiously opened her eyes.

Alex turned to McKenzie, her voice faltering. "I— I—can hardly see anything through the fog. I don't know where the homes and the docks and the resort are. Oh, McKenzie, I think we're lost!"

CHAPTER 2

Kidnapped!

A shiver ran down McKenzie's spine. "Shouldn't we just try to reach shore?" she asked, her voice higher than normal.

"The shoreline here is mostly rocks," Alex pointed out. "So there could be lots of underwater rocks to get caught up on. We don't want to get too close until I know just where we are."

The little sailboat floated listlessly. Only a few minutes earlier the sky had been clear. Now dense fog had settled over the cove, surrounding them in a white, swirling mist.

"What are we going to do?" McKenzie asked fearfully.

Alex chewed her bottom lip as she surveyed the situation. "Look!" she exclaimed, pointing at a flash of light cutting through the fog. "There's the light from the Heceta Head Lighthouse up the coast. We have to head back to our left to make sure we stay in the cove. I sure don't want to get out in the open waters."

McKenzie wasn't used to the ocean. The thought of being swept out into the rough waters scared her. "You don't think... we'll get washed away...." Her voice cut off.

"Oh, of course not," Alex said with a smile.

A fake smile, McKenzie thought. *She's trying not to scare me. She doesn't want me to know we're in big, big trouble.*

McKenzie's hand clutched the sides of the sailboat until her knuckles turned white.

"We can't even see where we are." McKenzie's voice trembled. "How will we know if we're being pulled out to sea?"

"The tide's coming in. It'll push us into the shore, not away from it," Alex reassured her.

"It'll push us into the rocks, you mean?" McKenzie shivered. *Why, oh why, didn't we tell Mr. C. we were going sailing?*

"I think we're just in a little pocket of fog. The sun is trying to break through," Alex said as she turned the sails, trying to catch what little breeze she could.

A seagull cried overhead, and a motorboat puttered in the distance.

At least someone else is out here. If we could only see, McKenzie thought, *then we could ask for help.*

"I'm really sorry I didn't pay more attention. I'm the one who got us lost," Alex said softly.

McKenzie smiled slightly. "It's not any more your fault than it is mine. I shouldn't have been gawking around so much. Anyway, I can't believe God would let us get lost at sea. I've been praying."

"Yeah, I have, too." Alex sighed. "I guess we have to trust Him."

McKenzie nodded. Though she still couldn't see the shoreline, she felt more relaxed than she had earlier. As she peered into the fog, a sleek gray object slid through the water beside her. She jumped. A whiskered nose popped through the water. For a second, McKenzie couldn't speak, then she cried, "Susie! Boy, am I glad to see you."

The sea lion spun in the water, twirling like a ballerina. Her flippers flapped up and down as she performed her water dance.

"Alex," McKenzie turned to her friend, "this is the sea lion I was telling you about."

"You mean her pups are the ones that are missing?" Alex asked, working the tiller.

"Yes," McKenzie said, relieved. "We can't be too far from Sea Lion Harbor."

Aaarrr! Aaarrr! Susie barked as she splashed the water with her flippers. With a final spin, the sea lion slipped away from the boat.

"I think she's calling for her pups," Alex said. "I hope she finds them."

A cool breeze brushed McKenzie's face. The bright sails snapped as they caught the breeze that suddenly rolled in across the cove.

"Hey, we're moving now." Alex grinned at McKenzie.

"Look." McKenzie pointed at Susie, barely visible in the fog. "Maybe we should follow her."

Alex steered in Susie's direction. The sea lion swam slowly, as if waiting for the sailboat to keep up.

"I think the fog is lifting. I see some trees on the shore." Alex brushed her damp hair out of her eyes.

McKenzie relaxed her grip on the sailboat and breathed deeply. She saw the vague outline of one the resort's beach homes. "God must have heard us. He sent good ol' Susie to show us the way back."

Minutes later Susie had disappeared, but the girls had sailed out of the cloud of fog. Alex steered the boat toward Becca's boat dock, clearly visible in the emerging sunlight.

After Alex hopped onto the dock, she tied up the boat.

McKenzie's knees wobbled as she tried to stand. She flailed her arms back and forth like a windmill as the skimmer teetered from side to side.

"Here, grab my hand!" Alex cried.

McKenzie grabbed Alex's fingertips and leaped onto the dock. "I've never been so glad to touch dry land before."

"I told you we'd get back okay," Alex said as she started up the dock. "I've never lost anyone yet."

McKenzie shook her head teasingly. "Okay, I'll never not trust you again."

As the girls approached their beach house, a voice called. Turning to the neighboring house, McKenzie saw Mr. Carney sitting in the shade in his lawn chair. A glass of iced tea sat in a wire cup holder beside him. The white stubble on his balding head contrasted with his black skin.

"Hi, Mr. C.," McKenzie called out, jogging over to him. "This is my friend Alexis Howell, but everybody calls her Alex. She came from Sacramento to spend the week with me."

Mr. Carney stood and shook Alex's hand, his teeth flashing a wide smile. "Nice to meet you, Miss Alex. You're quite the sailor."

"Thank you, I've had quite a bit of practice. Except I don't like sailing in the fog."

"You girls had me worried. I was about ready to call the Coast Guard. But then I saw your little skimmer. That fog can be tricky." Mr. Carney scratched his head with his pinkie finger. "And girls, this ocean is too rough to take a sailboat out of the protected bay and into the ocean."

"Lucky for us, we saw Susie and she led us back home." McKenzie unzipped her life jacket and slid it off.

"That wasn't luck, young lady." Mr. Carney's eyes grew serious. "The good Lord was looking after you two, He was. If I hadn't seen you leave, no one would have known where you went. You could have been in a heap of trouble out there if the fog hadn't lifted when it did."

McKenzie glanced sheepishly toward Alex and met her gaze. She knew Mr. Carney was speaking the truth. They could have been in serious trouble.

"I'm not scolding you girls, but I know your Aunt Becca had already left for work when you set out. She asked me to keep an eye out for you while she's gone. You just had me a bit worried, that's all."

"We're sorry we worried you. We were hoping to find Susie's pups. I want to show them to Alex," McKenzie explained. "Has anybody seen them yet this morning?"

Mr. Carney shook his head as he settled back in his lawn chair. "Not that I know of. It's strange, if you ask me. Those little pups are always with their momma. Don't know what could have happened to them."

"Do you think a whale or a shark could have gotten them?" Alexis shuddered.

Mr. Carney shrugged his shoulders. "I suppose that's possible, but I really don't think it's likely. Susie keeps a close watch over her pups."

The elderly man glanced at his watch and rose to his feet. "I'd better go check my lunch in the oven, then I'm heading to the gift shop. The book I ordered about caves came in this morning."

"We were going over there to shop for souvenirs," McKenzie said. "We could pick it up for you if you want."

Mr. Carney accepted the offer and pulled his wallet from

his back pocket. After he handed them a couple of bills, they ran across the sand to Aunt Becca's rental house. McKenzie found the key her aunt kept hidden on the front porch, and they slipped inside the back door.

Aunt Becca's golden retriever met them at the door. "Hey there, Mickey." McKenzie scratched the dog's head as she headed toward the computer in the corner of the living room.

"I'm going to check my e-mail before we go." McKenzie clicked the mouse until her account popped up.

"Hey, you've got a message from Inspector Gadget." Alex giggled as she peered over her shoulder and saw their friend Kate's name on the screen. "Oh, and there's another one from Elizabeth. But there's nothing from any of the other Camp Club Girls, though."

The Camp Club Girls were McKenzie's roommates from camp in Arizona. The six girls came from all parts of the country and had become best friends. While at camp they had solved a mystery together. Now when the girls visited each other, they always managed to solve some sort of mystery or riddle. They called their friend Kate Oliver Inspector Gadget because she had every new gadget or electronic device imaginable. Kate was eleven years old and lived in Philadelphia.

"I e-mailed all the girls as soon as I found out about the missing sea lion pups. Maybe Kate has some advice."

Kate had written:

Hey roomies, anything new about the pups? Dad gave me a pair of video sunglasses that are really cool. You can record sights and sounds when you're wearing them and nobody will know. I'm sending them to you so you should have them in a couple of days. They might come in handy to solve this mystery.

"Cool!" Alex said, peering over her shoulder. "I can't wait to see those."

"I didn't even know they made video sunglasses," McKenzie said, clicking on a message from fourteen-year-old Elizabeth Anderson, who lived in Amarillo, Texas.

Hi McKenzie and Alex,

Ever since you told me about the sea lion pups, I've been praying and praying. I have the strangest feeling that the pups are still alive. I think God wants you to save them, just like He does us. Keep all us Camp Club Girls posted so we can help.

Love, Elizabeth

McKenzie logged off, feeling relieved after reading Elizabeth's words. The older girl had an amazing faith. McKenzie often wished she was more like her. Elizabeth always remembered to turn to God, while McKenzie often forgot.

The girls changed quickly out of their swimsuits into shorts and T-shirts. Ten minutes later, they walked through the front door of the lobby to Emerald Bay Resort and Cottages.

Two employees stood behind a counter, busy with customers making reservations on computers. A rock fireplace stood at one end of the lobby with a leather couch and chairs nestled around it. A display of vacation brochures sat on the polished wooden coffee table in front.

A pamphlet caught McKenzie's eye as she approached the table. "Hey, look at this, Alex." She grabbed a colorful brochure and skimmed the front page. "Newport, a city just north of here, is having a photography contest during their festival later this week. Why don't you enter? You're a great photographer."

Alex took the brochure from McKenzie, her blue eyes sparkling. "Ooh. This would be fun. Maybe I could take pictures of some of the whales."

McKenzie grabbed a handful of various brochures and flicked through them. "We could go to the Heceta Head Lighthouse and Cape Perpetua. You should be able to get some really good shots up there."

The girls settled onto the couch with their heads together, poring over the brochures. McKenzie looked up when she heard loud voices at the counter.

"We reserved the Hideaway Bungalow more than three months ago." A dark-haired man with sunglasses perched on his head snapped at a young man behind the counter. A woman with blond hair stood beside him, shaking her head with exasperation.

They look familiar, McKenzie thought. *Where have I seen them?*

"I'm sorry, Mr. Franks," the clerk apologized. "Apparently there has been some confusion. We just gave that cabin to another party. But I'll tell you what I'll do. You can have the Beachside Cabin at the same rate as the Hideaway. That's quite an upgrade. The Beachside has a magnificent view of the cove."

Mr. Franks slapped his hand on the counter. "I don't want the Beachside Cabin. I reserved the Hideaway, and I demand that I get it!"

"Uhh," the clerk stammered as his face turned red. "But that's not possible."

"Young man," the bleach-blond woman said in a syrupy sweet voice. "I'm sure you don't understand our predicament. We're trainers at Sea Park, and we always reserve the Hideaway since it's away from all the hustle and bustle of the resort. It's an understanding we have with your manager, Mr. Simms. I'm sure you can make the necessary arrangements immediately, can't you?"

"Oh. . .uh," the clerk stuttered as he pecked on his computer keyboard. "I am so sorry. I didn't realize you were *the* Mel and Tia Franks. Let me double-check. Aah, yes, the Hideaway has just been cleaned, as a matter of fact. I can give you your keys now."

McKenzie raised her eyebrows as she met Alex's gaze. She tried to suppress a giggle as the irate couple grabbed their keys and marched out of the lobby.

"Now I know where I've seen them," McKenzie whispered to Alex. "Aren't they the couple in the motorboat that almost ran over us?"

"Yeah, I think you're right," Alex said, watching the couple through the window.

After shoving the free brochures in her back pocket, McKenzie headed across the lobby to the gift shop. Alex stopped to look at a postcard display, but McKenzie headed to an aisle filled with trinkets. She picked up a gray stuffed sea lion. It barked when she pressed its stomach.

Evan would like this, she thought, trying to decide what to get her little brother for a souvenir. *Or maybe he'd like the glow-in-the-dark Ping-Pong balls or a monster-sized stuffed whale.*

A rack held various hats with fake hair attached to the underside. An army-green fishing hat had stringy red hair hanging down. Black bushy hair stuck out from beneath an orange stocking cap. She picked up a baseball cap that had two long blond braids attached. Twisting her hair into a knot, she tucked it under the cap as she shoved it onto her head.

"Can I help you, ma'am?" McKenzie asked with a forced Southern drawl as she approached her friend in the next aisle.

Alex looked up from the postcard in her hand. Her blue eyes sparkled as she burst out laughing. "Where did you get that? You should see yourself."

McKenzie led Alex to the goofy hat display. The girls each grabbed a cap and giggled as they modeled for each other.

After they had tried on nearly every style, McKenzie decided to get a green fishing hat for Evan and a T-shirt for herself. Alex had a handful of postcards and a bag of gum balls. While the girls paid for their souvenirs, they inquired about Mr. Carney's book. The clerk located it beneath the checkout counter and handed it to them. After paying for it, the girls stepped outside.

"This looks like a cool book." McKenzie scanned the cover and read aloud, *"Secluded Caves along the Oregon Coast: Little-known Caves for Amateur Spelunkers."*

"What are spelunkers?" Alex asked, popping a gum ball in her mouth.

"Cave explorers." McKenzie flipped through the book as she walked across the parking lot, pausing to look at some of the pictures. "Maybe I can borrow this from Mr. C. when he's done."

McKenzie closed the book and stuck it back in the bag with her other purchases. The girls walked down the winding lane to Mr. Carney's cottage. After they delivered the book, he promised she could borrow it when he was finished.

Since Aunt Becca wouldn't get home from work for several more hours, the girls decided to have a picnic on the beach. They found a spot they liked in the bright sun and settled on the sand.

A woman stretched out on a lounge chair beneath a huge yellow beach umbrella. A girl who looked about six years old and a boy of about nine were building a sand castle near the water. The girl carried buckets of sand while the boy pounded the sand into shapes. So far, their castle looked like a bunch of lumps.

While the girls ate, the kids' voices drifted up the beach.

"I want to see the sea lion pups," the little girl said as she dumped a pail full of wet sand next to the castle.

"You can't see them," the boy said, patting the sand into a cone shape. "They're gone."

"Where did they go?" the girl asked. She plunked onto the beach and folded her arms across her chest.

"How do I know?" the boy answered, dumping another bucket of sand. "A man and woman took them away this morning."

McKenzie stopped chewing and leaned forward. She held her breath and a tingle ran up her neck as the boy continued. "I saw them. Mario and Bianca were kidnapped!"

An Intriguing Invitation

"Did that kid say what I think he did?" McKenzie asked, nudging Alex.

"Did he say somebody kidnapped Mario and Bianca?" Alex said, with her mouth full of sandwich.

A banana slice fell out of McKenzie's sandwich on its way to her mouth. It rolled down her front, smearing a glob of peanut butter down her swimsuit. "That's what I thought he said, too."

McKenzie plucked the banana off her lap and stuffed it in her mouth. She turned her attention back to the family building the lopsided sand castle.

The mother lifted her head from the lounge chair and turned toward her son. "Did you really see someone take the sea lion pups, Keaton?"

The boy nodded. "I went outside this morning before anyone was up. I saw some guy and a woman pull two little sea lions out of the water and put them into their boat. Two teenagers were helping."

"Did you see what they looked like?" the mom asked as she sprayed sunscreen on the boy's back.

The boy shrugged. He stuck a plastic shovel into the sand, scooping a trench around the castle. "Sort of, but not really. The guy had a really cool giant fish tattoo on his arm. Their boat was silver with red trim."

The mother turned from her son and tossed the sunscreen bottle to the ground. "Claire, get your life jacket on!" she yelled as she chased her daughter, who was running toward the water.

Standing, the boy tossed his shovel to the ground. He grabbed an inner tube and raced down the beach after his mother and sister.

Thank God Mario and Bianca are still alive, McKenzie thought with relief. *Elizabeth was right.* She glanced toward the boats sailing in the cove and sighed. *Five or six boats there now are silver with red trim. How can anyone figure out who took the pups if the boy can't remember what they look like?*

"Do you think someone really stole Mario and Bianca?" Alex took a gulp from her juice bottle.

"That kid seems to think so." McKenzie squirted sunscreen onto her leg and rubbed it in. "But he only remembers the guy's tattoo. Whoever stole them surely wouldn't come back around. They're probably long gone by now."

Alex stuffed her sandwich bags into her tote and nodded. "True. But maybe the kid is just making the whole thing up."

"He sure acted like he knew what he was talking about. I mean, he noticed the guy's tattoo and all. Why would he make that up?"

Alex rubbed sunscreen across her face. "Maybe we could go out there and talk to him. Ask him questions and stuff."

McKenzie looked down the beach and saw the woman gathering towels and sand toys. "I think we're too late."

The mother grabbed the little girl's hand, and the boy tagged along behind, dragging the beach chair. Minutes later they disappeared in the crowd of sunbathers near the resort. The girls ran to the cold water for a few moments then stretched out on their beach towels.

McKenzie closed her eyes against the sun. Then she remembered she hadn't told the Camp Club Girls about the boy's story of the sea lion pups' kidnapping. She dug her cell phone from her bag and texted a message. She sent it to Kate and Elizabeth, as well as Bailey Chang in Peoria, Illinois, and Sydney Lincoln in Washington, DC.

She propped herself up with her elbow and glanced at Alex. "Why don't we get your camcorder and walk down to Sea Lion Harbor? We might as well get started on the video report."

The girls quickly gathered their towels and bags and headed to the beach house. After changing their clothes, they grabbed their cameras and stepped out the back door. They set off down the road behind the row of beach homes that led to the Sea Lion Harbor observation area.

When they arrived at the overlook, McKenzie heard the sea lions before she saw them. Their barking was unlike anything she had ever heard. Even though she had heard them the night before with Aunt Becca, she was still shocked by the noise.

"Look at them all," McKenzie said, peering over the fence that overlooked the rocky ledge below. "There must be dozens of them. They're so cute when they play, and they're so noisy. Do you know what a group of sea lions is called?"

"A cluster?" Alex asked.

"No, a herd," McKenzie said. "When Aunt Becca told me that, I thought she was kidding. I thought she said it was a herd because I'm used to cows being in herds!"

"Well, I guess they're actually about as big as cows," Alex said.

"At least some of them. I never realized how big they can get," McKenzie agreed.

"Do you see Susie?" Alex leaned against the railing and watched the sea lions frolic in the water.

McKenzie squinted as she searched the herd for Susie. "There she is! On the ledge. That's not like her. Last night she was spinning like a ballet dancer while Mario and Bianca swam around her. She must not have found her pups yet. She looks sad now."

"Maybe she misses her babies." Alex lifted her camcorder and focused on the sea lions below her.

McKenzie focused her digital camera on Susie and snapped a picture. Several of the sea lions were chasing fish, catching them playfully, then letting them go. "Susie just doesn't act right. Do you think we could figure out what happened to the pups?"

Alex lowered her camcorder. "I think we should try, anyway. When I was doing my report for school, I learned it's illegal to capture sea lions. If we don't look out for them, who will? They're God's creatures, too."

"If someone stole Mario and Bianca, we need to find out who did it and what they did with the pups," McKenzie said, glancing at her watch. "It's hot out here. Do you want to go back to the beach for a while before Aunt Becca gets off work? That will give us time to figure out how to start this investigation."

Alex agreed as she shut off her camcorder. They hurried back down the road to the beach house. After grabbing their towels, they headed to the cove. While they were gone, sunbathers had flocked to the beach, spreading out colorful blankets and coolers. Rock music blared out of someone's boom box. A few kites dotted the sky.

McKenzie flung herself onto the sand.

Alex dropped down beside her and stretched out on her stomach with her arms folded beneath her chin. "Isn't it funny that a group of sea lions is called a herd, but baby sea lions are called pups?" Then without waiting for an answer, she asked, "Where should we begin, with this investigation, I mean?"

"Good question." McKenzie started digging in the sand. "We don't know much about the couple that the boy said stole the pups. All we know is that they drove a silver and red boat, and the guy had a fish tattoo. And they had two helpers. Maybe we should try to figure out why someone would want to steal the babies. You're the sea lion expert, Alex. What would someone do with a sea lion?"

Alex thought for a moment then answered. "Well, it's not to sell the fur, like some animals, because the sea lion doesn't have any fur. Some people in northern Alaska use the skins to make boats, but that would be dumb to steal pups for that."

"That's gross," McKenzie said, making a face. "Surely no one would be mean enough to do that. They wouldn't get much skin out of baby pups, anyway. There must be another reason. Why else would someone want a sea lion?"

"Hmm." Alex wrinkled her brow. "Mario and Bianca were twins, and that's very unusual. Maybe someone wants them for a zoo or something like that."

McKenzie scanned the people lounging on the beach. She wished she would see the mother and her two kids,

Keaton and Claire, again. If she did, she would talk to the boy. But she didn't see the family anywhere on this stretch of beach.

"Hey, look." McKenzie nodded in the direction of a boat. "Is that the boat that about ran us over this morning? It kind of looks like the same couple."

Alex turned in the direction McKenzie pointed. "It could be. It all happened so fast that I didn't get a good look at them. But it does look like the boat. It's silver and red, just like the one that kid, Keaton, saw."

The pilot of the boat steered it into the marina and cut the engine. A tall blond woman jumped onto the dock and tied the boat to the dock. They stowed their fishing gear in the back of the boat. Then they each grabbed an end of an old cooler and lugged it onto the dock.

"It is them. That's also the couple that got so mad because they wanted the Hideaway Bungalow so badly," Alex said.

McKenzie watched the couple carry the cooler across the beach and disappear on a narrow path through the trees. "I'm sure it's them, too."

A figure on the beach caught her attention. "McKenzie! Alex!"

A young woman with short dark hair called and waved at the girls.

"Alex, Aunt Becca's back." McKenzie stood and brushed sand off her legs.

"Hey, girls," Aunt Becca called out as they approached. "How's it going?"

Both girls began talking at the same time, telling Becca about the missing seal pups and the conversation they had overheard with the little boy and his mother.

"And when we were out on the skimmer, a couple that matched that description almost ran us over with their boat, tipping us over and everything," McKenzie explained.

"And then the fog got so bad we could hardly see to get back home. Mr. C. was almost ready to come looking for us," Alex said anxiously.

"What's this?" Aunt Becca frowned at the girls. "You were out and got lost in the fog? How far did you sail?"

"Uh. . ." McKenzie stammered, glancing sheepishly at Alex. "We're not sure. It was so foggy we couldn't see the landmarks."

Uh-oh. We're in trouble now. We've said too much, McKenzie thought. *I've seen that look before.*

Aunt Becca looked from one girl to the other, like she was trying not to get mad. "I know I told you girls you could take the sailboat out, but only if you stayed within a reasonable distance to the beach. You need to stay close enough to land so you can get back safely, even in a fog. I had asked Mr. Carney to keep an eye out for you two. I'm sure he was worried sick."

"We're sorry," both girls said awkwardly.

"Next time you'll need to tell either me or Mr. Carney when you go out. And you definitely need to stay very close. If you got pulled out into the ocean, you'd be in big trouble." Aunt Becca gave them a forced smile.

"Okay, enough of that," she continued. "Now, I'll tell you what I came out here for. How would you like to go flying with me in the Skyview plane? I'm taking a gentleman for a sightseeing tour in about thirty minutes. When I told him about you girls staying with me, he invited you to come along. I talked with my boss, and he said you could ride for free this once, since there's room."

Both girls jumped up and down with excitement as they hurried to the house. McKenzie couldn't wait to go flying. The girls quickly changed, and Aunt Becca drove the short distance to the small airport.

An older man introduced himself to the girls as Ted Lowry. He climbed into the front seat beside Aunt Becca. The girls settled into the backseat and fastened their seat belts. Aunt Becca taxied down the runway and expertly lifted the plane into the air.

"Yeee-iiikes!" McKenzie clutched her stomach as the plane climbed higher and higher. McKenzie had ridden in jets but never in a small plane like this. She felt weightless, sailing through the air. When Aunt Becca swooped low, McKenzie felt she was on an amusement ride.

Aunt Becca flew the plane along the coast, shouting above the roar of the engine, "You'll see the city of Florence to your right. The Emerald Bay Resort is just below us. You can see our cabin, girls, next to Mr. C.'s. Then the Hideaway Cabin is behind all those trees."

That's the Frankses' cabin, McKenzie thought. *Why would anyone want to stay in a cabin hidden in the woods like that? It's so isolated, no one would even know it's there.*

"Look at the people on the beach," McKenzie said, nudging Alex. "They look like tiny little bugs, and the homes and stores looked like miniature dollhouses. This is so cool!"

Aunt Becca flew the plane up and down the coast, pointing out various points of interest. "Cape Perpetua and the Heceta Head Lighthouse are just ahead a few miles," she said.

All too soon, the flight was over and Aunt Becca landed

the Skyview back on the runway. After they had taxied to the hangar, she cut the engine.

Mr. Lowry turned around in his seat to face the girls. "Becca here tells me you two are working on a special report on sea lions for your public TV station. That is quite an honor, McKenzie."

McKenzie felt her face flush as she thanked him.

He cleared his throat and continued. "I'm retired from the University of Oregon. I've spent years doing research on Steller sea lions. Tomorrow I'm going out on a boat with a crew that is training sea lions for use in government operations. I've already talked with Becca. She has given me permission to ask a favor of you girls."

McKenzie looked at Alex. "Okay," she stammered.

The older man grinned. "Don't look so worried. It's not every day kids your age get to ride along on one of these training sessions."

McKenzie stared at him as her pulse quickened. *Did I hear him right? Is he really asking us to come with him?*

"Are you serious?" she stammered.

Mr. Lowry chuckled. "Of course. I'm officially inviting you to be my guests. So, how about it? How would you girls like to go with me on the boat and videotape the crew as they work with the sea lions?"

McKenzie noticed that Alex looked as excited as she was.

How lucky can we get? McKenzie thought. *Maybe, just maybe, he can help us find Mario and Bianca!*

A Scream in the Night

For a minute McKenzie didn't know what to say. She still couldn't believe Mr. Lowry was serious.

McKenzie turned to Alex who was nodding, her dark ponytail bouncing up and down. "Well, sure. I mean, thank you, Mr. Lowry."

"Then it's all settled. I'll drop by about seven thirty tomorrow morning. We'll head to the port and meet the rest of the crew there."

The girls climbed out of the airplane and said good-bye to Mr. Lowry. They chatted excitedly on the drive back to the beach house. The sailing trip tomorrow would give them a great chance to film the report.

When McKenzie went to bed that night, scattered thoughts filled her mind. *I can't believe we're going in the sea with Mr. Lowry tomorrow. Hopefully we can get some great video footage of the sea lions.* She finally fell asleep to the sound of the waves rolling onto the beach.

McKenzie was the first one up in the morning. She woke Alex and by seven thirty, both girls were waiting outside when Mr. Lowry pulled up in his red pickup truck. They hollered good-bye to Aunt Becca and climbed into the car.

Twenty minutes later, he pulled into a parking spot at the port.

"What are we going to do today?" McKenzie asked after the three climbed aboard the largest boat at the docks.

Mr. Lowry pointed at a vessel out a little way in the Pacific Ocean. "That ship belongs to the United States Navy. The navy has trained sea lions to protect US ships from underwater terrorists. In their mouths, these sea lions carry a clamp that is attached to a rope. They fasten that to the leg of any diver approaching a ship. The sailors on the ship can then pull the person from the water."

"What does that have to do with us?" McKenzie asked.

"After we approach the ship, one of our men will dive into the water to test the sea lions," Mr. Lowry explained. "You girls will want to have your camera going. You should get some good footage."

Mr. Lowry handed each girl a life jacket. "I'll introduce you to our crew."

He called to a man in a blue jacket sitting behind the steering wheel. "Hey, Warren, I'd like you to meet my young friends, McKenzie Phillips and Alexis Howell. They're here to film a report for Montana Public TV."

The girls chatted with the captain. Then Mr. Lowry led them to the back of the boat where two more men waited. A blond-haired man, wearing a black scuba diving suit, turned as the girls approached. He shook the girls' hands and introduced himself as Josh.

The other man had dark hair and wore swimming trunks and a long-sleeved T-shirt. He ignored the girls as he focused binoculars on the navy ship. After a few seconds he turned to meet the girls.

McKenzie felt her jaw drop. Before she could speak, Mr. Lowry said, "McKenzie, Alex, I'd like you to meet Mel Franks, our sea lion expert and head diver today."

For a minute, McKenzie thought Mr. Franks wasn't going to respond. He stared at one girl and then the other, a crease forming on his forehead. *I wonder if he knows we're the ones he almost clobbered yesterday with his boat.*

"Nice to meet you, Mr. Franks," McKenzie said as she stuck out her hand.

He hesitated but shook her hand. He looked at her, as if he couldn't figure out where he'd seen her. McKenzie didn't know what to say or do. She didn't really want to ask him why he had almost flattened them.

Mel Franks glanced at his wristwatch and turned to Mr. Lowry. "Ted, why don't you go tell Tony to fire up the engine? It's time to move on."

The moment Mr. Lowry stepped away, Mr. Franks turned to the girls. "Didn't I see you girls out in the cove yesterday?"

McKenzie and Alex glanced sheepishly at each other. "Yes, our sailboat tipped," McKenzie explained. She left out the part that he was responsible for capsizing them.

"You girls stay away from that area. It's too dangerous in there, with all the rocks and churning waters. That can pull you right down. I can't believe your parents let you go out there," Mr. Franks scolded.

"Our parents aren't here," McKenzie said. "We're staying with my aunt in the Seaside Bungalow."

Mel Franks glanced around at the blond-haired man looking their way, then muttered, "Well, see to it that you stay away from that area, or I'll have a talk with your aunt."

McKenzie took a step backward, wishing Mr. Lowry

would return. She sighed with relief when the boat's motor rumbled to life, and the older man appeared.

"Hey, Mel," Mr. Lowry called. "Aren't you going down first? You'd better suit up."

"Yeah, yeah, I'm going," Mr. Franks said, suddenly in a lighthearted mood. He peeled off his shirt and strode to the back of the boat.

McKenzie stifled a gasp. She couldn't believe her eyes. She nudged Alex and nodded at the blue and green fish tattoo on Mel's arm!

Mr. Franks glared at her and slipped into his scuba suit. Alex opened her mouth to speak, but McKenzie shook her head. Her heart raced as she watched Mel.

"Come on up here with your camera, girls." Mr. Lowry motioned as the motorboat approached the navy ship. "Mel's going down. Then you'll see the sea lions go to work."

McKenzie wanted to talk privately with Alex but knew she couldn't do that while they were on the boat. *What is going on?* she wondered. *Is Mr. Franks the man that boy saw steal Mario and Bianca?*

When the boat was about fifty yards from the ship, Tony cut the boat's engine. A message crackled over his two-way radio. He spoke into the mouthpiece and turned to the crew on deck. "Captain said, 'anytime now.'"

With his breathing gear in place, Mr. Franks flipped backward off the side of the boat. McKenzie saw the outline of his body as he swam toward the ship.

"See the sea lion." Mr. Lowry pointed at a dark shadow beneath the water. "It's swimming to Mr. Franks with the clamp in its mouth. Watch what happens next."

McKenzie lost sight of Mel. Seconds later, the rope

hanging over the side of the navy ship jerked. The crew onboard the ship quickly reeled in Mr. Franks, hanging upside down with his leg attached to a rope. McKenzie laughed. Mr. Franks looked so funny as the navy guys hauled him onto the deck.

The rest of the crew cheered, declaring the practice mission a success. Then Josh took his turn diving. This time Alex filmed McKenzie explaining the role sea lions played in the military. In the background, Alex filmed Josh as he was jerked from the water.

They waited until a motorboat taxied Mr. Franks and Josh back to Mr. Lowry's boat. After the two men climbed aboard, Tony headed back to shore. Since these men knew a lot about sea lions, McKenzie asked the question that had been bugging her all morning.

"Mr. Lowry, have you heard about the twin sea lion pups that are missing?" She had to almost shout to be heard over the roar of the engine.

Mel Franks turned sharply, shooting McKenzie an angry look. Mr. Lowry didn't seem to notice as he offered the girls cold drinks from a cooler.

"Yes, I heard about that. I've heard talk that poachers got them," the older man said sadly.

"I'm guessing killer whales got them," Mel Franks said. "Poachers wouldn't have any use for sea lion pups."

Mr. Franks changed the subject back to the sea lion mission they had just finished. McKenzie's suspicions about him began to grow. He sure fit the description of the man the little boy had seen. And he obviously didn't want to talk about Mario and Bianca. *If he did steal them, why would he do it? If he's an expert on sea lions, surely he would want to keep them safe, though,* McKenzie thought.

The crew quickly arrived back in port. The girls thanked Mr. Lowry for letting them tag along. McKenzie noticed that everyone seemed happy they had come. Everyone, except for Mel Franks.

●—●—●

"Aunt Becca, may we use your computer to chat with the Camp Club Girls?" McKenzie asked.

"Sure. Is that the group of girls you met at camp awhile back?" Aunt Becca opened the refrigerator door and surveyed its contents.

"Yes, we have so much fun." McKenzie led the way to the computer.

"We're also really good at solving mysteries," Alex piped up. "We're going to try to figure out what happened to Mario and Bianca."

"That could be a tough job," Aunt Becca said, preheating the oven for a frozen pan of lasagna. "Lots of things could have happened to them. I know it's not a nice thought, but sea lions have natural predators. Like sharks and killer whales."

"That's what Mr. Franks said, too. But would an animal get both of them at the same time?" McKenzie logged on to the computer.

Aunt Becca shrugged. "I'm surprised Mr. Franks was on the boat this morning. He's one of Emerald Bay's regular customers."

McKenzie decided it was time to tell Aunt Becca everything they knew. "We heard a little boy on the beach say he saw a man and a woman steal Mario and Bianca yesterday morning. He said the man had a fish tattoo on his arm." She paused for a moment before continuing. "Mr. Franks has a tattoo just like that."

Aunt Becca looked startled. "I can't imagine why Mel Franks would steal sea lions. I know you girls like to solve mysteries, but when it involves other people, you have to be extra careful. After all, you didn't see the man steal anything. And remember to talk to God first before doing anything that might hurt someone."

"Oh, we will," Alex said as she pulled a chair up beside McKenzie. "That's one reason we like to talk to the other Camp Club Girls. We always pray for each other and help each other."

"Okay. I'll trust you girls to do the right thing. I guess I'm as curious as you are about those pups," Aunt Becca said before slipping out the front door with a book.

Mickey lay at the girls' feet as they signed in to the chat room. McKenzie told the girls about the conversation they had overheard on the beach earlier. Then McKenzie told them all about Mr. Franks capsizing their sailboat yesterday and the discovery of the cave on the inlet. She continued by sharing the news of their outing earlier that day with Mr. Lowry and his crew.

Bailey: *Maybe Mr. . .uh. . .what's his name. . .the cave man guy wanted to go to the cave and you were in his way.*

Sydney: *You mean, Mr. Franks? I don't know why he tipped McKenzie and Alex's sailboat, but we do have some clues already about the kidnappers. We know it was a man with a fish tattoo and a woman. Mr. Franks has a*

*tattoo like that, but some other guy could
have one, too.*

Elizabeth: *That's right. But don't forget the silver
and red boat.*

Kate: *You'll have to find the pups before you can
prove anything. Can you watch for silver and
red boats in the area? If that couple stole two
pups, they might be back for more.*

McKenzie: *That would be good, Kate. But maybe
we can watch Mr. and Mrs. Franks closely
and find out what is going on.*

Sydney: *Sea lions, like all animals, do best in
natural surroundings. Maybe the kidnappers
took them to a natural environment
somewhere to care for them, like a zoo.*

The Camp Club Girls discussed the disappearance awhile longer. Before signing off, McKenzie promised to keep them posted with any new information about the investigation.

After supper McKenzie and Alex stepped outside with their cameras. Sunset was near. Alex hoped to get some pictures of bounding whales for the photography contest. As they approached the dock, Mr. Carney called to them from his backyard.

"Hey, Mr. C.," McKenzie hollered, scurrying toward the older man sitting in his lawn chair reading in the fading light.

"I've been reading this book on local caves you picked up for me yesterday," he said as he snapped the book shut. "It's fascinating. According to the author, several little-known caves are on the Oregon coast. A couple of them are right around here."

"Really? Where?" McKenzie asked excitedly.

"I'm just getting to that part, but it's about too dark to read. Besides, I need to go in the house and finish packing my bag." He paused. "My son is taking me to his home. I won't be back until later tomorrow. I might have a few minutes to read before he gets here. Why don't I loan the book to you when I get back?"

The girls eagerly agreed and then headed to the dock. Alex took several pictures of the western sky, painted with streaks of pink, orange, and blue. McKenzie sat on the dock, dangling her legs over the side. She kicked her feet in the cool, clear water. Alex lowered her camera and pointed out a family of loons gliding through the shadowy water of the cove.

"Do you think Mel and Tia Franks stole the sea lion pups?" Alex asked as she sat down cross-legged beside McKenzie.

"I don't know. The evidence sure points to them." McKenzie scratched her arm. "That is, if we can believe the story that little boy told."

Alex sighed. "I wish we had seen the couple in the boat that morning. We only have a rumor to go on. We can't accuse anyone based on that."

McKenzie jumped as her cell phone rang. She pulled it from her pocket and flipped it open. "Hey, Sydney," she said after recognizing her friend's phone number. "What's up?"

"When Bailey called Mr. Franks 'Cave Man,' I started thinking. Maybe Mr. Franks tipped your sailboat over on purpose yesterday."

"Why would he do that?" McKenzie pulled her feet out of the water and tucked her wet legs beneath her.

"He tipped you over by the cave entrance, right? Maybe

he didn't want you to see something in that cave, like nets or something. I don't know how anyone steals a sea lion, but maybe there's stuff in there they use to capture sea mammals. If they stole two sea lions, they might steal more," Sydney explained.

McKenzie thought for a moment. "I didn't see anything in the cave. Except for a little bit of trash."

"I thought if the thieves stole two pups, they might come back for more. I mean, who would know if any other sea lion pups were missing? If Susie wasn't such a favorite for tourists, who would know Mario and Bianca were missing?" Sydney continued.

"I guess you've got a point," McKenzie answered. "But there's no way we can go back to the cave. Aunt Becca would never let us sail back over there."

"Oh, well. It was just an idea," Sydney said. "I'm just looking for clues."

By the time McKenzie hung up the phone, darkness had settled in and a cool wind had come up. A full moon and a sprinkling of stars lit up the sky. The lights of the resorts farther down the beach dotted the shoreline. Talking about Mr. Franks and his strange behavior on Mr. Lowry's boat made her feel uneasy. All the talk about thieves, missing sea lions, and dark caves made her shiver.

"Let's go in," McKenzie said as she stood and headed toward the light glowing in the kitchen window of the beach house.

"Good idea," Alex said, in close pursuit. "I need a snack before bed, anyway."

Hurrying up the sidewalk leading to the house, McKenzie set her camera on the porch railing. She kicked off her flip-flops and turned on the outside faucet. Then she stuck her foot under the stream of water to rinse the sand off her feet.

She jerked herself upright and froze in horror as a crazy, laughlike scream pierced the night!

CHAPTER 5

The Intruder!

A feeling like icy cold fingers rippled up McKenzie's neck as she lunged through the doorway. "What was that?" Her voice trembled as she turned to Alex.

A look of shock passed over Alex's face, then she giggled. "You should see the look on your face. That's just a loon calling for its mate."

McKenzie's face grew warm, and her breathing began to return to normal. "You mean that was a bird? It sounded like a maniac laughing and screaming at the same time."

"Oooh-ooh-ooh-OOOH!" Alex let out a mournful cry. She raised her arms high and bent her fingers like crooked claws. "I'm a scary loon, and I'm going to get you."

McKenzie playfully punched her friend in the arm. "That's the creepiest-sounding bird I've ever heard. It sounded like a scream."

"It used to scare me, too," Alex said, grabbing a box of cheesy crackers from a kitchen cupboard. "But now I love to hear the loons calling to each other."

McKenzie shivered as the loon's cry carried through the open windows of the sunporch. She rubbed her arms to chase away the chill. As she reached for the light switch, something warm and fuzzy brushed against her leg.

"Aaaahhh!" she screeched, jumping as something cold and wet touched her hand.

Glancing down, she sighed with relief. "Oh, Mickey. I'm glad it's you, boy." She patted the dog's head as he danced about her feet, whimpering.

"I think he needs to go out," Alex said, bending to scratch Mickey's ears. She held out a couple of crackers and dropped them, letting the dog catch them in his mouth. Then she reached up and grabbed a leash from a hook by the back door.

"You don't mean we're going back out there, do you?" McKenzie asked, feeling like a scaredy-cat.

"Aah, come with me." Alex snapped the leash onto the dog's collar. "Let's just take Mickey out for a minute."

McKenzie hesitated, but then followed Alex and Mickey out the door into the cool night air. The glow of the yard lights in front of each cabin lined the beach like a string of Christmas lights. The dog scampered about their feet, tugging the leash until Alex was almost running to keep up.

McKenzie scurried after them until Mickey stopped at the nearest tree and sniffed. Though the loons still called their eerie cry in the distance, she wasn't as scared as she had been earlier. *It still sounds creepy, but at least I know it's just a bird*, she thought.

"Uh-oh," Alex said, looking at McKenzie as she tugged on the leash. "What time is it?"

"Five after ten," McKenzie said after pushing the tiny button on the side of her watch so it would light up.

"I told Mom and Dad I'd call them at ten. I'd better do that now." Alex handed McKenzie the leash. "I'll be right back."

Operation: Excitement!

Alex sped toward the back steps and let the screen door bang behind her. McKenzie let Mickey pull her toward the next tree. *Come on, dog. Hurry up and do your business. I don't like it out here alone.*

McKenzie glanced around. The cabin to her right stood in darkness. Apparently the renters staying there weren't home yet for the night. She turned toward Mr. Carney's cabin on the other side of Aunt Becca's cabin. The dark windows reminded her that the older man was spending the night with his son.

Her gaze continued to the left, noting the dark grove of pine trees standing like a black forest separating Mr. Carney's cabin from the Hideaway. McKenzie had never seen the Hideaway except from Aunt Becca's airplane. Tucked behind the grove of trees, it was completely hidden from view. A maintenance road behind the cabins was the only entrance to the isolated cabin. Even then it was a quarter of a mile hike from the road to the Hideaway.

Mickey tugged McKenzie around the tree, sniffing the ground. An owl hooted somewhere in the top of a nearby tree. The wind whistled through the pine needles. McKenzie shivered while she watched Alex through the window, talking on the phone with her parents.

"Okay, Mickey," she muttered as she tied the dog's leash around a tree trunk. "I'm not waiting out here all night. It's too creepy out here for me. I'll be back in a few minutes."

McKenzie sprinted up the back steps and into the house, feeling like the biggest chicken ever. Normally, the dark didn't bother her, but too many weird sounds were freaking her out. Sounds she wasn't used to.

Once inside, she relaxed and grabbed a handful of

peanuts from a bowl on the coffee table. She settled onto the arm of the couch. Alex smiled and kept chatting into the phone's receiver.

Aunt Becca walked into the family room, wearing a purple terry-cloth bathrobe. She hugged McKenzie and whispered, "I'm going to bed. I've got to be at work early in the morning. Don't stay up too late."

McKenzie returned her hug and said, "Good night." Aunt Becca gave Alex a quick squeeze and went down the hall to her bedroom.

After Alex hung up, McKenzie stood and wiped her hands on her jeans. "Finally," she teased. "We'd better go get Mickey. He probably thinks we forgot him."

The girls scurried out the back door and raced down the steps. Moonlight flickered through the branches that rustled in the night. Gentle rolling waves in the cove lapped upon the beach. A screen door slammed shut somewhere down the beach, and a shadowy couple walked across the moonlit sand. The cluster of torchlights in front of the resort looked like tiny dots flickering in the wind.

"Where did you leave him?" Alex asked, interrupting McKenzie's thoughts.

McKenzie pointed at a tree bathed in the glow of the yard light. "Right there, next to the hammock."

"I don't see him," Alex said as she squinted into the darkness.

McKenzie ran toward the tree. *I'm sure this is where I left the dog.* "Oh, great! His leash must have come untied. Where did he go?"

"Here, Mickey!" Alex called, looking toward the beach and then back to the yard. "Here, boy."

McKenzie whistled. She paused and listened but didn't hear an answering bark. *Mickey, why did you have to run off?* she asked silently, glancing about for any sign of the dog.

The girls searched the yard, peering behind every shrub and tree. McKenzie had an uneasy feeling. Soon all she could hear was the loud thumping in her chest.

"We need a flashlight," Alex said, darting back inside the house.

Shivering as she waited on the back steps, McKenzie felt the cool breeze cut through her shirt. She considered going after a sweatshirt, but Alex bounded out the door and down the steps.

"Where should we look?" McKenzie asked, following her friend.

"How about that way?" Alex pointed toward Mr. Carney's yard. The yard light by the beach shone through the tree branches, casting eerie shadows on the ground.

Scritch! Scratch! The branches scraped against the metal light pole. Alex switched on the flashlight as the girls stepped across the yard. She shined the light around Mr. Carney's porch and peeked behind the bushes out front.

"Do you see him?" McKenzie whispered, peering over her friend's shoulder.

"No, but I did find this." Alex bent and picked up an object caught on the bush.

"That's Mickey's leash. He must have been caught and worked it loose." McKenzie frowned as she took the leash and wrapped it around her hand. "At least we know we're headed in the right direction."

Taking a deep breath, McKenzie huddled close to Alex. They crossed Mr. Carney's yard and approached the grove of trees. Wind whistled through the needles of the pines, standing like an army waiting to attack. Crickets chirped and bullfrogs croaked. A large bird swooped down from out of nowhere. And, of course, the crazy loons were still at it, making the hair on the back of McKenzie's neck twitch.

I know now why people who want a secluded cabin would come to this resort, McKenzie thought. *I'm glad our cabin is closer to the lodge where there are more people around.*

McKenzie felt a chill run up her back. She couldn't help feeling like Dorothy in *The Wizard of Oz.*

I'd better not see any flying monkeys, she thought with a tremble. She remembered how that part of the movie had terrified her when she was little.

She eyed the grove as if someone might be hiding there now. Every stump and shadow beckoned eerily. The sweet, tangy scent of the pine trees wafted over her in the night air. A faint whimper came from somewhere deep in the grove.

"I hear something." McKenzie paused and then called softly, just in case someone else was listening nearby. "Mickey, here boy."

Again, she heard the faintest whimpering cry. She clutched Alex's arm. "Did you hear that?"

"Yes. We'd better go look for him," Alex said, pointing the beam of light into the darkness.

Hanging on to each other, the girls stepped into the shadows. They ducked beneath branches as they called Mickey's name. Pine needles stung McKenzie in the face, and her shirt caught on a bramble. She tugged it loose and hurried onward.

She knew they had to be getting close to the Hideaway. When they came to the yard of the last cabin, the small, boxlike cottage stood dark and lifeless. McKenzie knew why it was given the name Hideaway. It was completely hidden from the rest of the cabins and the main stretch of beach. The moonlight shining on the windowpanes stared at her like glassy eyes. Once she thought she saw a flash of light inside, but when she looked again, everything was dark.

"So this is where the Frankses are staying?" Alex asked, pointing the flashlight at the house.

"Yeah, but shut your light off. There's enough moonlight coming through the trees so we can see without it," McKenzie whispered. "I don't think anybody's home, but if they are, I don't want to get caught out here."

McKenzie tipped her head as another whimper carried on the wind. "I heard it again!" McKenzie said. "It sounded like it came from over there—past the house."

Pulling Alex with her, McKenzie raced past the screened-in porch on the cabin to a cluster of bushes hugging the far side of the yard. A *yip* sounded—closer this time.

"Shine your light back here." McKenzie turned to Alex and knelt beside the shrubs.

McKenzie felt something wet on her arm as two beady eyes shone in the flashlight beam. A long slobbery tongue hung from a gaping mouth.

"Mickey!" Alex cried. "Oh, look, McKenzie. His collar's caught on a branch."

While Alex held the flashlight, McKenzie quickly untangled the dog. He jumped the moment he was free, yipping and licking the girls' faces. Despite being scared, she couldn't help but giggle with relief that they had found Mickey.

McKenzie clipped the leash back on the collar and pulled

the dog from his hiding spot. "We need to get out of here before the Frankses get home."

"Yeah, I'm never going to get to sleep tonight. I'm too antsy. I wish I had a good book to read. I only brought one with me, and I'm almost done with it," Alex said, clicking the flashlight off again and stepping away from the bushes. "Too bad Mr. C. didn't give us that book before he left. I'm dying to find out where those caves are around here."

"Me, too." McKenzie tugged Mickey's leash as they walked back across the Frankses' yard. "Maybe we could go exploring, but definitely in the daylight."

When they approached the dark grove of trees, the squeak of a screen door cut through the night. McKenzie froze and turned slowly toward the Frankses' sunporch. She saw nothing, but heard muffled voices from inside the house. Then all was silent again.

Had someone been on the screened-in sunporch all along? One of the voices sure sounded like Mrs. Franks, McKenzie thought anxiously. *And both voices sounded like women.*

McKenzie felt her pulse quicken. Alex stood motionless beside her. Grasping Alex's arm, McKenzie ran through the trees, pulling Mickey with her. The branches tore at her hair, and pine needles scratched her arm. They sped through the grove. The beam from Alex's flashlight bobbed up and down wildly as they dodged the maze of trees.

After darting across Mr. Carney's yard, the girls arrived, breathless, at their back porch. Once inside, McKenzie unhooked Mickey's leash. He trotted eagerly to his bowl in the kitchen and slurped the water.

"That was so-o-o weird!" Alex said after catching her breath. "Was Mrs. Franks watching and listening to us the whole time we were in her yard?"

McKenzie grabbed a tissue and dabbed at a bleeding scratch on her arm. "I don't know for sure, but I think she and someone else must have been out there."

"Why wouldn't she let us know she was there? It's almost like she was spying on us," Alex said while handing Mickey a dog biscuit.

McKenzie didn't answer. *It does seem like she was spying, but why?* Though McKenzie's breath had returned to normal, she still felt nervous. *God, forgive me if I'm wrong to suspect the Frankses, but something just doesn't seem right. I'm scared,* McKenzie quietly prayed.

Mickey settled onto his pillow in the corner of the kitchen. The girls headed down the hall to their bedroom. As McKenzie was about to slip under the covers, she suddenly remembered she had left her camera on the railing outside earlier in the evening.

"I'll be right back," she said to Alex and scurried down the dark hallway to the back door. With the moonlight shining through the window, she didn't need to turn on any lights. She quickly opened the door and grabbed the camera. As she turned to step back inside, she glanced toward Mr. Carney's cabin.

Was somebody on Mr. C.'s sunporch?

McKenzie slipped back into the shadows. The figure moved into the moonlight, bending over as if picking something up off the floor. Then the figure stepped back into the darkness. Someone, a woman, had just come out of Mr. Carney's cabin and was standing on the sunporch!

The Empty Cabin

McKenzie raced back into the bedroom she shared with Alex. "Someone is in Mr. Carney's house!"

Alex sat cross-legged in bed, wearing a pair of pink and blue polka-dot pajamas. She put down the mystery she was reading. She looked stunned at her friend's outburst. "Are you sure?"

"Positive." McKenzie felt her heart racing. "I saw her in the moonlight, standing on the sunporch."

Alex flung the covers back and jumped out of bed. "What do we do now?"

Without hesitation, McKenzie answered, "We'd better wake Aunt Becca. She'll know what to do."

McKenzie knocked on her aunt's bedroom door and flung the door wide open. The hall light spilled onto Aunt Becca's form lying on the bed.

"What's up, girls?" Aunt Becca said with a yawn as she rolled over, squinting at the bright light.

"There's a robber in Mr. C.'s cabin," Alex blurted out.

"What's this?" Aunt Becca swung her legs over the side of the bed and sat up. "What makes you think that?"

"I saw a woman on the porch," McKenzie explained, rushing her words. "I saw her, just now."

Aunt Becca slipped out of bed and scurried into the dark family room. Standing near the window, she peered cautiously toward the neighboring cabin. "I don't see anyone," she whispered.

"She must have left already," McKenzie spoke softly. "But someone was there. I saw her, plain as day. . .or night, whatever."

Aunt Becca moved quickly into the kitchen and switched on the light. "I really don't want to call the police. There could be a logical explanation for this. I think Mr. Carney gave me his son's phone number once. I'll try to find it and call him before it gets any later. I hate to worry him. But if someone is prowling, he needs to know."

Aunt Becca located the phone number and paced the room nervously after dialing. Moments later, McKenzie could tell that Mr. Carney's son had answered. Aunt Becca explained the situation. After a slight pause, she thanked the man and hung up.

"Well, you girls can sleep peacefully tonight. Al, Mr. C.'s son, said his dad had been having problems with his Internet. So he had asked the resort to send over a technician while he was gone. That must have been who you saw."

McKenzie looked quizzically at Alex. "What a weird time for someone to fix it."

"Mr. C. is a good, regular customer of Emerald Bay. He comes here every summer. If he wanted his Internet restored by the time he returns, I'm sure the staff would fix it." Aunt Becca seemed to accept the explanation without question. "They have a computer person on staff who probably just didn't get to it earlier today." With a yawn and a wave, she headed back down the hall.

McKenzie felt more relaxed since Aunt Becca had made the phone call, but something just didn't seem right. If the woman on the sunporch was working on a computer, wouldn't she be carrying some kind of bag or briefcase? But the woman McKenzie had seen wasn't carrying anything, at least nothing very big.

"That doesn't make any sense," McKenzie said. "Why would a repair person stand in the dark on the sunporch like she was trying to hide? I think something is going on over there."

●—●—●

When the girls awoke the next morning, Aunt Becca had already left for work. As they ate breakfast, McKenzie suggested that they tour the Sea Lion Harbor later in the day. She wanted to get some more footage of sea lions for her video report. By the end of the week, she would be on a plane back to Montana.

As the girls loaded the dishwasher, they heard a knock at the front door. A man wearing a brown uniform stood in the doorway with a package and an electronic clipboard.

McKenzie opened the door, and the man smiled at her. "I have a package for Mr. Lon Carney, but no one is home. My note says that it can be left with his neighbor. Could I get you to sign for me, please? Then I'll leave the package here with you."

"Sure," McKenzie said, signing her name on the pad.

The man handed her the package, thanked her, and went back to his truck. McKenzie watched the truck disappear down a bend in the road.

"Why don't we take this package over to Mr. C.'s house now and leave it on his porch?" McKenzie suggested. "We might not be here when he gets home this afternoon, and he might want it before we get back."

"Sounds good to me," Alex agreed while she wiped off the countertop.

A few moments later, the girls walked up the back steps of Mr. Carney's sunporch. Like McKenzie figured, the door was unlocked. They slipped inside and set the package by the door leading into his cabin.

McKenzie's mind went to the woman she had seen standing here last night. McKenzie glanced around the sunporch. She had only been here one other time, when she and Alex had brought the cave book over. But something seemed out of place. *What was different?*

She glanced at the little family of wooden loons clustered by the back door. She knew the loons had been lined up neatly when she had been here before.

Lots of people hide a spare key by the back door, she thought.

Instinctively, she picked up the largest loon and looked beneath it. A piece of clear tape hung loosely to the bottom.

She reached over to the middle-sized loon. Beneath it was a house key on the ground. It was the same size as the tape.

"Something is definitely not right, Alex. It looks like Mr. C. kept a spare key taped to the bottom of this loon. But it also looks like someone took the key and put it back under the wrong loon. And why would the resort staff need his key? Wouldn't they have their own?"

"Yes." Alex nodded. "But how would a thief know where Mr. C. kept his key?"

"She could have guessed. Lots of people hide their spare keys close to the door." McKenzie scratched at a mosquito bite on her arm.

"I guess that's true," Alex said with a sigh. "So, now what do we do? Aunt Becca and Mr. C. think a computer techie went into his cabin, but we think it was a robber."

McKenzie sighed and glanced out the screened-in porch. "I guess we'll have to wait until Mr. C. comes home and then tell him what we've found, and see if anything was stolen. I don't want to bother Aunt Becca about it at work. I didn't get a good look at the woman because it was so dark. But I think she was young."

"Did she look like Mrs. Franks?" Alex asked.

"A little bit. She was about her height, but I don't think it was her. It was dark, but I think she had short blond hair. Mrs. Franks has long hair." McKenzie shoved the loons back in place and stood up.

"Maybe she had her hair in a ponytail," Alex suggested.

"That's possible," McKenzie said.

After returning home, the girls spent the rest of the morning flying a bright, sea lion-shaped kite and hunting for seashells. They wanted to hang around the house so they could talk to Mr. Carney the minute he got home.

Soon after lunch, McKenzie heard a car door slam and voices outside Mr. Carney's cabin. She pulled the curtain back and glanced out the window as a black car pulled away from the cabin.

"Mr. C.'s home." McKenzie turned to Alex. "Let's go talk to him about the woman we saw last night."

Minutes later the girls stood on their neighbor's porch, knocking on the door.

"Well, well." Mr. Carney answered the door with a smile. "It's good to see you girls. I appreciate you keeping an eye on things for me last night. It's nice to know someone's watching out for me while I'm gone."

"That's what we wanted to talk to you about," McKenzie

said. "We think things look suspicious."

"Suspicious?" Mr. Carney frowned as he ushered the girls inside. "How?"

Both girls began talking at once. They told him about finding the spare key, the wadded-up piece of tape, and the misplaced wooden loons.

"Whoa, whoa, wait a minute. What's this about finding my spare key?"

McKenzie tugged his arm, leading him onto the sunporch. "We brought a package over for you this morning. I thought something looked strange, and I realized the wooden loons were out of order. They're always nice and neat. Then I saw the corner of the spare key sticking out from under one of them."

"We think someone found your spare key and went inside your cabin last night," Alex explained. "Then she got in a hurry and put it back under the wrong loon. You do hide a key there, don't you?"

Mr. Carney scratched his head. "I do hide it under the first loon. I reckon it's probably a little too obvious."

He paused, then continued, "Let me check inside. I'll see if anything is missing."

The girls followed him into the family room and waited on the couch. Mr. Carney went down the hallway and disappeared into a room.

A few minutes later he returned. "Nothing seems to be missing. I have no cash to speak of in the cabin. Did you see this woman carrying anything out?"

McKenzie met Alex's gaze. "I don't think so. Unless it was small and she hid it under her jacket."

"Well, I do know the resort staff came over sometime

after I left last night. My Internet is running. Could you have just seen the computer repair lady?"

"But McKenzie saw her bend down, like she was putting something on the floor by the back door," Alex reasoned. "Maybe she was putting the key back."

Mr. Carney smiled at the girls. "She probably accidently kicked the loons and bent over to shove them aside."

Hmm, McKenzie thought with a frown. *That makes sense. But there could still be a clue here. And I don't want to miss it.*

"I have an idea," McKenzie announced. "Why don't you call the resort office and ask them what time the computer techie came over? Then we'd know if it was the resort staff or someone else."

"Or Mrs. Franks," Alex piped in, hopping to her feet.

"Tia Franks?" Mr. Carney asked. "Is that who you thought you saw last night?"

McKenzie glanced at Alex, then turned back to her neighbor. "Well, it kind of looked like her, but her hair was different. Do you know her?"

"Everyone around here knows Mel and Tia Franks. She would have no reason to break into my cabin, girls." Mr. Carney smiled gently at them. "The Frankses are wealthy. They've done extensive research on sea lions and caves in the area. They're very well known in their field. I have nothing that would be of value to them. Besides, I see nothing out of place in here."

McKenzie began to feel a little foolish. Had she just imagined that the woman looked a little like Mrs. Franks?

"I'll tell you what. I'll go ahead and call the resort office to see if they keep a record of times their staff makes calls." Mr. Carney picked up his phone on the end table and punched in a few numbers.

He spoke to someone on the other end of the line for a few minutes and then hung up. "They don't keep track of the time service calls are made. All they know is a young female staff member got the Internet running last evening sometime."

McKenzie was beginning to wish she had never seen the woman. She felt there was something suspicious, but she couldn't prove it. *Why were there no lights on in the cabin when I saw her, not even on the sunporch? Because she didn't want to be seen, that's why!*

"I'm sorry we bothered you, Mr. C. Maybe I was mistaken," McKenzie said. "She just acted so. . .funny, you know?"

Mr. Carney put his arms around McKenzie's and Alex's shoulders. "Don't worry about it, girls. Like I said earlier, I'm glad you're looking out for me." He paused. "Hey, I was going to loan you that book about caves before you leave. I haven't finished it, but I'll let you read about the local caves. Let me get it."

The girls waited as Mr. Carney headed to his bedroom. After a few minutes, he returned. "I can't seem to find it. I thought I left it on the nightstand, but I'll have to look around for it and bring it over later."

As the girls headed to the back door, McKenzie turned to her neighbor. "I've been wondering. If Mr. and Mrs. Franks are so rich, why are they staying at this resort? There are a lot fancier resorts than this one."

"They come to this cabin every summer while they do work with the Sea Park and other sea lion projects. It's isolated and quieter than any other resort," Mr. Carney answered.

The girls told their neighbor good-bye and headed back to their own yard. They plunked down into the hammock, swinging it back and forth.

"Do you think we'll find out what happened to Mario and Bianca?" Alex asked as she pulled on a hangnail and made it bleed. "Or do you think it's too late. . .if you know what I mean."

McKenzie cringed at the thought. "I can't believe Mario and Bianca are dead. Surely God wouldn't let that happen to them, would He?"

"I sure hope not," Alex said glumly. "But it seems that some people are just born nasty."

"I know. But I don't think it's a coincidence that Mario and Bianca disappeared while we were out here doing a video report on sea lions. I think God allowed all this to happen so we can figure out what happened to them."

"Maybe," Alex said as she wrapped the hem of her blue T-shirt around her bleeding finger. "Maybe we could go look around the resort lobby sometime and see if there's an employee who looks like the woman you saw on the sunporch. At least then we'd know if it was Mrs. Franks or not."

"That's a good idea. And I've also been thinking," McKenzie said, chewing her bottom lip. "Maybe Mrs. Franks, or whoever that lady was, stole Mr. C.'s book on caves. He said he couldn't find it, and he was sure he left it on his nightstand."

"But he also said the Frankses were experts on sea lions and caves. Why wouldn't they buy their own copy? Mr. C. said they're rich." Alex tucked her legs beneath her.

McKenzie folded her arms behind her head and sighed. "I don't know why anyone would steal the book and leave Mr. C.'s valuables, but I'll do everything I can to find out!"

CHAPTER 7

A Cruel Hoax

"The tour doesn't start for twenty minutes," Alex said while the girls waited outside the Sea Lion Harbor lobby the next morning. "Why don't you stand by the sign, and I'll tape you. When I tell you to begin, start saying what we rehearsed."

McKenzie stood by the sign, trying to act like a professional news reporter. When Alex motioned for her to begin, she smiled at the camera and spoke. "Hi, I'm McKenzie Phillips, and I'm standing outside the Sea Lion Harbor observation area on the gorgeous Oregon coast. In just a few minutes, we'll go inside the cave and take a close-up look at the amazing Steller sea lions.

"The Steller sea lion is in the same family as the seal," McKenzie continued. "But the sea lion has an external ear flap while a seal only has a tiny opening for an ear. To move through the water, sea lions move their front flippers up and down. They walk on all four flippers on the ground, while seals scoot around. Let's go inside and take a look at the fascinating Sea Lion Harbor."

"Great!" Alex said, lowering the recorder. "I'll record more after we get inside."

A steady stream of people of all ages hurried past them, forming lines at the ticket booth. Others stopped to pose in front of the large brass sea lion statue out front and have their picture taken.

"Let's go." Alex grabbed McKenzie's arm. "People are lining up for tickets already."

After paying their admission, the girls stepped inside the lobby and waited for the tour to begin. A young man wearing a red polo shirt and matching cap approached their group of about fifteen people. He had long blond hair and looked about twenty years old.

"Hi. I'm Colby, your tour guide. If you've never been to Sea Lion Harbor before, you're in for a treat. I see most of you dressed warmly. That's good. It gets chilly down in the cave. Let's get started. Follow me, folks."

The girls hurried down the hall following Colby as he led the group down a set of stairs to an elevator.

"Once the elevator lowers us two hundred feet down, we'll take more stairs and climb farther down to the observation area," Colby explained as the elevator descended. "A few sea lions may be inside the cave, but most of them will be outside on the rocky ledges. In the spring and summer, sea lions prefer to be outside in the fresh air."

McKenzie felt her stomach twitch as the elevator dropped lower and lower into the ground. After they reached the bottom, they stepped out of the elevator. The girls followed Colby and the rest of the group down a set of stairs. Tiny lights set into the wall lit their way.

McKenzie peered over the railing into the darkness of the cave. The air smelled damp and musty. McKenzie shivered despite the sweatshirt she had worn. Alex was at the end of the line, recording every minute with her video recorder.

At the bottom of the stairs, they turned a corner and

stepped into a well-lit observation area. Water from the cove rushed through a tunnel, forming a natural pool at the bottom of the cave. Though only a few sea lions gathered in the pool, they sounded like a thousand. Their barking echoed off the cave walls.

McKenzie searched the group of sea lions, hoping to see Mario and Bianca. She was praying that the two pups had somehow gotten separated from their mother, Susie, and made their way in here. She knew it was not likely, but she couldn't help hoping. Scanning the herd of sea lions, she groaned inwardly.

They're not here, either, she thought dismally.

Down inside, McKenzie felt guilty for suspecting the Frankses of stealing the pups. Though the young boy claimed he had seen the theft, he could have been mistaken. But the description of the man's fish tattoo seemed too coincidental. McKenzie felt the boy was speaking the truth. *But why would anyone steal some of God's precious animals? If the Frankses actually stole them, surely they knew it was illegal*, McKenzie thought.

"Let's record some more here," Alex said as she tugged McKenzie into position in front of the railing.

"I can't hear a thing you're saying!" McKenzie yelled over the din of the barking sea lions behind them.

"This could be interesting!" Alex practically screamed in McKenzie's ear. "But let's try it."

After several attempts at recording McKenzie's report, Alex broke into a fit of giggles. "All I can see through the viewfinder is your mouth moving, while the sea lions are barking their heads off. It almost looks like you're barking your head off, too!"

"Maybe I can report separately, when we get away from all this noise," McKenzie said.

The girls hurried to catch up with Colby and the rest of the group who had left the observation area. The tour guide led the group outside, down another set of stairs to the outdoor viewpoint. As Alex recorded the herd of sea lions on the rocky ledge, McKenzie stepped closer to the tour group.

"Can sea lions be hunted?" a man asked.

"No, it is illegal to hunt sea lions," Colby answered. "The number of Steller sea lions have decreased over the years. But since laws are in place to protect all marine mammals, hopefully their numbers will increase."

McKenzie pulled a notebook from her backpack and scribbled notes in case she needed them later. As she turned to head back to Alex, Colby's voice caught her attention.

"Many people love to watch the sea lions at play. They adapt well to captivity and are natural entertainers." Colby pointed out several sea lions putting on a show for the audience by spinning in the water.

The group gathered at the railing, watching the sea lions frolic below them. Alex paced about the upper ledge, recording the animals from various angles.

McKenzie's mind was lost in thought when she felt her cell phone vibrate in her pocket. Stepping away from the barking sea lions, she saw Bailey's phone number on the screen.

"Hey, Bailey," McKenzie answered, plugging her other ear with her finger to drown out the background noise.

"I can hardly hear you," Bailey said. "What's all that noise?"

"We're at the Sea Lion Harbor taking a tour. That barking is from the sea lions," McKenzie explained.

"Well, I just wanted to tell you I've been researching sea

lions. I found an Internet article that says they make great performers in circus acts and marine shows," Bailey said.

"Really? That's cool," McKenzie said. "I wonder what kinds of acts they can do."

"I don't know," Bailey said. "The article didn't say. Maybe the thieves want to sell them for an act, though."

McKenzie thought for a moment. "That's an idea, anyway. Maybe I can ask our tour guide about it."

After saying good-bye to Bailey, McKenzie hung up and stuffed the phone in her pocket. The group had scattered about the observation area, many of them snapping pictures.

While she waited for Alex to finish taping the sea lions, McKenzie walked over to Colby. He was leaning on an iron railing, staring at the sea lions below. He looked up as she approached.

"My friend and I are doing a video report for a public TV station. Could I ask you a few questions?" McKenzie asked.

"Shoot," Colby answered, still leaning on the railing.

"We're trying to figure out what happened to the missing sea lion pups." McKenzie held her notepad and pen, poised to write. "A friend of mine said that sea lions are used for circus acts. Is that true?"

Colby's eyes narrowed. "Yes, some shows around the country use them for entertainment."

"How and where are sea lions trained?" McKenzie continued.

Colby stood up straight, looking at her with piercing eyes. He paused and asked, "What do you know about these missing pups?"

"Nothing, really," McKenzie said, wondering why he didn't answer her question. "We heard they might have been stolen, so we're trying to figure out where the thieves might have taken them."

"So, you think you can find these baby sea lions?" Colby smirked.

"Well, we're pretty good at solving mysteries," McKenzie explained. "We have some clues already."

Colby's eyes narrowed as he folded his arms across his chest. "What kind of clues?"

McKenzie suddenly felt uncomfortable. *Why is he so concerned about the information we have?* she wondered while Colby tapped his foot.

"Well, we have a description of the couple seen taking them. Since sea lions are used in circus acts, I'm wondering if the thieves are planning to train and sell them. If we could get inside a training center, maybe we could find the pups," McKenzie said.

Colby turned away and stared absentmindedly at the sea lions in the cove.

Did I say something wrong? McKenzie wondered. *He acts almost upset with me for asking about Mario and Bianca.*

After a minute, Colby turned back to McKenzie. "I know somebody who may have answers for you. Let me make a quick phone call."

McKenzie took a deep breath. *He must not be mad after all if he wants to help. Maybe he's just concerned about the sea lions.*

Colby walked to the far side of the observation area. He pulled a cell phone from a clip at his waist. He glanced at McKenzie then turned his back to her. The noise of the sea lions was so loud that she couldn't hear a word he said on the phone.

A movement behind McKenzie caught her attention. Turning, she saw Alex approaching. McKenzie quickly filled her in on her phone call with Bailey and her conversation with Colby.

The girls waited anxiously until Colby returned. "Well, girls, I have a surprise for you. I called Sea Park and told them about your video report and your questions. They are happy to help you out. The moment this tour is over, they want you to come for a special tour of the park. Someone there will have all the answers for you."

McKenzie's jaw dropped open as she looked at Alex then back at Colby. "Really? We can do that?"

"They're making an exception. Go through the main doors to the souvenir shop and ask for Nina. Don't mention this to anyone else, though. This isn't something they normally do. But since you're doing this special report, they wanted to help out."

"Do we need tickets?" McKenzie asked, glancing at her watch.

"No. Just tell the cashier I sent you. You should have no problem," Colby said with a pleased expression. "Oh, and be sure to bring your video camera. You'll want to take pictures of the marine animals."

"We'll have to ask my Aunt Becca first. She'll be here in a few minutes. But I'm sure it'll be okay," McKenzie said with excitement.

"All right, then. I'll call Sea Park and let them know it's all set," Colby said as he walked over to the railing and motioned for the tour group to gather.

McKenzie and Alex were so excited they barely heard Colby as he wrapped up the tour. "If the Frankses are hiding the sea lion pups there, maybe we'll find them," McKenzie whispered to her friend.

McKenzie called out "thank you" to Colby and headed to the parking lot as she saw Aunt Becca's car. Both girls began talking at once as they climbed in the backseat. They told her all about the Sea Lion Harbor tour and Colby's offer of a tour at Sea Park.

"I've never heard of them giving free tours," Aunt Becca said skeptically as she turned up the air-conditioning. "That must be something new they've started. I can drop you two off there while I run errands. After that, we're going on the Cape Perpetua tour. You'll love it. The views from the top of the lighthouse are amazing. You can see for miles."

A few minutes later Aunt Becca dropped them off at Sea Park. She promised to come pick them up the minute they called and told her they were finished.

A line was forming outside for the next show, so the girls moved around the crowd. The souvenir shop next to the lobby was busy with people waiting to get tickets. The girls passed row after row of sea lion knickknacks, T-shirts, and stuffed toy sea lions. Slinking through the crowd, the girls walked to the cashier's counter and waited their turn.

"We're looking for Nina," McKenzie said to a black-haired young man with "Warren" on his name tag.

"She stepped out for a while. Can I help you?" he asked as he tucked a receipt into the cash register drawer.

"We're here for a private tour of Sea Park," McKenzie explained.

Warren looked quizzically at the girls. "I've never heard of any private tours."

"Colby, the tour guide at Sea Lion Harbor, arranged it. He

set it up," McKenzie stated firmly. "He said to ask for Nina."

Warren reached for the phone. "That figures," he muttered. "Those Frankses are only here in the summer, but they're always pulling stuff like this, acting like they own the place."

The Frankses? Could Colby and Nina be related to Mel and Tia Franks? Oh no! McKenzie thought. *I told Colby we were trying to solve the mystery of the missing sea lion pups.*

McKenzie turned to Alex while she listened to Warren's phone conversation. "Hey, Nina. The kids are here that your brother sent over for a tour. Do you know anything about it?"

Warren listened and then turned his back to them, muttering into the receiver, "What do you mean, you want me to give the tour? Okay, okay. I'll show them the tanks."

Warren groaned as he hung up the phone. He motioned for the girls to follow him. "Come on. Let's go."

He told his assistant he was leaving and ushered the girls out a side door past the crowd of people lined up for the show. He led them down a long concrete hallway lined with several metal doors. A damp, fishy smell wafted up the empty corridor. The girls' footsteps echoed as their shoes slapped the cement floor.

Something is really strange, McKenzie thought. *No one seems to know anything about this tour.*

McKenzie swallowed and spoke to Warren, "I'm really sorry, but Colby set it all up. We're doing a video report for public TV, and we go home in a few days."

Warren turned and gave a slight smile. "It's not your fault. Colby and Nina think just because their parents are trainers that they can do anything they want. Actually, I need a break from the souvenir shop anyway."

"So Colby and Nina are Mel and Tia Franks' kids?" McKenzie asked.

"Yep," he said, stopping at a door with a tiny glass window in it. "They sure are. Nina wanted to make sure I showed you the inside of this room. In here you'll see the tank where we train some of our sea mammals."

Warren opened the door. Alex lifted her camcorder and swept the viewfinder across the room. A large tank sat in the center of the room, with ledges built along the sides. At first McKenzie thought the tank was empty, but then she saw dark shadows near the far end.

She stared at the two shimmering gray bodies beneath the water. Her jaw dropped open, and her heart pumped wildly. The two mammals swimming in the tank looked exactly like Mario and Bianca!

Suspicions!

McKenzie edged toward the tank for a closer look. The two mammals swam forward and raised their heads out of the water. McKenzie's heart sank. They weren't Mario and Bianca, after all. They weren't even sea lions; they were young seals.

"For a minute, I thought we'd found the missing sea lion pups," McKenzie said with disappointment.

"Yes, from a distance, seals look a little like sea lions." Alex stepped forward and stopped recording.

Warren grabbed a beach ball from a basket on the floor and tossed it into the tank. "Everyone seems concerned about Mario and Bianca. But you won't find them here, that's for sure. We get all of our mammals through reputable sources. Supposedly some kid saw the sea lion pups being stolen. If that's the case, the thief will probably sell them on the black market."

"Where?" Alex asked as she watched the seals playing.

"'Black market' means selling something illegally," Warren explained as he walked to the far side of the tank and leaned on the edge.

McKenzie thought about that for a moment. "Why would anyone want to steal a sea lion and sell it?"

Warren shrugged his shoulders and glanced at his watch. "It's hard to tell. Maybe some kind of collection. Twin sea lions are rare."

"What happens to the animals that are trained here?" McKenzie asked, watching the seals swim toward the beach ball.

"We only train animals we're going to use in our shows," Warren said. "We're planning to add these two seals to our main attraction."

"Are your trainers working with any sea lions right now?" McKenzie asked hopefully.

"No. We're concentrating on these two seals," Warren said. "Training is a lot of hard work."

McKenzie frowned. She watched Alex film the seals playing with the ball. *This isn't what I was hoping to find out. I really thought I would find Mario and Bianca in here. But all they have are seals,* she thought with dismay. *Maybe the Frankses aren't the thieves, after all.*

The seals flung their upper bodies from the water and popped the ball into the air. When it plopped back into the tank, they scooted it around and around. One seal came up beneath it and flung it in an arch toward the girls. McKenzie reached out her arms and caught it, showering Alex with a spray of water.

"Toss it back in," Warren said with a laugh.

The girls watched in amazement as the seals played with the ball. They were so absorbed in the show that they didn't notice anyone had arrived. Then a man called out. "Okay, Warren, I'll take over now."

McKenzie turned. Mel Franks stood in the doorway. Beside him stood a young woman with straight brown hair, wearing a khaki-colored fishing cap pulled low over her forehead. She disappeared through a door that looked like it led into a storeroom.

She looks familiar. McKenzie's stomach began to churn.

"Hey, Mr. Franks, I didn't know you were here," Warren said with surprise. "I'm giving these girls a behind-the-scenes tour. They said Colby arranged it. Do you know anything about it?"

"Of course," Mr. Franks said, smiling at the girls. "I'm glad we could accommodate you so quickly. Do you have any questions? We need to get busy with our training in here."

"I thought training was over for the day," Warren said with a confused look.

"These seals need more work," Mr. Franks said with an annoyed tone. "Why don't you head back to the lobby, Warren? We'll take over from here."

"Well, sure," Warren said, surprised. "I'll leave the girls to you then. We were just starting the tour. This was our first stop."

The girls thanked Warren and watched him head out the door. McKenzie suddenly had a funny feeling. *Was that girl his daughter, Nina?* she wondered. *She does kind of look like Mrs. Franks.*

Mr. Franks ignored the girls. He reached into the tank and retrieved the ball. He tossed it into the large basket against the wall.

"Did Warren answer all your questions?" Mr. Franks asked, turning to the girls.

McKenzie thought for a moment then spoke. "I thought for sure we had found the missing sea lion pups when we first came in here. These seals look so much like them."

Mr. Franks' tone of voice softened. "Seals and sea lions can easily be confused. Like I told you the other day, killer whales probably got the pups. You should probably give up on ever seeing them again. It's just one of those things."

I think he's trying to convince us that the pups are dead, McKenzie thought. *Does he have something to hide?*

"Are you guys the only trainers at Sea Park?" McKenzie asked, forcing herself to look Mr. Franks in the eye.

"Yes, my wife and I train most of the sea mammals, but we're teaching our daughter here to help out," Mr. Franks answered with a stern gaze.

Nina emerged from the storeroom carrying two wet suits. After tossing the suits on top of a black duffel bag, she glanced at her watch. "Don't you think we should start training, Dad? It's getting late."

"Good idea." Mr. Franks kept his gaze fixed on the girls. "I hate to cut your tour short, girls, but we've had a change of plans. We have to do one more training session today, and the seals train better without an audience. Why don't you scoot on out of here?"

Mr. Franks seemed almost anxious to get rid of them. *Is he upset with Colby for arranging this tour without their permission?* Their tour had amounted to viewing seals in a tank, and now they were finished. *This is too weird. Something is going on here, but what?*

She knew she should leave. But she also knew this might be her only chance to ask a few questions about the missing sea lion pups.

Taking a deep breath, she forced herself to get straight to the point. "Do you have a permit to capture sea mammals for your show at Sea Park?"

Nina glared at her and disappeared into the storeroom again.

211

Mr. Franks walked toward McKenzie, his dark eyes blazing. "What's this all about?"

McKenzie took a step backward. "Some kid said he saw a man with a fish tattoo and a woman take the sea lions. And you have a fish tattoo."

The moment the words came out of her mouth, McKenzie wished she could take them back. *I can't believe I just accused them of stealing!*

Mr. Franks was silent. Then he threw his head back and laughed. "So that's what you two are getting at. You think we stole the sea lion pups?"

McKenzie's face burned with embarrassment as Mr. Franks turned to his daughter, standing just inside the storeroom door. Nina chuckled.

"I admire your spunk, kiddo," Mr. Franks said. "But the kid was mistaken. He saw Tia and me getting these two little seals. And, yes, we have a permit to capture them.

"You might as well forget about Mario and Bianca, or whatever their names are," he said. "I'm sure they're long gone."

McKenzie touched Alex's arm lightly and turned back to the Frankses. "I'm sorry. We just care about Susie's pups, that's all."

"No harm done," Mr. Franks said as he ushered the girls to the door. He still acted cheerful. But a flash of anger remained in his eyes. "Can you find your way out?"

McKenzie assured Mr. Franks they knew the route back to the lobby.

"Let's go," Alex said softly, tugging McKenzie's arm. "We need to get to Cape Perpetua so I can photograph the whales. By the time we get there, it will be time for the tour."

The girls stepped into the hallway and let the heavy door close behind them.

"Oh, Alex! I was awful," McKenzie said, guilt bubbling inside of her. "I accused them without evidence. I feel terrible."

"If it makes you feel any better, I was thinking the same thing," Alex said sympathetically. "We thought because he had a fish tattoo that he was the thief. I can see now that the little boy was mistaken. Seals look a lot like sea lions. He probably didn't know the difference. Don't feel bad. You did the right thing and apologized."

McKenzie nodded but didn't feel any better inside. When they came to a corner, she realized she didn't know which hall they had taken. She looked at Alex. "Do you know how to get out?"

"I was too busy filming to pay attention." Alex looked both ways down the hall.

"I thought I knew," McKenzie said, peering down the hall to her right. "But now I'm not sure."

While they considered their next move, Alex pointed to her left. "I think I hear voices. Let's see if we can find someone to ask."

The girls headed toward the voices and stopped when they came to an open door. An angry voice floated out. "These coolers were full of fish yesterday. Now this one is half empty. And one of our portable coolers is missing, too."

Another voice responded, "You know, I thought there were fish missing a couple of days ago. Our animals can't eat that much. Where's it all going?"

McKenzie peered through the doorway and saw two teenage boys surveying the contents of the coolers on the back wall. At first the boys didn't notice them, but then the taller one turned and glanced at them.

"Do you know how to get out of here?" McKenzie called across the room. "We're sort of lost."

The shorter boy waved a fish in one hand as he spoke, "If you're looking for the front door, you're way off track. You probably don't want to go that way, though. A show is going on and is about to let out. But if you want the back door leading to the employee parking lot, head down the hall to your right and go through the exit door."

After thanking the boys, the girls hurried down the hallway and out the door with EXIT lit in red letters. They walked between the parked cars toward a stone wall that separated the lot from the street. Finding a shady spot, the girls hopped onto the wall, while McKenzie called Aunt Becca.

"She'll be here in about ten minutes," McKenzie said, flipping her phone shut.

While they waited, movement at the far end of the lot caught McKenzie's eye. A short-haired blond woman had come from behind the far end of the building carrying a large duffel bag. She climbed into a white pickup parked nearby and backed it up to a door on the side of the building. McKenzie recognized the man who quickly stepped out and loaded a portable cooler into the truck. After throwing a tarp over it, he climbed into the front seat.

Nudging Alex, she said excitedly, "Look. Mr. Franks is leaving. But who was that girl with him? He told us he had to train the seals. That didn't take long."

"Maybe Nina is training them," Alex suggested.

The girls watched the pickup disappear down the street into the busy flow of traffic.

"That woman was too far away to get a good look at her," McKenzie said, frustrated. "But wasn't she dressed like Nina?"

Alex thought for a minute. "I think you're right. Do you think the woman in the pickup was Nina? But her hair was different. Do you think she was wearing a wig earlier?"

"You know, that hat looked like one of those funny disguises we saw in Emerald Bay's gift shop the other day. Maybe she was trying to disguise herself." McKenzie grew excited.

"Why would she do that?" Alex asked.

McKenzie thought for a moment. "The person I saw in Mr. C.'s cabin had short blond hair, and so did the girl we saw in the truck."

"So you think Nina was the person you saw on Mr. C.'s sunporch?" Alex asked.

"It could have been her. When I stepped outside that night to get my camera, I bet she saw me. That's why she was wearing a disguise earlier—so I wouldn't recognize her."

"Wow!" Alex's eyes flashed. "Maybe we're on to something."

"Something is definitely funny about them, whether they know anything about Mario and Bianca or not." McKenzie pulled her legs beneath her on top of her rocky perch. "Do you remember when Nina brought those two wet suits out of the storage room? She threw them on top of a black duffel bag. The girl we saw just now was carrying a black duffel bag."

Alex's eyes grew wide as she suddenly remembered something. "That one guy in that room said fish and a portable cooler were missing. Maybe that was the missing cooler that Mr. Franks carried out. Maybe it was filled with fish."

"Yeah. I just thought of something else. Those seals were tossing beach balls with their noses. Could they be trained to do that already if the Frankses had just captured them a few days ago, like they said they did?"

Alex shifted her position on the rock wall. "Hey, good point. They must be some really talented seals if they can learn that quickly." She hesitated and added, "Do you think that little boy really did see them steal Mario and Bianca after all?"

McKenzie sighed. "It seems possible, but I felt so horrible when I accused them. We don't know that they had fish in the cooler they carried out or that it was even the missing cooler. We still don't have evidence."

"I also think it's weird that Colby arranged this tour that amounted to practically nothing. Something is so strange about this whole thing," Alex said, swinging her legs.

"Yeah, he was so anxious to help us get the answers we needed for our report, but then Mr. Franks acted like he couldn't wait to get rid of us," McKenzie said.

McKenzie's mind whirled. Pieces of the puzzle were beginning to fall into place, but something still wasn't right. *We've missed something, but I don't know what,* she thought.

"I don't get it. Why would Colby plan this tour?" Alex shooed a fly away. "It's almost like he wanted us to see those seals."

That's it! McKenzie's pulse quickened. "You're right, Alex. The Frankses are all working on this together. When I told Colby we were trying to find Mario and Bianca, he called someone at Sea Park—probably his dad. They *did* want us to see the seals—seals that could be mistaken for Mario and Bianca from a distance. He thought if he could convince us they captured seals instead of sea lions, we would no longer suspect them. This whole tour was rigged to throw us off, so we'd give up on the investigation."

Alex stared at McKenzie with bewilderment in her eyes. "So, what now?"

"I bet Mario and Bianca are alive and well. We just have to find out where!"

CHAPTER 9

Terror at Devil's Churn!

"If the man at the cave did steal Mario and Bianca, where would he take them?" Bailey asked.

McKenzie pushed her phone's speaker button and settled into a lawn chair beside Alex.

McKenzie dug her feet into the sand absentmindedly, eating her last bite of a ham sandwich as she talked. "That's a good question. We know they aren't at Sea Park. Even if they were in a tank we didn't see, some employee there would have seen them. If the Frankses have them, they must be hiding them somewhere else."

"But what would they want the pups for? Sea Park already has lots of marine animals. So why would they steal animals when they can capture them legally?" Alex twisted the cap off a juice bottle and sipped.

McKenzie leaned back in her chair, flicking the sand with her toes. "Maybe they're doing something illegal—like selling them on the black market. You know, like Warren was talking about earlier."

"But how can we prove any of this?" Bailey said, sounding frustrated. "We have no idea where the sea lion pups are or even if they're still alive."

"We'll both be going home in a few days. If we don't find

them soon, nobody will. We're the only ones who think they might still be alive," Alex said.

"You know more about sea lions than we do, Alex," McKenzie said. "Where do they live around here besides Sea Lion Harbor?"

Alex thought for a minute and then answered, "There are probably other caves along the coast where they could live. But I don't know how anyone would keep the pups from swimming away. If the Frankses stole the pups, I would think they would steal more. After all, more sea lions, more money. Right?"

"Could be," Bailey said. "If the Cave Man knows all about sea lions, he would know the best place to hide them."

The three girls chatted longer then hung up. McKenzie glanced up the beach. They had planned to keep an eye on the Frankses. But so far, that hadn't worked out. She hadn't even seen the couple on the beach or out in the cove in their boat. As far as McKenzie could tell, they simply went to work.

"We could go see if their boat is docked. If it's gone, maybe the Frankses are hunting more sea lions," McKenzie said.

"Or maybe they're just taking a break from work to go out in their boat," Alex said.

McKenzie sighed and leaned her head back. A screen door slammed. Turning, McKenzie saw Mr. Carney coming down his back steps. "Hey, Mr. C.," she called out.

The older man raised his hand in greeting as he strolled across the yard to the girls. "I've been looking all over for that book on caves, and I just can't find it. I must have laid it down somewhere and forgot where I put it. Those maps in it were really interesting. You girls would have fun looking for those old caves. The minute I find it, I'll bring it over."

"Thanks Mr. C.," Alex said. "But we're leaving at the end of the week."

"So soon?" he asked, frowning. "I'll miss you girls. I like being around young 'uns. I don't feel quite so old then."

"We'll miss you, too," McKenzie said. After a moment, she continued, "Do you remember where any of the cave entrances were around here?"

"I didn't have a chance to look at the map before I lost the book," Mr. Carney said, rubbing the back of his neck. "But in the last chapter I read, I learned there are several cave entrances on public land near the Sea Lion Harbor area and Emerald Bay Resorts."

"Is there another copy of the book somewhere? Maybe at the public library?" Alex asked, popping a grape in her mouth.

"No. It has to be special ordered through the bookstores. I guess I'd better get busy looking for it." He scratched his head as he muttered about where he might have left it. Then he headed back to the house.

McKenzie felt sorry for Mr. C.

"Alex, do you think the book was stolen?" she asked.

"Maybe," Alex said. "You mean by the woman in his cabin. But how would she know about the book, and why would she steal it?"

McKenzie heard Mickey bark and Aunt Becca's door slam. She turned around. There was Aunt Becca, coming out of the house. The dog bounded down the steps, his slobbery tongue dangling out of his mouth. Seconds later he put his paws on McKenzie's lap and licked her face.

"Girls," Aunt Becca called, "I just got a call from my boss. The other pilot scheduled to work this afternoon called in with an emergency. So I need to go in right away and take a tour group up in the Skyview."

"What about Cape Perpetua and the Heceta Head Lighthouse?" McKenzie asked.

"I'm sorry I can't drive you two up there like we planned. But I called the resort and got you on the next tour bus. It leaves in half an hour, so if you've finished lunch you can go over to the parking lot and meet the bus. You'll need to go inside to the front desk and pick up your tickets."

McKenzie pushed Mickey off her lap and stood. "Thank you, Aunt Becca, but I'm really sorry you can't go with us."

"Me, too," Aunt Becca said as she let Mickey back in the house. "You'll love the lighthouse. The view from the top is breathtaking."

Within minutes the girls climbed aboard the waiting charter bus. McKenzie slid into a window seat as Alex slipped in beside her. Tourists of all ages filled the seats. An elderly man with powdery white hair ushered his wife into a window seat before sitting beside her.

Across the aisle, a young mother held a baby on her lap. A brown-haired preschool-aged girl wearing a yellow sundress dug around in the diaper bag until she pulled out a small green plastic pouch. As she ripped the top off, McKenzie caught a whiff of grape fruit snacks.

A group of teenagers scurried toward the back of the bus, filling the last seats. Chattering voices filled the bus as the tourists settled in for the ride.

As the bus traveled up the highway, the tour guide, a college-aged girl named Ally, started giving the tourists facts about what they'd see along the road. Soon the bus pulled into a parking lot of a scenic overlook.

Operation: Excitement!

"We'll take about thirty minutes here to look around and take pictures. For those of you who want to hike a bit, I'm taking a group down to the beach to see the sights. It's a fairly steep hike, but it's not long, maybe a half mile down and back," Ally said as she stepped off the bus. "Those who don't want to hike can feel free to wait here at the overlook. It's a beautiful photography spot."

McKenzie and Alex headed for a hike with the group of teenagers and Ally. A few middle-aged couples and families brought up the rear. As they hiked down the rocky trail, Ally pointed out vegetation around the beach. McKenzie breathed in the salty smell of the ocean and various wildflowers growing along the trail. After the group hiked about fifty yards, they reached the beach.

"This is gorgeous!" McKenzie exclaimed, peering at the rocky, jagged coastline. The waves crashed against the cliffs, spewing fountains of water high into the air.

Ally gathered the tour group close. She pointed to a large dark opening in the face of the cliff about a hundred yards away. "On your left, you will see one of the most notorious caves in our area. Hundreds of years ago, it was common to see shipwrecks along these rocky shores. According to a legend, a band of thieves scoured the wreckage searching for valuables. They would then fill their boats with these treasures. During high tide, the caves would fill with water. The thieves would then sail their boats into these underground water passages and deposit their valuables, hiding them until they could return."

"So the thieves had to wait for high tide again, before they could sail back into the caves and get their loot?" one of the teenage boys asked.

"No," Ally explained. "These caves were the perfect hideaway. Most of these underground caves have another entrance, usually higher up the cliff. The thieves knew these underground passages like the backs of their hands. They would enter the caves from inland and haul their treasures out."

"Wow! Is that story for real?" Alex asked, snapping a picture with her camera.

"No one knows for sure. It's the stuff legends are made of—stories that get passed down through the generations." Ally held up her hand and called the group together. "We need to head back to the bus now. So watch your step, folks."

The trek back up the trail was harder than going down. By the time they reached the bus, McKenzie was breathing hard. She slumped into her seat with relief. The bus pulled back onto the highway. McKenzie's mind raced with jumbled thoughts of Ally's story.

Alex leaned over in her seat, her eyes dancing with excitement. "That legend reminds me of the book I've been reading. A man tried to scare all the people out of an old western town because he was storing oil in the mines. He didn't want anyone to find out about his treasure. He wanted it all for himself. Just like the thieves in Ally's story."

McKenzie glanced around to make sure no one was listening. "You know that cave we went in the other day while we were sailing? It was low tide when we were there. Do you think the water would get deep enough to sail a boat in there during high tide?"

Alex looked questioningly at McKenzie. "I don't know. But a boat could definitely get farther into the inlet, anyway."

"I keep thinking about Mr. Franks capsizing us. Do you think he really was trying to scare us away from that inlet so we wouldn't find that cave?" McKenzie said softly. "Maybe there is a clue in there that would help us find Mario and Bianca."

"Oh, no!" Alex's eyes grew wide. "You don't think he's got, uh, you know. . .skins in there, do you?"

McKenzie shook her head. "No. You were the one who pointed out that no one would steal sea lion pups for their skins. Adult sea lions maybe, but not pups."

"I just started thinking about how sometimes rich people wear exotic furs. Sometimes for trimming on their clothes. Baby sea lion fur would certainly be exotic," Alex pointed out. "Let's hope he's not doing that! But there's no way we can go back to the cave from the cove. Maybe there's another entrance, like in the story Ally told."

"But how in the world could we find it? We might have a chance, if Mr. C. could find his book with the maps." McKenzie sighed.

"If that woman you saw in his cabin stole it, we'll never find another cave entrance." Alex drummed her red painted fingernails on her camera.

"We can't give up. We have to figure out what happened to Mario and Bianca so it doesn't happen to any other sea lion pups. We owe it to Susie to find her babies."

Ally rose from her seat as the bus rolled into another parking lot off the side of the highway. She announced that the tour had arrived at the Heceta Head Lighthouse.

"Maybe I can get some whale shots from the lighthouse with my zoom lens," Alex said as she climbed off the bus. "I really wanted to enter one in the photography contest in Florence. But my time is running out."

"I would enter something, too, but I'm not a very good

photographer. I'll just take pictures to put in my scrapbook when I get home." McKenzie pulled her camera from its case and looked up. "Wow! I've never seen a real lighthouse."

In front of them, perched high on a rocky cliff overlooking the ocean, sat a tall, round white tower with red trim. A matching keeper's house and other buildings sat nearby, while spruce trees loomed on the cliff above the lighthouse. Waves crashed against the rocky shoreline far below.

Several tourists settled onto benches overlooking the ocean, while others headed for the trail that led to the lighthouse. McKenzie and Alex brought up the rear, stopping now and then to take pictures of the coast as well as pelicans and bald eagles flying overhead.

"I see whales!" Alex exclaimed as she focused on two bounding gray spots in the ocean. She groaned as she lowered her camera. "Even with my zoom lens, they're still too far away."

"Hey, we'd better hurry and catch up. Everyone else is already going into the lighthouse." McKenzie tugged Alex's arm and they raced past the lighthouse keeper's house toward the Heceta Head Lighthouse.

They slipped through the door as the rest of the group began climbing the spiral staircase to the top. McKenzie peered out a narrow window, feeling dizzy as she stared down at the top of the lighthouse keeper's house. Even inside the tower she could hear the crashing of the waves on the rocky shore far below. *I wonder how many secret caves are hidden in those cliffs,* she thought.

After taking pictures at the top, the group headed back down the stairs to the trail leading to the parking lot. When the bus was loaded, the driver headed toward Cape Perpetua for the final tour stop.

After the bus parked, the girls followed the group and the tour guide down the trail to the shore. McKenzie breathed in the tang of the ocean as they approached a black rock ledge. The woman with the two small children pushed the baby in a stroller and held the hand of her young daughter.

Crash! The waves hit the rocks below them, exploding over the sides and sending a towering spray of water high into the air. A fine mist floated on the breeze. Despite the warmth of the day, McKenzie shivered as the cool droplets touched her skin.

"Wow! I see why they call this Devil's Churn," McKenzie said as wave after wave struck the rock. The spewing water reminded her of erupting volcanoes she'd seen on TV.

Alex clicked away on her camera, focusing on the spraying water. She snapped shots of the craggy cliffs. On the distant beach, McKenzie saw a group of sea lions gathered on a ledge and heard their barking. She zoomed in with her camera and snapped a picture.

Stepping away from the group, McKenzie wandered down the rock to a tidal pool set back from the shoreline. She noticed a small pool left behind from the high tide. It was filled with sea stars and shells.

McKenzie reached into the cool water and pulled out a shimmering white stone. As she turned the rock over in her hand, she heard a cry from above.

She turned to see a look of horror etched on the face of the woman. The woman screamed again. Her outstretched arm pointed to the Devil's Churn.

McKenzie gasped. A flash of a yellow dress disappeared beneath the surface of the spouting, churning water!

The Hero

McKenzie froze as shrieking voices cut through the roar of the crashing waves.

"Help!" the woman screamed, trying to dash down the steep path with the stroller.

Everything seemed to move in slow motion. Out of the corner of her eye, McKenzie saw someone jump into the water. She gasped as she recognized Alex's thin figure plunging into the water and disappearing beneath the surface.

"Alex!" she screamed. Her knees trembled as she ran toward the Devil's Churn.

Oh, dear God, save them both! McKenzie prayed urgently. McKenzie's heart raced.

Alex, where are you?

She scanned the dark water. Her stomach twisted like the fury of the Devil's Churn.

Please, please, please, God. Don't let the little girl or Alex drown. Help them!

Suddenly Alex's dripping form rose from the churning black waters, clutching a small figure. The little girl's tiny arms clung to Alex's throat like a necktie. Her dripping yellow dress was plastered to her tiny body.

"I'm coming!" the mother yelled.

"Somebody grab the little girl!" another voice cried.

All around her, people scurried, frantically trying to help. McKenzie heard an ambulance siren. Someone had called for help. She realized she needed to stay out of the way.

Instinctively, McKenzie raised her camera to her eye. She snapped a picture seconds before a teenage boy jumped into the water. He pulled the little girl from Alex's grip and carried her to safety. A middle-aged man grasped Alex's arm and pulled her out of the swirling water.

The crowd cheered as the mother grabbed the soaked child. An older woman stood a distance away with the stroller. The mother stroked the little girl's wet hair, clinging to her sobbing daughter.

Scampering up the rock, McKenzie threw her arms around Alex's trembling body. "Are you okay?"

Alex nodded and panted. Water ran down her legs. She flung her wet hair out of her eyes and shivered.

"I'm fine," she said through chattering teeth.

A white-haired man slipped his jacket around Alex's trembling shoulders. He guided her to a rock out of the wind so she could sit in the warmth of the sun.

"You were quite the hero, young lady," he said patting her shoulder.

"Are you all right, dear?" his wife asked, settling beside her.

Alex simply nodded as a crowd of people gathered around, fussing over her. She kicked off her tennis shoes. After pouring a stream of water out of them, she set them on the bench beside her. A young man in a blue uniform arrived with a first-aid bag. He raced to the little girl, still huddled in her mother's arms.

Another young man in a blue uniform appeared at Alex's

side with a blanket. The bus driver rushed up with a thermos and poured some coffee into a Styrofoam cup. "Take a drink of this. It'll warm you up."

Alex lifted the steaming cup to her mouth. She shuddered as the liquid touched her lips. "Yuck," she cried.

Everyone laughed as Alex handed the cup back to the driver. A man came out of the visitor's center with two T-shirts from the gift shop, and handed them to Alex and the little girl to put on.

"Some people will do anything for a free T-shirt," he said with a grin.

Alex thanked him and slipped into the visitor's center to change. When she returned, she carried a large bag of caramel popcorn and an orange slushy.

"It pays to be a hero—you get all sorts of goodies," she said with a giggle.

Now that the little girl had been pronounced okay, the young mother pushed through the cluster of people and hugged Alex tightly. The little girl shyly clutched her mother's legs. Alex bent over and hugged her.

When Ally announced it was time to leave, everyone climbed onto the bus and found seats. The other passengers smiled at Alex as they walked down the aisle. Several shook her hand.

"You were so brave, Alex," McKenzie said, turning to her friend. "I just stood there and did nothing. You saved that little girl's life."

Alex brushed her damp hair out of her eyes and blushed. "I guess because I've grown up around the water I jumped in automatically."

"Weren't you afraid you might drown?" McKenzie asked,

taking a handful of popcorn that Alex offered.

Alex's eyes grew serious. "I didn't have time to think about it. I could only think about that little girl."

McKenzie shuddered at the thought of what might have happened. Gazing at the camera in her lap, she thought, *I sure hope the picture turns out. I want to surprise Alex with it.*

As the bus traveled down the road, McKenzie rested her head against the seat back and stared out the window. She watched the waves crash against the jagged rocky shoreline. Beside her, Alex leaned her head to one side, her eyes closed.

McKenzie's eyelids began to droop. *Beep!* Her eyes popped open as she dug her cell phone out of her pocket.

The message read that one message was stored.

How did that happen? Maybe it rang during the excitement, and I missed it, she thought.

She punched buttons on the phone and listened to Kate's message. "Hey, McKenzie. I've been doing some research and have found out some weird things. I did a background search on Mel and Tia Franks and printed off tons of articles.

"I wasn't going to be able to look at them until later, but guess what. Biscuit the Wonderdog pulled a page out of the printer and brought it to me. There was a picture of the Frankses and a story about them leading a spelunking expedition about ten years ago. You know, they explore caves and stuff. They even helped that guy write the book of Mr. C.'s that is missing. Give me a call when you can. Bye."

"Who was that?" Alex asked, opening her eyes and yawning.

"Kate." McKenzie snapped her phone shut. She glanced about at all the tourists and then said softly, "Biscuit has done it again. Finding that dog at Discovery Lake Camp is the best thing that ever happened to us—next to all of us meeting each other. I'm so glad Kate kept him. I'll tell you about it when we get home. We're almost back to the resort."

After the bus had parked, the girls said good-bye to the woman and her children. The woman asked Alex her name and where she was staying. Then she hugged her once more.

"Okay, what was the call from Kate all about?" Alex asked as the girls walked to their beach house.

McKenzie relayed the message to Alex and said, "So, now I'm really confused. I thought for sure that strange woman I saw in Mr. C's cabin was the Frankses' daughter, Nina. And I'm sure she tucked something under her arm that night. When he told us his book was missing, I was positive she had stolen it. But why would she want it if her parents helped write it? It doesn't make any sense."

"It is weird," Alex said, trudging up the back steps.

"Kate wanted me to call her when I had a chance," McKenzie said as she unlocked the door to the beach house.

"Why don't you do that now? I can't wait to get out of these wet clothes." Alex headed down the hall. "I'm taking a shower."

McKenzie grabbed her camera and settled in front of the computer while she called Kate. The line was busy, so McKenzie put down the phone to try again in a few minutes.

Mickey trotted over and laid his head on her lap while she downloaded snapshots from the tour. She glanced at each one quickly, stroking Mickey's head with her free hand. When she got to the one of Alex rescuing the little girl, she stopped and examined it.

I'm not the best photographer in the world, but this one is pretty good. At least, I think it's good enough for the contest.

231

She smiled as she unhooked the camera from the computer.

McKenzie glanced at the clock on the wall. She picked up her phone and clicked on Kate's name again.

"I'm so glad you called," Kate said. "I've been thinking about this whole thing. Maybe the Frankses' daughter did steal the book on caves from Mr. C."

"But why would she steal a copy? She must have one of her own. After all, her parents helped write it," McKenzie said.

"I found a summary of the book online. It's supposed to be one of the best ever written on caves along the Oregon coast. I also read that the maps are thorough. Maybe Nina Franks didn't steal the book for herself," Kate explained. "Maybe she doesn't want you to have the maps. Didn't you say you were talking about borrowing the book from Mr. C. the night you discovered someone was listening from the Frankses' back porch?"

McKenzie thought for a moment. Then her pulse began to quicken. "That's right. She and Mr. Franks know we're looking for Mario and Bianca. Do you think they've got the sea lions hidden in a cave somewhere, and they don't want us to find them?"

"That's what I'm wondering," Kate answered. "I've contacted Sydney, Bailey, and Elizabeth. Everybody is searching the Internet trying to find a copy of those maps. So, check your e-mail often. If any of us finds anything, we'll let you know."

McKenzie's mind whirled as she hung up the phone. *Could it really be that simple? Are the Frankses trying to hide the maps from us so we can't find the pups?*

She looked up as Alex walked into the room drying her hair on a towel. McKenzie relayed everything she and Kate had discussed.

"So, what now?" Alex asked, pulling a brush through her damp hair. "We just can't sit and wait for them to find the maps. We could search the Internet, too."

McKenzie drummed her fingers on the desk. "I agree. We need to actually be out *doing* something. We see the Frankses a lot, so they can't be going too far. We have to come up with a way to watch them and find out where they're going."

"You mean spy on them?" Alex asked.

The back door banged, and the girls turned around. Aunt Becca stepped inside and set a pizza on the counter. McKenzie sniffed the cheese and Canadian bacon wafting across the room.

"How's the celebrity?" Aunt Becca asked, grinning at Alex.

"How did you find out?" Alex asked with a shocked expression.

"The whole resort knows. Everybody is talking about it. They're all saying, 'You should have seen that little girl jump in the water to save that preschooler from drowning.'" Aunt Becca's eyes sparkled.

Alex groaned. "They called me a 'little girl'? That's disgusting. I'm twelve—almost a teenager."

"Hey, I am so proud of you," Aunt Becca said, giving Alex a hug. "That woman was so thankful that she wanted to do something for you. She wants you and McKenzie to take your pick of the tours the resort offers, and she will pay for both of you. You only need to decide what tour you want and pick your tickets up at the resort lobby."

Alex looked at McKenzie, her eyes wide with surprise. "Really? We can go on any tour we want?"

"That's what she said. So, talk it over and decide what

you want to do. Then we'll set it up." Aunt Becca placed three paper plates around the table and poured two glasses of milk for the girls.

After saying the blessing, the girls each grabbed a slice of pizza. While eating, Aunt Becca talked about her day at work.

"I even learned a few things today," she said, laying down her fork. "I took an older gentleman, Mr. Tagachi, up today for a Skyview tour. Years ago, before Emerald Bay Resort was built, he ran a fishing boat off the coast here. He told me about an old sea lion harbor just up the beach a little ways. People used to go there and watch the sea lions."

"Yes, we went there the other day," McKenzie said. "Remember? You picked us up."

"No, not that one," Aunt Becca said. "That's the tourist one. This is another one that sea lions hang out at. The fishermen used to refer to it as a sea lion harbor."

"Where is it?" McKenzie asked with her mouth full of pizza.

"Just up the coast a little ways, but the sea lions no longer use it," Aunt Becca said. "When the state blasted dynamite through the rock for a new highway, the ledge the sea lions used for nesting collapsed. That's when the sea lions migrated farther down the beach to the current Sea Lion Harbor."

"What else did this guy tell you?" McKenzie asked as she flicked a piece of cheese at Mickey. He snapped it between his jaws and stared at her, waiting for more.

"All sorts of stuff. He was quite the history buff." Aunt Becca picked up her empty paper plate and stuffed it in the trash. "He knows all about sea lions and their habitats. I'd introduce him to you girls, but he's heading back to his home in Texas in the morning."

Aunt Becca grabbed the leash from the hook by the back door. "Will you girls finish cleaning up? I need a good long walk before dark. I'll take Mickey with me."

The girls agreed. Aunt Becca stepped outside with the dog dancing and yipping about her feet.

McKenzie sighed as she sat in silence with Alex.

"Maybe this guy would know where someone might hide sea lions, but now we can't ask him," she said. She popped a cookie in her mouth and thought for a moment. She pushed her chair back, propping her legs on the corner of the table. Then she glanced at Alex, and their eyes met.

"Are you thinking what I'm thinking?" Alex asked after downing her last swig of milk.

McKenzie grinned. "I'm thinking we need to use our free tour and go up with Aunt Becca in the Skyview. If we can't talk to that guy, she can at least show us the old sea lion harbor!"

Up, Up, and Away!

"Are you sure you want to take the Skyview for your free trip?" Aunt Becca asked after breakfast the next morning. "I might be able to arrange a free trip if the plane isn't already full and the other tourists agree."

"We know," McKenzie said, "but then we'll have to fly the regular routine. We just want you to fly us along the coast and look for caves. You can do that, can't you?"

"Sure, all flights are paid by the hour. So we can fly anywhere you want to go as long as we're back in one hour. I can take you up later this morning." Aunt Becca glanced at the clock. "But right now I need to run to the grocery store. Anyone want to ride along?"

"Not me," Alex said, sitting at the kitchen table in her pajamas. "I want to take pictures this morning while the light is good. I'm still not sure what picture I'm going to enter in the contest."

"I'll go," McKenzie announced, thinking of the picture she wanted to print as a surprise for Alex.

"Okay," Aunt Becca said as she cleared the table. "When you're dressed, we'll go."

Twenty minutes later, McKenzie entered the supermarket and headed for the customer service department. While

Aunt Becca shopped, McKenzie stuck her camera card in the machine and printed off a large picture. She quickly chose a mat frame from the rack and paid the cashier for both items.

When she and Aunt Becca arrived back home, Alex was standing on the dock taking nature pictures. After hiding the framed photo under her bed, McKenzie joined her friend on the beach.

Later that morning, Aunt Becca took the girls to the airport as promised. Within minutes the Skyview took off into the clear morning sky. The plane skimmed the treetops, and Aunt Becca circled above the resort before heading north along the beach.

"Okay, look to your right," Aunt Becca said as she managed the controls. "It's high tide, but you can still see the cave in the side of the cliff that Mr. Tagachi told me about."

McKenzie peered out the window. At first she couldn't see the cave, but then she spotted a dark hole in the rocks. Water from the cove rushed through the entrance, disappearing into darkness.

"Doesn't that look like the cave we found the other day?" McKenzie asked quietly, so her aunt wouldn't hear. "Right after the Frankses about ran us over."

"Yeah, I think you're right," Alex answered, lifting her camera and snapping a picture.

"So there used to be a ledge there for sea lions?" McKenzie asked. She tried to imagine what the cove might have looked like years ago.

"That's what Mr. Tagachi told me," Aunt Becca answered from the front seat. "When the ledge was destroyed, the sea lions moved farther south."

McKenzie thought for a moment. *If sea lions used to live*

in the cave, maybe the Frankses could be hiding Mario and Bianca there. We thought maybe there were clues hidden in the cave, but maybe it's the sea lions. That would make sense. The Frankses really were trying to scare us away that day when they tipped our sailboat over.

McKenzie's mind wandered as she tried to put the pieces of the mystery together. When she and Alex had entered the cave the other day, she had heard no sea lions barking. *Surely we would have heard them echoing in the cave,* she thought. *Unless there's another entrance! That must be it! But where?*

The roar of the plane made it difficult to talk, so McKenzie decided to wait until the plane landed to discuss her ideas with Alex. The hour passed quickly, and soon the Skyview touched down at the airport.

"I have another tour going up shortly," Aunt Becca announced when they climbed out of the plane. "These tourists are from our resort, so you two can catch their shuttle bus back to Emerald Bay. Okay?"

As the girls rode to the resort, McKenzie's cell phone rang, signaling a new text message. "It's from Sydney. She said she sent us an important e-mail message."

McKenzie couldn't wait to get back to the beach house. *What in the world is so important? Could it be something about the maps?* she wondered.

The girls hurried home from the resort, stopping at the mailbox. McKenzie pulled out a thick, brown padded envelope addressed to her.

Ripping it open, she cried, "The video sunglasses are finally here!"

Alex snatched them from her, and they raced inside to the computer. Two messages waited for them—one from

Sydney and one from Elizabeth. Eager to see their messages, McKenzie opened Sydney's first.

This took some digging on the Internet, but I finally got it done! Check out the attachment.

The moment McKenzie opened the attachment, her jaw dropped open. "Look, Alex! She found maps of caves in this area!"

After printing the maps, McKenzie laid them out on the desk. She quickly located the old sea lion harbor. She traced the dark line that represented the underground cave. It curved and then branched off into two different directions. One tunnel appeared to stop at a dead end. The other one ended near the north end of the Emerald Bay Resort.

"There's the other entrance." Alex jabbed her finger at a dark spot on the map. "Isn't that up by the Hideaway?"

McKenzie squinted at the tiny markings on the map. "It sure looks like it. Maybe we can find it."

Now that she had the map, McKenzie started feeling nervous. *What if we go to all this work searching for the cave and Mario and Bianca aren't even there?*

Alex tapped her on the shoulder. "See what Elizabeth has to say."

With a click of the mouse, McKenzie opened Elizabeth's e-mail.

Hey guys. Thought you might need a little encouragement. I really feel you're getting close to solving this thing. Don't give up. Think how Susie will feel when you find her pups. Proverbs 12:10 says, "The

righteous care for the needs of their animals, but the
kindest acts of the wicked are cruel."
    Let me know the minute you find them.

"I don't know about you, Alex, but I really needed to hear that right now. I was starting to think this was too much for us to handle. But now I know we can do it." McKenzie grinned at her friend.

"I agree. We have to try," Alex said, flipping her hair over her shoulder. "We don't have much time left. We leave the day after tomorrow."

McKenzie glanced at the clock. "We need to look for it while the Frankses are gone. Surely they would be at Sea Park now, training the animals. Even if they come home for lunch, that shouldn't be for a while yet. I think we'd better go for it."

"I'm game. Let's go," Alex said, her eyes flashing with excitement.

McKenzie grabbed Alex's backpack by the door. She shoved in two flashlights she found in the kitchen cupboard and the pair of video sunglasses.

Alex raced to their bedroom and returned with sweatshirts.

"Since we know caves can get pretty cold," she said, shoving them into the backpack with her cell phone. She slung the strap of her camera around her neck. "Just in case I need to take pictures of the evidence."

"Good idea, but we'd better get going." McKenzie scribbled a note to Aunt Becca and left it on the table. Then she folded the cave map and stuck it in her pocket.

Minutes later, they walked down the service road past Mr. Carney's cottage and the lot of spruce trees. A wooden sign reading HIDEAWAY CABIN marked the narrow drive through the trees.

"I hope they're not home," McKenzie said. The girls couldn't see the Frankses' cabin through the forest of evergreen trees until they rounded several curves.

Alex whispered, "This doesn't look like any resort cabin I've ever seen. Look, it has a storage shed. I didn't see it the other night."

"Aunt Becca told me that the three cabins on this end—ours, Mr. C.'s, and the Hideaway—are for renters staying awhile. Maybe that's why this one has a shed. Or maybe it's just an old equipment shed," McKenzie said.

"Their car isn't here," Alex noted.

McKenzie spoke softly as she stepped behind a stand of flowering shrubs. "I hope we don't have to go into their yard to find a trail to the cave. If one of them is home, we could be in big trouble."

Alex tugged on McKenzie's arm. "See that break in the shrubs on the far side of the yard? Could that be a start to the trail?"

McKenzie peered in the direction Alex pointed. "It could be. Let's stay in the trees and circle around that way. Then if someone is home, they won't be able to see us."

Together the girls walked through the trees. They ducked behind the shrubbery in case someone was watching from the house. Moments later they stepped onto a faint trail leading from the yard of the Hideaway through the trees.

"It looks like somebody has driven back here," Alex said as she snapped a picture.

McKenzie glanced at the double row of tracks leading over a hill and then disappearing from sight. "These are tracks from an ATV."

She peered back toward the cabin. Only a portion of the

Hideaway was visible through the trees. If anyone was home, they weren't outside. She didn't see any signs of an ATV at the house.

"If they have an ATV, I guess it could be parked in the shed," she said.

"It's not big enough for a car, but an ATV could fit easily," Alex said. "Let's go before it gets any later."

McKenzie hurried down the trail, deeper into the timber with Alex close behind. The wind whistled through the evergreens. Though McKenzie couldn't see the seagulls, she heard them calling. The track twisted through the trees before dropping into a narrow valley strewn with sand and rocks.

"Hey, look over there!" Alex grabbed McKenzie's arm and pointed to a dark opening in a rocky cliff. "There's the cave!"

McKenzie scurried to the entrance and peered inside. "Someone drove the ATV in here, at least for a little ways. It's a pretty wide tunnel."

Alex slipped her backpack off and pulled the sweatshirts out. After slipping hers on, she retrieved the two flashlights and handed one to McKenzie. She hoisted the backpack onto her shoulders and said, "I have a funny feeling about this. I hope we don't get caught, especially by the Frankses."

"There's no way they'll catch us. Nobody saw us come back here. The Frankses will be at work until later this afternoon," McKenzie said with certainty.

McKenzie took a deep breath and stepped inside the cave entrance. She flicked on her flashlight and swept the beam back and forth. Shadows danced eerily on the rough stone walls as she pointed the beam down the tunnel.

"Are you ready for this?" she asked, her voice trembling and echoing off the cave walls.

Alex edged closer to her friend. "I guess, but I'm only doing this for Mario and Bianca."

"They'd better be here," McKenzie said softly as she crept down the tunnel.

McKenzie shivered beneath her sweatshirt and breathed in the damp, musty smell. When they approached a bend in the tunnel, she turned and looked behind her. The cave opening, now far behind them, was no more than a dot of light. The tire tracks that had led them into the cave continued deep into the tunnel.

"This is *soooo* creepy!" Alex said in a loud whisper, clutching McKenzie's arm.

"Yeah. We had better find the sea lions, or I'll really be mad." McKenzie's teeth began to chatter.

"We'd better not be doing this for nothing." Alex paused, turning on her flash and taking a picture of the tire tracks on the ground.

The girls crept onward. The tunnel turned and sloped downward. *Whoosh!* McKenzie jumped when something fluttered above her head and she felt a quick rush of air on her face.

"What was that?" she cried.

"I think it was a b–b–bat!" Alex stammered, huddling closer to McKenzie.

Don't look up! McKenzie thought, trying to calm herself. *Then I won't see a gazillion red, beady eyes staring at me.* She scrunched her shoulders and linked arms with Alex, keeping her flashlight focused in front of her.

"I don't like bats. I don't like bats. I don't like bats," she muttered anxiously.

As they rounded a corner in the cave, McKenzie stopped

and flashed her light around. The tunnel had opened into a large, high-ceilinged room. *Something sounds different,* she thought. A strange gurgling and splashing sound came from the center of the room.

Stepping forward cautiously, she pointed her flashlight down into a large gaping hole. A rock ledge about ten feet down ran around the edge, surrounding a small underground pool.

McKenzie swept her flashlight beam across the pool and two grayish brown masses lay on the ledge above the pool. She edged closer and peered downward. Her skin felt clammy, and her voice trembled. "Look, Alex. There are two sea lion pups down there!"

"Are they Mario and Bianca?" Alex asked, aiming her light on them, too.

"I'm not sure. It's too dark in here." McKenzie pointed her light at the far end of the pool. "Look over there. There is some kind of a wire gate on that end. An underground stream feeds into this pool, and someone has made a type of cage to trap the sea lions.

"This is a pretty fancy setup," she continued as she swept her light along the floor of the cave surrounding the pool. "Look! There are lights set up all around the pool. There must be a portable generator somewhere."

The girls scanned the room with their lights.

"There it is!" Alex cried, hurrying to a large metal box on wheels. She leaned over and flicked a button on top.

Ka-chunk! McKenzie jumped as the generator powered up with a bang. Spotlights lining the edge of the pool flickered on. Their humming echoed in the vast cave. The two sea lion pups on the ledge lifted sleepy eyes.

McKenzie's heart raced as she stared at the animals. *I would know these two little guys anywhere*, she thought. "Oh, Alex. We've found them. Mario and Bianca are alive!"

Alex raced to McKenzie's side, bubbling with excitement. "I don't believe it! We really found them." She lifted her camera and clicked photos of the sea lions and their surroundings. When she finished, she tucked the camera into her backpack.

McKenzie hurried to the ledge above the sea lions and peered down at them, calling them by name. As if answering her, they slipped one by one into the pool with a splash.

McKenzie jerked her head up as a rumble echoed from somewhere deep in the cave. She felt a vibration beneath her feet.

"Alex!" she cried. "Somebody is coming on the ATV! We've got to get out of here!"

CHAPTER 12

Mission Possible!

Glancing around, McKenzie spied a dark tunnel on the opposite side of the chamber. "In here!"

She darted into the inky darkness with Alex close behind. Scurrying, McKenzie searched for a place to hide.

The roar of the ATV grew louder as it approached the pool chamber. Fleeing deeper into the cave, McKenzie grabbed Alex's arm and pulled her into an alcove. She flattened herself against the wall, relieved by the temporary safety of the darkness. Peering around the corner, she saw headlights of the ATV reflecting off the rock walls.

"Oh, no!" she whispered with disgust. "We left the lights on! They'll know someone's here."

Alex tugged McKenzie's arm. "Get back! We don't want them to see us."

McKenzie shined her light down the tunnel before her then turned back to Alex. "Let's go. We can't stay here or we'll get caught!"

The girls fled down the dark, sloping floor of the cave. McKenzie stopped when she heard the rumble of the ATV shut off behind them. Muffled voices echoed down the tunnel. She strained to make out the words, but the people were too far away. Boots thumped on the stone floor, growing louder as the intruder approached the tunnel where the girls hid.

"Someone's over here," a woman's voice called. "I see flashlights down this passageway."

A man's voice yelled something while heavy footsteps clamored across the chamber floor.

A shiver ran down McKenzie's spine as she recognized the voices of Mel and Tia Franks.

"We have to find a place to hide," she whispered. "Turn your light off. One light won't be as bright as two."

"Where are we going to go?" Alex whispered fearfully as they hurried deeper into the cave.

"I don't know."

McKenzie stopped. The tunnel branched into two different directions.

The ATV rumble had started again.

It's coming our way! her thoughts screamed as the roar grew louder. *Dear God, help us get out of here,* she prayed.

She quickly scanned one trail and then the other.

A sudden idea came to her. She pulled a piece of gum out of her pocket and tossed it just inside the entrance to the narrower tunnel.

"That way is too narrow for the ATV. Hopefully, they'll see the gum wrapper and go that way on foot. Then we'll have a few extra minutes to get away."

McKenzie darted into the other entrance, pulling Alex by her sweatshirt.

The girls turned a corner and flattened themselves against the cold, clammy wall. Without the light, McKenzie couldn't see Alex but heard her rapid breathing. The roar of the ATV grew louder as it neared the intersecting tunnels.

"Get out and see what that paper is on the ground!" the man's voice boomed over the idling motor.

A moment later, Tia's voice cried out. "It's bubble gum. I bet those two girls—whatever their names are—are sneaking around here! I knew they were up to no good. They must have gone this way."

Mr. Franks grumbled and shut off the ignition. "Grab that spotlight and let's get going!" he yelled, his boots pounding the cave floor.

McKenzie took a deep breath as the Frankses' voices and footsteps grew fainter. Stepping back out into the main tunnel, she turned to Alex. "Come on! We have to move fast. We're taking the ATV and getting out of here."

"Have you ever driven one?" Alex asked fearfully.

"Lots of times. We drive them every day on our farm." McKenzie flicked on her flashlight and ran toward the ATV with Alex in close pursuit.

As McKenzie approached the vehicle, a spotlight blinded her in the eyes. "Stop, right now!" a raging voice commanded.

Shielding her eyes, McKenzie made out the forms of Mel and Tia Franks as they beamed their lights on the girls. McKenzie swallowed the lump in her throat.

A plan quickly formed in her mind. She leaned toward Alex and whispered, "Now's the time to try out Kate's video sunglasses."

Alex nodded. McKenzie stepped away from Alex and moved toward the ATV. The Frankses followed her with their light, leaving Alex in the shadows. Out of the corner of her eye, McKenzie saw her friend slip the backpack off and fumble inside.

"Just what do you think you're doing here?" Mrs. Franks said angrily.

McKenzie cleared her throat, and her voice came out all squeaky. "We were looking for the missing sea lion pups, and we found them. You stole them, didn't you?"

I can't believe I actually accused them! My plan had better work, she thought. Her knees began to tremble.

"Oh, I see you found cute little Mario and Bianca," Mr. Franks said sarcastically. "Well, you'll never be able to prove it. We've got a truck coming any minute now to take them away."

"Where are you taking them? You won't hurt them, will you?" McKenzie stepped toward Alex.

"Of course we won't hurt them." Mrs. Franks laughed crazily as she kept the light focused on McKenzie. "But I think we need to turn you two over to the cops. This cave is private property, and you're trespassing."

"But you stole the sea lion pups. You just admitted it," McKenzie said, watching Alex return the backpack to her shoulder.

"No one will believe you. Like we told you a minute ago, we're taking the sea lions away. We'll have this setup torn down in minutes," Mr. Franks continued.

"You know, girls," Mrs. Franks explained in a sickly sweet voice. "We're very well known around here as sea lion experts. No one will believe you. Don't even try to convince anyone, or you'll be the talk of the town. And not in a good way, if you know what I mean."

Bzzzzz! Bzzzzz! Mr. Franks grabbed the walkie-talkie on his belt and answered. "We'll be there in a sec. Over."

He walked to the ATV and climbed on. "How lucky can I get? The truck is already here," he said to Mrs. Franks.

Mr. Franks started the ATV, and Mrs. Franks climbed in

beside him. He shoved it in reverse and turned it around. As he headed for the glow from the brightly lit pool chamber, Mrs. Franks motioned for them to follow on foot.

"You girls might as well sit tight for a while," she said when they arrived back at the sea lions' makeshift pool. "You're not going anywhere until we're out of here."

McKenzie's mind raced. *We have to find some way to get out of here, but we'll never get by them if we try to go out the way we came in.* She reached into her jeans pocket and felt the cool touch of her cell phone.

As if reading their minds, Mrs. Franks said, "Forget about your cell phones working down here. That's why we have these walkie-talkies." Turning to Alex, she added, "What's with the sunglasses, girlie?"

McKenzie groaned. Alex slipped the glasses back into the backpack. Mrs. Franks walked away, helping her husband move boxes and trunks full of supplies.

Alex leaned over and whispered in McKenzie's ear. "How will we get out of here?"

"I'm working on it," McKenzie said. As she wiped her sweaty palms on her jeans she felt a slight bulge in the pocket. *The cave map!* She had forgotten all about it. Leaning toward Alex, she whispered and nodded toward the passageway they had just traveled, "Let's head back down that tunnel. It's our only chance."

The girls stood and edged back toward the gaping black hole. When they arrived at the entrance, McKenzie flicked on her flashlight and ran. Her tennis shoes pounded the rocky floor while Alex sprinted beside her.

"Hey, get back here!" Mrs. Franks screamed.

"Aah, leave them alone," Mr. Franks answered. "They'll

never find their way out. We'll come back for them later."

When the girls reached the fork in the tunnel, McKenzie stopped to catch her breath. She pulled the map out of her pocket. "Let's see if we can find another way out. We'll have to hurry if we want to save Mario and Bianca before the Frankses take them away."

Alex beamed her flashlight at the map. "We must be here." She pointed her finger at a fork in the tunnel just off the main chamber.

"I think you're right. This tunnel will lead to the entrance by the cove. We don't want to go that way, or we'll be stranded." McKenzie traced her finger along another line on the map. "If we take the tunnel on the right, there's another way out. It looks like it comes out about a half mile north of here, just off the main road. I think it's our only chance."

"Let's go. I don't want to be trapped in here," Alex said with a trembling voice. "What if they don't come back for us?"

"It doesn't matter. They don't know we have a map. We'll be out of here in no time," McKenzie said, trying to convince herself.

The girls hurried as fast as they dared down the passageway. The chill had crept into McKenzie's bones. She walked faster, trying to warm up. A horrible thought crept into her mind. *What if the map is wrong?*

She pushed the thought away and kept walking. *How far underground are we?* A new thought rushed in. She had never before been claustrophobic, but the farther they walked, the more the walls seemed to close in on her. *Dear God, get us out of here, please!*

She halted suddenly when they came to another fork in the tunnel. Turning to Alex, she pulled her map out again. "Oh,

251

no. The map only shows one tunnel. Which way do we go?"

Alex squinted, peering at the map. Then she turned and shined her light back and forth between the two tunnels. "The tunnel to the right looks like it curves back quite a bit. The other one goes straight like the one on the map. I think it's the one we want."

McKenzie glanced in both directions. "Okay, let's go. We can always come back."

McKenzie started down the left passageway, the beam from her flashlight bouncing off the dark, musty walls. The circle of light began to grow smaller and dimmer. "Oh, no, Alex. My batteries are going dead! We should have only been using one flashlight."

"Shut yours off. We'll use mine." Alex moved closer to McKenzie.

With Alex holding the light, the girls crept farther down the tunnel. *Thump-thump! Thump-thump!* McKenzie's heart felt like it could burst out of her chest. Water gurgled somewhere ahead.

"Do you hear that?" she stopped and asked. "Maybe we're coming to an underground stream."

McKenzie stared ahead and didn't see the drop-off until it was too late. Her foot slipped. Her body crashed to the floor, twisting and bouncing as she slid down a wet embankment.

McKenzie screamed.

"McKenzie!" Alex shouted.

Cold air rushed at McKenzie's face. She shot down the slippery slope on her backside. She flailed her arms, feeling like she was on a giant waterslide in complete darkness. A dot of light in the distance grew bigger and bigger.

Bouncing over a bump at the bottom, she sailed through the air like a rag doll. She splashed into a pool of icy water. She stood in the knee-high water, turning as a scream pierced the silence. A beam of light flew down the hill behind her. Seconds later, Alex landed with a splash at McKenzie's feet.

McKenzie sputtered and caught her breath. A beam of light waved eerily beneath the water. Reaching in, she pulled out Alex's waterproof flashlight.

"Are you okay?" McKenzie pulled her friend to her feet.

"I think so," Alex said in between coughing fits. "But where are we?"

McKenzie saw daylight coming through the opening of the tunnel about thirty yards away. Pulling her cell phone from her pocket, she held it above the water, hoping it wasn't too wet to work. She plodded toward the light as the water grew deeper. When she reached the opening, she stood in waist-high water, staring into the bright sunlight.

"We're at the inlet in the cove, Alex!" she cried.

Seconds later, the girls climbed onto the large boulder outside the cave entrance they had climbed the other day. The warmth of the rock felt good beneath McKenzie's cold, wet body. "See if your phone stayed dry inside the backpack."

McKenzie sighed with relief as she punched in a number on Alex's phone. After a few seconds a voice answered on the other end. "Mr. C. This is McKenzie. We need you to come get us in your boat, but first, please call the police. I'm losing my signal. We've found Mario and Bianca. . ."

●—●—●

"Look at Susie," Alex said after she snapped a picture. "She's so happy to have her pups back."

Aunt Becca smiled as she stood beside the girls at the Sea

Lion Harbor observation area. "If you hadn't found the pups when you did, the Frankses would have gotten away. The police got to the cave as the truck was ready to leave. Though your video sunglasses worked like a charm, the Frankses confessed again to the police. They planned to train the pups and then sell them to a circus, just like you thought."

McKenzie felt a little sorry for the Frankses when she heard they were arrested. But when she saw Susie playing with her pups again, she knew they had done the right thing by calling the police. She thanked God silently. Without His help they never could have saved Mario and Bianca.

"If I hurry, maybe I can enlarge this picture of Susie and her pups at the photo shop for the contest tomorrow," Alex said, "since I never got a shot of the whales."

I think I'll submit the photo of Alex to the contest, too, McKenzie thought.

Later that evening, both girls handed their photos over to the contest chairman inside the community building in Newport. "You can't see mine until tomorrow," McKenzie said with a grin. "It's a surprise."

After breakfast the next morning, Aunt Becca drove the girls to the festival in Newport. McKenzie held the morning paper in her lap. A picture of the two Camp Club Girls graced the front page. VACATIONING GIRLS CRACK SEA LION SMUGGLING RING, the headline read.

"Wow, we're famous," Alex said with a giggle.

"I can't believe the owners of Sea Park invited us to swim with the sea lions today. The owners are bringing some new trainers in," McKenzie said excitedly.

After Aunt Becca parked the car, the three hopped out. Music blared over the loudspeakers as they walked down the crowded sidewalks. McKenzie could detect wonderful smells from popcorn, hot dogs, and nachos to caramel apples and ice cream. Little kids stood in line to get their faces painted.

"Here we are, girls," Aunt Becca said, ushering them into the community building.

A mingling of voices echoed throughout the hall as people walked about, looking at the pictures on display racks. The girls walked through the crowd, peering over shoulders, and looking for their photos.

"There's mine," Alex exclaimed, ducking beneath a man's arm. "I got second place!" Her fingers touched the red ribbon hanging on the side of her picture of Susie and the pups.

"Congratulations!" McKenzie said, "Now, let's look for mine."

Dodging in between spectators, she finally found her picture. A red, white, and blue honorable mention ribbon hung beside it. Alex's eyes grew wide.

Alex grinned. "I didn't even know you took my picture that day."

Aunt Becca stood behind the girls, admiring McKenzie's picture of Alex saving the little girl from drowning in Devil's Churn. No one spoke for a minute, but then Aunt Becca glanced at her watch. "We'd better head back toward Florence. We don't want the staff at Sea Park to wait on us."

On the way to the park, McKenzie suddenly understood the importance of caring for God's creatures. At times she had thought they would never find the pups. But God had strengthened her faith by keeping them safe until they could be rescued.

Later, McKenzie and Alex stood beside the sea lion arena, wearing black wet suits. McKenzie beamed as a national TV news crew focused their cameras on Alex, reporting on her rescue of the little girl in Devil's Churn.

Minutes later, the crew followed Alex as she approached McKenzie, their cameras still rolling. Aunt Becca stood beside them, holding Alex's camcorder.

"Hello. I'm McKenzie Phillips and this is Alexis Howell, coming to you live from Sea Park in Florence, Oregon. Today we're going to help train sea lions for the park's most famous show. Want to join us?"

McKenzie slid her goggles on and turned to the two sea lions floating in the pool behind her. She climbed onto the ledge and held her breath. With a lunge, she leaped into the air, landing in the pool with an ungraceful cannonball splash.

Camp Club Girls

Bailey's
ESTES PARK EXCITEMENT

Linda McQuinn Carlblom

Two Mysteries, Five Days!

Crsiiish!

The ground shook.

Bailey Chang grabbed her father's arm.

"Does Colorado have earthquakes?" she shouted over the sudden noise.

"Stampede!" someone yelled.

Bailey's dad grabbed her. With his other hand he snatched her friend Kate Oliver. He dragged them to the safety of the Stanley Hotel's front porch. Bailey's mom and older sister, Trina, ran up the steps.

A herd of beautiful elk thundered across the lawn of the old hotel. Within seconds, only a cloud of dust and an unnatural silence remained.

Moments earlier Bailey's greatest fear was of the historic Stanley Hotel itself. Nestled in the majestic Rocky Mountains in Estes Park, Colorado, it had stared menacingly at Bailey, each window a glaring eye, as her family drove up and parked. Its deathly white walls and blood-red tile roof eerily reminded her of the ghosts rumored to live in it. The bright sun hid behind clouds on this early October afternoon.

Bailey swallowed hard, her dark brown almond eyes wide. In her nine years, she had never stayed in a haunted hotel. Nor had she almost been trampled by a stampeding herd of elk.

"Is everyone okay?" Mr. Chang asked as the dust settled.

"I think so," Mrs. Chang answered. "Are you girls all right?"

"Except for being almost killed in a stampede, we're great!" fourteen-year-old Trina mouthed off.

"A—Are we really going to stay here?" Bailey asked her father, George Chang, who had brought the family along on a business trip.

"Yes," he answered matter-of-factly. "It's a well-known hotel, highly recommended. I'm sure that stampede was merely a fluke."

Bailey looked at her eleven-year-old friend, Kate Oliver. Kate's eyes were as big as twin full moons behind her black, rectangular glasses. She nervously tucked her sandy, shoulder-length hair behind her ears. Biscuit the Wonder Dog whined and hid behind Kate's leg. Bailey, Kate, and the other four Camp Club Girls had rescued Biscuit when they first met at Camp Discovery. Though Biscuit lived with Kate, he still took part in some of the girls' mysteries.

"But what if it's true, Dad?" Bailey asked.

"What if what's true?"

"What if there really are ghosts in there?" Bailey pointed at the hotel.

"Bailey." Mrs. Chang's hands rested firmly on her hips, her blond head tilted. "Do you really think your father would let you stay in a dangerous place?"

"Think about it, Bales," Trina said, relaxing now that the threat had passed. "Mom and Dad barely let us go to sleepovers without interrogating our friends' parents first. They're pretty picky about where we sleep."

Bailey's shoulders slumped slightly. "I guess you're right."

Kate looked over a pamphlet for the hotel that she'd picked up at the Denver, Colorado, airport. "Maybe we can study this brochure about the hotel and investigate the ghost sightings and mysterious sounds people have reported."

She grinned at Bailey and grabbed Biscuit. "And Biscuit the Wonder Dog will sniff out clues for us." Biscuit's whole body wriggled and wagged as he licked Kate's face.

With the stampede over, Bailey's family returned to unloading their Honda CR-V in front of the hotel. "Come on. Let's go get checked in," Mr. Chang said, starting toward the main entrance.

The huge front porch seemed friendly enough, Bailey thought, now that she didn't need to escape from rampaging elk. Cushioned white wicker rocking chairs, love seats, and tables sat waiting for people to relax in their comfort. *Maybe it won't be so bad.* Bailey took a deep breath and stepped through the doorway.

Bailey smelled old wood and lemon oil as she entered the magnificent lobby, pulling her pink camouflage suitcase. Gleaming hardwood floors reflected her awestruck face. She was so busy looking around that she nearly ran into an enormous flower bouquet on a round, glass-topped table.

A wide, grand staircase with a white banister and glossy wood handrail invited—or dared—guests to go upstairs and explore ghostly nooks and crannies. On each end of the lobby overstuffed couches and chairs rested on large area rugs in front of fireplaces. An old green car with yellow wooden wheels in mint condition stood on display near one of the fireplaces, protected by thick red velvet ropes.

"That car's called the Stanley Steamer," Kate explained to

Bailey. "Here's a picture of it in this brochure. The guy who started this hotel, F. O. Stanley, invented it. See, there's his picture."

The girls surveyed antique black-and-white portraits of F. O. Stanley on gray-green wallpapered walls.

"Wow," Bailey said. "This looks like where a movie star would stay."

"I've never stayed in a place this fancy before." Kate shoved her glasses up her small, roundish nose. "Sure beats the Super Six where we usually stay."

"Sure does." Mrs. Chang turned a slow circle to take it all in. "I'm glad George's company is paying for this."

Bailey parked her suitcase and joined her dad, who was standing at the registration desk. Her mom, Trina, and Kate followed close behind.

"Usually the elk are quite friendly as they roam about the town," the clerk with a name badge that said "Barbara" was saying. "But for some reason they've become aggressive in the last few weeks, so be cautious around them."

"What made them become so aggressive?" Bailey asked, standing on tiptoe to see over the counter.

The registrar shrugged her shoulders. "One minute they're calm and the next thing you know, they're charging. No one knows why."

"That's unusual." Kate scratched her head. "There must be a reason for their sudden change."

"Don't worry," Mrs. Chang said, putting one protective arm around Bailey's shoulder while patting Kate's back with the other. "We'll be careful. Right, girls?"

The two nodded but smiled at each another. Biscuit yawned and whined at the same time.

Barbara leaned over the counter. "Is that your dog?"

"He's mine." Kate smiled proudly then picked up the wiggly fur ball. "This is Biscuit." The dog's whole body wagged in a friendly Biscuit greeting.

Barbara frowned. "Is he house-trained?"

"Of course!" Kate answered.

"Does he bark?"

Bailey almost blurted out, "Not as much as you!" but Kate answered coolly, "Only when threatened."

Mr. Chang quickly stepped in. "I'm sure Biscuit will be no trouble. We'll make sure he stays quiet and doesn't make a mess. And if he does, we'll take full responsibility for any extra cleaning charges."

"Just make sure you keep him on a leash." Barbara gave the Changs their keys and a map of the hotel, and then she called a bellhop to take the suitcases to room 412. "The elevator is right over there or you can take these stairs," she instructed the Changs, pointing to her left.

"Let's ride the elevator," Kate suggested after hooking a leash to Biscuit's collar.

"After walking through the airports, I'll be glad to take the easy way to our room." Mrs. Chang smiled. "I can't wait to get out of these shoes!"

The five climbed into the elevator and Bailey pushed the button for the fourth floor. A ding signaled their arrival. The doors opened to a long hallway with plush burgundy carpet.

"Look at that wallpaper," Bailey said in awe. The lower portion of the wall was painted white, and the upper was papered with a white-on-white embossed design. Bailey touched it. "It's not wall*paper*—it's wall *fabric*!"

"Whoa!" Kate reached out to feel it, too, before following

the arrow directing them to room 412.

As the girls walked down the hall, two boys who looked about their ages came out of one of the rooms. Lunging, Biscuit growled and barked at them.

Kate yanked him back with the leash. "Biscuit!" She picked up the little dog and looked at the boys. "Sorry."

One of the boys shrugged while the other gave her a fiery glare.

"I hope that isn't any indication of how this week will be." Mr. Chang stopped outside of room 412. He slid his magnetic card through the slot and pushed the door open.

Bailey walked in and eyed the sparsely furnished room. "Cool! It looks so old-fashioned!" Two full-size beds with tall posts at each corner stood against one wall. A wooden table and chair sat in another corner. Bailey looked around. "Look how high these beds are! They even have little steps to help you get into them!"

A rollaway bed was pushed along one wall, ready to open.

"Let me guess," Trina said. "That's my bed."

"You girls can trade off if you want." Mrs. Chang looked softly at her older daughter.

"That's okay. At least I won't have to sleep with anyone."

"I'll let you use our stairs if you want help getting into your rollaway," Bailey offered.

Trina laughed. "I think I can get into this bed without steps. But thanks."

"No way!" Kate shouted. "Come see this bathroom!"

Bailey hustled to the door and peered in. A claw-foot bathtub sat next to the toilet. A freestanding toilet paper holder and a pedestal sink completed the decor.

"I can't wait to take a bath in that tub," Bailey said. "It's just like in the old movies. I'll need lots of bubbles."

Back in the bedroom, Mrs. Chang put her suitcase on the bed and began to unpack. "Dad and I will take this bed and you can have the one by the window," she said to Bailey and Kate.

"I have a meeting this afternoon, but you can get settled while I'm gone," Mr. Chang said. "I should be back before supper."

"Okay. See ya later, Dad." Bailey hugged her dad's neck. "Don't get run over by any wild elk!" she joked.

Kate climbed onto the bed by the window. "Let's look at this brochure to see what we can find out about this place."

"Yeah, maybe we'll learn where the ghosts hang out." Bailey shuddered, then grinned. She sprawled out on the bed beside Kate.

"Let's see." Kate laid out the brochure before her like a map. "This tells the history of the hotel and about F. O. Stanley, inventor of the Stanley Steamer automobile, who came to Estes Park for health reasons. He and his wife spent a summer here in 1903 and fell in love with the area. Because of his health improvement and the beauty of the valley they decided to stay and opened the Stanley Hotel in 1909."

"Interesting," Bailey remarked.

"Sorta, but listen. . ." Kate's eyes sparkled. "The hotel was the inspiration for a novel by Stephen King. It's also been used as a location for a bunch of films."

"Cool! We're actually staying where they made movies!" Bailey exclaimed. "Maybe we'll see some stars. Or *maybe* some of their stardom will rub off on *me!*"

"You don't need anything to rub off on you to become a star," Mrs. Chang said. "You're special in your own right. But remember, you need to finish your education before you run off to Hollywood."

Bailey laughed and sat up. "But wouldn't it be awesome? To be a famous actress making big movies?"

Trina rolled her eyes as she hung one of her sweaters in the closet. "You've dreamed that dream for s–o–o–o long."

Bailey glared at her sister. "So what?"

"So you have to do something besides sit around and dream about it, that's what." Trina poked her younger sister in the ribs. Bailey rolled to her side, giggling.

Biscuit jumped onto the bed to check out the commotion then nested comfortably against Bailey's back.

"All right. Now, where were we?" Kate asked, looking at the brochure. "Oh yeah! I was just getting to the part about the ghosts!"

"Oooooo!" Bailey gave her best ghost shriek, making Biscuit howl.

Kate laughed as she scooped the little dog into her arms. "Don't worry, boy. Ghosts aren't real."

"What's it say?"

Kate pushed up her glasses. "It says F. O. Stanley's ghost is the most notable one seen. It usually appears in the lobby or the Billiard Room, which was his favorite room when he was alive. His wife, Flora, has been seen playing the piano in the Music Room. Cleaning crews also have heard strange noises coming from room 418, as well as finding the bed rumpled when the room has been empty. And guests say they hear children playing in the halls at night. One guest saw a man wearing a cowboy hat and a mustache staring out of the window of room 408 when no one was in the room."

"Since even numbers are on one side of the hall and odd

on the other, that makes room 408 only two doors down from ours!" Bailey exclaimed. "Do you think we'll see any of the ghosts?"

Kate answered in her scariest voice, "You never know," then laughed evilly.

"Stop it! You'll scare Biscuit." Bailey petted the dog.

"Biscuit?" Trina glanced sideways at her sister. "You sure he's the only one you're worried about Kate scaring?"

"Well, I'm not scared of any fake ghosts, if that's what you mean." Bailey crossed her arms defiantly and lifted her chin.

Trina smirked. "Right."

Kate pushed her glasses up. "Since ghosts aren't real, these sightings and sounds must be done by some special effects." Bailey could see the wheels turning in Kate's head. "Maybe we can uncover how they do them."

"Yeah!" Bailey agreed. "Another Camp Club Girls mystery! Does the brochure say anything else that might help us figure it out?"

"Not much. Just that room 401 is usually the ghost hunters' favorite room." Kate put the pamphlet on the nightstand.

"Hey, check this out," Trina called, pulling back the curtains.

Bailey and Kate jumped up from the bed.

"Awesome!" Bailey pressed her nose to the window. Below their fourth floor window was a grassy courtyard where elk wandered among the guests as if they'd checked in and paid for a room themselves.

"They don't seem aggressive," Kate said.

"Maybe not now, but you can't be too careful around wild animals," Mrs. Chang warned.

"I wonder what they eat," Bailey said. "Maybe we could get some elk food and feed them."

"No way." Mrs. Chang shook her head in no uncertain terms. "You heard what the lady at the desk said. They can become aggressive without warning. Wildlife can be very unpredictable."

Trina moved away from the window and went back to unpacking her suitcase. "I wonder what makes them get angry and charge people."

"Maybe they're afraid the people will hurt them," suggested Bailey.

"Or maybe someone did hurt them and it has made them skittish," Kate offered.

"Maybe they've got some hideous sickness like mad elk disease and it will gradually infect the whole elk population!" Bailey grimaced.

Trina laughed. "You two have a lot of crazy ideas. Maybe they're just sick of tourists like us invading their town."

"Looks like we'll have two mysteries to work on while we're here." Bailey held up one finger. "One, what makes the ghosts and spooky sounds, and two, what made the elk turn mean."

Bailey looked at Kate, two fingers still raised like a peace sign. A grin spread slowly across her face. Kate beamed back then raised her hand and Bailey high-fived it. The Camp Club Girls had two mysteries and only five days to solve them.

Ghost Hunt

"Mom, can Kate and I go explore the hotel?"

Placing clothes into the dresser drawers, Bailey's mother answered, "I suppose. But take the hotel map with you and your cell phone, just in case you get turned around."

"Okay, thanks!" Bailey turned toward the door.

"And don't forget Biscuit," Trina added with a smile.

"We would never forget you!" Kate cooed in a baby voice to her dog.

"And stay together," Mrs. Chang warned.

"We will," Kate promised.

"You still have the brochure about the hotel?" Bailey asked her friend.

"Right here." Kate patted her back pocket before hooking Biscuit's leash to his collar. "Let's go, boy."

"Don't let any ghosts sneak up on you!" Trina called as they left.

Bailey laughed. "That shouldn't be a problem since ghosts don't exist!"

"Let's find room 401 while we're on this floor," Kate suggested as the door closed behind them. "Since it's the ghost hunters' favorite room, maybe we'll see something that will explain how they do some of the special effects."

"Good idea." Bailey looked both ways down the hall. "Our room number is 412, and I think the numbers were smaller nearer the elevator, so let's go that way."

"Even-numbered rooms are on our side, and odd on the other."

Bailey studied the oval plates outside each door that showed the room numbers. "Here it is," she whispered when she spotted room 401.

"Why are we whispering?" Kate asked.

Bailey laughed. "I don't know. I feel like I'm spying or something."

Kate examined the walls and then inspected the carpet. "I don't see anything suspicious. Do you?"

Bailey shook her head as she inspected the hallway. "There's a speaker, but that's where the music is coming from. Nothing weird about that."

"We'll have to keep our eyes and ears open," Kate said, still searching. "I'm sure this isn't that complicated if we just keep thinking."

Trying to peer underneath the door, Bailey ventured, "The tricks could be hidden inside the room." She stood back up. "I can't see anything. Maybe we'll have better luck at room 217, the room where they say the author of that scary book stayed."

"It's worth a try," Kate said.

The girls found an elevator and stepped inside.

"Did you read that book or see the movie that was made from it?" Bailey asked as the doors closed.

"No, it's a horror movie. My parents won't let me watch scary movies like that. Did you see it?"

"Nope." Bailey grinned mischievously. "I think our

parents are just alike. Mine would never let me see scary movies, either."

"Hey, I wonder if Elizabeth saw it." The elevator bell dinged as the doors opened onto the second floor. Kate stepped out first with Biscuit in tow. "She's fourteen. Maybe her parents let her watch those kind of movies."

Bailey flipped open her cell phone and pushed *E* in her contacts. Elizabeth's number showed up and Bailey pushed TALK. Kate spotted a sign that pointed to room 217 and they followed its arrow.

"Elizabeth? It's Bailey."

"And Kate!" Kate shouted into the phone.

"Well, this is a surprise!" Elizabeth said. "What are you two up to? Are you really together or are we conferenced in?"

"We're together," Bailey said, and went on to explain where they were and why. "And guess what? We've already got two mysteries to solve!"

"Two?" Elizabeth asked.

"Yeah, the elk here have gone bonkers," Bailey explained. "I think they might need a counselor or something!"

Elizabeth laughed. "Maybe we should have them talk to McKenzie. She's good at figuring people out, maybe she could help the elk, too!"

"Maybe! So that's our first mystery." Bailey's voice rose with excitement. "Our second one is hunting ghosts. People say ghosts live in this hotel. But since we know ghosts aren't real, we're trying to figure out who is making them seem real, and what special effects they use."

"Wow! Sounds exciting!" Elizabeth paused a moment. "So how can I help? You know I love a good mystery."

Bailey told her that a book by Stephen King was inspired by the hotel, and that a movie had been made from the book.

"Have you ever seen it?" Bailey looked expectantly at Kate.

"If it's a Stephen King movie, I haven't seen it," Elizabeth answered. "My folks won't let me. Too scary." She added, "And I'm glad."

Bailey laughed and then shook her head at Kate to relay Elizabeth's answer. "Yeah, I know what you mean. I don't really want to see those scary movies, either. We just thought since you're older you might have seen it."

"Let me talk!" Kate grabbed the phone. "Hi, Elizabeth! Biscuit says hi, too."

The girls chatted for a minute and then Elizabeth said, "Well, you know I'm praying for you two! Keep me posted on what you find out."

"We appreciate your prayers," Kate said. "We'll let you know what we find out and if you can help out on anything else. If you talk to any of the others, let them know we'll be calling or e-mailing them soon with all the mystery details."

Kate flipped the phone closed just as they came to the end of the hall.

A metal room plate by the door read 217.

"Here we are! Just think. Movie stars stood at this very place we're standing." Bailey nearly felt faint from the rush.

"And just think," Kate repeated just as dreamily. "A future movie star is standing here right now!"

"Oh, stop." Bailey waved her hand. "You're just saying that."

"You never know. It could happen." Kate dug in her pocket and brought out a pen. "Here. Let me take your picture, just in case. Then we can say I predicted your fame on this very day at this very moment outside this very door!"

"Hold it! That's not a camera. It's a pen." Bailey shook her head.

"Ah, you *think* it's a pen, but it's really a tiny camera!" Kate smiled brightly. "I've been dying for the right moment to show you my latest gadget!"

"Let me see that." Bailey took the pen from Kate. She clicked the top of it, and the ballpoint came down just like a real pen. She scribbled on the corner of the brochure. Blue ink looped round and round. "So it's a real pen *and* a camera. How does it work?"

"You look into the silver clip to see what the camera sees. Then click the top and it takes the picture."

"Did I take a picture when I clicked it before?" Bailey asked.

Kate shook her head. "It only functions as a camera when it's held on its side. Up and down, it's just your ordinary, average blue pen. Turn it over and it switches to camera mode."

"That's awesome!" Bailey squealed. "Let's try it. Take my picture." She struck her most glamorous pose.

Kate held the pen on its side and clicked the top.

"How do we see the picture?"

"We have to unscrew the pen and remove the memory chip inside. I have a special stick to put it into that will fit the computer, then we download the pictures."

"I can't wait to see how it turns out." Bailey bounced up and down on her toes.

"Me, too." Kate looked around. "Let's see if we can find any clues here."

A door burst open down the hall and a man bolted out. "Oh no! We've got to go help them!" he shouted to the woman behind him.

"I hope no one was hurt!" she cried as she and the man ran past the girls.

Bailey looked at Kate and they took off after the man and woman, who had stopped in front of the elevator. The elevator doors opened just as the girls caught up and they all climbed inside.

"What's going on?" Bailey asked.

"We were looking out our window when we saw an elk run through the courtyard knocking a boy to the ground," the man answered. "We're going to see if he needs help."

"My husband is a doctor," the woman explained.

Bailey nodded somberly, and Kate petted Biscuit.

The elevator door opened into the main lobby. The doctor and his wife rushed to the courtyard where the elk had charged.

Bailey and Kate stood a short distance away but stayed close enough to see and hear what was going on. In the courtyard, a boy who looked about six years old was stretched on the ground. He didn't appear to be injured, but his father was kneeling over him. The doctor hurried to them.

"Sir, I'm Dr. Gibbins," the man said, kneeling by the father. "I saw what happened from my room and came immediately in case the boy was injured. Is he your son?"

"Yes," the father answered. "Thank you."

The boy moaned and turned his head.

"Did the elk step on him or just knock him down?" asked Dr. Gibbins.

"He was knocked down and bumped his head."

The little boy tried to sit up.

"Hold on there, son." The doctor gently checked his arms and legs to make sure no bones were broken.

"Daddy!"

"I'm right here, Robby," his father answered tenderly.

"I think he's going to be fine," the doctor told him.

"Seems to have gotten the wind knocked out of him and a good bump on his head when he went down, but nothing too serious." He helped the child sit up.

"Thank you," the father said again, clasping the doctor's hand.

Robby's dad stood up and picked up his son. "Let's go see Mommy."

From the sidelines, Bailey looked at Kate. "Wow! That was scary."

"Guess what they said about the elk was true." Kate stuffed her pen back in her pocket.

"Did you have that out the whole time?" Bailey asked.

Kate nodded. "I took a few shots just in case it turned into a major news story or something." She laughed. "They might need some pictures for the evening news."

Bailey rolled her eyes. "You're always thinking."

"It'll be a good test to see how well the pictures turn out since we were farther away."

"I wonder what made the elk run like that?" Bailey eyed the courtyard.

"Something must have set him off."

The two girls strolled through the courtyard looking for any clue of what might have spooked the elk but found nothing.

"This really is a mystery." Bailey sighed. "A mystery with no clues."

"There's bound to be something we're missing," Kate encouraged. "We'll figure it out."

"Come on. Let's head back to the room."

◆━━◆━━◆

That night, while Mr. Chang and Trina went to get ice, and Mrs. Chang read a book, the girls reviewed their day.

"After looking around here a bit I think we're starting to learn our way around, don't you?" asked Bailey.

"Yeah, the map in the brochure was helpful," Kate replied. Then wrinkles lined her forehead. "I felt bad about that little boy getting hurt by the elk."

"I know. Me, too," Bailey said.

"I'm glad he seemed to be all right."

"That camera-pen of yours is awesome!" Bailey grinned like she'd just won a prize at the fair. "I can't wait to see the pictures you took today."

The hotel room door opened and Mr. Chang and Trina walked in with a full ice bucket. "Anyone want some ice for a bedtime drink of water?"

"Yeah!" Bailey ran into the bathroom to grab the plastic-wrapped glasses. They scooped ice into each one and added water from the tap. "Thanks!"

"Are we ready for lights-out?" Mr. Chang asked.

"Just a minute," Kate replied. "Let me spread Biscuit's blanket at the foot of the bed." She and Bailey laid out the paw-printed fleece blanket, and Biscuit turned a tight, complete circle before plopping down on it. "All set!"

Mr. Chang flipped off the light. "Good night."

"'Night, Dad." Bailey lay in the dark with her eyes open. Moments later, she heard soft giggling.

"Girls, get to sleep." Mrs. Chang used her no-nonsense voice.

"We're *trying* to," Bailey answered, confused.

The giggling came again, this time followed by childlike voices.

"Bailey, you heard your mother," Mr. Chang warned sternly.

"Dad, it isn't us!" Bailey complained.

"Then who is it?" Trina smarted off.

"How should I know?"

The voices came again, the words unclear, but sure.

"It's the ghost children in the hallway!" Bailey yelled, sitting straight up.

Ghost Children of the Night

Biscuit gave a low, throaty growl.

"Ghost children?" Mrs. Chang said, getting up. "Really, Bailey, I think you've been reading too many mysteries."

Bailey switched on the bedside lamp. "Hand me that hotel brochure, Kate." She pointed to Kate's suitcase, where she could see the brochure sticking out.

Again they heard faint laughing and children's voices.

"Did it ever occur to you that those could be real children out there, rather than 'ghost children,' as you call them?" Trina leaned on one elbow in her bed.

"Listen to this," Bailey said, folding the pamphlet back. "Guests often say they hear children playing in the hallway at night. One couple even checked out of the hotel very early in the morning complaining that the children in the hallway kept them up all night. However, there were no children booked in the hotel at the time. The children have since been called 'ghost children of the night.'" Bailey lowered the hotel brochure and nodded emphatically. "See? Ghost children."

"I seem to recall seeing some boys in this hallway when we brought our luggage to our room," Mr. Chang said. "Two boys. We could be hearing them, or any other children who are checked in."

"If we hear the voices again, can I peek out the door to see if anyone's out there?" Bailey asked.

"If you promise to get right to sleep afterward," Mr. Chang answered with a yawn.

"Me, too?" Kate asked.

"You, too."

"Yeah, that way there'll be a witness when the body snatchers grab Bailey," Trina teased.

"Trina!" Mrs. Chang scolded. "That will be enough from you. Can we all just relax and get to sleep?" She flipped the light off.

Hee-hee-heeeeee!

"That's them!" Bailey said, jumping into her slippers and bathrobe. "I'm out of here!"

Trina groaned. Biscuit barked fiercely then bounded off the bed and ran to the door.

"Me, too!" Kate felt her way through the dark after Bailey.

Cautiously, Bailey slid the security chain off the door and slowly opened it. Light from the hallway spread into the room in a giant wedge. She poked her head out into the hall and looked from side to side. "I don't see anyone."

"No surprise there," Kate said, joining her in the doorway.

"Mom, can we go down the hall?" Bailey whisper-yelled.

"Just grab the key off the table first. And stay in our hall," Mrs. Chang instructed in a tired mumble. "I don't want you wandering the entire hotel in your pajamas."

Bailey felt her cell phone on the table and opened it, shining its light to find the key. "Got it," she told her mom. "We'll be back in just a minute."

"Stay, Biscuit," Kate commanded. "We'll be right back."

With the phone lighting their path, the girls crept back to

the door and stepped into the lighted hallway. Bailey shoved her phone into her bathrobe pocket. A high-pitched giggle greeted them, followed by muffled children's voices that sounded like they were telling secrets.

"There it is again!" Kate's eyes scanned the walls then moved up and down from floor to ceiling as if looking for some clue as to where the voices came from.

"Sounds like they're coming from down here," Bailey whispered loudly, walking to the far end of the hall. The voices spoke again, though still not clearly.

"There must be wires to a speaker somewhere," Kate said. She ran her hand along the wall, stopping at the corner. "Here!"

Bailey hustled over to her friend.

"Feel right here," Kate instructed.

Bailey touched the wallpaper on one wall then continued around the corner. "Aha! A bump!" She ran her hand vertically along the bump and found that it went higher than she could reach. "Our wire!"

"Now we just have to figure out where it runs to and we may have our first solution to the ghost sounds." Kate's eyes sparkled like diamonds, and she gave Bailey a victorious high five.

"Come on," Bailey said. "We'd better go back so my mom doesn't worry."

The two tiptoed back to the room. Bailey lit her cell phone up again once they arrived in the dark room and led the way to their bed. Biscuit jumped at their legs, excited to see them as if they'd been gone for months. Kate and Bailey pulled back the sheets and climbed in, followed by Biscuit, who snuggled into his little nest of blankets on the bed.

"We'll have to investigate some more tomorrow," Kate whispered.

"Should be a great way to start the day!" Bailey smiled and then drifted off to sleep.

●——●——●

The next morning, Bailey woke to the sound of the phone and her father's voice. She rolled over and pulled her pillow over her head.

"Yes, I'll be available in an hour. Thank you. See you then."

Mr. Chang flipped his cell phone closed and said to Mrs. Chang, "William Perkins will meet me in the hotel lobby in an hour for our conference. His wife and children are here with him, and he's bringing them to meet us. They're also staying at this hotel."

"Guess I'd better clean up." Mrs. Chang sprang from the bed and headed to the shower.

"Will has two boys, so I don't imagine the girls will be too interested in hanging out with them much."

"Or will they?" Mrs. Chang said with a sly smile. She laughed and shook her head. "Probably not, but it will be nice to meet them anyway. It's always nice to have a friendly face, just in case you need something." Mrs. Chang turned on the water. "Will you get the girls up while I shower?"

Mr. Chang moved to the girls' bed and whispered, "Biscuit!" The dog stretched and yawned, but soon he was prancing all over Bailey and Kate, nudging Bailey's pillow off her head, licking hands, faces, and feet.

"Biscuit! Stop!" Kate howled, hiding her face in the covers.

"We're too tired. Go away." Bailey rolled over.

"Come on, girls," Mr. Chang said. "Time to get up. Some people are meeting us downstairs in an hour."

"Ugghh," Bailey moaned.

"You, too, Trina." Mr. Chang shook his older daughter's shoulder. "Mr. Perkins is bringing his family to meet us."

"How could you do this to me?" Trina wailed, with all the dismay she could muster at 7:00 a.m.

"Easy!" Mr. Chang chuckled. "Watching you writhe around and moan is good early morning entertainment."

Trina threw a pillow at her father, which he deftly dodged. When she saw him pick up the pillow and pull his arm back to throw it, she jumped up. The pillow landed with a *whoosh* in her empty bed.

"Ha!" Trina laughed. "Missed me!"

"Ha, yourself." Mr. Chang laughed. "I got you up."

Bailey and Kate had pillows in hand ready to throw but put them back down when the action wound down so quickly. "Shucks," Bailey said. "We missed our chance."

An hour later, they stepped out of the elevator into the hotel lobby.

The Perkins family was looking at the old Stanley Steamer car in the lobby when the Changs arrived.

"Will! Great to see you." Mr. Chang and Will Perkins shook hands.

"George, I'd like you to meet my wife, Janice, and my sons, Joseph and Justin."

Bailey inhaled sharply and elbowed Kate. Joseph and Justin were the two boys Biscuit had nearly attacked in the hall the day before. Good thing they'd taken Biscuit for an early morning walk and left him in the room before coming to meet the Perkinses.

"It's a pleasure to meet you," Mr. Chang replied, shaking each of their hands. "This is my wife, Dory, and my two daughters, Trina and Bailey. And this is Bailey's friend Kate."

Bailey smiled politely.

"Hey, aren't you the ones who had that dog in the hallway yesterday?" Justin asked.

Mr. Chang cleared his throat. "I guess we are. I'm sorry, I didn't recognize you. We're terribly sorry about Biscuit barking at you. He's a little skittish being in a new place and off his usual routine."

"No harm done," Mr. Perkins assured him.

Bailey noticed that Justin, the older of the two, was scowling. *What's his problem?*

Her thoughts were interrupted by a friendly looking older man and his wife approaching them. "There they are!" the man said.

"Grandpa!" Joe ran to the couple, who greeted the boy with warm hugs.

"Hungry for some breakfast?" Grandpa asked him.

"Starving!"

Mr. Perkins introduced his parents, Glen and Clara Perkins, to the Changs.

"They live here in Estes Park. That's why I brought the family along," Mr. Perkins explained.

"We're off to have breakfast at the Waffle House," Grandma Perkins said. "You're welcome to join us."

"George and I need to get to our conference," Mr. Perkins said. "But maybe Dory and the girls would like to."

"That would be lovely," Mrs. Chang said before Bailey could signal that she did not want to eat with these grouchy boys. She turned her back to the group and rolled her eyes at Kate.

After getting directions to the Waffle House, Mrs. Chang, Trina, Bailey, and Kate piled into the car. "That was nice of them to invite us to join them for breakfast," Mrs. Chang said.

"Nice if you like eating with Oscar the Grouch," Bailey retorted.

"Bailey!" her mother warned.

Bailey looked down at her lap. "But Mom, those boys are so rude!"

"Maybe they're not morning people," Mrs. Chang said.

"Apparently they're not afternoon people either, since they were so grouchy yesterday when Biscuit barked at them."

"Maybe they're afraid of dogs," Trina said.

"Who could be afraid of sweet little Biscuit?" Kate asked.

"As I recall, Biscuit wasn't exactly his usual, sweet little self when he barked at the boys." Mrs. Chang turned into the Waffle House driveway. "Let's just give them a chance. We don't know what's going on in their lives. Maybe they're having some kind of problems at home or something."

Bailey nodded. She never thought of that.

"Right this way." The hostess grabbed menus and motioned for them to follow her to two tables pushed together.

Bailey sat next to Kate, with Justin and Joe directly across from them. While the adults chatted pleasantly, the children were silent. Bailey cleared her throat. "So how old are you?"

The dark-haired boys shifted in their seats. They seemed uncomfortable making conversation with the girls.

"I'm twelve," Justin said, eyes narrowed.

"And I'm ten," Joe added less than enthusiastically.

"You're about our ages, then," Kate volunteered. "I'm eleven and Bailey's nine."

"What about her?" Justin nodded in Trina's direction.

"That's Trina. She's fourteen."

"Umph," Joe said.

Whatever that means, thought Bailey. She eyed the boys more closely. They weren't bad looking. They could even be considered cute if they smiled more. Freckles sprinkled Joe's nose and round cheeks. Justin's face was more chiseled and his build was more muscular than his younger brother's. His eyes burned with anger or hurt or something Bailey couldn't quite identify. His eyebrows pointed downward in what looked like a permanent frown.

"Did you hear about the elk problem they're having?" Kate asked, trying to be polite.

"Of course we did," Joe snapped. "Our grandparents live here."

"Oh, right," Bailey said. She added, "Did we say something wrong?"

"What do you mean?" Justin placed his hands on the table, palms down as if he were about to jump up.

Bailey shrugged. "Well, you just seem mad at us."

"Why should we like you?" Joe scowled.

"Why shouldn't you?" Kate smiled in spite of herself.

"We don't have anything against you. We just don't like your dog." Justin leaned back and folded his arms.

"Have you had a bad experience with dogs before?" Bailey asked.

Joe watched his older brother, waiting for his answer. "Maybe, maybe not."

"Well, I'm sorry if you did," Kate said. "Biscuit is a really nice dog, and he'd never hurt a flea."

"Whatever." Justin picked up his menu and hid behind it.

"Have you eaten here before?" Bailey asked, changing the subject.

"Our grandparents bring us here all the time," Joe said, suddenly sounding almost friendly.

"What do you recommend?" Kate asked.

"I usually get the Belgian waffles with strawberries and whipped cream." Joe licked his lips.

"What about you, Justin?" Bailey asked.

"I don't have a favorite," he said from behind his menu.

"I'm thinking of the ham and cheese omelet," Kate said. "Ever had it?"

Justin lowered his menu slowly. Bailey saw his jaw clench. "I've had it and it's fine," he said through gritted teeth.

Were those tears in his eyes? Bailey blinked to see more clearly. Too late. The menu was back up again.

The waitress took their orders and they ate their breakfast without much conversation.

Afterward, Mrs. Chang and Trina went to do some shopping while Bailey and Kate took Biscuit for a walk and talked about their strange encounter with the Perkins boys.

"Something was definitely bothering Justin," Kate said.

"No kidding!" Bailey's eyes nearly popped out of her head. "Did you see when you asked him if he'd had the omelet before? I thought he was going to cry!"

"We need to get on our Camp Club Girls website to let the other girls know what's going on around here. So far we have elk gone mad, unexplained ghost noises, and two crabby boys who hate us for no reason." Kate stopped to let Biscuit sniff some bushes.

"Maybe Justin and Joe don't hate us, but they sure do act weird," Bailey said.

Back at their room, Bailey opened her laptop and signed on to the CCG website then clicked on the chat room. Kate pulled out her cell phone and also went to the site.

Bailey: *Hi CCGs. Who's out there?*

Elizabeth: *I'm here.*

McKenzie: *Me, too.*

Sydney: *Me three!*

Alex: *Me four!*

Bailey: *Perfect! Kate and I are in Estes Park and have some weird stuff we may need your help with. We're staying at the Stanley Hotel, which is supposedly haunted. We've heard some strange noises and voices and are trying to find out what causes them.*

McKenzie: *Oooo! Sounds spooky!*

Elizabeth: *How can we help?*

Bailey: *We heard the ghost children of the night in our hall last night.*

Kate: *I found a wire running along the wall under the wallpaper. It probably goes to a speaker somewhere. It was higher than I could reach, so I lost track of it.*

Alex: *Sounds just like a* Scooby Doo *episode! They always have fake ghosts. Maybe you'll run into Shaggy and Scooby while you're there!*

Bailey: *Any hints you can give us?*

Alex: *I think you're on the right track with the speaker wire. You just have to find the speaker.*

Kate: *I figure it's probably a recording. Something probably trips a circuit to start it. But what would be tripping the recording to play?*

Alex: *Look for a switch of some kind. It will most*

> *likely be hidden. Something people would touch unknowingly. Or at least that's how they did it in Scooby.*
>
> Kate: *Great. We'll look around some more.*
>
> Bailey: *We also are trying to find out why the elk (which roam around town just like people!) are suddenly going crazy and are charging for no reason.*

Kate told Bailey, "Tell them about Justin and Joe."

> Bailey: *Kate wants me to tell you about these two boys we met.*
>
> Alex: *Oooo! Sounds interesting!*

Kate rolled her eyes at Bailey. Leave it to Alex to get the wrong idea about boys.

> Bailey: *It's not like that. These boys are crabby. Even Biscuit doesn't like them. We're not sure what's up with them, but we hope to find out.*
>
> Kate: *Bailey has already nicknamed the older one Oscar the Grouch.*
>
> Alex: *And the younger one?*
>
> Bailey: *I'm thinking of Slimey, you know, like Oscar's worm friend on Sesame Street.*
>
> McKenzie: *LOL. Maybe they're insecure and trying to make up for it by being tough.*
>
> Bailey: *Maybe. We don't know too much about them yet except their dad works with my dad*

and their grandparents live here in Estes Park.

Elizabeth: *Do you know much about elk? What would spook them?*

Bailey: *We haven't researched elk yet. Any volunteers?*

Sydney: *I can check them out. My Uncle Jerome lives in a cabin on South Twin Lake near the Nicolet National Forest in Wisconsin and has elk around his property.*

Bailey: *Great. Thanks. If anyone reads anything about special effects that could be used to make ghost sounds, let us know. We'll keep you posted on any new developments. Bye!*

Bailey closed the laptop and sighed. "I wish we could all be together to work on our mysteries."

"It's great that we can at least stay in touch so easy, though." Kate suddenly sat up straight. "Hey! We never finished exploring the wire we found under the wallpaper last night."

"Let's go!" Bailey was off the bed faster than you could say "ghost children of the night."

"You stay here, Biscuit," Kate said. "We won't be long."

Kate brought along her camera-pen, and Bailey her camera-watch. There were no ghost noises in the bright sunlight of afternoon. A neighboring door opened and Justin and Joe came out, binoculars hanging around Justin's neck. They stopped short when they saw Bailey and Kate.

"Hi, Justin. Hi, Joe," Bailey said. "Where you going?"

"Hiking." Justin kept his eyes to the floor.

"That sounds like fun," Kate said. "Maybe we can go with you sometime."

289

"Yeah, maybe," Joe answered, his eyes meeting Bailey's.

"We don't know our way around the trails like you probably do since your grandparents are from here," Bailey said, trying to build the boys up just in case McKenzie's idea about them being insecure had any truth to it.

"Hmmph," Justin grunted. He pushed past them.

"What's that long thing under your jacket?" Bailey asked.

"Huh? Oh this?" Justin looked flustered and pulled his jacket closed even more. "It's just my walking stick."

Bailey and Kate nodded as the brothers dashed to the elevator.

The girls turned to each other.

"That was no walking stick," Kate said. "It was way too short."

"And it looked like it was made of metal." Bailey frowned.

"Bailey!" Kate's eyes were wide with alarm. "I think you're right! That metal walking stick was really the end of a long gun!"

CHAPTER 4

The Angry Elk

When the elevator doors closed behind Justin and Joe, Bailey and Kate went to a hallway window to see if they could spot the brothers leaving the hotel. They were about to give up when the boys came into view and walked across a grassy field into a wooded area.

"Where do you think they're going?" Bailey asked.

"And why do they need that gun?" Kate added.

Bailey turned from the window and started back down the hall. "Those two are up to no good."

Kate followed then stopped. "Bailey, look!" She pointed to a high corner where the hall had a sudden small turn.

Bailey's eyes followed Kate's finger to a flat circle with tiny holes in it. "A speaker!"

"Exactly!" Kate ran her hand along the wall. "Aha!"

"Aha what?" Bailey asked.

"What do you wanna bet our wire ends there? I can see a bump under the wallpaper up higher than I can reach, but then it snakes over from the corner to the speaker."

"They probably put it there figuring no one would look up since the hall jogs to the left here. People would have to watch where they're going so they don't run into the wall."

"Perfect reasoning!" Kate high-fived Bailey. "I mean, look

how they wallpapered the edges of the speaker so you barely even see it. A definite attempt to hide it."

"If we hear those ghost children again tonight, let's see if the voices are coming from this speaker."

The elevator dinged, and Mrs. Chang and Trina stepped out, arms loaded with shopping bags. "Oh, Bailey! I thought you and Kate were taking Biscuit for a walk."

"We already did," Kate said. "Now we're investigating the ghost children's voices we heard last night. We think we may have figured it out!"

Bailey wound her hand through the crook of her mom's arm and pulled her toward the corner speaker. "See that flat, round thing up there?"

"Yeah," Mrs. Chang said, craning her neck.

"It's a speaker," Bailey whispered.

"No!" Mrs. Chang responded dramatically.

Bailey giggled. "Yes!"

"Does that mean you won't be spirited away after all?" Disappointment dripped from Trina's voice.

Bailey glared at her.

"Anyway," she continued, turning back to her mom, "if we hear the voices again, can we come down here to see if that's where they're coming from?"

"I suppose," Mrs. Chang answered. "But right now I have to go put these packages down. They're about to break my arm!" Mrs. Chang and Trina wrestled their bags to the room.

"Wait a minute," Bailey said to Kate. "We know where the speaker is, but how does it come on? Like, is it on a timer or does it have a motion sensor that sets it off? What trips it to play the sounds?"

"We'll have to look for a hidden switch like Alex said."

Kate scratched her head. "That will be our next step."

Kate pulled out her camera-pen and snapped a few pictures of the speaker.

"Now that Mom and Trina are back, let's go see what they're going to do this afternoon," Bailey suggested. "Maybe they would take us into town to do some sightseeing." Bailey raised her eyebrows at Kate.

"That would be fun," Kate agreed. "We haven't had a chance to see the town of Estes Park yet."

"Let's go ask," Bailey said, already hurrying down the hall.

●—●—●

An hour later, Mrs. Chang pulled into a parking place outside a row of shops and Trina, Bailey, and Kate, with Biscuit in tow, climbed out of the car. A gentle breeze blew Bailey's hair in her face. She shaded her eyes from the bright sun.

"Did you see those banners hanging over the street?" Bailey asked.

Trina looked around. "Which ones?"

"One said the Elkfest starts tomorrow, and another one said something about a film festival!"

"Elkfest?" Trina looked at her sister like she had sprouted antlers.

"I don't know what it is, but that's what the sign said." Bailey pulled out her cotton candy lip balm and generously applied it.

"I read about that on the web before we left for our trip," Kate said. "It's a celebration of the elk that live here. There are classes, bugling contests, elk tours, entertainment, and all kinds of activities."

"Bugling contests?" Bailey asked.

"That's the sound the elk make," Kate informed her. "I

guess the contest is to see which person can sound most like a real elk."

"Now that would be fun to see!" Trina said, laughing. "Maybe we could get Dad to enter."

"I seriously doubt that." Mrs. Chang smiled. "But it would be funny."

"Can we go, Mom?" Bailey pleaded.

"We can pick up some information about it," Mrs. Chang said. "If it works out, I suppose we could."

"Cool." Bailey started down the sidewalk with Kate and Biscuit, while Mrs. Chang and Trina trailed behind. They looked in shop windows, exploring the stores that interested them. Elk and bighorn sheep leisurely roamed the streets, not nearly as hurried as the humans around them.

"Be careful around those animals!" Mrs. Chang yelled ahead to them. "No fast moves that might spook them."

"Okay," Bailey answered, her eyes glued to the window displays.

"Here's a rock store!" Bailey squealed. "Maybe I can find a good one to add to my collection."

Inside, Bailey buried her hands in the barrels of polished stones, letting them trickle through her fingers, cool and slick. She inspected row upon row of shelves that held rocks and gift items. Impressive displays of quartz, geodes, and turquoise glittered from every aisle. Jewelry cases boasted the authenticity of the gems.

"Wo—o—ow!" Bailey said, taking it all in. "This must be heaven!"

"If you can't find something for your rock collection here, you never will," Kate said.

Bailey gasped. "Look at this!" She held a shimmering rock

in her hand. "Gold!"

"That can't be real gold," Kate said. "They wouldn't have it in an old barrel."

"But it looks just like gold," Bailey said. "Even the sign says it's gold."

"Yeah, fool's gold," Trina said from nearby.

Bailey whirled around to face her. "Gold is gold."

"And a fool is a fool," Trina muttered.

"Girls," Mrs. Chang warned.

"Bailey, check out this poster." Kate stood by a large wooden pillar on which a poster had been stapled. "Estes Park Film Festival, a weekend of stars."

"Stars? Here?" Bailey's knees nearly buckled.

"That's what it says," Kate replied.

"We've got to keep our eyes open!" Bailey exclaimed. "This could be my big break!"

"Or heartbreak," Trina mumbled.

"I've got to look my best at all times, just in case!" Bailey looked down at her sweatshirt and jeans with holes in the knees. "This will never do!" Her voice rose ever higher, approaching the panic level.

"Deep breath, Bailey, deep breath," Kate coached her. She picked up a brochure from a rack of tourist information and fanned her friend. "Do you need your inhaler?"

"What's wrong?" Mrs. Chang asked, rounding the corner.

"Bailey just found out there's a film festival here this weekend and the streets will be swarming with stars." Kate smiled sweetly and pushed up her glasses.

Mrs. Chang put her arm around Bailey. "I hate to break this to you, but we're going home on Thursday."

"Some of the stars may come early. I've got to be ready,"

Bailey replied breathlessly. "Kate, will you be my manager?"

"Of course," Kate answered.

Bailey eyed her friend's mismatched outfit. "But we may need to work on your wardrobe."

Kate smoothed her clothes out with her hand. "What's wrong with this?" Kate asked.

"Nothing for your everyday girl look," Bailey said. "But if you want to be a Hollywood agent, it doesn't quite cut it."

"*Hollywood* agent?" Kate scrunched up her nose. "You're from Peoria, Illinois, and I'm from Philadelphia, Pennsylvania!"

"But you have to dress for success." Bailey waved her arm with a flair. "You have to act the part of who you *want* to be, not just who you are."

Biscuit yawned loudly.

"Hmm. Maybe I'm not ready for this Hollywood agent thing."

"Of course you are!" Bailey patted Kate on the back. "You just have to believe in yourself."

Suddenly, a commotion outside drew Bailey and Kate to the store window. People scattered from the streets, revealing two enormous elk standing on their hind legs pawing at each other as if they were boxing. When Mrs. Chang and Trina hurried over to see what was going on, Mrs. Chang put her arms protectively around the girls.

"Must be two males fighting over a female," Bailey overheard a man say.

"But they usually do that in the hills, not right here in the middle of town!" said another.

"I see Justin and Joe out there!" Bailey yelled and pulled away from her mother.

"Bailey! Don't go out there!" Mrs. Chang screamed.

Biscuit barked wildly, each bark almost lifting him off his feet.

Bailey flung open the door and as she did, the elk bolted toward the hills, leaving only dust to prove their presence. Coughing, Bailey tried to spot Justin and Joe. Kate, Mom, and Trina appeared at her side.

"I don't see them!" Bailey wailed, beginning to wheeze. She pulled her inhaler from her pocket and breathed in the asthma medication.

As the dust settled, people began talking excitedly. No one had been hurt, just shaken. Bailey, from the corner of her eye, saw two figures running down the street.

"There they go!" she said. "Justin! Joe!" she called. But the two kept on running.

"Guess they're in a hurry to get out of here," Kate said.

"I can't blame them," Trina replied. "Are we ready to move on? I looked at all the rocks I can stand."

"I guess." Bailey gave a longing glance back at the rock shop. "I didn't get anything for my collection, but I'm not exactly in the mood anymore. I think I'm ready to go back to the hotel."

"I'm more than ready," Mrs. Chang said with a shiver. "Too many elk around here for my taste."

"Look at this," Kate said. "This sign says there's a free shuttle a few blocks down the street that can take us back."

"Mom, can Kate and I take the shuttle back?" Bailey begged.

"I suppose," Mrs. Chang answered. "Just stay on the sidewalk and keep your eyes open for running elk."

"I doubt there will be any more since those two just went

through," Bailey said. "But we'll be careful."

Mrs. Chang and Trina went back to their car and the girls walked to the shuttle stop.

"I wonder what made the elk come into town like that?" Bailey thought aloud.

"Me, too."

"I hate to say it, but it almost seemed like Justin and Joe were ahead of the elk, like they were leading them here." Bailey grimaced at the thought.

"That doesn't seem likely," Kate said. "They were probably just at that end of the street when it all began."

"Yeah, you're probably right."

When the girls neared the shuttle stop, Bailey stuck her arm out in front of Kate to stop her. "Look!" Bailey pointed to the bench at the shuttle stop. "It's them!"

"Let's go!" Kate took off running.

The boys didn't see the girls until Bailey poked Justin's arm.

"What'ja do that for?" Justin snarled.

"We wanted to surprise you." Bailey flashed her sweetest smile.

"Are you guys okay?" Kate asked. "We saw you running from the elk."

"Yeah, we're okay." Justin studied his tennis shoes.

"How was your hike?" Bailey asked.

"Hike?" Joe said.

"I thought you hiked here," Bailey said.

"Oh yeah, we did," Joe said. "But we're taking the shuttle back."

"Where's your hiking stick?" Kate noticed Justin's jacket was unzipped all the way down and hanging open.

"Hiking stick?" Justin's eyebrows descended like dark

clouds on a mountain, confusion filling his eyes.

"Yeah, you said the long thing you were carrying in your coat at the hotel was your hiking stick." Bailey crossed her arms and waited for an answer.

"Oh, that!" Justin laughed as if he'd just been told the world's funniest joke. "We left it on our way down from the hill. Got tired of carrying it."

"Hmm," Bailey said, hardly convinced. "Here comes the shuttle."

●—●—●

Back at the room, Bailey sat on the floor with her suitcase and sorted through her clothes looking for just the right outfit for her "Hollywood Moment." A pile of rejected items surrounded her as she pulled out another shirt. "Mom, would you let Kate and me go hiking on one of the trails by ourselves?"

Trina strolled by her and rolled her eyes but held her tongue.

"Only if you promise to stay on the trail," Mrs. Chang replied.

"We will, won't we, Kate?" Bailey tossed a tie-dyed shirt on the floor.

Kate nodded her approval. "And Biscuit could be our guide dog."

"Let's try it tomorrow!" Bailey said, suddenly feeling she'd just been set free.

"Tomorrow's the Elkfest," Kate reminded her. "We'll have to go the next day."

"Shucks," Bailey whispered, her voice registering her dismay. "I wanted to look for that 'hiking stick' Justin left behind."

"Exactly what I was thinking," Kate said with a nod.

"We'll just have to pray it's still there when we go."

"There!" Bailey said, holding up a red long-sleeved T-shirt with rhinestones that spelled "sweet," and a pair of new jeans with flowered embroidery down the leg. "I have my Hollywood outfit figured out for wearing to the Elkfest tomorrow. You never know, there may be a talent scout there for the film festival, too!"

●—●—●

That night, Bailey could hardly wait for lights-out in their room. "Hurry up, Trina!" she ordered. "How long can it take for you to brush your teeth and wash your face?"

Trina stuck her head out from the bathroom, growling with her foamy, white mouth.

"Patience, Bales, patience," Mr. Chang said calmly from behind a business report.

"We never hear the children of the night until the lights are out and everyone's quiet," Bailey tried to explain. "We need to get to bed so we can listen."

Kate was already beneath the covers, which she'd tucked snugly under her chin. Biscuit puttered around her feet, making his bed just right. He plopped down with a giant sigh just as Trina finally emerged fresh-faced and ready for bed.

"Okay, lights out!" Bailey said. Mrs. Chang flipped the switch and the room went dark. Silence flooded the room like billowing smoke, filling every corner until Bailey could hardly breathe. "I don't hear anything, do you?" she whispered to Kate.

"Uh-uh."

"Maybe no one's out there to trip the switch." Sweat beaded on Bailey's upper lip. A door in the hallway creaked then slammed. Bailey raised her head to listen even harder, if that was possible.

"We'll just have to wait it out," Kate whispered.

Bailey nodded in the dark and lay perfectly still. Then she heard it.

Elkfest!

A muffled, high-pitched giggle seeped into the room. Bailey and Kate sprang from their bed like jack-in-the-boxes.

"We'll be back in a few," Bailey said breathlessly. She grabbed her robe, then her cell phone for light. Biscuit let out a yip but then settled back into his cozy blanket.

"He must be getting used to us jumping out of bed," Kate said softly.

When Bailey opened the door, Trina groaned and pulled the covers over her eyes as the wedge of light poured in from the hall. Kate followed Bailey to the door but then took the lead once it closed behind them. They hurried to the speaker they'd seen in the hall earlier and waited. Nothing.

"Something has to be tripping this thing to set it off." Kate looked around.

A ding alerted the girls that someone was about to get off the elevator. The doors opened, and a middle-aged couple emerged and went to their room at the far end of the hall in the opposite direction from the girls. Their door closed with a bang.

Hee-hee-heeeeee!

Bailey saw Kate's eyes widen and a grin spread across her friend's face. The laugh had come from the speaker above them. The two jogged down the hall. Bailey looked in all the potted plants in the hallway for a switch of some kind that the couple might have brushed against. Kate got on all fours and felt the carpet from the elevator to the couple's room.

"I found something!" she said in a loud whisper. "Feel right here."

Bailey joined Kate on her hands and knees and ran her hand along the carpet. "A bump!" she said.

"I think it's the switch that turns on the ghost children's laughter. It comes on when someone steps on it."

"Let's try it." Bailey scrunched up her shoulders. "I can't wait to tell Alex about this since she's the one who told us to look for a switch." She stood and stepped on the bump.

Almost a full minute of silence passed. "It didn't work!" Bailey moaned.

Hee-hee-heeeeee!

"It's on a delay!"

"Kate! You're a genius!" Bailey hugged her friend.

"They must have delayed the ghost recording so when people hear the children laughing and look out into the hall, whoever tripped the switch would have had enough time to get to their room."

"Yeah, so no one would be there when they checked!" Bailey gave Kate a high five.

"Well, that solves that one!" Kate said.

"Now if we can just figure out why the elk are going nuts."

"Yeah, that's a tougher one to pin down."

Bailey scratched her head. "Maybe Sydney will have discovered some information about elk behavior that will help us. Let's call her tomorrow."

"We'd better get back," Kate said.

They returned to their room, the sound of *Hee-hee-heeeeee!* echoing in their heads.

— • — • —

The next morning, Bailey awoke to a deep, reverberating sound that rose quickly to a high-pitched squeal and was followed by a series of low grunts. Biscuit sat up, ears twitching. Bailey rubbed her eyes. "What was *that*?" Mr. and Mrs. Chang were already up and dressed. Trina obviously slept through anything.

"Not another ghost, I hope," Mrs. Chang said with a smirk.

"Sounds like a wounded elephant," Kate said, stretching.

"I think it's coming from outside." Bailey went to the window to investigate. "There's a guy out here blowing some kind of horn."

"I know what it is," Mr. Chang said. "I read about it in the newspaper this morning. Today is the start of the Elkfest, and he's bugling like an elk to begin the festivities."

"Oh yeah!" Bailey said. "We saw a poster about that in town yesterday and we picked up a flyer that told all about it. We thought you should enter the bugling contest, Dad." She cast a mischievous look his way.

"Sure thing. I'll get right on that," Mr. Chang teased back. "It would be fun to watch some of it, though," he admitted.

"Do you have meetings today?" Kate asked.

"Just one. After that, I'm free." Mr. Chang looked at his watch. "I'd better get going. I hope to be back around ten. We can go into town then if you'd like."

"Yeah, if Trina ever gets up!" Bailey yelled, hoping to wake her sister.

Mrs. Chang gave her a look. "You didn't make it any too easy for her to sleep last night with your ghost capers," she said. "Did you figure anything out?"

Bailey and Kate filled Mrs. Chang in on how the ghost children's voices were activated. "Pretty smart of you to figure all that out," Mrs. Chang said. "I'm impressed."

"We need to send an e-mail to the other CCGs to let them know." Bailey turned on the laptop. "Hopefully, they'll have some elk info for us."

Bailey opened her e-mail and found a note from Sydney. Kate read over her shoulder.

Hi. An elk's #1 defense is his sense of smell. He can spook at the scent of a human as far as a mile away. Hunters have to keep checking the wind to make sure it isn't blowing their scent toward where the elk gather.

Elk also have excellent hearing and can be spooked by a car or an ATV miles away. Of course I'm talking about wild elk. Sounds like the elk in Estes Park are used to people and vehicles, unless they possibly feel threatened by someone and remember their scent.

"That's interesting," Bailey said. "Maybe the elk are catching the scent of someone who's been mean to them and that's what's making them charge."

"Maybe," Kate replied. "Anyway, it gives us something to start with. If there's another incident, we'll have to keep our eyes open for any similar circumstances."

—●—●—

Bailey stepped out of the car at the Elkfest in her favorite jeans with flowers embroidered down the sides of each leg and sequins in the centers of each flower. Her long-sleeved red, rhinestoned T-shirt had thumbholes at the end of each cuff. Large white sunglasses and shiny pink lip gloss completed her Hollywood outfit. Kate, unaffected by Bailey's pleas that she dress like an agent, wore green plaid pants and a Hawaiian print shirt.

Bailey felt the same excitement when she looked around at the Elkfest as she did her first time at the circus. The sweet aroma of hot Indian fry bread mingled with corn dogs and cotton candy. Elk roamed freely among the crowd, eating the food people dropped. Live country-western music filled the air and a festive mood settled over the town.

"When's the bugling contest?" Bailey asked, looking for movie stars.

Mr. Chang looked at a schedule he'd picked up. "At one o'clock."

Bailey looked at her watch. "It's only eleven thirty now."

"Maybe we should get some lunch then head over that way so we get good seats," Mr. Chang suggested.

"Hey, there are the Perkinses!" Mrs. Chang said. She waved to the family.

"Hi, Dory," Mrs. Perkins said to Mrs. Chang. "What do you think of the Elkfest?"

"It's terrific! We're interested in the bugling contest, but we see it isn't until one o'clock," Mr. Chang told them.

"Yeah, they always have it in the afternoon," Mr. Perkins said. "My dad is in the competition again this year." He motioned to Justin and Joe's grandpa. "He won it a couple years ago."

"No kidding!" Mr. Chang said.

"Now we'll have someone to cheer for." Bailey wished she could turn a flip like Alex could. She would have done one on the spot.

"We'll see if I'm worth cheering for in a couple hours, won't we?" Grandpa Perkins winked at Bailey. "I appreciate your enthusiasm and support."

Bailey turned to Justin and Joe. "You must be excited to see your grandpa in the contest, huh?"

"Sure," Joe said. "He'll win, I just know it." He smiled at his grandpa, and Bailey thought it was the happiest she'd ever seen Joe. Justin shrugged and kicked a rock in the dirt.

"We were just getting ready to eat a bite of lunch," Mrs. Chang said. "Would you like to join us?"

"We can't eat until after Grandpa's contest is over," Justin glowered at the Changs. "He can't bugle on a full stomach."

"Oh, I see," Mrs. Chang said, hesitation marking her words as she looked uncertainly at Justin.

"Actually, we had a late breakfast so we could eat lunch later after Dad's big performance." Mr. Perkins's face seemed a bit redder than usual. "But thanks anyway."

"Good luck on the contest!" Bailey said as the families parted. "We'll be rooting for you!"

"Thanks!" Grandpa Perkins replied. "I'll need all the help I can get!"

The Changs found a hot dog stand and ordered five hot dogs and drinks. The aroma had tempted Bailey since they arrived. She loaded her dog with ketchup, mustard, and relish.

While they ate, they watched Native American dancers perform. Bailey was enthralled by the unusual dance style—the silent tap, tap, tapping of their moccasin-clad feet and the leaning and swaying of their bodies. They moved to the beat of a tom-tom drum, its leather top being struck hard, then soft, to make different rhythms and sounds.

A medium-skinned man with a long ponytail of black hair streaked with gray sang in his Native American language. The young dancers especially impressed Bailey. Some of them looked much younger than her. She clapped hard when their performance ended.

"Trina and I are going to run to the restroom before going to the bugling contest," Mrs. Chang told the girls. "Do you want to come?"

"I'm okay," Bailey said.

"Me, too," Kate agreed.

"That sounds like a good idea," Mr. Chang added. "You girls stay right here until we get back."

Kate grabbed Bailey's arm when the family left. "Look!"

The Perkins family was down the street, and Justin and Joe appeared to be telling their parents something. Then the boys ran toward one of the hills surrounding the town.

"Looks like they're going to do some hill climbing." Bailey frowned. "I wonder if they picked up their 'walking stick' from the area they hiked yesterday."

"You mean *gun*?" Kate snorted. "Those guys are either avid hikers or they are up to something. What time is it?"

Bailey checked her watch. "Twelve fifteen."

"Their hike will have to be short, or they'll miss their grandpa's bugling performance."

"And Joe seemed excited about seeing it." Bailey remembered Joe's unexpected smile. "I don't think he'd want to miss it."

"Justin, however, is another matter." Kate pushed her glasses up. She dug in her pocket and pulled out her camera-pen. Holding it horizontally, she twisted the pointed end to zoom in as close as possible. Justin and Joe's image got larger on the metal clip. She quickly clicked the end. Bailey joined in with her camera-watch.

"Between the two of us, we should have some good shots to share with the Camp Club Girls." Kate returned her pen to her pocket.

"Are we ready?" Mr. Chang said when the family met up again.

"Ready!" the girls shouted in unison.

"Let's go cheer Grandpa Perkins on!"

The Changs sat in the grass near the front and sipped on their sodas. A magician entertained the crowd gathering for the bugling contest.

"I need a volunteer," the magician said. "Who will help me?"

Bailey's hand was up like a rocket.

"You, there, in the red sparkly shirt." The magician pointed to Bailey.

"He's pointing at you, Bailey!" Kate pushed her friend to her feet. "If there are talent scouts out there, they'll all see you on stage. It could be your big break!"

Bailey ran up to the stage, her family applauding her all the way.

The magician asked Bailey her name and age. Then he looked confused. "Hmm. That's unusual," he said.

"What?" Bailey asked.

"You seem to have something on the back of your shirt."

"I do?" Bailey twisted to see.

The magician reached behind her and pulled out a bouquet of flowers. "Oh, I'm sorry. I hope I didn't spoil the surprise you were hiding for your mother."

Bailey squealed and clapped.

The magician handed the flowers to Mrs. Chang. "Let's

hear it for my lovely assistant, Bailey! Thank you for your help, miss."

Bailey curtsied grandly and took her seat. "Do you think anyone famous saw me?" she asked Kate.

"If they were here, they totally saw you," she replied.

Soon, the contest began. A panel of judges sat in front of the stage and took notes on each contestant's bugling ability. Bailey scanned the crowd a short time later and spotted the Perkins family, including Justin and Joe, sitting on the other side of the bugling area.

"I guess they made it back in time," Bailey whispered to Kate. She nodded in the boys' direction.

"Guess so," Kate said. "And Justin actually looks almost happy."

"Amazing!" Bailey joked.

Grandpa Perkins's name was announced, and he went to the microphone. "I've been in this bugling contest five years running and only won once, two years ago. But this is the first time I've ever had two cheering sections." He waved his arm toward his family and then the Changs. They all yelled their loudest. Grandpa gave them an informal salute then cleared his throat and got down to business. He let out two low, resonant tones that quickly rose to a high-pitched squeal, followed by three deep grunts. He sounded just like one of the elk!

The crowd went wild. Even the elk in the park stopped and looked. Grandpa bowed before waving and taking his seat on the stage with the other contestants.

Bailey clapped wildly. "Grandpa Perkins was fantastic!"

Kate nodded. "I bet he wins the grand prize."

The bugling contest continued, but after about the fifth

person, Bailey thought she felt a slight tremor. She looked at Kate, who looked back at her, questions in her eyes. The shaking increased and soon people were on their feet running and yelling, "Stampede!"

Elk ran through the crowd on their long, knobby legs, more elk than Bailey had ever seen at one time before. Dust flew and parents snatched small children to safety. When the rumbling and shaking ended, Bailey noticed some people lying on the ground injured.

"The Perkinses! Where are they?" Bailey wondered aloud. As much as she didn't like Justin and Joe, she didn't want any of them to get hurt. The dust cleared and she caught sight of them. "There they are! By the stage."

Mr. Perkins was helping a shaken Grandpa Perkins off the stage. "They look like they're okay," Kate said. "We're lucky we weren't hurt."

Bailey listened to conversations around her.

"What do you think caused the elk to run through town this time?"

"I bet it was the bugling contest. Probably drew them right in."

"They've never done that before."

"Had some mighty good buglers this year."

"They're probably nervous with all these people around."

"They're trying to protect their young."

"Protect their young? They were born in May, five months ago."

"I think they're aggressive because it's mating season."

"Could be. Peak mating is September and October."

"But they've never been this aggressive in mating season before. Something got them stirred up."

"Seems like they show up only to charge lately. They don't roam around as freely as they once did."

"True enough. And they seem to come out more in the evenings than they used to."

"Where did they come from?"

"From that hill," one said, pointing to where Bailey and Kate had seen Justin and Joe hiking.

"That's the opposite direction from where they came out of the woods last time."

Bailey looked at Kate as they took in all the talk. "What do you think, Kate?"

"I don't know," she said thoughtfully. "I think we need to talk to the other girls. Seems when we work together, things come together faster."

"Two heads—or six—are better than one!" Bailey agreed.

As the people gathered, leaders announced that the bugling contest would resume in an hour and the winner would be declared shortly after that. The Changs walked over to where the Perkins family stood.

"Everyone all right here?" Mr. Chang asked.

"Yes, a bit shaken, but not injured," Mr. Perkins answered. "Your family okay?"

"We're fine, too," Mr. Chang replied.

"Mr. Perkins," Bailey said to Grandpa, "you were awesome!"

"Yeah, you sounded like a real elk!" Kate agreed.

"I bet you're going to win." Bailey grinned as if she'd just won a prize herself.

"Of course he'll win," Justin said, surprising Bailey. "No *tourist* should win the local contest."

"Well, now, I wouldn't say that," Grandpa said, patting his

grandson's back. "The best bugler should win, wherever he's from."

"A tourist doesn't know the elk bugle as well as the locals," Justin maintained. "They should just give up and go home."

Bailey almost laughed until she saw how serious Justin was. No hint of a smile crossed his face, no look of pride in his grandpa. Just the usual anger. Was it her imagination or was that jab at tourists targeted at her and her family?

"Come on, Bailey," Kate said, hooking her arm through her friend's. "I'm so sure Grandpa Perkins is going to win, we may as well go see some more of the Elkfest."

Bailey glanced at her mother. "Is it okay, Mom?"

"Sure, go have fun," Mrs. Chang replied.

Target Practice

When Bailey and Kate returned from the Elkfest that evening, they made a conference call to the other Camp Club Girls. Leaving Trina to watch TV in the hotel room, the two friends sat on an overstuffed couch in the lobby. Biscuit, on his leash, sat quietly between them. After all the girls were on the line, Bailey explained the children of the night mystery. Kate supplemented the story with technical details.

"You were right about the hidden switch, Alex," Bailey told her. "Kate found it under the hallway carpet."

"But what we hadn't counted on," Kate added, "was that it was on a timer, so it didn't go off immediately when stepped on."

"Wow! You guys are awesome!" Alex exclaimed. Bailey imagined her doing a backflip with her typical cheerleader enthusiasm. "Scooby Doo would be proud. Next thing you know they'll be asking you to be on their show!"

McKenzie giggled. "Now *that* I'd like to see! Bailey and Kate as cartoon characters!"

"Anything to report on the elk research, Syd?" Bailey asked.

"Yeah. Hold on. I've found out a few things."

Bailey heard papers rustling, and then Sydney continued. "The elk in the Estes Park Rocky Mountain area are called wapiti elk. Wapiti means 'white rump' in the Shawnee Indian language."

Bailey laughed. "Yep. That's them, all right."

"Like I mentioned before, adult elk have an awesome sense of smell, but they also have excellent hearing and can run up to thirty-five miles an hour. They're well equipped to avoid the cougars and bears that prey on them. Strong animals like elk don't need much cover except during extreme weather, to avoid hunters, or when they're harassed."

"Harassed?" McKenzie asked.

"You know, if people or other animals bother them," Sydney explained. "They're very social animals and live in herds most of the year. They're mostly active at dawn and dusk, but when it gets hot or when they're harassed, elk may become more active at night. When they're not being hunted, elk get along well with humans so lawns and golf courses become some of their favorite restaurants."

The girls giggled and Biscuit joined in with happy barks.

Sydney continued reading. "September and October are good months to observe them because the boy elk—or bulls, as they're called—are battling over the girl elk, so they aren't as worried about being seen. You'll hear the bull's bugle usually near dusk or dawn. You should be careful around the male elk during mating season, especially in areas where they're used to being around people, because they tend to be more aggressive."

"So maybe it *is* because of mating season that the elk have been acting so strange," Kate said. "We heard someone say that at the Elkfest today."

"But from hearing the townspeople talk, it seems they're more aggressive than usual this year." Bailey sighed.

"Sydney said they become more active at night if they're harassed," Elizabeth added.

"Good point," Bailey said. "We overheard someone mention that after the elk stampede today."

"But who or what is harassing them?" McKenzie asked.

"That's the question." Kate stroked Biscuit, her face thoughtful.

Silence filled the phone line for a moment.

"Not to change the subject, but have you seen those boys anymore?" Alex asked.

"Yeah, we've seen them a couple of times," Bailey answered. "They went on a hike yesterday."

"With a very unusual walking stick," Kate added, concern clouding her face.

"Oh yeah." Bailey's eyes sought Kate's. "We didn't get a good look at it, but Justin, the older boy, had something hidden in his coat. When we asked him about it, he said it was his walking stick."

"But it looked like it was made out of metal," Kate chimed in, "and though it *was* sort of long, it was still too short to be a walking stick."

"Then we saw them out the window as they left the hotel and walked to a wooded area. Justin's walking stick was in plain view by then and it turns out. . ." Bailey paused dramatically, ". . .it was a gun!"

The other girls gasped in unison.

"What kind of gun?" Elizabeth asked.

"It looked like an air pellet gun or whatever those are called," Kate said.

"It's called an airsoft gun," Sydney said. "My older brother has one. It's kind of like a BB gun, but smaller, and the pellets can sting but not do serious damage."

"But get this," Bailey's voice rose in excitement. "When they came back, they didn't have it with them. When we asked them about it, they said they got tired of carrying it and left it behind."

"Well, they said they left their walking stick behind, since they just claimed they had a walking stick," Kate said.

"Yeah, right!" McKenzie said. "That doesn't seem likely."

"Bailey, you and Kate have to be careful around those two," Elizabeth warned. "Avoid them if you can. First Corinthians 15:33 says, 'Do not be misled: Bad company corrupts good character.' Don't take any unnecessary chances."

"We won't," Kate assured her.

Bailey stood and stretched. "We'd better get to bed. But if any of you think of anything that could help us, let us know. And Sydney, thanks for the great info on elk. Keep up the good work."

●—●—●

The next morning, Bailey and Kate started out on their hike with Biscuit, taking their secret cameras, water, cell phones, binoculars, and some trail mix. Both girls wore hoodies to ward off the early morning chill.

Rather than taking the free shuttle, Bailey and Kate decided to hike into town. They passed the rock shop and lots of cute restaurants they hoped Bailey's parents would take them to before their vacation ended. The girls lingered outside the fudge and ice cream shop, their mouths watering. They enjoyed seeing the sleepy town wake up, its stores just opening.

"Hey, look! A miniature golf course!" Kate pushed her glasses up.

"Want to play a round before we head up the hill?" Bailey asked.

"Sure!" Kate reached down and picked up her dog. "Reminds me of the day we found Biscuit at Camp Discovery!"

The two grinned and rubbed the wiggling fur ball.

"You were so cute," Kate cooed to him.

"And dirty and stinky!" Bailey plugged her nose at the memory.

Kate covered the dog's ears. "Don't you listen to her. You've always been a prince." She set Biscuit back down.

Bailey paid the man at the counter for the round of golf and they chose clubs that were just their sizes.

"What do you think Justin and Joe are up to today?" Bailey asked.

"Probably still sleeping." Kate stepped up to the first hole and teed off.

Bailey looked at her watch. "I guess it *is* only nine o'clock." She took her turn.

"Look at that huge elk!" Kate pointed to the street. Biscuit barked and pranced around Kate's feet.

Just as Bailey turned to look, the elk raised his head and let out a shrill bugle.

"Wow! He sounds just like Grandpa Perkins!" Bailey said seriously and then laughed at how it must have sounded. "From what we just heard, I bet he won that bugling contest yesterday. We'll have to find out today."

Bailey and Kate moved to the next hole, a miniature Rocky Mountain peak with tunnels for the ball to go through in the middle of the base, and one on either side.

Kate stuck out her neck and squinted through her glasses.

"What are you looking at?" Bailey asked when she realized her friend was looking into the distance rather than at the golf tunnels.

"I think I'm looking at Justin and Joe," Kate replied, pointing toward the hill they hoped to hike later. She pushed her glasses up and squinted to get a better look.

Bailey's head swung in the direction Kate's finger pointed. She snatched the binoculars out of their case and peered through them. Focusing in, she found the boys. "That's them all right, and it looks like they got to the 'walking stick' before we did."

"Really?" Kate sounded disappointed, but then her voice perked up. "Can you see the 'walking stick' clearly?"

"*Very* clearly, and we were right—that's no walking stick."

Kate grabbed the binoculars from her friend and looked. "No, it isn't. That is definitely a gun, and it looks like they're doing some target practice."

"What are they shooting at?" Now it was Bailey's turn to squint.

"Looks like they have empty soda cans lined up on a tree stump," Kate said. "It's hard to tell since the trees are so thick there." Kate lowered the binoculars.

"So we were right," Bailey repeated, her hands on her hips.

Kate nodded. "They were lying, just as we thought."

"Maybe we're jumping to conclusions," Bailey said solemnly. "Just because they're shooting a gun doesn't make them bad people. As long as they're being careful and shooting at things like cans. And it's probably an airsoft gun like Sydney told us about—the kind that just shoots little plastic pellets."

"But why would they try to cover it up by lying?" Kate

pointed her golf club at Bailey. "That's what makes it suspicious."

Bailey sighed. "I suppose you're right. Although many people don't approve of kids using even plastic pellet guns."

"Let's hurry up and finish this golf game and get over to that hill," Kate said. "Maybe we'll see what they're up to."

"Yeah," Bailey agreed. "It's your turn."

Bailey and Kate finished their round of golf and hurried to the hill, where elk and bighorn sheep roamed around its base. Biscuit ran ahead of them, causing the big animals to scatter. The air smelled crisp and fall-like, red and gold leaves crunching under their feet as they walked.

"It smells so good out here!" Kate said as she stared at a towering pine.

"If nothing else, maybe we can learn some more about the elk's behavior while we're out here," Bailey said. She moved close to a pine tree and sniffed the bark.

"What are you doing?" Kate looked at her friend like she'd gone crazy.

"Smelling the bark," Bailey answered matter-of-factly.

"Well, I can see that. But why?"

"Come see for yourself." Bailey motioned her over. "Sniff."

Kate looked around then put her nose close to the tree and inhaled. Biscuit came back and sniffed all around the tree, too.

"Well?" Bailey asked.

"Smells like vanilla!" Kate cried.

"See? Aren't you glad you tried?" Bailey took another sniff. "Sometimes I can't decide if it smells like vanilla or butterscotch, but either way it smells good."

"Where'd you learn that?" Kate asked.

"Sydney, of course," Bailey answered. "She showed me at camp the first day she and I went out hiking."

"I should have guessed Syd would have taught you that."

The two walked on. Biscuit trotted alongside the trail just a few feet ahead.

"What's that?" Bailey took a few steps off the trail and stopped by a bathtub-size, shallow hole in the ground.

"I don't know, but it smells awful!" Kate covered her nose and mouth with her hands. Biscuit scampered into the sunken earth, sniffing furiously.

Bailey took a few steps closer. "It's so muddy I can hardly get any closer."

"Biscuit's going to be a mess!"

"He already is." Bailey bent down and looked at the huge indentation. "There are light brown hairs in the mud. And look at all these tracks around it."

Kate stooped to look at the four-inch footprints that looked like a long heart shape cut down the middle. "Do you think these are elk tracks?"

Bailey shrugged. "We'll have to check on the Internet."

"Or ask Sydney."

"Let's get some pictures of it and we can send them to her to see." Bailey aimed her camera-watch at the indentation and Kate pulled out her camera-pen.

"These hairs sure look the same color as elk fur," Kate said.

"Come on. Let's keep going." Bailey stood and walked back to the trail, trying not to sink into the mud. "Must be so muddy because of that pond over there."

The girls looked at a small pool of water almost hidden by reeds. It sat just yards beyond the smelly indentation.

"Let's go, boy," Kate called to Biscuit. The mud-covered

dog plodded his way out of the bog to her side.

"I guess today we'll find out who won the bugling contest." Bailey kicked some fall leaves that covered the trail.

"If anyone can bugle better than Grandpa Perkins, he's probably part elk!"

Bailey suddenly stopped and listened.

"Wha—?" Kate began, but Bailey held her hand up to stop her and put her finger to her lips.

Bailey tiptoed to the right of the trail and hid behind a tree, motioning Kate to join her. When Kate reached her, she whispered, "I think I hear Justin's and Joe's voices."

Kate nodded silently. She picked up Biscuit and reattached his leash, his muddy feet leaving marks all over her light pink hoodie. She didn't dare complain or make a sound.

The girls stayed still as stones but heard nothing more.

"Apparently they've moved farther up the hill from when we saw them earlier. Let's keep going," Bailey whispered. "But stay off to the side of the trail so if they come down this way, they won't see us."

"We told your mom we'd stay on the trail," Kate reminded her.

"We'll be right beside it," Bailey said. "We'll keep it in sight. She just didn't want us wandering and getting lost."

The girls crept silently, like spies, hopping from behind one tree to the next. The boys' voices grew louder.

"Look over there," Bailey exclaimed.

Kate nodded. Justin and Joe had moved their target practice off the trail.

"I can barely hear them," Kate said. "And I don't have a clear view of them."

Bailey scurried to the next tree, which took her several

feet closer to the boys. Kate followed carefully. She pulled out her camera-pen and snapped a few pictures of the boys. Bailey did the same with her camera-watch, just for good measure. Biscuit caught sight of what the girls were looking at and a low growl rumbled in his throat.

"Shhhh," Kate said softly as she scratched the dog's head to try to calm him.

Justin stopped mid-aim and looked around as if he'd heard something. Then he refocused his aim at the pop cans lined on a tree stump.

Bailey strained to hear what they said.

"We'll show them," Justin said to his younger brother. "We'll have them so scared they never come back!" With that, he pulled his trigger and a loud pop rang out.

Biscuit barked and leaped from Kate's arms. He ran in the boys' direction, leash dragging behind him.

"What in the wo—" Justin turned and saw Biscuit flying at him, barking wildly.

"It's those girls' dog!" Joe yelled. He spun in circles, eyes searching the woods.

"Biscuit!" Kate jumped from behind the tree and raced after the dog, with Bailey close behind.

"Get that dog away from me!" shouted Justin.

"Biscuit! Come here!" Kate screamed.

The girls reached the boys just as Justin raised his airsoft gun and pointed it at Biscuit.

CHAPTER 7

Lost!

"NOOO!" Kate shrieked.

The gun went off. Biscuit yelped and darted into the woods.

"Biscuit!" Kate rushed through the trees after her dog.

Bailey strode squarely to confront Justin, whose gun hung limp in his hand. "Why did you do that?" she demanded, tears stinging her eyes.

"He was going to attack me!" Justin yelled.

"He was barking around your feet! If he wanted to attack you, he would have jumped at you."

"Well, I wasn't going to wait to find out." Justin ran his hand through his short hair, his face flushed. "It would have been too late to do anything by then." He looked at his younger brother, who stood dazed nearby. "You okay, Joe?"

"I—I think so," he stammered.

"Let's get out of here before that dog comes back and attacks us again." Justin set his gun on the safety setting and stuffed it into his jacket as Joe gathered their targets and supplies.

Bailey wanted to grab the gun and knock both boys senseless with it. Instead she turned and dashed into the woods. "Kate?" she called. The wind in the trees was her only reply. "Kate!" Nothing.

Bailey looked back and realized she could no longer see the trail they'd been on. She stood for a few minutes, trying to push down her fear. *What should I do?* All she could think of was Kate and Biscuit, but she didn't know how to find them. In the shadows of the towering pines, the air felt chilly, even with her hoodie on.

Which way should I go? Bailey looked around her again. *I can't think!*

"Kate!" Still no reply.

Bailey sucked in a deep breath and let it out slowly. *Help me think, God. Show me what to do.* She tucked her icy hands into her hoodie pockets and fingered her cell phone. *That's it! Thanks, God!* Snatching it out, she dialed Kate. Thank heavens she could pick up a signal. One ring. Two rings.

"Hello?"

"Kate! Thank goodness! Where are you?"

"I'm not sure."

Bailey heard Kate's voice tremble. "Did you find Biscuit?"

"Yeah, he's here with me."

"Is he okay?"

"I think so. I looked over him and didn't see any injuries. I guess he was just spooked by the noise of the gun."

Bailey closed her eyes and sighed. "I about let Justin have it when you and Biscuit disappeared into the woods. He claimed Biscuit was about to attack him. I nearly decked him, even if he is bigger than me."

Kate laughed. "Well, I'm glad you held yourself back. That's all we need is for him to say Biscuit attacked him and then you assaulted him."

The girls grew silent. "Bailey, we have to find each other

and get back to the trail."

"I don't know which way to go." Bailey's voice rose, fear once again curling within.

"Hang on a second."

Bailey could hear rustling, as if Kate were looking for something. "Here it is."

"What?"

"My mini-GPS. It's a trial product my dad brought home from work one day. What better time to try it out than now?"

"Trial product? GPS units have been around awhile."

"But this one is tiny. It fits into the palm of my hand. I can clip it onto my belt if I want."

"That's fantastic!"

"Let's see, I'll put in Estes Park, Colorado, and see what it brings up." Kate punched in the city and state. "It worked! Now I just have to zoom in to find that street we were on."

"I'm glad you're the one trying to figure this out," Bailey said. "I'm directionally challenged."

"Here we go," Kate said. "Looks like we walked north to get to this hill from town. The sun was to our right, so that must be east since it rose only a few hours earlier, right?"

Bailey relaxed. "You're starting to sound like Sydney!"

"So to get back we need to go south, so the sun is to our left."

Bailey looked up and shielded her eyes from the sun. "I'll hang up and yell for you. Hopefully, you'll hear me as you get closer. Then we can look for the trail together from here."

"Okay," Kate said, "but if I don't hear you soon, I'm calling you back."

"Deal." Bailey stuffed her phone back in her pocket and yelled, "Kate! Kate, I'm over here!"

She yelled for what seemed like a full minute, stopping only to listen briefly for an answer. A cool breeze swirled dry leaves around her feet, and she zipped her mud-splotched hoodie clear to the neck.

"Kate!" Leaves crunched behind her and Bailey swung around. "Kate?" No answer, but the crunching drew closer. "Kate, if that's you, you'd better answer me!" Silence. "Kate, this isn't funny!"

From behind a clump of trees, a huge elk with enormous antlers stuck out his head and looked at Bailey. She froze, not sure if the elk would charge or if he was as afraid as she was. They stood, eyes locked, neither one moving a muscle. Finally, the elk seemed satisfied that the girl meant no harm and munched on a nearby shrub. Bailey exhaled a breath she didn't realize she'd been holding and inched forward to get a better view of the elk.

Suddenly Bailey was startled by her cell phone ringing. "Kate? I'm watching a big elk eat. You should see him!"

"You're supposed to be calling for me, remember?"

"I did, but then the elk scared me and I was afraid to make much noise."

Bailey heard rustling again and turned to look. The elk turned his head, too, ears twitching. "Kate! Over here!"

At the sound of Bailey's voice, the elk turned toward her and narrowed his eyes. He lowered his head, those gigantic antlers pointing in her direction, then took a few steps toward her. Hardly daring to take a breath, Bailey froze. Images of charging elk filled her mind.

Biscuit sniffed the air and leaped out of Kate's arms, barking wildly. The tiny dog ran at the towering elk, who seemed momentarily confused by all the excitement. He tried to keep his eye on the dog prancing at his feet, one minute in front of him and the next behind. In apparent exasperation, the elk turned and lumbered off into the woods.

Kate came through the trees. "Bailey! I was so afraid for you." She hugged her friend. "Are you all right?"

"I'm fine. But my legs felt like noodles for a minute there."

Biscuit scampered up to Bailey and jumped to get her attention.

"I see you! Thanks for scaring that elk away. You really are a wonder dog!" She gave the dog a friendly rub. "But you scared us when you ran off into the woods!" Bailey slipped her lip balm from her pocket and applied some. "Now all we have to do is find the trail."

"Shouldn't be too hard with this GPS."

"Let's see that thing." Kate placed the tiny device in Bailey's palm. "I've never seen one this small."

"Dad says it still has a few glitches, but it works well for the most part." Kate took the GPS back. "See? It shows where we are. It looks like this squiggly line might be a trail."

"So we need to turn around and go to our right to find it. Let's try it."

Kate started off in the direction the GPS indicated. Bailey and Biscuit followed close behind. She kept her eye on the device and could see the distance between them and the trail diminishing. "We're almost there!"

"I think I see it!" Bailey went running, Biscuit barking excitedly beside her.

"I was thinking," Kate said when they were back on the trail. "I wonder if Justin and Joe know something about the elk being so agitated."

"Maybe. They sure are angry themselves."

"Maybe Justin is giving anger lessons to the elk."

Seeing the twinkle in Kate's eyes, Bailey laughed. "Yeah, they were probably just waiting for their class to gather when we snuck up on them."

"They seem to spend a lot of time on this hill."

"Yeah. And with that 'walking stick' that looked just like the gun they were shooting pop cans with today."

Just then the ground trembled.

"Did you feel that?" Kate asked.

Before Bailey could answer, the trembling became stronger. "Don't tell me it's another—"

The girls heard loud rustling and soon Bailey spotted a herd of elk running through the forest toward them. "Stampede!"

Kate snatched up Biscuit, grabbed Bailey's arm, and pulled her behind a tree. About twenty elk thundered by so close Bailey thought she could stick out her hand and touch them as they passed. She saw what looked like fear in their eyes and heard their snorts and panting. When the last one was out of sight, the fading rhythm of hooves was all that remained, followed by an eerie quiet. Bailey and Kate cautiously stepped out from behind the protection of the tree and looked around. A cloud of dust marked the path the elk had taken.

"I hope they don't run clear into town." Kate's eyes registered her concern.

"Something back there in the woods scared them. Why else would they run like that?"

"I don't know, but I think you're right."

"Y–You don't think it was a wild animal, do you?" Bailey forced the words from her mouth, barely daring to speak them.

Kate turned to her friend, eyes wide. "Let's get out of here!"

The girls ran down the trail until they could see the town. "We're almost there," panted Bailey.

"Are you okay? Do you need your inhaler?"

Bailey shook her head. "I'm okay. Just winded."

They slowed down and walked the rest of the way to town. When they got on Main Street, they heard people talking about the elk.

"I can't believe they came through here again!"

"This is the worst it's ever been."

"What are we going to do about them?"

"The elk are becoming too dangerous."

"Something has to be done."

Bailey pulled Kate aside where no one would hear them. "Do you think we should tell them what happened on our hike?"

"You mean our encounter with the elk, the elk stampede, getting separated and lost, or seeing Justin and Joe target practicing?"

Bailey giggled. "I guess we did have a lot going on, didn't we? Should we tell any of it?"

"I'm not sure. It might not have anything to do with the stampede through town."

"Then again it might." Bailey let out a giant sigh. "Maybe we should just go back to the hotel."

"Yeah. We need to gather more evidence before we point fingers at people."

"Let's take the shuttle back. I'm tired of walking."

"Me, too." Kate hooked Biscuit's leash on him and set him down. "It's a wonder you didn't get trampled by that huge elk or the stampeding herd," she said in his pointy little ear. "You are so brave!"

"It's amazing none of us did," Bailey added. "God must be working overtime keeping an eye out for us."

"As usual."

The girls joined a couple of people who were waiting at the shuttle stop.

Kate plopped down on the bench. "We should get in touch with the other Camp Club Girls when we get back."

"Yeah, they'll want to hear about our adventure."

A voice interrupted their conversation, and Justin and Joe's grandma joined them under the shelter. "Oh, hi girls!"

"Mrs. Perkins! What are you doing here?"

"I've been doing a little shopping this morning." She held up her bags as proof. The shuttle pulled to the curb and the group boarded. Bailey and Kate sat across the aisle from Grandma Perkins and her shopping bags. Biscuit sniffed them curiously.

"What have you girls been up to?" Grandma Perkins asked.

"We went for a hike this morning and now we're heading back to the hotel."

"Justin and Joe were hiking today, too!"

Bailey bit her lower lip. "Yes, we saw them."

"My stomach is growling." Kate put her hand on her tummy.

Bailey, relieved at the change of subject, looked at her watch. "That's because it's lunchtime. It's almost twelve o'clock."

"Guess we timed that right."

When the shuttle parked in front of the hotel, Bailey, Kate, Biscuit, and Grandma Perkins got off.

"Oh, Mrs. Perkins! Did Mr. Perkins win the bugling contest?" Kate asked.

"No, someone else won," Grandma Perkins replied.

Bailey could hardly believe her ears. "That's impossible! He was the best one there!"

"Well, I'm glad you thought so, but the judges didn't agree." Grandma Perkins's voice was kind. "It's all right. He just did it for fun. He didn't care if he won."

"I bet Justin and Joe were really disappointed," Bailey said quietly as they walked down the hotel sidewalk.

"Yes, they were." Mrs. Perkins shook her head. "Especially Justin."

Bailey suddenly stopped and gasped.

"What's the matter?" Kate's eyes followed Bailey's line of vision toward the old historic building.

"I thought I saw a ghost in that window."

"Bailey! You know better than that!" Kate laughed but then paused. "You're as white as a sheet!"

"Which window?" Grandma Perkins asked.

"The fourth floor, four windows over from the right."

"Ah, yes. The famous room 408. And what did this ghost look like?"

"Like a cowboy. He had a cowboy hat and a mustache and he just stared out the window then faded off to the left."

"That must be the old cowboy ghost we read about in the brochure!" Kate kept her eyes on the window.

"Legend has it that a guest thought he saw the same thing years back," Grandma Perkins explained. "But the front desk confirmed that the room was vacant. They said no one could have stood in that window because it was over the bathroom sink, and he couldn't have faded to the left because it would have taken him through the wall. That was the first reported sighting of the cowboy ghost. Many people have seen him since then, but only at this time of the year."

"Are you telling me I saw a real ghost?" Bailey's voice trembled.

"Bailey! You're not going to fall for that, are you?"

"All I'm saying is that you're not the first to have seen it—whatever it is." Grandma Perkins patted Bailey on the back. "You want me to walk you to your room?"

"That's okay. We don't believe in ghosts, do we, Bailey?"

"N–no. We don't."

"Okay, then. I'll see you later." Mrs. Perkins left with a friendly wave.

Bailey and Kate stood in the hotel yard, still trying to absorb what had just happened.

"Do you believe that? I mean, really. Who would believe in cowboy ghosts?" Kate snickered as she looked up at the fourth floor window again.

Bailey stood silent beside her, but then she noticed Kate's face grow pale. Bailey followed Kate's eyes and this time they both saw the cowboy. "There he is! I told you it was real!" Bailey's voice quivered.

Kate reached for Bailey's hand. Her mouth moved, but no words came.

Now it was Bailey's turn to reassure Kate. "It has to be special effects, don't you think, Kate? Remember, there are no such things as ghosts."

No sooner had she said those words than the cowboy faded away to the left of the window just as he had done before.

"That is definitely a special effect. It's identical to the movement I saw before!" Bailey squeezed Kate's hand. "Come on. We've got another mystery to figure out. Hopefully, it will be as easy as finding out where the ghost children's laughter came from."

Kate nodded mutely as Bailey led her to the hotel entrance.

Mystery Music

Back in the hotel room, Bailey and Kate bathed Biscuit in the sink. Water sprayed everywhere when he shook himself. The girls screamed with laughter and wrapped the dog in a hotel towel.

"There you go!" Kate dried him off. "Nice and clean."

While the girls fixed sandwiches from food the Changs had put in the minifridge, they told Mrs. Chang about their hike and the beautiful scenery. They left out the parts about Justin and Joe, getting lost, and how close they were to the elk stampede.

"When we got back to town, the elk had just stampeded again and everyone was talking about it," Bailey told her.

"Oh no! Not again." Mrs. Chang shook her head. "Was anyone hurt?"

"I don't think so." Kate's green eyes were serious behind her dark-rimmed glasses. "They say it's the worst it's ever been and that they're going to have to do something about it because it's getting too dangerous."

Mrs. Chang nodded as she straightened up their room. "I can believe that. They can't just let the elk run wild in town."

Bailey plugged in the charger for her laptop. "I still think there has to be a reason they're acting so crazy this year. We just have to uncover it."

"Sounds like you had a nice morning, in spite of the stampede," Mrs. Chang said.

"We did!" Bailey replied enthusiastically. "Grandma Perkins rode home on the shuttle with us."

"And when we got to the hotel, we saw the cowboy ghost of room 408!" Kate squealed.

"Cowboy ghost?" Mrs. Chang got that you've-got-to-be-kidding-me look on her face.

Bailey nodded. "We know he's not real, Mom. We just want to figure out how they do the special effect."

"Yeah, like the ghost children. We figured *that* one out." Kate reached for her laptop.

"Well, I guess there's no harm in that." Mrs. Chang glanced at her watch. "Oh, it's time for me to pick up Trina. She and a girl she met here at the hotel went to a movie. Will you be all right for a little while?"

"Yeah. We're going to get online and chat with the other Camp Club Girls."

"Okay. See you later." Mrs. Chang dropped a kiss on Bailey's nose and left.

"Let's download the pictures we took to send the other girls before we chat with them," Kate suggested. "Then they'll have them to look at while we talk."

Bailey and Kate each downloaded their photos and then logged into the CCG website chat room.

Bailey: *Hi! Anybody there?*
McKenzie: *I'm here.*
Sydney: *Me, too.*
Kate: *Hang on. I'll call the others to get them to log on.*

Elizabeth: *I'm here now.*

Alex: *Me, too.*

Bailey: *We found something weird on the hike we went on this morning.*

Elizabeth: *What was it?*

Kate: *We don't know. But we're hoping some of you might help us figure it out. We sent you some pictures of it.*

Bailey: *We hiked up a trail and found this weird, huge indentation in the ground. It was about the size of a bathtub. It had what looked like elk hair and tracks around it and it smelled awful. Sydney, we were hoping you could tell us if the tracks look like they belong to an elk. You'll see them in the pictures, too.*

Sydney: *I'll look and see. And I bet I know what that indentation was, too.*

Kate: *What?*

Sydney: *Hang on. I'll look at the picture to be sure. There it is. Yep. Was there any water nearby?*

Bailey: *Yeah, we saw a scummy pond with grass growing in it a few feet away.*

Sydney: *It was probably an elk wallow. And those are definitely elk tracks in the picture. My uncle hunts elk and he told me about them. Usually the male elk, the bulls, roll in wallows to cover their bodies with the scent of urine and droppings so they'll attract the female elk.*

Elizabeth: *Gross! What nasty cologne!*

Operation: Excitement!

Sydney: *You think that's bad? The female elk then roll in the wallow to get the same scent on them and let the bull know they're interested.*

Alex: *I'd rather pass notes.*

Sydney: *One thing's for sure. If you have wallows, you have elk.*

Bailey: *Anyway, back to the hike. We caught Justin and Joe shooting airsoft guns at some empty pop cans. We sent you a few shots of that, too, no pun intended! Just look at the pictures. They're a little blurry. The noise from the gun scared Biscuit to death!*

Kate: *Yeah, he flew out of my arms and ran at them, barking his head off.*

Bailey: *Justin, or should I say Oscar the Grouch, was so scared he aimed his gun right at poor little Biscuit and shot!*

McKenzie: *Oh no! Is he okay?*

Kate: *Yeah, he wasn't hurt. Apparently our wonder dog is faster than a speeding bullet or else Oscar the Grouch is a lousy shot. Biscuit must have just been freaked out over the sound of the gun because he ran into the woods and I ran after him.*

Bailey: *And I stayed to give those boys a piece of my mind!*

Sydney: *LOL. Careful. You might need that piece of your mind later.*

Elizabeth: *Guess you forgot the Bible says, "A gentle answer turns away wrath, but a harsh word stirs up anger."*

Bailey giggled.

Bailey: *Guess I did.*

Kate: *I found Biscuit after calling for him awhile. But then I realized I had wandered off the path and didn't know how to get back.*

Bailey: *In the meantime, I had gone to find Kate and Biscuit and I realized I was lost, too. But I asked God to help me. Then He gave me the idea to call Kate on her cell.*

Kate: *Boy, was I glad to hear from her. We remembered what Sydney taught us about using the position of the sun to figure out what direction we needed to go.*

Sydney: *Wow! I'm impressed!*

Kate: *So when we got back together, we used my dad's mini-GPS I had in my pocket to find the trail so we could get back to the town.*

Sydney: *Wait a minute. Back up. What do you mean "caught" the boys shooting their airsoft gun at the pop cans? They weren't really doing anything wrong.*

Bailey: *No, but they sure acted like they got caught at something.*

Kate: *They were defensive and angry.*

Elizabeth: *Maybe they didn't like being spied on.*

Kate: *Or maybe they're up to no good since they act that way no matter when we see them or what they're doing.*

Bailey: *Wait! I just remembered something I heard Justin say to Joe before he knew we were there.*

> *He said something like "We'll*
> *make them sorry they ever came here."*
> McKenzie: *Who do you think they were talking*
> *about?*

Bailey suddenly felt like a rock dropped to the bottom of her stomach.

> Bailey: *I hope he wasn't talking about Kate and*
> *me, but he sure seems to hate us.*
> Kate: *But why?*
> McKenzie: *You must be a threat to them in*
> *some way.*
> Bailey: *How can we be a threat to them when*
> *they don't even know us?*
> McKenzie: *They're obviously insecure. You just*
> *have to figure out why.*

For just a second, Bailey felt sorry for the boys, especially Justin. She remembered her mom saying maybe they had problems at home or something. Maybe they just needed someone to care about them. Bailey's loud sigh drew Kate's eyes from her computer.

> Bailey: *Maybe we just need to keep being nice to*
> *them. Find out what they're interested in and*
> *stuff like that. They could be going through a*
> *rough time or something and that's what*
> *makes them so grouchy.*
> Elizabeth: *That's a good idea. I'm proud of you,*
> *Bailey.*

Bailey: *I'm not saying it'll be easy. But I'll try.*

Kate: *Guess what?*

Alex: *I'll bite. What?*

Kate: *Bailey and I saw a new ghost at the hotel today.*

Sydney: *No way!*

Bailey: *Room 408. The room with the cowboy ghost.*

Kate: *Of course it has to be another special effect. It moves exactly the same every time it's seen. We're going to figure out how they do it.*

Bailey: *Yeah. He shows up in the window and stares out a minute then fades away to the left. The only problem is that if he was a real person, he'd plow into a wall if he turned that way.*

Alex: *Didn't they use some sort of projection system to make it look like there were ghosts in the movie* Casper? *They could be using one in that room, too. Or once I saw a movie where an image was etched onto a window and the sun shining on it made it come to life. Maybe you should look more closely at the window.*

Kate: *We'll do that. Bailey and I need to take a tour of that room to see if we spot anything unusual. Anyway, we just wanted to update you. Let us know if you have any more ideas about how ghosts could be created or any new information about elk.*

Bailey logged off and closed her laptop.

"All right." Kate exited the chat room and brought up a

blank document. "Let's see what we have so far in the elk mystery. One. We know the elk are spooked but don't know why." She typed the entry into the blank document.

Bailey jumped in. "Two. We know Justin and Joe have an airsoft gun and were in the woods today before the stampede."

Kate typed the second entry. "But then again, so were we."

"Three. Justin has a grouchy attitude all the time."

"Four. They visit their grandparents here every year." Kate continued typing but stopped. "We don't even know if any of this has anything to do with the elk problem."

"No, but a good sleuth follows hunches," Bailey said. "And I have a hunch it does."

"I hope we're not going down the wrong path." Kate looked thoughtful. "What about what we know about elk?"

"Well, we know they make wallows during mating season," Bailey offered.

"And we know they are more aggressive during that time as well."

"But not usually this much."

"We know they have a great sense of smell and can run really fast," Kate said as she typed.

"Boy, do we know that!" Bailey laughed. "We learned they're usually most active in the early morning and later in the evening, unless they're being harassed."

"That may be a key to this mystery."

"We know the male elk are the ones with that shrill bugle." Bailey did her best impersonation of an elk bugle, starting with the low grunts and ending with a high shriek.

Biscuit sat up and howled while Kate covered her ears and laughed. "You aren't quite ready for that bugling contest yet!"

"I still can't believe Grandpa Perkins didn't win that."

"I can't either. I wonder if that's why Justin was so grouchy today."

"Maybe. Something must be making him mad." Bailey felt a little sad inside, like when she knew a friend was going to do something wrong but she couldn't talk her out of it. She turned at the sound of the key card sliding in the door.

"Hey!" Mrs. Chang gave her standard greeting. "What are you two up to?"

"We just finished chatting with the other Camp Club Girls," Bailey said. "How was your movie, Trina?"

"Not bad." The teenager flipped on the TV.

"We told the other girls all about our hike and seeing the cowboy ghost," Kate told Mrs. Chang.

"Sounds like you had fun. By the way, Bailey, Dad and I are going out to a business dinner tonight."

"What about us?" Bailey stuck out her lower lip.

"Adults only, I'm afraid." Mom's eyes brightened. "But how about a pizza party? We can have it delivered to our room."

"Yeah!" Bailey and Kate gave each other a high five.

"How 'bout it, Trina?" Bailey asked.

"Fabulous." Trina said in a monotone, still channel surfing.

"It'll be fun!" Bailey informed her sister brightly.

"Whatever." Trina gave up on finding something to watch and turned off the TV. She flopped on the bed and started listening to her iPod.

"I'm going to get cleaned up and then I'll call in the pizza." Mrs. Chang headed for the shower.

A while later, Bailey whistled when her mom emerged looking fresh and pretty in her black dress, dangly earrings, and strappy heels. The familiar smell of her mom's perfume made Bailey want to snuggle in her lap like she did when she was a little girl.

"What kind of pizza do you want?"

"Pepperoni!" Bailey shouted.

"With black olives?" Kate asked.

"Sure, I like olives and so does Trina."

"Pepperoni and black olives it is." Mrs. Chang phoned in the order.

While they were waiting for the pizza, Mr. Chang came home and spruced up, too.

"You guys look great!" Bailey said.

A knock at the door signaled the beginning of the pizza party. Mr. Chang paid for the food and set it on the small table. Then he tapped Trina on the shoulder and she took out her earphones.

"We should be home between nine and ten," he told her. "You're in charge while we're gone. You hear that, Bales?"

Bailey and Kate both nodded.

The Changs blew the girls a kiss good-bye and told them to call on the cell phone if anything came up.

"We can handle this, Mom," Trina said.

"Good. I know you can. Have fun."

As soon as the door closed, the trio playfully shoved their way to the pizza. Trina lifted the lid. "Mmmm. Smell that."

They each took a slice and chatted and giggled as they ate. Kate fed Biscuit a couple of pieces of pepperoni.

"Trina, did you leave your iPod on?" Bailey asked.

"No. Why?"

Bailey cocked her head to listen. "I thought I heard piano music."

Trina put one earphone in. "Nope. It's not this."

"Listen. There it is again." Bailey craned her neck forward.

"I hear it, too." Kate said. "It's very soft, though."

"Sounds like old-fashioned music to me." Bailey went to the window to see if anyone was playing music outside but saw only people quietly strolling in the courtyard.

The music became louder.

"I hear it now." Trina joined Bailey at the window.

"It's not coming from outside." Kate put her ear to the air vent on the floor. "It sounds like it's coming through the vent!"

"It sounds. . .spooky." Kate shivered.

"Let's just turn on the TV and forget about it," Trina suggested.

The girls all sprawled out on the beds as Trina flipped through the channels.

A romantic comedy came on. "Oooo. This looks good." Trina fluffed her pillow and put it behind her back against the headboard.

"Didn't our hotel brochure say that F. O. Stanley's wife played the piano and sometimes guests still hear her music?"

"I think you're right! But would we be able to hear it clear up here?"

The eerie music continued.

Finally Bailey couldn't stand it anymore. "I don't know, but I'm going to find out where that music is coming from!"

"I'll come with you!" Kate announced.

"Fine with me," Trina said, still glazed over by the TV. "Just don't leave the building."

"Deal." Bailey grabbed another slice of pizza to munch on while they investigated.

Grabbing Biscuit, they walked down the hallway. The music seemed to get louder. Reaching the elevator, they pressed the DOWN button. When they reached the hotel lobby, the music was much louder.

Bailey marched to the front desk. "Excuse me."

Barbara, the surly hotel clerk, scowled at Biscuit.

"Can you tell me where that music is coming from?" Bailey smiled sweetly.

"From the Music Room, to your right." Barbara pointed to the room at the end of the lobby.

"The Music Room. Of course. Thank you." With a polite nod, Bailey turned to leave.

"And keep that dog under control."

"I will." Kate gave the woman a thumbs-up and raised Biscuit's paw in a wave.

Bailey and Kate walked on the lobby's shiny wooden floor to the doorway of the Music Room, the piano music growing ever louder. Stopping at the door, they peeked inside and saw that the room was unfurnished except for a grand piano at the far end. It sat in a raised alcove, almost a small, rounded room in itself. Its lid was propped open to allow the beautiful music to flow unhindered. A huge fireplace with white columns upholding the mantel took up most of the left wall. A giant mirror hung above it. Arched windows lined the other walls, with square-paned ones in the piano alcove. The piano sat sideways, but Bailey could clearly see the keys moving up and down from the door, though no one appeared to be playing it.

Bailey swallowed hard and looked at Kate, who had just used her free hand to remove her glasses and rub her eyes. She put them back on, steadying herself against the door frame. She and Bailey nodded pale-faced at each other. A ghost!

Trampled!

Kate, carrying Biscuit, followed Bailey cautiously across the threshold onto the glossy-wood Music Room floor. Immediately, the music stopped. Bailey grabbed Kate's arm. They tiptoed toward the piano, as if they were sneaking up on the ghost.

"Maybe whoever was playing will appear," Bailey whispered.

"I doubt it. But maybe we'll be able to see how they're doing the special effect."

"Yeah. I have to keep reminding myself it isn't real."

The girls stepped up into the alcove and inspected the piano.

"I wish I'd brought Biscuit's leash." Kate shifted the dog to her other arm and looked closer. "Aha! Just as I thought. It's a player piano."

"Huh?"

"A player piano. You know, the kind that has songs programmed into it so it plays by itself."

"Oh, I've seen those in stores. But doesn't someone have to start and stop it?"

"Usually." Kate continued checking all angles of the piano. She wrestled with Biscuit who was getting wiggly. "I

347

bet this one has an automatic switch or sensor somewhere that turns it on and off."

Bailey helped her search for a switch, even crawling underneath for a look. "I don't see anything."

Kate studied the strings and hammers for each key inside the piano. "There's so much stuff in here it's hard to tell what doesn't belong. But I think I may see something. Come over on this side for a better look."

Bailey was next to her in a flash.

"See that switch close to the hinge where the piano lid opens?"

"Yeah, I see it."

"I think it may be the culprit. And I think that box next to it is a timer that makes the music play only every so often."

"But how does it stop when someone comes in the room?"

Kate cocked her head and squinted her eyes. Bailey could practically see the wheels turning in her brain. "Maybe a motion sensor that's set to turn it off when someone comes through the door?"

"But we have to find it to be sure." Bailey's eyes started scanning the room. "There!"

Kate followed Bailey's finger to a small device mounted in the ceiling corner of the room. It was pointed directly at the doorway. "Yep, I bet that's our motion sensor."

"Let's go back out to the lobby and try it out." Bailey and Kate walked out to the lobby. They passed the time by looking at the Stanley Steamer car as they waited for the music to begin again.

Soon the melodious sound of the piano wafted into the lobby.

"There it goes!" Bailey made a beeline for the Music

Room and stopped abruptly outside the door.

"Okay. Ready?"

"Ready." Kate grabbed Bailey's hand and together they walked into the room. The music stopped. "I'm sure the motion detector saw us."

"I wonder how sensitive it is," Bailey said. "Like, I mean, do we have to enter the room or just move in the doorway?"

"Interesting. Let's find out." Kate, Biscuit, and Bailey filed back out to the lobby so the piano could reset.

Soon the music began again.

"Let's go!"

Bailey and Kate stopped in front of the doorway. "Let's try just kicking our foot through the doorway, but not actually going in," Bailey suggested.

Kate giggled and locked arms with Bailey in chorus line fashion. "Okay. On three. One. . .two. . .three!"

Kate and Bailey each kicked one foot out. Once again, the music stopped.

"Wow! Pretty sensitive!" Bailey grinned from ear to ear.

"Guess we've pretty much solved this mystery. Might as well go back to the room."

"Hey, there goes Justin and Joe across the yard." Bailey pointed toward the window. The floodlights shining on the yard spotlighted the two boys as they walked away from the hotel. One turned around as if to see if anyone was following them.

"Is that their gun he's carrying?" Kate asked.

"Couldn't be. It's too dark for target practice."

"Weird."

The boys disappeared into the shadows.

"Know what I was thinking?" Bailey asked.

"What?"

"I wonder if anyone's staying in room 408."

Kate headed for the front desk. "We could check. And if no one is, we could ask if we can go see it tomorrow."

"Exactly what I was thinking." Bailey asked Front Desk Barbara if the room was vacant.

"Hmmm. Let me check." Barbara typed something into her computer and waited. She ran her finger down the screen until she came to the line she wanted. "Yep. Looks like it's vacant."

"Can we go look at it tomorrow?" Kate asked.

"What for?"

"We're curious about Tex." Bailey smiled knowingly at Kate.

"Tex?" Barbara smirked.

"Yeah. You know. The cowboy ghost. We think we saw him this afternoon from the front lawn."

"Well, I'm off tomorrow, so you'll have to check back with whoever's working then."

"Okay. Thanks." Kate gave a friendly wave as they walked off.

Bailey let out a laugh. "I just had a crazy idea."

"Oh no. What?"

"Let's see if Justin and Joe want to see the room with us tomorrow."

"No way!"

Bailey put her hand out. "Aw, come on. We just talked to the other girls today about trying to get to know them better. What if they really are going through something bad and just need a friend?"

"I seriously doubt that."

"Well, so do I. But what's the harm in asking them? They'll probably just say no anyway."

"That's true. All right. Let's do it."

Suddenly, a man burst through the front door of the lobby. "The elk! They're stampeding again, and this time someone's hurt!"

Bailey and Kate hurried outside. Elk ran frantically in front of the hotel, sending some of the guests scrambling for cover on the porch. Biscuit leaped out of Kate's arms and darted right into the herd.

"Biscuit!" Kate screamed. The dust settled from the stampede, and people ran in all directions. Kate and Bailey sprinted to the yard where Biscuit lay motionless.

Kneeling beside the little dog, Bailey saw blood pooling beneath his right front paw. Ragged breaths puffed from his open mouth, and his tongue hung out one side. His eyes were open, but he didn't appear to see anything. "Oh, Biscuit!" Kate cried.

Shivering from the cold, Bailey pulled her cell phone from her pocket and steadied her finger to dial.

"Hello?" Trina said.

"Trina! The elk stampeded and Biscuit got trampled." Bailey choked down a sob. "We're on the front lawn. We need help."

"I'll be there as soon as I call Mom and Dad."

Bailey returned her phone to her pocket and wrapped her arms around herself to ward off the night chill.

Kate gently stroked the injured dog's side. "Hang on, Biscuit. Help's coming."

Bailey heard a siren in the distance. "Sounds like help is on its way for the people who were injured. I don't know if

351

they'll help dogs, too, or not."

Within minutes, a red and white ambulance screeched to a halt at the far side of the lawn where a group of people gathered. Medics knelt on the ground next to their patient then lifted him onto a stretcher and loaded him through the open back doors of the vehicle. Just as Bailey and Kate turned their attention back to Biscuit, they heard another siren. Looking back, they saw a second, and then a third ambulance arrive and take away two more people. Police cars began to filter in also, as well as news reporters.

"Those elk must have really been mad to run right into all those people," Bailey said sadly. "Or scared out of their wits."

"I hope the people who got hurt will be all right." Kate's forehead wrinkled with concern.

"We need to pray for them tonight—and Biscuit."

"Bailey!" Trina ran to them from the porch, carrying sweatshirts for both girls. "Thought you might need these."

"Thanks." Bailey slipped into her hoodie. "Biscuit's hurt bad. We don't know if we should move him or not. We don't want to injure him any more than he already is."

"That was smart of you." Trina put her arm around Kate, who wiped her eyes and nose with the sleeve of her sweatshirt. "I called Mom and Dad," Trina told her. "They heard about the stampede at the restaurant and were on their way home before I called. They'll know what to do."

"I think we need to say a prayer right now for Biscuit." Bailey laid her hand on the injured dog.

Trina took Kate's left hand, leaving her right hand free to continue comforting her dog.

"God, we're scared for Biscuit. Help him to be strong and brave. Help Mom and Dad to get here fast so it's not too late."

Bailey felt her face get warm.

"Well, that was nice of you to think of them. I think those boys need some good friends like you." Mrs. Chang reached back between the front seats and patted Bailey's knee.

Mr. Chang pulled into a parking space in front of the hotel. "It's been quite a night. You girls handled the events of the evening very well."

Bailey pulled her hoodie closer around her and huddled against the cold night air as the group hustled into the hotel lobby. Mr. Chang walked directly to the front desk, Bailey and Kate close behind, while Mrs. Chang and Trina waited by the elevator.

"Do you have any information about the condition of the people who were injured in the stampede this evening?" he asked Front Desk Barbara.

"Only what the news has been reporting." Barbara pointed to the small TV in the corner of the reception desk. "They say three people were taken to the hospital. A man is in serious condition and the other two were treated and released."

"Something is going to have to be done to make sure this doesn't happen again."

"I heard the news reporter saying there's talk of putting up a fence along the wooded areas at the base of the hills to try to keep the elk from coming into town so easily."

Mr. Chang nodded and turned to leave. "Thanks for the information."

"What'd she say?" Trina asked when Mr. Chang joined them at the elevator.

The elevator dinged and the doors opened for them to get on. Bailey pushed the button for the fourth floor.

"Three people were hurt, but only one is still in the hospital. He's in serious condition."

"Wonder who it was." Bailey felt the elevator whisk them up to their floor.

The doors opened on the fourth floor and there stood Grandma Perkins.

"Mrs. Perkins! Good to see you again," Mr. Chang said.

"It's nice to see you, too." Grandma Perkins seemed to be in a hurry to get on the elevator and leave. Bailey noticed her eyes looked teary.

"Is everything all right?" Mrs. Chang asked her.

Grandma Perkins shook her head and turned her eyes away. "It's Glen. He was hurt in the elk stampede tonight. We thought it would be fun to surprise our grandsons with their favorite ice cream before they went to bed. When we got out of the car and were walking across the lawn, the elk charged through. Glen pushed me out of the way, but he got trampled. He's still in the hospital." Tears brimmed in her eyes.

"Grandpa Perkins was one of the people who got hurt?" Bailey cried.

Grandma Perkins nodded and wiped her eyes.

"I'm so sorry to hear that," Mrs. Chang said. "We heard someone was seriously hurt, but we didn't know it was him. We'll be praying for his quick recovery."

"Thank you." The older woman had a faraway look. "I just wish we could figure out what's causing those elk to act like this."

"I hope they come up with a solution before anyone else gets hurt," Mr. Chang said.

"I'd better get home. I'm about worn out from being at the hospital and from all the stress. I got a few bumps and bruises myself. My son sent me home and promised he'd stay with Glen tonight. Janice offered to drive me home, but I told her I was fine."

Mrs. Chang took Grandma Perkins's hands in hers. "Of course. Please let us know if we can do anything to help you or your family."

"Thank you so much." She pushed the button and the doors closed.

—•—•—

"I can't believe it." Bailey shook her head as they entered their room. "Grandpa Perkins is such a nice man. I wish he hadn't gotten hurt."

"We have lots of things to pray about tonight, don't we?" Mrs. Chang said. "Including thanking God that none of us were injured. You girls were pretty close to the action. I'm glad you're all right." She kissed all three girls on the head.

"Mom, do you think we could go see Grandpa Perkins at the hospital tomorrow?" Bailey asked.

"That would be nice, if they let kids in. I'll have to check the hospital rules first. We wouldn't stay long. He needs his rest to get better."

"I feel sorry for Justin and Joe. They must be really sad." Kate pulled out her pajamas and headed for the bathroom to change.

Bailey's eyes met Kate's. She suddenly thought, *I hope they weren't responsible for that elk stampede!*

CHAPTER 10

The Cowboy Ghost

The next morning, through a fog of sleepiness, Bailey heard her dad leave for one of his meetings. She had an uneasy feeling but couldn't put her finger on what it was. Then it came to her—the stampede the night before. Biscuit was hurt and so was Grandpa Perkins. It seemed like a bad dream.

Kate rolled over and stretched. "Biscuit?" Still half-asleep, she felt around the bed for him.

"Kate, Biscuit's not here, remember?" Bailey whispered, not wanting to wake the others.

Kate sat up, worry lines creasing her forehead. She rubbed her eyes, blew her nose, and put on her glasses. Her shoulders slumped like she held the weight of the world on them. "Oh yeah. I forgot."

"I was thinking," Bailey said softly, looking to see if her mom and Trina were still asleep. "The elk stampeded shortly after we saw Justin and Joe walking toward the hills last night."

"I know. I thought the same thing."

"I think they've been shooting at the elk and making them charge into town."

Kate thought on that a moment. "The elk are being harassed and it's making them more aggressive, just like Sydney said."

"I bet if Justin and Joe caused the stampede, they're sorry for it now that their grandpa got hurt."

"If it's them, I hope they've learned their lesson." Kate's eyes blazed fiercely.

"But why would they want to make the elk stampede in the first place? I don't get it."

"I don't know, either. I have a feeling there's a whole other piece of this mystery that we haven't begun to figure out yet."

"I'm starting to think they're really messed up. They seem to have a nice family, so I don't think that's the problem." Bailey propped herself up on her elbow.

"No, it must be something else. McKenzie mentioned that they might feel threatened in some way. Maybe we need to think about what it could be."

"I know," Bailey replied. "I wish there was some way she could talk to Justin and Joe. She's so good at figuring people out."

"Guess for now we'll just have to rely on her suggestions and figure it out ourselves."

"I think we need to pray for them," Bailey said. "And we need to ask God to show us if there's some way we can help them."

"Maybe if we invite them to see room 408 with us today, we'll have a chance to learn more about them." Kate put her hand over her mouth and sneezed, waking Trina and Mom. She smiled sheepishly. "Sorry."

"Good morning to you, too," Trina mumbled then buried her head under her pillow.

"Do you know when we can go get Biscuit?" Kate asked Mrs. Chang.

"I'll call to find out." She looked at the clock. "They're

probably just opening." She picked up the vet's business card and dialed the number. "Yes, this is Dory Chang and I was wondering how our dog, Biscuit, is doing and when we might pick him up." Mrs. Chang covered the mouthpiece of the phone and whispered to Kate, "They're checking."

Kate nodded.

Mrs. Chang directed her attention back to the person on the phone. "Okay. Thank you. We'll see you later. Bye."

"What'd they say?" Bailey asked.

"They said Biscuit is doing fine and we can pick him up this afternoon. They need to change his bandage this morning and check his vital signs. If something doesn't check out, they'll give us a call. Otherwise, he's good to go."

"Good. I can't wait to have him back," Kate said, beaming.

"Let's get dressed so we can ask the front desk if we can see room 408 before we get Biscuit." Bailey hopped off the bed and grabbed some clothes.

"Good idea. You think the boys will want to come after what happened last night?" Kate asked.

"Hard to say. But it could be a nice distraction for them." Bailey slipped into her jeans and T-shirt. "I'm ready."

"Wait just a minute, missy," Mrs. Chang said in her mom voice. "You need to eat something and brush your teeth and hair before you go anywhere."

"Aw, Mom. We have ghosts to chase down." Bailey smirked at her mom.

"Then you'll need all the energy you can get from breakfast. Have a seat." Mrs. Chang set the box of cereal in front of her daughter and grabbed a carton of milk from the minifridge.

Kate quickly dressed and joined Bailey at the table. "Did

the vet say anything else about Biscuit?"

"No, I'm afraid not."

"I can't wait to see him."

"We should turn on the morning news to see if there are any new developments about the stampede." Mrs. Chang grabbed the remote and pushed POWER.

"Witnesses say they observed some young men with guns just before the stampede. . . ," the newscaster said.

Bailey froze, her spoon halfway between her open mouth and her bowl. Kate choked on the bite she'd just taken. Coughing, she snatched a napkin from the table.

"Are you okay?" Mrs. Chang asked her.

"Y–Yes. I'm fine."

Bailey glimpsed her friend's worried eyes. They finished breakfast, brushed their teeth and hair, and were out the door to go see if Justin and Joe wanted to go ghost hunting with them. Kate grabbed a small pad of paper and a pen in case they needed to take notes.

"I can't believe our suspicions about Justin and Joe were on the news!" Bailey said as they walked down the hall.

"I hope they didn't do anything." Kate knocked on the Perkinses's door.

A moment later, Mrs. Perkins answered. Bailey told them why they were there.

"Well, how thoughtful. Just a minute, I'll ask them."

A moment later she returned. "Thank you, girls, for thinking of them, but with all that's happened, they think they'll pass this time. We're going to go to the hospital to see their grandpa later. He was hurt in the stampede last night."

"Yes, we heard. I'm sorry." Bailey shifted her weight from one foot to the other. "Mrs. Perkins, do you know if they'd let us see Grandpa Perkins if we went? If children are allowed in the hospital?"

"Yes, I saw children visiting other patients last night."

Kate brightened up. "That would be great. We'd like to go visit him."

"That would be lovely. I know he'll be glad to see you."

"Okay. Well, tell Justin and Joe hi and that we're sorry about their grandpa."

"I'll do that." Mrs. Perkins closed the door.

Standing on tiptoe a short time later, Bailey leaned against the tall front desk. "Excuse me. We were wondering if we could see room 408, please."

The man at the counter smiled. "Barbara told me some young gals might be coming to ask about that."

Bailey looked at Kate, eyebrows high with surprise.

"Let me see. Yes, it's vacant, though I can't let you in without an adult. Would you like me to get a bellhop to take you?"

"Yes, please!" Bailey could hardly contain her excitement. They were going to get to see the haunted room!

"And what are your names?" the front desk clerk asked.

"I'm Bailey Chang, and this is Kate Oliver."

"Very good. I'll get someone to take you up."

"Thank you."

"Now remember," Kate said, pulling Bailey aside while they waited for the bellhop. "We need to look for anything that could be used to make it look like the cowboy appears in the window then fades to the left."

"Got it." Bailey turned at the sound of footsteps. A young man Bailey guessed to be in his twenties approached them.

"You must be Bailey and Kate." He stuck out his hand and shook Bailey's hand first, then Kate's. "I'm Lance. Nice to meet you. So you're interested in the cowboy ghost of room 408, huh?" he asked as they walked to the elevator.

Kate nodded. "We saw him from the front yard yesterday."

"What time of day was it?" The elevator doors opened and they stepped in.

"Around noon. Why?"

"Seems like that's the time most people see him these days."

Kate looked at Bailey, who widened her eyes.

"Why do you suppose that is?" Bailey asked, fishing for more information.

"It has something to do with the lighting. You know, the sun being directly overhead and all."

"Interesting." Kate pulled her pen and paper from her pocket and jotted down the lighting clue. The elevator doors opened, and Lance led them down the hall to room 408. He slid his key card through the slot and they heard it unlock, the tiny green light flashing. "Here we are! I'll wait here by the door for you. Take your time looking around."

Bailey gazed at the room that looked remarkably like their own room down the hall. Nothing special or haunted about it.

Kate walked slowly around the room, inspecting every wall and corner. Bailey followed her as she went to the window over the bathroom sink. It overlooked the front yard where they'd been standing yesterday when they saw the ghost.

"If the ghost looked like it faded to the left from out there," she said to Bailey, "then it would have to move to the right from in here, since it faced the window." Sure enough, the bathroom wall was right there, making it impossible to move in that direction.

"Alex thought we should feel the glass, remember?" Bailey asked.

Kate leaned closer to the window and ran her fingers over the glass. "There are definitely scratches or etching or something. I can feel them." She moved her open hand along the window's surface.

Bailey felt it, too. "Maybe people tried to claw their way out of here to escape the ghosts!"

Kate laughed. "I doubt that. I think Alex may be right. It's some kind of etching."

"Sometimes they put etched glass or thick blocks of glass in bathroom windows so no one can see in." Bailey scratched her head. "But who could see in way up here on the fourth floor?"

"We did! Or we thought we saw the cowboy ghost, anyway."

"Let's go out on the lawn at noon again today so we can check it out. We'll see if we see that cowboy ghost again. Maybe Lance will even bring us back up here then so we can see what it looks like from the inside."

Kate high-fived Bailey. "Let's go ask him."

Lance was leaning against the door frame listening to his iPod. He snatched the earphones from his ears when he saw the girls. "All done?"

"For now," Bailey replied. "But we were wondering if there's any chance you could bring us back up here around noon. We want to see what the room looks like at the time of day we saw the cowboy."

"If I'm not busy with any other guests, I'll be glad to."

"Great! Thanks!"

"I'll walk you back down to the lobby." Lance extended his arm to show the way.

"Oh, thank you," Kate said, "but we're going back to our room now. It's just down this hall. Thanks for letting us in."

"No problem. I'll try to meet you in the lobby around noon."

Bailey followed Kate to their room. "Why did you want to go back to our room? There's not much to do there."

"We need to tell the other girls what happened last night." Kate's eyes grew serious.

"Oh, yeah. I almost forgot they don't know about Biscuit or Grandpa Perkins yet."

"Or that we're pretty sure Justin and Joe were involved in the stampede and that the news talked about boys with guns going into the hills just before the stampede."

"We do have a lot to cover with them!" Bailey slid her key card in the door.

"We're back," Bailey announced when they entered the room.

"I was just getting ready to call you." Mrs. Chang bustled around tidying up and then grabbed her purse. "Trina and I are going shopping. Do you want to go?"

Bailey looked at Kate to see if she wanted to go. She detected the slight shake of her head. "No. I don't think so. We were just there yesterday when we went hiking."

"Okay. You'll be all right here?"

Bailey nodded. "We're going to call the Camp Club Girls to tell them about last night's stampede and that Biscuit got hurt."

Mrs. Chang kissed Bailey on the cheek. "Sounds good. We'll probably be back around one o'clock or so. There are sandwich makings in the fridge if you get hungry. We'll go get Biscuit after Trina and I get home."

"Okay. See you later. Have fun!"

Kate dialed Elizabeth then conferenced in all the other girls, including Bailey.

"Everyone there?" Each one confirmed they were there and could hear each other.

"Good. We have a lot to tell you about since yesterday," Bailey said.

"Really? How much could have happened in less than twenty-four hours?" Alex asked.

"A lot! We'll start at the beginning. We heard creepy ghost music last night and went to investigate," Kate began. "Legend says it's the ghost of F. O. Stanley's wife, Flora, playing the piano. Turns out the ghost music came from the Music Room where she always played, but it's really just a piano player on a timer. If anyone comes into the room when it's playing, the music stops."

Bailey picked up the story. "We discovered it's on a motion sensor that's tied into the timer. So if the detector senses motion in the doorway, it turns off the timer and player piano, stopping the music."

"Awesome! You guys are getting good at this!" Sydney exclaimed.

Bailey laughed. "But that's not all! While we were still in the lobby, there was another stampede in front of the hotel."

"I was carrying Biscuit because I'd forgotten his leash," Kate added. "He heard the noise and bolted from my arms and ran outside."

"No!" Alex said.

"We chased after him, but it was too late." Kate's voice shook as she relived the horrible evening. "He'd been trampled by the elk and was lying in the grass with a bloody paw."

"It was terrible!" Bailey wailed. "Poor Biscuit could hardly breathe he hurt so bad."

"What did you do?" Elizabeth asked.

"We had to take him to the hospital," Kate said.

"And get this," Bailey said. "Someone had just told my parents where the closest one was and which vet to ask for!"

"Wow," Elizabeth said. "That sounds like a real God-thing!"

"Totally." Kate cleared her throat. "And the hospital was pretty close, too!"

"You did the right thing by not picking Biscuit up to comfort him," McKenzie said. "A loving touch is all anyone really needs as they wait for help in a time like that. So how is he now?"

"Well, the doctor checked him over," Kate told her. "He had a crushed paw and some broken ribs. They wrapped his paw up in a big bandage and gave him some pain medicine to make him sleep so he could heal easier. We had to leave him at the hospital overnight, but we're going to get him this afternoon." Kate grinned triumphantly.

Sydney sighed. "That's a relief."

"Give the puppy a hug for me when he gets home," Alex said.

"And an extra treat from me!" McKenzie added.

"I'm glad he's going to be okay," Elizabeth said. "I'll be sure to remember him in my prayers. You know, in Proverbs, the Bible tells us a righteous man cares for the needs of his animals. I'd say you've done exactly that."

"Thanks, Lizzy." Kate smiled shyly at Bailey.

"But that's not the worst of it!" Bailey continued. "Three people were hurt in that stampede, too!"

"Oh no!" Sydney cried.

"Here's the sad part—the one hurt the most was Justin and Joe's Grandpa Perkins." Bailey couldn't bring herself to call Justin "Oscar the Grouch" under the circumstances.

"That is sad," McKenzie said. "How are they taking it?"

"We don't really know." Bailey shrugged, even though the others couldn't see it through the phone.

"We haven't actually talked to them ourselves yet."

"But here's the creepy part," Bailey continued. "We saw Justin and Joe walking toward the hills the night of the stampede."

"And it was only a few minutes later that the stampede happened." Kate bit her lower lip.

"We think they had their gun with them even though it was way too dark for them to do any target practice."

"Not only that," Kate added, "the news station this morning reported that witnesses had seen two young men with guns before the stampede. So we weren't the only ones who noticed."

"Man," Sydney said. "Those boys are going to have some explaining to do."

"You're telling me." Bailey pulled her lip balm out of her pocket and smoothed some on.

"We want to try to get to know them better to see if we can help them in any way," Kate said.

"They must be really afraid and lonely right now. Not to mention sad about their grandpa," McKenzie added. "They really do need some good friends like you."

Bailey and Kate then briefly told the Camp Club Girls about their trip to room 408 that morning.

"So we're hoping to go back up to see it around noon," Kate said.

"And we want to look at that window from the lawn at that time to see if the cowboy ghost shows up."

"Keep us posted," Alex said. "That sounds like an awesome hotel!"

"We will!" Bailey said. "And in the meantime, we have to figure out what the boys are so angry about."

"Maybe you'll remember something they said that will give you a clue," McKenzie said.

"Yeah, we'll have to think back about our conversations with them," Kate agreed.

Someone knocked at Bailey and Kate's hotel door, ending the conference call. Bailey made sure the chain was latched on the door before opening it the three inches it allowed. She inhaled sharply when she saw who stood on the other side.

Confession

Kate came to the door and peered out over Bailey's head to see Justin and Joe.

"Justin! Joe! What are you doing here?" Bailey unhooked the chain and opened the door.

"W–We just wanted to see if you want to go to the hospital with our family." Justin inspected his black and red Nikes as he spoke. "My mom said you wanted to visit my grandpa."

"Yes, we do," Kate said. "We're sorry he was hurt."

"The only problem is that my parents aren't here for me to ask permission right now." Bailey frowned.

"Can you call them?" Joe asked.

"Yeah. Sure." Bailey was so surprised by this unexpected invitation she could hardly get her words out. "When are you leaving?"

"Later this afternoon," Justin replied. "We just wanted to give you a heads-up in case you wanted to come along."

"I'll call my mom right now." Bailey grabbed her phone from her pocket and speed-dialed. "Mom? Can we go with the Perkinses to the hospital later today to see their grandpa? Okay. That should work. Thanks. Love you, too."

"Well?" Justin asked.

"She said yes. She'll pick us up at the hospital when she and my sister are done shopping, and then we'll pick up Kate's dog from the vet. Plus, she also wants to see your grandpa."

"Why's your dog at the vet?" Joe asked.

"He got trampled in the stampede, too," Kate said.

"He did? Is he all right?" Justin seemed genuinely concerned about the little dog.

"He broke some ribs, and his paw got messed up." Kate grimaced. "He had to spend the night there, but he's getting out today."

"He might not be quite as fast as he was when he saw you in the hills yesterday," Bailey teased the boys.

"Thank goodness for that!" Justin cracked a shy smile, the first Bailey had ever seen on his face. It was a nice smile, she decided, looking at his straight white teeth. He was cute.

"Thanks for inviting us to go with you," Kate said.

"We'll knock on your door when we're ready to leave." Joe seemed more relaxed than Bailey remembered him being before, maybe because Justin wasn't so irritable.

"Wait!" Bailey called. "We're going to check out room 408 where the cowboy ghost is always seen today at noon. You wanna come?"

Justin looked at Joe and shrugged. "Sure."

"We're meeting the bellhop, Lance, in the lobby then if you want to meet us there, too."

"Okay, we'll see you in the lobby at twelve o'clock," Joe said.

"Great. See you then." Kate shut the door and latched the chain.

"Can you believe that?" Bailey exploded.

"They're like different people today!"

371

"Well, they can't help but be changed by what happened to their grandpa." Bailey shook her head. "But I never dreamed the change would be this dramatic."

"Let's tell the girls we're going so they can pray that we have an opportunity to share our faith with the boys," Kate suggested. "This could be just the chance we've been waiting for."

Bailey snatched her laptop from the bed, and Kate grabbed hers off the nightstand. "We'll just have to tell whoever's online since we don't have time to get everyone together before they pick us up." Bailey logged on.

Bailey: *Anyone out there?*
Elizabeth: *Hi! I'm here.*
McKenzie: *Me, too.*
Kate: *Of course, I'm here.*

Bailey looked from her computer to Kate and they traded grins.

Bailey: *You'll never guess who was just here.*
McKenzie: *The ghost of Christmas past?*
Kate: *LOL. No, but a very good guess considering where we are.*
Bailey: *It was Justin and Joe!*
McKenzie: *No way! What'd they want?*
Kate: *They invited us to go with them to the hospital to see their grandpa.*
Elizabeth: *That's a miracle!*
Bailey: *That's what we thought. And they were actually nice to us, not grouchy at all.*

Kate: *We told them about Biscuit getting hurt
and Justin asked if he was going to be okay.*

Bailey: *And he smiled a really nice smile when I
teased him.*

McKenzie: *LOL. You're funny.*

Kate: *Anyway, we wanted you to be praying for us.*

Bailey: *Those boys really need Jesus in their
hearts so they'll be happier.*

McKenzie: *And they'll need good friends to
support them if they were involved in the
stampedes.*

Elizabeth: *You can show them God's
unconditional love. I'll be praying.*

Kate: *Thanks. We knew we could count on you.*

Bailey: *Plus, we invited them to go with us to
check out the cowboy ghost and they said yes!*

McKenzie: *You're kidding!*

Kate: *I know. We can hardly believe it.*

Bailey: *We have to eat before then, so we'd better
go. But maybe you can get the word out to the
other girls so they can pray, too.*

Elizabeth: *Okay. We'll try. But about these ghosts
you're chasing—just remember that Hebrews
9:27 says that man is destined to die once,
and after that to face judgment.*

Bailey: *What's that supposed to mean?*

Elizabeth: *It means ghosts aren't real. Once we
die, we're dead. We don't come back to haunt
people as ghosts.*

Kate: *We know they're not real, Elizabeth,
but thanks for the reminder.*

Operation: Excitement!

Bailey: *Yeah, thanks. It's easy to get carried away with this stuff sometimes. We'll keep you posted. See ya.*

Bailey logged off and closed her laptop. Kate got out the bread and started making a peanut butter and jelly sandwich.

"Something Justin said at the Elkfest just came to me," Bailey said.

Kate spread the peanut butter on her bread. "What was it?"

"I think it may be what McKenzie was talking about when she said the boys must feel threatened somehow. Remember how Justin was so mad when we said we hoped Grandpa Perkins would win the bugling contest?" Bailey grabbed the peanut butter jar. "He said something about how the tourists shouldn't be able to win and should just go home."

"I thought he was just kidding," Kate said around a bite of sandwich.

"So did I until I looked at him. He was mad and dead serious." Bailey finished making her sandwich and poured a glass of milk.

"That could be it, Bailey!"

"Justin and Joe used to visit their grandparents here before all the tourists started coming. Maybe Estes Park has changed so much from all the tourists that Justin wants them to leave."

"He could be angry that their quiet vacation spot is now crowded and busy." Kate took another bite. "I bet the tourists don't take care of the place like the locals, either."

"I know I've seen some of the tourists littering and leaving messes behind," Bailey said.

"That would explain why Justin didn't like us at first. If he feels threatened by tourists, he'd feel threatened by us since we're tourists!"

Bailey stopped eating. "Maybe he's using that gun to scare the elk into town so they'll scare the tourists away."

"But how did he always know where to find the elk?" Kate asked.

Bailey bit into her sandwich and thought a second. Then her eyes lit up. "Sydney said one thing's for sure. If you have wallows, you have elk."

"That's it!" Kate yelled. "The wallows! The boys are finding the elk by finding the wallows. Bailey, I think we may have just figured out our mystery."

"Now we just have to prove it."

"Come on, we have to get down to the lobby. It's almost noon!"

As they exited the elevator, they saw Lance waiting for them. The Perkins boys showed up moments later.

"Everyone ready to check out room 408?" Lance asked.

"Can we start by looking at it from the courtyard first to see if we can see the cowboy ghost?" Bailey asked.

"Sure," Lance said. "I'll wait here for you."

The foursome went to the front yard and looked up to the fourth floor window.

"There he is!" Kate pointed at the image.

"Cool!" Justin said. "I've never actually seen him before."

"We've always heard about this, but never saw it for ourselves!" Joe added.

"Okay, so we know he's showing up right now," Bailey said. "Let's go to the room to see if we can figure out how it's happening."

Lance escorted them to the fourth floor and unlocked the door. The room was bright, flooded with sunlight.

"Look at the etching on the glass now," Bailey said. "You can see a lot more of it with the sun shining directly on it."

"Yeah," Kate agreed. "I can see the whole image of the cowboy now."

"Why couldn't we see it before?" Bailey asked Lance.

He smiled. "You were right about the etching on the glass. When the sunlight shines directly on it, you can see all of it. But some of the etching is done so lightly that it only shows up under bright light. That's why you couldn't see the whole image this morning."

"Look!" Joe said. "A shadow is starting to move across the window."

Bailey and Kate looked at each other, eyes wide. "That must be what makes it look like the cowboy's turning toward the wall before he disappears!"

"Exactly," Lance said. "You guys are pretty smart."

"But wait a minute," Kate said. "If it depends on the sunlight to make it appear, then wouldn't it show up at different times of day depending on the time of year? You know, with the rotation of the earth and all."

Lance laughed. "Now you're really thinking! And you're right. You just happen to be here when the sun shines on it around noon. Other times of the year it's earlier or later in the day." He leaned toward Bailey and said in a mock whisper, "That makes it more mysterious."

"Wow." Bailey walked to the window and ran her hand over the etching. "I can't believe we figured that out."

"Well, we might not have if it weren't for Alex's help about the etchings," Kate reminded her.

Lance looked at his watch. "I'd better get back to work."

"Thanks for showing us all this and confirming our theory," Kate said as they all left the room.

Closing the door behind him, Lance said, "My pleasure!"

Bailey turned to the boys. "I think we'll go out on the porch for a while. If we're not in our room when you're ready to go to the hospital, you can find us down there."

Joe nodded. "Okay, see you this afternoon."

●—●—●

At the hospital, everyone grew quiet. They'd chatted all during the ride, but when they turned into the parking lot, Justin and Joe were back to their usual grouchy faces. Justin's eyebrows made a sharp V-shape over his eyes.

Bailey and Kate walked in silence with the boys' family. When they came to Grandpa Perkins's room, Bailey could hardly believe it was him in the bed. Tubes snaked from his arms and nose. His face was bruised and swollen. His silver hair stuck out in odd places and lay too flat in others.

Grandma Perkins was sitting in a chair by the bed but stood when they entered the room. She motioned for Justin and Joe's dad to take her seat. The others sat on chairs that were brought in and put around the room. Bailey and Kate sat on the far side of the room while Justin and Joe parked themselves close to the door. Their mother stood on one side of Grandpa's bed and Mr. Perkins, now in Grandma's chair, took his father's hand.

"Hi, Dad. We're all here—Janice, Justin, Joe, and even our friends, Bailey Chang and Kate Oliver from down the hall at our hotel. Remember? They cheered you on during the bugling contest at the Elkfest."

Grandpa Perkins's eyelids fluttered then opened slightly.

A faint smile crossed his lips.

"You don't have to say anything, Dad. Save your strength for getting better."

Bailey heard a chair scrape and saw Justin leave the room, followed by Joe. She looked at Kate, wondering if they should go. Kate nodded and they went into the hallway where they found Justin and Joe arguing in loud whispers.

"We can't tell!" Justin snapped.

"We have to," Joe said. "They'll find out sooner or later and it would be better if they heard it from us."

"Justin? Joe?" Bailey said.

The brothers' heads jerked toward them in surprise, their eyes blazing.

"Look, we don't mean to intrude, but maybe we can help." Bailey walked closer to Justin and Joe.

"What do you know about anything?" Justin barked.

Kate spoke gently. "We know you seem to be in trouble and we'd like to help."

"No one can help us," Joe said, tears filling his eyes.

"That's not true. If we can't help, we know who can." Bailey's voice was strong and confident.

"But first you have to tell us the problem." Kate stood waiting for their reply.

The boys remained silent.

Justin drew in a deep breath and blew it out slowly. He eyed Joe, who nodded. Justin looked at Bailey and she noticed his chin quiver. Tears pooled in his eyes. "It's our fault. My fault, really. Joe tried to talk me out of it," he finally whispered.

"What's your fault?" Bailey thought she knew, but she figured it was important for Justin to say it himself.

"The stampede. All of them. And Grandpa's injuries."

"How is it your fault? What did you do?" Kate asked.

"We—I—scared the elk. I shot around them with my airsoft gun to spook them. I never shot directly at the elk. Only in the trees and bushes around them. Joe came along because I pressured him. He didn't want to be involved."

"Why did you want to scare the elk? Didn't you see how it made them stampede?"

"Yeah, I saw," Justin replied. "That was the point. I remember when Joe and I were little and we'd come here to visit my grandparents. This place was awesome. It was so beautiful. But over the years the tourists began coming and it started to change. They didn't care about taking care of this place since they'd be going home in a week or two. They acted like they owned the place just because they threw their money around in all these shops.

"The Elkfest used to be just for the locals," he continued, "but now all these fancy tourists were joining it. It made me sick. I wanted Estes Park to be peaceful like it used to be. It was our special place with our grandparents until those tourists ruined it. So I hoped the elk would scare them away."

"How did you know where to find the elk? It seems like you always knew where they were."

"I just looked for a wallow and knew they'd be close by."

"Just as we thought," Bailey said.

"Where there are wallows, there are elk." Justin smiled, but his eyes were sad. "Wait a minute. You *knew* that? Did you know what we were doing, too?"

Bailey nodded. She turned to Justin and put her hand on his arm. "It's okay, Justin. We're still your friends. We'll explain later. But you need to tell your parents."

Justin shook his head. "I can't."

"Sure you can. We'll go with you," Kate said. "And God will give you the strength to do what you need to do."

"You talk about God like He's standing right here with us," Justin said.

Bailey laughed. "That's because He is!"

"I wish I had faith like that," Joe said.

"You can!" Kate assured him. "You just have to ask God for it. He loves to help people believe."

Justin shook his head. "Seems like God wouldn't want anything to do with someone like me."

"That's the cool thing about God," Kate said. "He's not like people who only love popular, nice-looking people, or those who never mess up. He especially loves those who need help and who have done things they shouldn't."

"When you really think about it, that includes all of us." Bailey could hardly believe they were having this conversation. She knew the Camp Club Girls' prayers were giving her and Kate the courage to tell the boys about God.

Justin looked at them. "Maybe you're right." He looked toward the hospital room door. "I guess it's time to tell them."

Bailey and Kate followed Justin and Joe back into Grandpa Perkins's room.

"I—I have something I need to say," Justin began. "I owe you a huge apology. I don't know if you'll be able to forgive me."

"Forgive you for what?" Mrs. Perkins looked surprised.

"For causing all this trouble."

"This isn't your fault, son," Mr. Perkins said. "No one could have stopped those elk."

"That's where you're wrong." Justin told the story to his parents and grandparents. "So if I hadn't been so stupid and wanted everything the way it used to be, I wouldn't have shot at the trees and bushes around the elk to spook them and this never would have happened. Grandpa's hurt because of me, and I'm so sorry."

Mr. Perkins's forehead creased with worry, but his words were gentle. "I'm disappointed in what you did, Justin. I always taught you to be responsible with guns and never to use them for harm. You used your airsoft gun inappropriately, and there will be consequences." Mr. Perkins put his arm around his son's shoulder. "But it takes a strong man to admit when he's wrong. I'm glad you told the truth."

"You know you could never do anything to make us stop loving you," his mother said. "Not even this."

"I know." Justin's face relaxed. "You guys are the best."

Mr. Perkins turned to his younger son. "And Joe. I'm proud of you for not taking part in this. Even though you went with him, you did try to talk him out of it."

Joe ran to his father's arms and hugged him.

"However," Mr. Perkins added, "even if you couldn't stop Justin, you should have come to Mom or me. You should always speak up and tell an adult if you know someone is involved in dangerous activities. Maybe none of this would have happened." Justin's face was white, and Joe's ears went red. "You will both have consequences."

A tap at the door shifted their attention in that direction. "Hello?"

"Mom!" Bailey cried, glad to have the tension broken.

Mrs. Chang and Trina entered.

"How is he doing?" she asked.

"The doctor says he's making progress," Mr. Perkins said.

"His vital signs are good. It's just a matter of time and healing now."

"He certainly is in our prayers," Mrs. Chang said.

"We appreciate that," Mrs. Perkins replied.

Mrs. Chang turned to the girls. "Kate, are you ready to go get Biscuit?"

"I'm more than ready!" Kate replied. "I can't wait to see him."

"Where is that cute little dog?" Mrs. Perkins asked. "On a playdate?"

"Oh no," Kate said seriously. "He's at the animal hospital. He was hurt in the stampede."

"No!" Mrs. Perkins went to Kate and took her hands in hers. "You were kind to come see Grandpa Perkins when Biscuit had an injury to be concerned about. I'm sorry I didn't know about it sooner."

"At least Biscuit is recuperating." Kate looked at Grandpa Perkins. "I wish Grandpa could go home today, too."

"He'll be home before we know it," Grandma Perkins piped in. "And stirring up trouble, no doubt."

"We'd better go," Mrs. Chang said. "You girls ready?"

"Yeah," Bailey said. Then turning to Justin and Joe, she said, "We'll be around if you want to talk or anything."

Justin smiled. "Thanks. We just might."

●—●—●

On the way to the vet, Bailey and Kate told Mrs. Chang and Trina what they'd learned.

"You're kidding!" Mrs. Chang said.

"Nope. And here's the cool part," Bailey said. "We got a chance to tell them about God and how He loves them no matter what they've done." Bailey's smile was as big as a watermelon slice.

"That is cool," Trina said.

"What did they say?" Mrs. Chang asked.

"Joe said he always wanted to have faith like that," Bailey said.

"And I told him God would help him believe if he just asked Him."

"You girls amaze me." Mrs. Chang looked at them in her rearview mirror. "I'm proud of you. And I bet God's smiling pretty big right now, too."

"I hope so," Bailey said. "We told them we would be around if they wanted to talk or anything."

"You've done what you can for now," Mrs. Chang said. "Now God will do His part and help them sort it all out." She pulled the car into a parking space in front of the animal hospital.

Bailey and Kate jumped out of the car and ran to the door. Mrs. Chang and Trina met them inside.

"The nurse is getting Biscuit," Kate said. "We already gave them our name."

Soon, the nurse came out with Biscuit on a leash. He limped on his bandaged paw, but when he saw Kate he hobbled on three legs to her, straining the leash.

"Hey, buddy!" Kate knelt so Biscuit could lick her face. "I missed you!"

"Looks like he missed you, too!" the nurse said. "As you can see, we've bandaged his middle so his ribs will heal faster. Since the bandage only sticks to itself, you can remove it in a week or two. Just try to keep him as calm as possible for the next couple of weeks. No jumping up or down onto furniture."

"What about his paw?" Bailey asked. "Do we need to know anything about that?"

"We had to stitch it up. Remove the bandage tomorrow and see how it looks. If the wound isn't oozy or bleeding, you don't need to rebandage it. But if it is, go ahead and bandage it up for another day. I'll send an extra one home with you." The nurse handed the bandage to Kate. "Just wrap it with the gauze and tape it so it's secure."

"Thank you for taking such good care of Biscuit," Kate said.

"We were happy to do it," the nurse replied. "If you have any questions about caring for his injuries, give us a call."

"We will," Kate said.

Mrs. Chang went to the counter and paid the bill while the girls headed to the car with Biscuit.

"I can't believe all that's happened this week." Bailey petted Biscuit, who laid his head on Kate's arm as she held him. "Do we have some things to tell the Camp Club Girls tonight!"

CHAPTER 12

Solutions

Back at the hotel, Kate made Biscuit a little bed of blankets on the floor and gently laid him on it. "I'm so glad to have you back, Biscuit," she cooed as she stroked his head. "You be a good boy and stay here while Bailey and I call the girls. We won't be long."

"Mom, Kate and I are going to sit in the lobby to call the Camp Club Girls."

"Okay," Mrs. Chang said and waved them out.

Bailey pulled her phone from her pocket and conferenced everyone in. "We've had quite a day," she told them.

"What's going on?" Sydney asked.

"Oh, nothing," Kate answered casually. "We came up with a solution to the elk mystery we've been working on all week."

Four girls screamed, and Bailey held the phone away from her ear and laughed.

"How'd you do it?" McKenzie asked.

"Actually, we figured it out earlier, but we still had to prove we were right," Bailey said.

Kate laughed and jumped into storytelling mode. "We went to the hospital to see Justin and Joe's grandpa. Just after we got to his room, the boys went into the hall."

"We decided to follow them to make sure they were okay," Bailey said. "You know, in case they were upset by seeing their grandpa or something."

"We found them in the hall," Kate said. "We overheard Joe telling Justin that they had to tell what happened."

"We didn't know what to do at first." Bailey took up the story. "But pretty soon we asked if we could do something to help."

"We got them to tell us what the problem was." Kate looked at Bailey.

"So? What was it?" Alex asked.

"Justin admitted he'd been shooting at the elk to scare them into stampeding," Bailey blabbed.

"No way! Oscar the Grouch confessed?" Alex screeched.

"You were right all along!" Elizabeth said.

"I feel bad about calling him Oscar now," Bailey said. "He's really not so bad after you get to know him."

"What about his brother?" McKenzie asked.

"Joe tried to talk Justin out of doing it, and went with him," Kate said. "So he was involved, but not really."

"Except by association," Elizabeth said. "Proverbs says a person is known by the company he or she keeps."

"Yeah, but when it's your brother, it's hard to stay away from him." Bailey felt sorry Joe had gotten mixed up in his brother's mess.

"I wonder how they knew where to find the elk," Sydney said.

"Remember the smelly wallow we told you about that we found on our hike?" Bailey pulled her lip balm from her pocket and put some on. "We realized the boys must be using them to find the elk."

"But here's the good part," Kate said. "We encouraged Justin to tell his parents and told him we'd even go with him. He was afraid to. But then I told him God would give him the strength."

"So did he do it?" Sydney asked.

"Yep," Kate replied. "He walked right in there and told them everything."

"How'd they take it?" Alex asked.

"Pretty well, considering," Bailey said. "But they'll both have some kind of consequences."

"Guess that's to be expected," Elizabeth said.

"Wow," Sydney said. "You guys *have* had quite a day."

Bailey shifted her phone to the other ear. "We got Biscuit back."

"Already?" McKenzie asked. "How is he?"

"He's bandaged to keep him from moving too much," Kate answered. "That will give his ribs a chance to heal. We're supposed to keep him quiet. We can take the bandage off in a week."

"What about his foot?" Sydney asked.

"It's still wrapped up," Kate replied. "But we're supposed to look at it tomorrow to see if we can leave the bandage off."

"Wow, God really answered our prayers that he would heal fast," Elizabeth said. "I'm still surprised he wasn't killed in that stampede. God sure watched out for him."

Kate inhaled deeply. "I've thought the same thing. It's a relief to have him back home. I must have told God thank You a bazillion times already!"

The girls laughed.

"Now we'll just pray that God keeps working on Justin and Joe," Elizabeth said.

"Funny how we were so afraid of them before and now we're hoping they'll come to talk," Bailey said. "God sure turns things upside down."

"I've got to go," Sydney said. "But keep me posted."

"We should get going, too," Bailey said. "We'll let you know if anything more happens."

Bailey and Kate went back into their hotel room. Biscuit slept on the little bed Kate made him on the floor and hadn't moved at all. He lifted his shaggy head when they came through the door.

Mrs. Chang was lost in a book and Trina was looking out the window. "Hey, the Perkinses are coming back from the hospital," she said.

Bailey and Kate went to the window and saw the family walk up to the main entrance.

"Hey, maybe we can introduce Justin and Joe to the ghost in the Music Room tomorrow," Kate said.

"Mom, can we go ask when they get up here?"

"I think that would be a nice gesture," Mrs. Perkins said, "just so they don't wonder if we think less of them after what happened."

Bailey and Kate waited until they heard the Perkinses' voices in the hall before going out to greet them.

"We were wondering if Justin and Joe would like to come to the Music Room with us tomorrow," Bailey said. "There's a ghost who lives there!"

The Perkins family laughed.

"That would be fun, but we can't," Justin said. Then he looked at his parents and gave a sheepish grin. "We're pretty much grounded for the rest of our lives."

"Ohhh," Kate said. "We hadn't thought about that. Sorry."

"It's okay." Joe elbowed his older brother. "He's grounded longer than I am. Maybe if you come back again next year about this time I'll be free to go with you. But Justin probably can't for a few more years."

Justin playfully punched Joe in the arm.

"But we told our parents that you talked to us about your faith," Justin said. "They said we could have you over to talk to us again if you wouldn't mind."

"Mind?" Bailey said, her eyes growing to the size of tennis balls. "We'd love to!"

●—●—●

"So that pretty much covers it," Bailey told the Camp Club Girls. "We're going over to talk to them tomorrow afternoon, and our parents might even come, too."

"That is so cool," Elizabeth said. "You really let your light shine. Knowing Jesus and living a life of faith will be the best solution for their lives."

"For sure," Kate agreed. "And thanks to all of us working together, we have a solution to our mysteries."

Bailey giggled. "I can't wait to see what our next one will be!"

The Camp Club Girls
are on the case!

Don't miss these other exciting
3-in-1 story collections...

Available wherever Christian books are sold.

Introducing
God ♥s Me

A series for girls ages 10 to 14

God Hearts Me New Life Bible for Girls

God Hearts Me: A Bible Promise Book for Girls

God Hearts Me: A Devotional Journal for Girls

God Hearts Me: Daily Devotions for a Girl's Heart

God Hearts Me: Daily Prayers for a Girl's Heart

Coming Soon!

God Hearts Me Perpetual Calendar

God Hearts Me: My Prayer Journal

God Hearts Me: My Secret Diary

God Hearts Me:
3-Minute Devotions for Girls on the Go!

the S.A.V.E. Squad

Since they can't save the whole world, what about a small piece of it? Sixth-graders Sunny, Aneta, Vee, and Esther join together as the S.A.V.E. Squad and set out to rescue homeless dogs, Dumpster cats, retired thoroughbreds, and injured owls.

diary of a
REAL PAYNE

These pages from EJ Payne's diary will have you ROTFL!

Check out the entire series. . .

Available September 2014
Oh Baby!